With high-tension suspense and cutting-edge technology, Patricia Cornwell—the world's #1 bestselling crime writer—once again proves her exceptional ability to entertain and enthrall in this remarkable novel featuring chief medical examiner Dr. Kay Scarpetta.

On her quest to find out exactly what happened to her recently murdered former deputy chief, Jack Fielding, Scarpetta drives to the Georgia Prison for Women to meet a convicted sex offender and the mother of a vicious and diabolically brilliant killer. Against the advice of her FBI forensic psychologist husband, Benton Wesley, Scarpetta is determined to hear this woman out.

Scarpetta has both personal and professional reasons to learn more about a string of grisly killings: the murder of a Savannah family years earlier, a young woman on death row, and then other inexplicable deaths that begin to occur at a breathtaking pace. Driven by inner forces, Scarpetta discovers connections that compel her to conclude that what she thought ended with Fielding's death and an attempt on her own life is only the beginning of something far more destructive: a terrifying terrain of conspiracy and potential terrorism on an international scale.

And she is the only one who can stop it.

Praise for the novels of Patricia Cornwell

PORT MORTUARY

"With *Port Mortuary*, Cornwell has presented a gift to her readers—a return to over-the-top forensics and bigger-than-life characters that drew us to the Scarpetta series in the first place."
—*The Jackson Clarion-Ledger*

"Entertaining . . . Scarpetta is one of the most believable characters in crime fiction because her many strengths are tempered by true human frailties . . . a must-read for crime fiction fans."
—*The Vancouver Sun*

continued . . .

THE SCARPETTA FACTOR

"[An] insistent and gripping thriller."　　　*—The Star-Ledger*

"A finely crafted, pulse-racing thriller that readers won't want to put down."　　　*—Library Journal*

SCARPETTA

"When it comes to the forensic sciences, nobody can touch Cornwell."　　　*—The New York Times Book Review*

"The coolly graphic autopsy scenes are classic Scarpetta, but new elements . . . keep this tale fresh."　　　*—People*

THE FRONT

"[A] classically written crime novel."　　　*—USA Today*

AT RISK

"Highly entertaining."　　　*—St. Louis Post-Dispatch*

"Scary."　　　*—The Boston Globe*

BOOK OF THE DEAD

"Compelling."　　　*—Richmond Times-Dispatch*

"What a walloping, riveting mix of . . . adventure and psychology. Author Cornwell certainly is skilled at dissecting the not always attractive innards of human nature."　　　*—Forbes*

PREDATOR

"A fine psychological thriller."　　　*—The Denver Post*

"Sensationally plotted, with a twist at the end that will leave you gasping for breath."　　　*—Daily Express* (U.K.)

TRACE

"Cornwell gets her Hitchcock on . . . [She] can generate willies with subtle poetic turns." —*People*

"Fun [and] flamboyant." —*Entertainment Weekly*

BLOW FLY

"[A] grisly fast-paced thriller . . . utterly chilling." —*Entertainment Weekly*

"A story so compelling that even longtime readers will be stunned by its twists and turns." —*Chicago Tribune*

THE LAST PRECINCT

"Ignites on the first page . . . Cornwell has created a character so real, so compelling, so driven that this reader has to remind herself regularly that Scarpetta is just a product of an author's imagination." —*USA Today*

"The most unexpected of the Kay Scarpetta novels so far . . . Compelling . . . Terrific." —*The Miami Herald*

BLACK NOTICE

"Brainteasing . . . one of the most savage killers of her career . . . [a] hair-raising tale with a French twist." —*People*

"The author's darkest and perhaps best . . . a fast-paced, first-rate thriller." —*The San Francisco Examiner*

POINT OF ORIGIN

"Cornwell lights a fire under familiar characters—and sparks her hottest adventure in years." —*People*

"Packed with action and suspense." —*Rocky Mountain News*

TITLES BY PATRICIA CORNWELL

SCARPETTA SERIES

ANDY BRAZIL SERIES

WIN GARANO SERIES

NONFICTION

BIOGRAPHY

OTHER WORKS

BERKLEY BOOKS   NEW YORK

RED MIST

PATRICIA CORNWELL

THE BERKLEY PUBLISHING GROUP
Published by the Penguin Group
Penguin Group (USA) Inc.
375 Hudson Street, New York, New York 10014, USA
Penguin Group (Canada), 90 Eglinton Avenue East, Suite 700, Toronto, Ontario M4P 2Y3, Canada
(a division of Pearson Penguin Canada Inc.) • Penguin Books Ltd., 80 Strand, London WC2R 0RL,
England • Penguin Group Ireland, 25 St. Stephen's Green, Dublin 2, Ireland (a division of Penguin
Books Ltd.) • Penguin Group (Australia), 250 Camberwell Road, Camberwell, Victoria 3124, Australia
(a division of Pearson Australia Group Pty. Ltd.) • Penguin Books India Pvt. Ltd., 11 Community
Centre, Panchsheel Park, New Delhi—110 017, India • Penguin Group (NZ), 67 Apollo Drive,
Rosedale, Auckland 0632, New Zealand (a division of Pearson New Zealand Ltd.) • Penguin Books
(South Africa) (Pty.) Ltd., 24 Sturdee Avenue, Rosebank, Johannesburg 2196, South Africa

Penguin Books Ltd., Registered Offices: 80 Strand, London WC2R 0RL, England

This is a work of fiction. Names, characters, places, and incidents either are the product of the author's
imagination or are used fictitiously, and any resemblance to actual persons, living or dead, business
establishments, events, or locales is entirely coincidental. The publisher does not have any control over
and does not assume any responsibility for author or third-party websites or their content.

RED MIST

A Berkley Book / published by arrangement with Cornwell Entertainment, Inc.

PUBLISHING HISTORY
G. P. Putnam's Sons hardcover edition / December 2011
Berkley premium edition / September 2012

Copyright © 2011 by Cornwell Entertainment, Inc.
Cover design by Richard Hasselberger.
Stepback photograph copyright © Mark Coggins.

ISBN: 978-0-425-25043-3

BERKLEY®
Berkley Books are published by The Berkley Publishing Group,
a division of Penguin Group (USA) Inc.,
375 Hudson Street, New York, New York 10014.
BERKLEY® is a registered trademark of Penguin Group (USA) Inc.
The "B" design is a trademark of Penguin Group (USA) Inc.

PRINTED IN THE UNITED STATES OF AMERICA

10 9 8 7 6 5 4 3 2 1

ALWAYS LEARNING   **PEARSON**

My thanks to the Navy and Marine Corps Public Health Center, and also to Dr. Marcella Fierro, Dr. Jamie Downs, and other experts who were so helpful with my research, including Stephen Braga, who generously shared his expertise in criminal law.

As always, I am grateful to Dr. Staci Gruber for her incredible technical skills and expertise, and her patience and encouragement.

This book is dedicated to you, Staci.

And I heard a great voice out of the temple saying to the seven angels, Go your ways, and pour out the vials of the wrath of God upon the earth.

—REVELATION 16:1

1

Iron rails the rusty brown of old blood cut across a cracked paved road that leads deeper into the Low-country. As I drive over train tracks, it enters my mind that the Georgia Prison for Women is on the wrong side of them and maybe I should take it as another warning and turn back. It's not quite four p.m., Thursday, June 30. There's time to catch the last flight to Boston, but I know I won't.

This part of coastal Georgia is a moody terrain of brooding forests draped with Spanish moss and mudflats etched with convoluted creeks that give way to grassy plains heavy with light. Snowy egrets and great blue herons fly low over brackish water, dragging their feet, and then the woods close in again on either side of the nar-

row tar-laced road I'm on. Coiling kudzu strangles underbrush and cloaks forest canopies in scaly dark leaves,
and giant cypress trees with thick gnarled knees rise out
of swamps like prehistoric creatures wading and prowl-
ing. While I've yet to spot an alligator or a snake, I'm
sure they are there and aware of my big white machine
roaring and chugging and backfiring.

How I ended up in such a rattletrap that wanders all
over the road and stinks like fast food and cigarettes with
a whiff of rotting fish, I don't know. It's not what I told
my chief of staff, Bryce, to reserve, which was a safe,
dependable, mid-size sedan, preferably a Volvo or a
Camry, with side and head air bags and a GPS. When I
was met outside the airport terminal by a young man in
a white cargo van that doesn't have air-conditioning or
even a map, I told him there had been an error. I'd been
given someone else's vehicle by mistake. He pointed out
the contract has my name on it, Kate Scarpetta, and I
said my first name is Kay, not Kate, and I didn't care
whose name was on it. A cargo van wasn't what I ordered.
Lowcountry Concierge Connection was very sorry, said
the young man, who was quite tan and dressed in a tank
top, camo shorts, and fishing shoes. He couldn't imagine
what happened. Obviously a computer problem. He'd be
glad to get me something else, but it would be much
later in the day, possibly tomorrow.

So far nothing is going the way I'd planned, and I
imagine my husband, Benton, saying he told me so. I see
him leaning against the travertine countertop in the

kitchen last night, tall and slender, with thick silver hair, his chiseled handsome face watching me somberly as we argued again about my coming here. It's only now that the last trace of my headache is gone. I don't know why a part of me still believes, contrary to evidence, that half a bottle of wine will resolve differences. It might have been more than half. It was a very nice pinot grigio for the money, light and clean with a hint of apples.

The air blowing through the open windows is thick and hot, and I smell the pungent, sulfuric odor of decomposing vegetation, of salt marshes and pluff mud. The van hesitates and surges by fits and starts around a sun-dappled bend where turkey buzzards forage on something dead. The huge ugly birds with their ragged wings and naked heads lift off in slow, heavy flaps as I swerve around the stiff pelt of a raccoon, the sultry air carrying a sharp putrid stench I know all too well. Animal or human, it doesn't matter. I can recognize death from a distance, and were I to get out and take a close look, I probably could determine the exact cause of that raccoon's demise and when it occurred and possibly reconstruct how it got hit and maybe by what.

Most people refer to me as a medical examiner, an ME, but some think I'm a coroner, and occasionally I'm confused with a police surgeon. To be precise, I'm a physician with a specialty in pathology, and subspecialties in forensic pathology and 3-D imaging radiology, or the use of CT scans to view a dead body internally before I touch it with a blade. I have a law degree and the special reservist rank of colonel with the Air Force, and therefore an affiliation with the Department of Defense, which last year appointed me to head the Cambridge Forensic Center it has funded in conjunction with the Commonwealth of Massachusetts, the Massachusetts Institute of Technology (MIT), and Harvard.

I'm an expert at determining the mechanism of what kills or why something doesn't, whether it is a disease, a poison, a medical misadventure, an act of God, a handgun, or an improvised explosive device (IED). My every action has to be legally well informed. I'm expected to assist the United States government as needed and directed. I swear to oaths and testify under them, and what all this means is that I'm really not entitled to live the way most people do. It isn't an option for me to be anything other than objective and clinical. I'm not supposed to have personal opinions or emotional reactions to any case, no matter how gruesome or cruel. Even if violence has impacted me directly, such as the attempt on my life four months ago, I'm to be as unmoved as an iron post or a rock. I'm to remain hard in my resolve, calm and cool.

"You're not going to go PTSD on me, are you?" the chief of the Armed Forces Medical Examiners, General John Briggs, said to me after I was almost murdered in my own garage this past February 10. "Shit happens, Kay. The world is full of whack jobs."

"Yes, John. Shit happens. Shit has happened before, and shit will happen again," I replied, as if all were fine and I'd taken everything in stride, when I knew that wasn't what I was feeling inside. I intend to get as many details as I can about what went wrong in Jack Fielding's life, and I want Dawn Kincaid to pay the highest price. Prison with no chance of parole forever.

I glance at my watch without taking my hands off the wheel of the damn van with its bad case of the damn shakes. Maybe I should turn around. The last flight out of here to Boston is in less than two hours. I could make it, but I know I won't be on it. For better or worse, I'm committed, as if I've been taken over by an autopilot, maybe a reckless one, possibly a vengeful one. I know I'm angry. As my FBI forensic psychologist husband put it last night while I was cooking dinner in our historic Cambridge home that was built by a well-known transcendentalist, "You're being tricked, Kay. Possibly set up by others, but what concerns me most is you setting yourself up. What you perceive as your wish to be proactive and helpful is in fact your need to appease your guilt."

"I'm not the reason Jack is dead," I said.

"You've always felt guilty about him. You tend to feel guilty about a lot of things that have nothing to do with you."

"I see. When I think I can make a difference, I should never trust it." I used a pair of surgical scissors to cut the shells off boiled jumbo prawns. "When I decide that taking a risk might produce useful information and help bring about justice, it's really my feeling guilty."

"You think it's your responsibility to fix things. Or prevent them. You always have. Going back to when you were a little girl taking care of your sick father."

"I certainly can't prevent anything now." I pitched shells into the trash and dashed salt into a stainless-steel pot of water boiling on the ceramic-glass induction cook-top that is the hub of my kitchen. "Jack was molested as a boy, and I couldn't prevent that. And I couldn't prevent him from ruining his life. And now he's been murdered and I didn't stop that, either." I grabbed a chef's knife. "I barely prevented my own death, if we're honest about it." I diced onion and garlic, the fine steel blade clicking quickly against antibacterial polypropylene. "It's a lucky accident I'm still around."

"You should stay the hell out of Savannah," Benton said, and I told him I had to go and to please open the wine and pour us each a glass, and we drank and disagreed. We picked distractedly at my *mangia bene, vivi felice cucina,* or eat well and live happy cooking, and neither of us was happy. All because of her.

It's been a hellish existence for Kathleen Lawler. Currently serving twenty years for DUI manslaughter, she's been locked up longer than she's been free, going back to the seventies, when she was convicted of sexually molesting a boy who grew up to be my deputy chief medical examiner, Jack Fielding. Now he's dead, shot in the head by their love child, as the media refers to Dawn Kincaid, given up for adoption at birth while her mother was in prison for what she did to conceive her. It's a very long story. I find myself saying that a lot these days, and if I've learned nothing else in life it's that one thing can and will lead to another. Kathleen Lawler's catastrophic tale is a perfect example of what scientists mean when they say that the beat of a butterfly wing causes a hurricane on another part of the planet.

As I drive the loud, lurching rental van through an overgrown marshy terrain that probably didn't look all that different in the age of dinosaurs, I wonder what beat of a butterfly wing, what breath of a disturbance, created Kathleen Lawler and the havoc she has wrought. I imagine her inside a six-by-eight-foot cell with its shiny steel toilet, gray metal bed, and narrow window covered by metal mesh that looks out over a prison yard of coarse grass, concrete picnic tables and benches, and Porta-Johns. I know how many changes of clothing she has, not "free-world clothes," she's explained in e-mails I don't answer, but prison uniforms, trousers, and tops, two sets of each. She's read every book in the prison library at least five times, is a gifted writer, she's let me know, and some months ago she e-mailed a poem she says she wrote about Jack:

FATE

he came back as air and I as earth
and we found each other not at first.
(it wasn't wrong in reality,
just a technicality
that neither of us heeded
or god knows needed).

fingers, toes of fire.
cold cold steel.
the oven yawns
the gas is on—
left on like the lights of a welcoming motel.

I've read the poem obsessively, studied it word by word, looking for a buried message, concerned at first that the ominous reference to an oven with gas turned on could suggest that Kathleen Lawler is suicidal. Maybe the idea of her own death is welcome, like a welcoming motel, I offered to Benton, who replied that the poem shows her sociopathy and disordered personality. She believes she did nothing wrong. Having sex with a twelve-year-old boy at a ranch for troubled youths where she was a therapist was a beautiful thing, a blending of pure and perfect love. It was fate. It was their destiny. That's the deluded way she views it, Benton said.

Two weeks ago her communications to me abruptly stopped, and my attorney called with a request. Kathleen Lawler wants to talk to me about Jack Fielding, the protégé I trained during the early days of my career and worked with on and off over a span of twenty years. I agreed to meet with her at the Georgia Prison for Women, the GPFW, but only as a friend. I will not be Dr. Kay Scarpetta. I will not be the director of the Cambridge Forensic Center or a medical examiner for the Armed Forces or a forensic expert or an expert in anything. I will be Kay this day, and the only thing Kay and Kathleen have in common is Jack. Whatever we say to each other will not be protected by privilege, and no attorneys, guards, or other prison personnel will be present.

A shift in light, and the dense pine woods thin before opening onto a bleak clearing. What looks like an industrial area is posted with green metal signs warning me that the rural road I'm on is about to end, no trespassing allowed. If one isn't authorized to be here, turn back now. I drive past a salvage yard heaped with twisted and smashed-up trucks and cars, and then a nursery with greenhouses and big pots of ornamental grasses, bamboos, and palms. Straight ahead is an expansive lawn with the letters GPFW neatly shaped by bright beds of petunias and marigolds, as if I've just arrived at a city park or a golf course. The white-columned redbrick administration building is grandly out of context with blue metal-roofed concrete pods enclosed by high fences. Double coils of razor-sharp concertina shine and glint in the sun like scalpel blades.

The GPFW is the model for a number of prisons, I've learned from the careful research I've done. It's regarded as a superior example of enlightened and humane rehabilitation for female felons, many of them trained while in custody to be plumbers, electricians, cosmetologists, woodworkers, mechanics, roofers, landscapers, cooks, and caterers. Inmates maintain the buildings and grounds. They prepare the food and work in the library and in the beauty salon, and assist in the medical clinic and publish their own magazine and are expected to at least pass the GED exam while they're behind bars. Everyone here earns her keep and is offered opportunities, except those housed in maximum security, known as Bravo Pod, where Kathleen Lawler was reassigned two weeks ago, about the same time her e-mails to me abruptly stopped.

Parking in a visitor's space, I check my iPhone for messages to make sure there is nothing urgent to attend to, hoping for something from Benton, and there is. "Hot as hell where you are, and supposed to storm. Be careful, and let me know how it goes. I love you," writes my matter-of-fact practical husband, who never fails to give me a weather report or some other useful update when he's thinking about me. I love him, too, and am fine and will call in a few hours, I write him back, as I watch several men in suits and ties emerge from the administration building, escorted by a corrections officer. The men look like lawyers, maybe prison officials, I decide, and I wait until they are driven away in an unmarked car, wondering who they are and what brings them here. I tuck my phone into my shoulder bag, hiding it under the seat, taking nothing with me but my driver's license, an envelope with nothing written on it, and the van keys.

The summer sun presses against me like a heavy, hot hand, and clouds are building in the southwest, boiling up thickly, the air fragrant with lavender mist and summersweet as I follow a concrete sidewalk through bloom-ing shrubs and more tidy flower beds while invisible eyes watch from slitted windows around the prison yard. In-mates have nothing better to do than stare, to look out at a world they can no longer be part of as they gather intelligence more shrewdly than the CIA. I feel a collec-tive consciousness taking in my loud white cargo van with its South Carolina plates, and the way I'm dressed, not my usual business suit or investigative field clothes but a pair of khakis, a blue-and-white striped cotton shirt tucked in, and basket-weave loafers with a matching belt. I have on no jewelry except a titanium watch on a black rubber strap and my wedding band. It wouldn't be easy to guess my economic status or who or what I am, ex-cept the van doesn't fit with the image I had in mind for this day.

My intention was to look like a middle-aged casually coiffed blond woman who doesn't do anything dramati-cally important or even interesting in life. But then that damn van! A scuffed-up shuddering white monstrosity with windows tinted so dark they are almost black in back, as if I work for a construction company or make deliveries, or perhaps have come to the GPFW to trans-port an inmate alive or dead, it occurs to me, as I sense women watching. Most of them I will never meet, al-though I know the names of a few, those whose infa-mous cases have been in the news and whose heinous acts have been presented at professional meetings I attend. I resist looking around or letting on that I'm aware of anyone watching as I wonder which dark slash of a window is hers.

How emotional this must be for Kathleen Lawler. I suspect she has thought of little else of late. For people like her, I'm the final connection to those they've lost or killed. I'm the surrogate for their dead.

2

Tara Grimm is the warden, and her office at the end of a long blue hallway is furnished and decorated by the inmates she keeps.

The desk, coffee table, and chairs are lacquered honey-colored oak and have a sturdy shape and for me a certain charm because I almost always would rather see something made by hand, no matter how rustic. Vines with heart-shaped variegated leaves crowd planters in windows and trail from them to the tops of homebuilt bookcases, draping over the sides like bunting and tumbling in tangled masses from hanging baskets. When I comment on what a green thumb Tara Grimm must have, she informs me in a measured melodious voice that inmates tend to her indoor plants. She doesn't know the name of the creepers, as she calls them, but they could be philoden-dron. "Golden pothos." I touch a marbled yellow-green leaf. "More commonly known as devil's ivy."

"It won't stop growing, and I won't let them cut it back," she says from the bookcase behind her desk, where she is returning a volume to a shelf, *The Economics of Recidivism*. "Started out with one little shoot in a glass of water, and I use it as an important life lesson all these women chose to ignore along the path that landed them in trouble. Be careful what takes root or one day it will be all there is." She shelves another book, *The Art of Manipulation*. "I don't know." She scans vines festoon-ing the room. "I suppose it's getting a bit overwhelmed in here."

The warden is somewhere in her forties, I deduce, tall and svelte and strangely out of place in her scoop-neck black dress that flows midcalf, with a gold coin lariat wrapped around her neck, as if she paid special attention to her appearance this day, perhaps because of the men just leaving, visitors, possibly important ones. Dark-eyed, with high cheekbones and long black hair swept up and back, Tara Grimm doesn't look like what she does, and I wonder if the absurdity occurs to her or others. In Bud-dhism, Tara is the mother of liberation, which one might argue this Tara certainly is not. Although her world is grim.

She smooths her skirt as she sits down behind her desk and I take a straight-backed chair across from her. "Mainly I needed to go over anything you might intend to show Kathleen," she informs me of the reason I was directed to her office. "I'm sure you know the routine."

"It's not routine for me to visit people in prison," I reply. "Unless it's in the infirmary or worse." What I mean is if an inmate needs a forensic physical examination or is dead.

"If you've brought reports or other documents, anything to go over with her, I need to approve them first," she lets me know, and I tell her again that I've come as a friend, which is legally correct but not literally true.

I am no friend to Kathleen Lawler and will be deliberate and cautious as I extract information, encouraging her to tell me what I want to know without letting on I care. Did she have contact with Jack Fielding over the years, and what happened during episodes of freedom when she was on the outside? An ongoing sexual affair between a female offender and her younger male victim certainly has occurred in other cases I've researched, and Kathleen was in and out of prison the entire time I knew Jack. If there were continued romantic interludes with this woman who molested him as a boy, I wonder if the timing of them might be related to those periods when he went haywire and vanished, prompting me to find him and eventually hire him back.

I want to know when he first discovered that Dawn Kincaid was his daughter and why he recently connected with her in Massachusetts, allowing her to live in his house in Salem, and for how long, and was this related to his walking out on his wife and family? Did Jack know he was being altered by dangerous drugs, or was that part of Dawn's sabotage, and was he aware his behavior was increasingly erratic, and whose idea was it for him to engage in illegal activities at the Cambridge Forensic Center, the CFC, while I was out of town?

I can't predict what Kathleen might know or say, but I will handle the conversation the way I've planned and rehearsed with my lawyer, Leonard Brazzo, and give her nothing in return. She can't be required to testify against her own daughter and wouldn't be credible in court, but I won't reveal a single fact that could find its way back to Dawn Kincaid and be used to help her defense.

"Well, I didn't suppose you'd bring anything relating to those cases," Tara Grimm says, and I sense she is disappointed. "I confess to having a lot of questions about what went on up there in Massachusetts. I admit I'm curious."

Most people are. The Mensa Murders, as the press has dubbed homicides and other vicious acts involving people with genius or near-genius IQs, are about as grotesque as anything one might ever conjure up. After more than twenty years of working violent deaths, I still haven't seen it all.

"I won't be discussing any investigative details with her," I tell the warden.

"I'm sure Kathleen will be asking you, since it is her daughter we're talking about, after all. Dawn Kincaid supposedly killed those people and then tried to murder you, too?" Her eyes are steady on mine.

"I won't be discussing any details with Kathleen about

those cases or any cases." I give the warden nothing. "That's not why I'm here," I reiterate firmly. "But I did bring a photograph I'd like her to have."

"If you'll let me see it." She reaches out a fine-boned hand with perfectly manicured nails painted deep rose as if she just had them done, and she wears many rings and a gold metal watch with a crystal bezel.

I give her the plain white envelope I'd tucked into my back pocket, and she slides out a photograph of Jack Fielding washing his prized '67 cherry-red Mustang, shirtless and in running shorts, grinning and glorious, when he was captured on camera some five years ago, between marriages and deteriorations. Although I didn't do his autopsy, I've dissected his existence these five months since his murder, in part trying to figure out what I could have done to prevent it. I don't believe I could have. I was never able to stop any self-destruction of his, and as I look at the photograph from where I sit, anger and guilt spark, and then I feel sad.

"Well, I guess that's fine," the warden says. "He was easy on the eyes, I'll give him that. One of these obsessive bodybuilders, good Lord. How many hours in a day would it take?"

I look around at framed certificates and commendations on her walls because I don't want to look at her looking at that photograph, uncertain why it's bothering me so much. Maybe it's harder to see Jack through a stranger's eyes. *Warden of the Year. Outstanding Merit. Distinguished Service Award. Meritorious Service Award, Continuing Excellence. Supervisor of the Month.* Some of them she's won more than once, and she has a bachelor's degree cum laude from Spalding University in Kentucky, but she doesn't sound like a native, more like Louisiana, and I ask her where she's from.

"Mississippi, originally," she says. "My father was the superintendent of the state penitentiary there, and I spent my early years on twenty thousand acres of delta land as flat as a pancake, with soybeans and cotton that the inmates farmed. Then he got hired by Louisiana State Penitentiary in Angola, more farmland far away from civilization, and I lived right there on the grounds, which might seem strange. But I didn't mind living in the lap of my father's work. Amazing what you get used to as if it's normal. It was his recommendation that the GPFW be built out here in the middle of scrubland and swamps, and that the women take care of it and cost the taxpayers as little as possible. I guess you could say that prisons are in my blood."

"Your father worked here at some point?"

"No, he never did." She smiles ironically. "I can't imagine my father overseeing two thousand women. He would have been a bit bored with that, although some of them are a whole lot worse than the men. He was sort of like Arnold Palmer giving advice about golf-course design, no one better, depending on your vision, and he was progressive. A number of correctional institutions called upon him for advice. Angola, for example, has a rodeo stadium, a newspaper, and a radio station. Some of the inmates are celebrated rodeo riders and experts in leather, metal, and woodworking design that they're allowed to sell for their own profit." She doesn't say all this as if she necessarily thinks it's a good thing. "My worry about these cases you have up north is did they get everyone involved?"

"One would hope."

"At least we know for sure Dawn Kincaid is locked up, and I hope she stays locked up. Killing innocent people for no good reason," the warden says. "I hear she's got mental problems because of stress. Imagine that. What about the stress she's caused?"

Some months ago, Dawn Kincaid was transferred to Butler State Hospital, where doctors will determine whether she is competent to stand trial. Ploys. Malingering. Let the games begin. Or as my chief investigator, Pete Marino, puts it, she got caught and caught a case of the crazies.

"Hard to imagine she was all on her own when she was coming up with ways to sabotage and destroy innocent lives, but the worst is that poor little boy." Tara is talking about what is none of her business, and I have no choice but to let her. "Killing a helpless child who was playing in his backyard while his parents were right there inside the house? There's no forgiveness for harming a child or an animal," she says, as if harming an adult might be acceptable.

"I was wondering if it would be all right for Kathleen to keep the photograph." I don't verify or refute her information. "I thought she might like to have it."

"I suppose I can't see any harm in it." But she doesn't seem sure, and when she reaches across her desk to hand the photograph back to me, I catch what is in her eyes.

She's thinking, *Why would you give her a picture of him?* Indirectly, Kathleen Lawler is the reason Jack Fielding is dead. *No, not indirectly,* I think, as anger simmers. She had sex with an underage boy, and the child they produced grew up to be Dawn Kincaid, his killer. That's about as direct as anything needs to get.

"I don't know what Kathleen has seen that's recent," I offer as an explanation, returning the photograph to its envelope. "It's an image I choose to remember him by, the way he was in better times."

I can't imagine Kathleen looking at this photograph and not opening up to me. We'll see who manipulates whom.

"I don't know how much you were told about why I moved her into protective custody," Tara says.

"I simply know that she has been." My answer is intentionally vague.

"Mr. Brazzo didn't explain?" She seems dubious as she folds her hands on top of her tidy square oak desk.

Leonard Brazzo is a criminal trial lawyer, and the reason I need one is that when Dawn Kincaid's attempt on my life goes to trial, I don't intend to entrust my welfare to some overworked or green assistant U.S. attorney. I have no doubt the team of lawyers who have taken her on pro bono will make my being attacked inside my own garage somehow excusable. They'll claim it was my fault she ambushed me from behind in the pitch dark. I'm alive because I was bizarrely lucky, and as I sit inside Tara Grimm's ivy-infested office, it bothers me more than I care to admit that I'm really not responsible for saving myself.

"As I understand it, she's been moved into protective custody for her own safety," I reply, as I envision the level-four-A camouflage vest with its inserted Kevlar-ceramic plates. I remember the body armor's tough nylon texture, the new smell of it, and its weight as I draped it over my shoulder inside my dark, frigid garage that night after retrieving it from the backseat of the SUV.

"Seems like my moving her to Bravo Pod might have made you hesitant about what you might be walking into down here in Savannah," Tara comments. "Seems like you might not be inclined to seek out anything *unsafe* after what you've been through."

I envision the blizzard of intense white specks as small as pollen on the MRI scan of the first victim Dawn Kincaid stabbed with an injection knife. Bright white particles densely concentrated around a buttonhole wound and blasted deep inside the organs and soft tissue structures of the chest. Like a bomb going off internally. If she'd finished what she'd started when she came after me with that same weapon, I would have been dead before I hit the ground.

"Not that I understand why you were wearing body armor at your own house." The warden probes because she can.

I don't offer that part of my job with the Department of Defense is medical intelligence, and that General

Briggs wanted my opinion of the latest level of body armor developed for female troops. I happen to know for a fact that the vest can stop a steel blade. Luck, dumb luck, and I remember being shocked by what I saw in the mirror after it was over. My red-tinted face. My red-tinted hair. For an instant I smell the iron smell and hear the hissing red mist as it landed warmly, wetly, all over me inside my cold, dark garage.

"I understand the dog was out there in the garage with you when it happened, if what's been in the news is true. How is Sock?" I hear the warden say, as I look down at my hands. My clean hands with their functional unpolished short squared nails. I take a deep breath and concentrate on any odors in the room. No iron bloody smell, just the hint of Tara Grimm's perfume. Estée Lauder. Youth-Dew.

"He's doing quite well." I focus on her again and wonder if I missed something. How did we get on the subject of a rescued greyhound?

"So you still have him?" She looks steadily at me.

"Yes, I do."

"I'm glad to hear it. He's a very good dog. But they all are. Just as sweet as they can be, and I know Kathleen didn't want to give him up to just anyone and is hoping she'll get him back when she's out."

"When she's out?" I ask.

"Dawn adopted Sock because Kathleen didn't want anyone else to have him, she loved that dog so much," Tara says. "Good to animals, I'll give her credit for that, at least, and knowing all this should have alerted you that the two of them have a connection, an alliance. Kathleen and Dawn, even though Kathleen will lead you to think otherwise, as you're about to find out. Since I've been the warden here, Dawn's been a fairly frequent visitor, coming to see her mother three or four times a year, making deposits in her commissary account. Of course, that's stopped. The two wrote to each other, but the police took those letters, although it doesn't prevent the two of them from communicating now, one inmate writing another. You probably know all that."

"I'd have no reason to."

"Kathleen lies about it now that Dawn's in trouble. Doesn't want any guilt by association when it comes to someone who might be in a position to help her. You, for example. Or a prominent lawyer. Kathleen will say what she thinks is to her advantage."

"What do you mean 'when she's out'?" I repeat.

"You know, everybody's wrongly convicted this day and age," she says.

"I didn't realize there's any suggestion Kathleen Lawler might have been."

"She won't get Sock back unless he lives to be a very old dog," Tara Grimm says, as if she'll make sure of it. "I'm glad you're keeping him. I'd hate for one of the rescues we train here to be homeless again or end up in the wrong hands."

"I can assure you Sock won't ever be homeless or in the wrong hands." I've never had a pet so bonded to me, following me everywhere like a needy shadow.

"Most of our greyhounds come from a racetrack in

Birmingham, the same one Sock came from," she says. "They retire them, and we take them so they aren't euthanized. It's good for the inmates to be reminded that life is a God-given gift, not a God-given right. It can be given or taken away. When you acquired Sock, you didn't know he belonged to Dawn Kincaid, I assume."

"He was inside a back room of an unheated house in Salem in the winter and had no food." She can interrogate all she wants. I'm not going to tell her much. "I took him home with me until we could figure out what to do with him."

"And then Dawn showed up to get him," the warden says. "She came to your house that same night to get her dog back."

"It's interesting if that's the story you've heard," I reply, and I wonder where she might have gotten an absurd idea like that.

"Well, your interest in Kathleen is a mystery to me," she says. "I wouldn't think it was the wisest move for someone in your position. Now, I said so to Mr. Brazzo, but, of course, he wasn't going to elaborate on your real motive for agreeing to meet with Kathleen. Or why you've been so kind to her."

I have no idea what she means.

"Let me be a little more blunt," the warden says. "At certain times during the day, inmates with e-mail privileges are allowed to use the computer lab, and whatever they send to pen pals or receive from them has to go through our prison e-mail system, which is monitored and has filters. I know what she's e-mailed to you over recent months."

"Then you're also aware I never answered."

"I'm aware of all inmate communications to and from the outside world, whether it's e-mail or letters written on stationery and sent by post." She pauses, as if what she just said is supposed to mean something to me. "I have an idea what you're after and why you're being friendly and accessible with Kathleen. You want information. What should concern you is who's really behind Kathleen's invitation. And what that person might want. I'm sure Mr. Brazzo told you the troubles she's had."

"I'd rather hear your account of them."

"Child molesters have never been particularly popular in prisons," she says slowly, thoughtfully, in her blunted drawl. "Kathleen served her sentence for that long before I came here, and after she got out the first time, she got into one bad mess after another. She's served six different sentences since her first incarceration, all of them right here at the GPFW, because she never seems to drift any farther away than Atlanta when she gets out. Drug crimes, until this most recent conviction for killing a teenage boy who had the misfortune of riding a motor scooter through an intersection at the moment Kathleen ran a stop sign. It's a twenty-year sentence, and she's required to serve eighty-five percent of it before she's eligible for parole. Unless there's intervention, she's likely to spend the rest of her natural life here."

"And who might intervene?"

"Are you personally acquainted with Curtis Roberts? The Atlanta lawyer who called your lawyer to invite you here?"

"No."

"I don't think the other inmates knew about Kathleen's early conviction of child molesting until your cases up there in Massachusetts started hitting the news," she says.

I don't recall there being anything about Kathleen Lawler on the news, and the explanation I was given about why she'd been transferred to Bravo Pod was that she'd angered other inmates.

"Some of them decided they were going to teach her a lesson for what she did to your murdered colleague when he was a boy," Tara adds.

I'm quite certain Kathleen Lawler's illicit relationship with Jack Fielding has not been in the news. I would know. Leonard Brazzo didn't mention this, either. I don't think it's true.

"That, added to the boy on the scooter she ran over while she was driving under the influence. There are a lot of mothers in here, Dr. Scarpetta. Grandmothers, too. Even a few great-grandmothers. Most of these inmates have children. They don't tolerate anyone who harms a child," she goes on in a slow, quiet voice that is as hard as metal. "I got wind of a plot, and for Kathleen's own protection I transferred her to Bravo Pod, where she'll remain until I feel it's safe to move her."

"I'm curious about what's been in the news, exactly." I try to draw out details of what I suspect is a complete fabrication. "I don't think I've heard this same news. I don't recall hearing Kathleen's name mentioned in connection with the Massachusetts cases."

"Apparently one of the inmates, or maybe it was one of the guards, someone here caught something on TV about Kathleen's past," Tara says evasively. "About her being a sex offender, and it spread like wildfire. It's not a popular thing to be at the GPFW. Harming a child isn't forgiven."

"And you saw whatever this was on the news as well?"

"I didn't." She watches me as if trying to figure out something.

"I'm just wondering if there's another reason," I add.

"You think there might be." It's not a question the way she says it.

"I was contacted about this visit two weeks ago, or, more accurately, Leonard Brazzo was," I remind her. "Which was around the time Kathleen was moved to protective custody and lost e-mail access. What this suggests to me is the rumor started spreading like wildfire about the same time I was asked to meet with her. Would that be correct?"

She holds my gaze, her face inscrutable.

"I'm just wondering if there really was anything in the news." I go ahead and say it.

3

The slayings began in northeastern Massachusetts about eight months ago, the first victim a star college football player whose mutilated nude body was found floating in Boston Harbor near the Coast Guard Station.

Three months later a young boy was killed in his own backyard in Salem, assumed to be the victim of a black-magic ritual that involved hammering nails into his head. Next an MIT graduate student was stabbed to death with an injection knife in a Cambridge park, and finally Jack Fielding was shot with his own gun. We were supposed to believe that Jack killed the others and himself, when in fact his own biological daughter is to blame, and perhaps she would have gotten away with it had she not failed in her attempt on me.

"There's been a lot about Dawn Kincaid in the media," I continue making my point to Tara Grimm. "But I haven't heard anything about Kathleen or her past. For that matter, what happened to Jack as a boy hasn't been in the news. Not that I'm aware of."

"We can't always stop outside influences," Tara says cryptically. "Family members are in and out. Lawyers are. Sometimes powerful people with motives that aren't always obvious, and they get something started, place someone in harm's way, and next thing that person loses what few privileges she had or loses a lot more than that. I can't tell you how many times these liberal crusader types decide to set things right and all they do is cause a lot of harm and put a lot of people at risk, and maybe you should ask yourself what business it is of someone from New York City to come down here and meddle in things."

I get up from a prison-built chair that is as hard and rigid as the warden who ordered it made, and through open blinds I see women in gray prison uniforms working in flower beds and trimming grass borders along sidewalks and fences and walking greyhounds. The sky has gotten volatile and is the color of lead, and I ask the warden who from New York City? Who is she talking about?

"Jaime Berger. I believe the two of you are friends." She steps out from behind her desk.

It's a name I haven't heard in months, and the reminder is painful and awkward.

"She's got an investigation going on, and I don't

know the ins and outs of it, and shouldn't," she says, about the well-known head of the Sex Crimes Unit for the Manhattan District Attorney's Office. "She has big plans and is insistent that nothing is leaked to the media or to anyone. So I didn't feel comfortable mentioning anything about it to your lawyer. But it did occur to me you might have found out anyway that Jaime Berger has an interest in the GPFW."

"I know nothing about an investigation and have no idea." I'm careful not to let what I'm feeling register on my face.

"You seem to be telling me the truth," she says, with a glimmer of defiance and resentment in her eyes. "It seems what I've just said is new information to you, and that's a good thing. I don't appreciate people telling me one reason for something when they really have another. I wouldn't want to think your coming here to visit Kathleen Lawler is a ruse to cover up your involvement with another individual I'm responsible for at the GPFW. That you're really here to help Jaime Berger's cause."

"I'm not part of whatever she's doing."

"You might be and not know it."

"I can't imagine how my coming to visit Kathleen Lawler would have anything to do with something Jaime is involved in."

"I'm sure you're aware that Lola Daggette is one of ours," Tara says, and it's a strange way to phrase it, as if the GPFW's most notorious inmate is an acquisition like a rescued race dog or a rodeo rider or a special plant cultivated in the nursery down the road.

"Dr. Clarence Jordan and his family, January sixth, 2002, here in Savannah," she continues. "A home invasion in the middle of the night, only robbery wasn't the motive. Apparently killing for the sake of killing was. Hacked and stabbed them to death while they were in bed, except for the little girl, one of the twins. She was chased down the stairs and got as far as the front door."

I remember hearing Savannah medical examiner Dr. Colin Dengate present the case at the National Association of Medical Examiners annual meeting in Los Angeles some years ago. There was a lot of speculation about what really happened inside the victims' mansion and how access was gained, and I seem to recall the killer made a sandwich, drank beer, and used a bathroom and didn't flush the toilet. It was my impression at the time that the crime scene raised more questions than it answered and the evidence seemed to argue with itself.

"Lola Daggette was caught washing her bloody clothing and then made up one lie after another about it," Tara says. "A drug addict who had problems with anger and a long history of abuse and run-ins with the law."

"I believe there's a theory that more than one person could have been involved," I reply.

"The theory around here is justice was served, and this fall Lola should get to explain herself to God."

"DNA, or maybe it was fingerprints, was never identified," I begin to remember the details. "Opening up the possibility of more than one assailant."

"That was her defense, the only remotely plausible story her lawyers could come up with that might explain how the victims' blood could be all over her clothes if she wasn't involved. So they manufactured an imaginary accomplice to give Lola someone to blame." Tara Grimm walks me out into the hall. "I wouldn't like to think of Lola being free in society, and it's a possibility she could have that opportunity even though her appeals are used up. Apparently new forensic tests of the original evidence were ordered, something about the DNA."

"If that's true, then law enforcement, the courts, must have a substantive reason." I look down the hallway to the checkpoint, where guards are talking to each other. "I can't imagine the Georgia Bureau of Investigation, the police, the prosecution, or the court would allow evidence to be retested unless there were legitimate grounds for it."

"I suppose it's within the realm of possibility that her conviction could be overturned. Could be others getting out early on good behavior, for that matter. Could be one big jailbreak here at the GPFW." The warden's eyes are hard, the glint in them now undisguised anger.

"Jaime Berger's not in the business of getting people out of prison," I reply.

"That seems to be the business she's in now. She's not paying social calls on Bravo Pod."

"This was how long ago, exactly? When she was here?"

"I understand she has a place in Savannah, a getaway. It's just something I've heard." She dismisses the information as gossip, while I'm certain it's more than that.

If Jaime came here to the GPFW to interview someone on death row, she didn't do so without going through exactly what I am right now. She sat down with Tara Grimm first. *Social calls,* as in more than one. A getaway from what, and for what purpose? It seems completely out of character for the New York prosecutor I used to know.

"She's been coming here, and now you're here," the warden says. "I have a suspicion you're someone who doesn't believe in coincidences. I'll let the officers know it's all right to take that photograph in and leave it with Kathleen."

She steps back inside her office, and I follow the long blue hallway, returning to the checkpoint, where a corrections officer in a gray uniform and baseball cap asks me to empty my pockets. I'm told to place everything in a plastic basket, and I hand over my driver's license and the van keys and explain the photograph has been approved by the warden, and the officer says he's aware and I can carry it in with me. I'm scanned, patted down, and given a clip-on red badge that says I'm official visitor number seventy-one. My right hand is stamped with a secret code word that will show up only under ultraviolet light when I'm leaving the facility later today.

"You might get in this place, but if your hand isn't stamped, you're never getting out," the officer says, and I can't tell if he's being friendly or funny or something else.

His name is M. P. Macon, according to his nameplate, and he calls on his radio for Central Control to open the gate. A loud electronic buzz, and a heavy green metal door slides open and clacks shut behind us. Then a second one opens, and visitation rules posted in red warn that I'm entering a zero-tolerance workplace for inmate-employee relationships. The tile floor has just been waxed and is tacky beneath my loafers as I follow Officer Macon along a gray corridor where every door is metal and locked and every corner and intersection are hung with convex security mirrors.

My escort is powerfully built and has a vigilant air that borders on combat wariness, his brown eyes constantly scanning as we reach another door that is remotely opened. We emerge into the yard in the heat, and low, ragged clouds stream overhead as if fleeing some encroaching danger. Lightning shimmers in the distance, thunder cracks, and the first drops of rain are the size of quarters on the concrete walkway they smack. I smell ozone and freshly cut grass, and the rain soaks through the thin cotton of my shirt as we walk fast.

"I was thinking this would hold off for a while." Officer Macon looks up at a dark churning sky that any second is going to split open directly over us. "This time of year, it's every day. Starts out sunny with a blue sky, just pretty as can be. Then we get us a bad storm, usually by four or five in the afternoon. Clears the air, though. This evening it will be cooled off nice. At least for this time of year in these parts. You don't want to be here in July and August."

"I used to live in Charleston."

"Well, then you know. If I could take summers off, I'd head up to where you just came from. Probably a good twenty degrees cooler in Boston," he adds, and I don't like it that he knows where I started out this morning.

Not exactly a difficult deduction to make, I remind myself. Anyone who checks would find out I work in Cambridge, and the nearest airport is Logan in Boston. He unlocks an outer gate and leads me along a walkway with high fencing and rolls of razor wire on either side. Bravo Pod looks no different from the other units, but when the outer door clicks open and we step inside, I feel a collective misery and oppressiveness that seems to seep from gray cinder block and polished gray concrete and heavy green steel. The control room on the second level is behind one-way mirrored glass directly across from the entrance, and there is a laundry room, an ice machine, a kitchen, and a grievance box.

I wonder if it's true, that this is where Jaime Berger came when she was here. I wonder what she talked about with Lola Daggette and if it is connected to Kathleen Lawler's being moved into protective custody and how any of it might relate to me. For Jaime to come here and deliberately place someone in harm's way doesn't sound like her, either. It's inconceivable to me that she could have been the source of a rumor about Kathleen Lawler's past that engendered hostility among the other inmates. Jaime is smart, shrewd, and exceedingly cautious. If anything, she is careful to a fault. Or she used to be. I haven't seen her in six months. I haven't a clue what is going on in her life. My niece, Lucy, never mentions her or what happened, and I don't ask.

Officer Macon unlocks a small room that has large plate-glass windows flanking the steel door. Inside are a white Formica table and two blue plastic chairs.

"If you just wait here, I'll bring in Miss Lawler," he says. "I may as well warn you, she's a talker."

"I'm a pretty good listener."

"The inmates sure do love attention."

"Does she have visitors often?"

"She'd like that, all right. An audience around the clock. Almost all of them would." He doesn't answer my question.

"Matter where I sit?"

"No, ma'am," he says.

Typically in interview rooms if there is a hidden camera it will be mounted diagonally across from the subject, which in this instance would be the inmate and not me. There is no camera in here, I'm fairly certain, and I sit down and scan for hidden audio surveillance microphones, fixing my attention on the ceiling directly over the table, noticing the metal fire sprinkler and next to it a tiny hole surrounded by a white mounting ring. My conversation with Kathleen Lawler will be recorded. It will be listened to by Tara Grimm and possibly others.

4

Since Kathleen Lawler was moved into protective custody, she has been locked up twenty-three hours a day inside a cell the size of a toolshed with a view through metal mesh of grass and steel fencing. She can no longer see the concrete picnic tables, benches, or flower beds she's described in e-mails to me. She rarely catches a glimpse of another inmate or a rescued dog.

The one hour she is allowed out for recreation she walks in "boring perfect squares" inside a small caged area while a corrections officer watches from a chair parked next to a bright yellow ten-gallon cooler. If Kathleen wants a drink of water, a small paper cup is pushed through chain link. She's forgotten the human touch, the brush of fingers against hers or what it's like to be hugged, she says, with a dramatic flair, as if she's been in

Bravo Pod most of her life instead of only two weeks. Being in PC, or protective custody, is the same thing as death row, she says about the new situation she finds herself in.

She no longer has access to e-mail, she explains, or to other inmates unless they yell cell to cell or stealthily carom folded notes called "kites" under the doors, a feat that requires rather remarkable ingenuity and dexterity. She's allowed to write a limited number of letters each day but can't afford stamps and is very grateful when "busy people like you bother to think about people like me and pay a little attention," she makes a point of saying. When she isn't reading or writing she watches a thirteen-inch TV built of transparent plastic with tamper-resistant screws. It has no internal speakers and the signal is weak, the reception very poor in her new confines, the worst ever, and she conjectures it's because of "all the electromagnetic interference in Bravo Pod."

"Spying," she claims. "All these male guards and a chance to see me with my clothes off. Locked up in here all by myself, and who's going to witness what really goes on? I need to move back to where I was."

Allowed only three showers per week, she worries about her hygiene. She worries about when she will be allowed to get her hair and nails done again by inmates who aren't the most skilled stylists, and she irritably indicates her overprocessed short dyed blond hair. She complains bitterly about the toll incarceration has taken on her, about what it's done to her looks, "because that's the way they degrade you in here, that's the way they get you good." The polished-steel mirror over the steel sink in her cell is a constant reminder of her real punishment for the laws she's broken, she says to me, as if it is the laws themselves that are her victims, not human beings she has violated or killed.

"I keep trying to make myself feel better by thinking, *Well, Kathleen, it's not a real glass mirror,*" she muses from the other side of the white Formica table. "Everything that reflects anything in this place must cause distortion, don't you think? The same way something is distorting the TV signal. So maybe when I look at myself, what I'm seeing is distorted. Maybe I don't really look like this."

She waits for me to affirm that her beauty really isn't lost, that her steel mirror is guilty of fraudulent reflections. Instead I comment that what she describes sounds terribly difficult and if I found myself in a similar situation I'm sure I'd share many of her same concerns. I would miss feeling fresh air on my face and seeing sunsets and the ocean. I would miss hot baths and skilled hairstylists, and I sympathize with her about the food especially, because food is more than sustenance to me and I feel comfortable talking about it freely. Food is a ritual, a reward, a way of soothing my nerves and brightening my mood after all I see.

In fact, as Kathleen Lawler continues to talk and complain and blame others for her punishing life, I think about dinner and look forward to it. I won't eat in my hotel room. That would be the last thing I feel like doing after being trapped in a dirty stinking cargo van and now inside a prison with an invisible code word stamped on my hand. When I check into my hotel in Savannah's historic district, I will wander along River Street and find something Cajun or Greek. Better yet, Italian.

Yes, Italian. I will drink several glasses of a full-bodied red wine—a Brunello di Montalcino would be nice, or a Barbaresco—and I will read the news or e-mails on my iPad so no one tries to talk to me. So no one tries to pick me up, the way people often do when I travel alone and eat and drink alone and do so many things alone. I will sit at a table by a window and text Benton and drink wine and tell him that he was right about something being very wrong. I've been set up or manipulated, and I'm not welcome here, and the gloves are off, I'll let him know. I intend to grab the truth with my bare hands.

"Well, imagine not really knowing what you look like anymore," says the shackled woman sitting across from me, and her physical appearance is her biggest heartbreak, not the death of Jack Fielding or the boy she ran over when she was drunk.

"There was tremendous opportunity for me. I missed a very real chance to be somebody," she says. "An actress, a model, a famous poet. I have a damn good singing voice. Maybe I could have composed my own lyrics and been a Kelly Clarkson. Of course, they didn't have *American Idol* when I was coming along, and Katy Perry is a closer fit, more what I used to look like if she was blond.

I suppose I could still be a famous poet. But success and acclaim are much more reachable if you're beautiful, and I was. Back in the old days, I'd stop traffic. People would gawk. The way I looked back then, I could have what I wanted."

Kathleen Lawler is unnaturally pale from years of being shielded from the sun, her body soft and shapeless, not overweight but broken down and doughy from a life that has been chronically inactive and unavoidably sedentary. Her breasts sag, and her upper thighs spread widely in the plastic chair, her former attention-getting figure as formless now as the white prison uniform she and other inmates wear in segregation. It's as if she's no longer physically human, as if she's evolved backward, returned to a primitive stage of existence like a platyhelminth, a flatworm, she says sardonically with a thickly elastic Georgia drawl that makes me think of taffy.

"I know you're probably sitting here looking at me and wondering what I'm talking about," she says, as I recall pictures I've seen, including mug shots from her arrest in 1978 after she and Jack were caught having sex.

"But when I met him at that ranch outside of Atlanta?" she says. "Well, I was something. I don't mind saying it, because it's true. Long corn-silk hair, big-busted, with an ass like a Georgia peach and legs that wouldn't quit, and huge golden-brown eyes, what Jack used to call my tiger eyes. It's funny how some things get passed on, like you've been programmed in the womb or maybe at conception and there's no escaping. The roulette wheel spins and stops and your number comes up and that's what you are no matter how hard you try or even if you don't try at all. You are what you are, you are what you're not, and other events and other people just enhance the angel or devil, the winner or the loser in you. It's all about the spinning of the wheel, whether it's hitting the winning home run in the World Series or being raped. Decided for you, and forget undoing it. You're a scientist. I'm not telling you anything you don't know about genetics. I'm sure you agree you can't change nature."

"What people experience also has significant impact," I reply.

"You can see it with the dogs," Kathleen continues, not interested in my opinions unless she tells me what they are. "You get a greyhound that was mistreated, and it's going to react to certain things a certain way and have its sensitivities. But it's either a good dog or a bad dog. It was either a winner on the track or wasn't. It's either trainable or not. I can bring out what's already there, encourage it, shape it. But I can't transform the dog into something it wasn't born to be."

She finishes telling me that she and Jack were two peas in the same pod and she did to him exactly what was done to her, and she didn't recognize it at the time, couldn't possibly have the insight, even though she was a social worker, a therapist. She was molested by the local Methodist minister when she was ten, she claims.

"He took me out for ice cream, but that's not what I ended up licking," she puts it crudely. "I was crazy in love. He made me feel so excited and special, except in retrospect I don't think *special* is what I really was feeling." She goes into graphic detail about her erotic relationship with him. "Shame, fear. I went into hiding. I can see that now. I didn't associate with other kids my age, spent huge amounts of time by myself."

Her unrestrained hands are tense in her lap, only her ankles shackled, and the chains clink and scrape against concrete whenever she restlessly shifts her feet.

"Hindsight is twenty-twenty, as they say," she continues, "and what was really going on was I couldn't tell anyone the truth about my life, about the lying, the sneaking around to motels and pay phones and all sorts of things a little girl shouldn't know about. I stopped being a little girl. He took that from me. It went on until I was twelve and he got a job with a big church in Arkansas. I didn't realize when I got involved with Jack, I basically did the same thing to him because I was encouraged and shaped in a certain way to do it, and he was encouraged and shaped in a certain way to accept it, to want it, and oh, yes, he sure did. But I see it now. What they call insight. It's taken me a lifetime to figure out we don't go to hell, we build it on a foundation already laid for us. We build hell like a shopping mall."

So far she has avoided telling me the minister's name. All she's said is he was married with seven children, and he had to have his God-given needs met and considered Kathleen his spiritual daughter, his handmaiden, his soul mate. It was right and good that they were joined in a sacred bond, and he would have married her and been open about his devotion but divorce was a sin, Kathleen explains to me in a flat, dead voice. He couldn't abandon his children. That was against God's teachings.

"Fucking bullshit," she says hatefully.

Her tiger-eyed stare is unwavering, her once lovely face peanut-shaped and haggard now, with a spiderweb of fine lines around a mouth that once was pouty and voluptuous. She is missing several teeth.

"Of course, it was unadulterated bullshit, and he probably moved on to some other little girl after I started shaving my parts and hiding from him when it was my period. Being beautiful and talented and smart didn't land me anywhere good, that's for damn sure," she emphasizes, as if it is imperative I understand that the ruin sitting across from me isn't who she is, much less who she was.

I am supposed to imagine Kathleen Lawler as young and beautiful, wise and free, and well intentioned when she began her sexual relationship with twelve-year-old Jack Fielding at a ranch for troubled youths. But what I see before me is the wreckage caused by one violation that caused another and another, and if her story is true about the minister, then he damaged her the same way she damaged Jack, and the destruction still hasn't ended and probably never will. It is the way all things begin and continue. One act, one deception. A chronic lie that escalates to critical mass, and lives are disabled, disfigured, and defiled, and hell is built, lights on and welcoming and like that motel Kathleen described in the poem she sent.

"I've always wondered if my life would have turned out different if certain other things hadn't happened," she ponders depressively, resentfully. "But maybe I'd be sitting right here anyway. Maybe God decided while my mama was pregnant with me, *This one's going to lose everything. Some have to, may as well be her.* I'm sure you understand what I mean. You see it enough in the morgue."

"I'm not a fatalist," I answer.

"Well, good for you, still believing in hope," she says snidely.

"I do." *But I don't believe in you,* I think.

I slip the plain white envelope out of my back pocket and slide it across the table to her. She takes it in small hands with translucent white skin that pale blue veins show through, and her unpolished nails are pink and clipped short. When she bows her head to look at the photograph, I notice the gray in the mousy new growth of her dyed short hair.

"I'm guessing this one was taken in Florida," she says, as if she's talking about more than one photograph. "That might be a gardenia bush I'm seeing in the background, through the spray of water from the hose he's using? Well, hold on. Hold on one damn minute." She squints at the photo. "He's older in this. It's more recent, and those little white flowers are meadowsweet. There's a lot of meadowsweet around here. You can't walk a city block without seeing meadowsweet, and now I'm thinking Savannah. Not Florida but right here in Savannah."

After a pause, she adds in a strained tone, "You happen to know who took this?"

"I don't know who took it or where," I reply.

"Well, I want to know who took it." Her eyes change. "If it's Savannah or somewhere around here, and that's what it looks like to me, well, maybe that's why you're showing it to me. To upset me."

"I have no idea where it was taken or by whom, and I'm not trying to upset you," I tell her. "I had the photograph copied and thought you might like it."

"Maybe right here. Jack was here with that car of his and I didn't know." Pain and anger sharpen her tone. "When I first knew him, I told him how much he would love Savannah. What a nice place to live, and I said he should join the Navy so he could be stationed nearby at the new submarine base they were building at Kings Bay. You know at heart Jack had a wanderlust, was someone who should have sailed around to exotic parts of the world or taken up flying and been the next Lindbergh. He should have joined the Navy and gone around the world on ships or in planes instead of being a doctor to dead people, and I wonder whose influence that was."

She glares at me.

"I wonder who the hell took this picture and why I wouldn't have known he was here if he was," she says acidly. "I don't know what you think you're up to, springing something like this on me, making me think he would come here and not try to see me. Well, I do know, too."

I wonder where Dawn Kincaid was five years ago,

around the time I speculate the photograph was taken, and how often she might have come to Savannah to see Kathleen, and might Jack have come here to see Dawn but wasn't interested in seeing her mother while he was in the area? Now that I'm confronted with Kathleen in the flesh, this woman I'd heard so much about but had never met, I seriously doubt Jack was driving his Mustang here or anywhere to see her as recently as five years ago or even ten years ago. It's almost impossible for me to imagine that after a point he would have loved Kathleen Lawler anymore or bothered with her. She is remorseless and pitiless, completely lacking in empathy for anyone, and decades of substance abuse and self-destructive living and incarceration have taken their toll. She hasn't been charming or beautiful in a very long time, and that would have mattered to my vain deputy chief.

"I don't know where the photograph was taken or any of the details," I repeat. "It was a photograph in his office, and I thought you'd like a copy, and this one is yours to keep. I didn't always know where he was during the more than twenty years we worked together on and off." I offer an opening for her to give me more information about him.

"Jack, Jack, Jack," she says and sighs. "All you did was move. Here one minute and gone the next, while I stayed in the same damn black hole. I've been right here in one cell or another most of my life, all because I loved you, Jack."

She looks at the photograph, then at me, and her eyes are harder than sad.

"I can't seem to last on the outside for long," she adds, as if I came here today to learn all about her. "Like any other addict who keeps falling off the wagon, only the wagon I fall off of isn't abstinence. It's the wagon of success. I've never been able to allow myself the success I'm capable of because it's not in the cards for me to have it. I set myself up for failure every time. It's what I mean about genetics. Failure is part of my DNA, what God decided for me and everyone who comes after me. I did to Jack what was done to me, but he never blamed me. He's dead and I may as well be because the things that matter in life have a mind of their own. Both of us victims, maybe victims of the Almighty Himself.

"And Dawn?" Kathleen goes on. "Well, I knew she wasn't right from day one. She never had a chance. Born prematurely, a tiny little thing tethered to lines and leads and tubes in an incubator, or so I was told. I didn't see it. I never held her, and how's a little thing like that going to learn to bond with other human beings when she spends the first two months of her life in a Crock-Pot and Mama's in the big house? Then a series of foster families she couldn't get along with, finally ending up with a couple in California who got killed in a car wreck, went over a cliff, something tragic like that. Fortunately for Dawn, by that point she was already at Stanford on a full scholarship. Then Harvard, and that's where she ended."

Dawn Kincaid was at Berkeley, not Stanford, before transferring to MIT, not Harvard. But I don't correct her mother.

"Like me, she had all the possibilities in the world,

and her life is over, ended before it began," Kathleen says. "No matter how it turns out in court, just being a suspect is all anyone will remember about her. Her goose is cooked. You can't have the kind of jobs she did in top secret labs, not if you've been a suspect in a crime."

Dawn Kincaid is more than a suspect. She's been indicted on multiple charges, including first-degree murder and attempted murder. But I don't say a word.

"And then what happened to her hand." Kathleen holds up her right hand, her eyes boring into me. "The kind of technology she's into, where she has to work with nanotools and whatever else? She's permanently impaired now because of losing a finger and the use of her hand. Seems like she's gotten her punishment. I imagine it must make you feel kind of bad. Maiming someone."

Dawn didn't lose a finger. She lost the tip of it and suffered tendon damage, and her surgeon thinks she will regain total functioning of her right hand. I block out the images as best I can. The gaping black square where the window had been and the wind blowing in, and a rapid shifting of the dark, frigid air as something slammed me hard between my shoulder blades. I remember losing my balance as I wildly swung the metal flashlight and feeling it crack against something solid. Then the garage lights were on and Benton was pointing his pistol at a young woman in a big black coat, facedown on the rubber flooring, bright wet blood drops near the severed tip of an index finger with a white French nail, and near it, the bloody steel knife that Dawn Kincaid tried to stab into my back.

I felt sticky all over, smelling and tasting blood as if I'd walked through a cloud of it, and I was reminded of accounts I've heard from soldiers in Afghanistan who witnessed a comrade being blown up by an IED. There one minute. A red mist the next. When Dawn Kincaid's hand slipped down the razor-sharp blade of that injection knife as it was hissing out compressed carbon dioxide gas at eight hundred pounds per square inch, I was airbrushed with her blood, and I feel stained by it in places I can't reach. I don't correct Kathleen Lawler or offer the smallest fact, because I know when I'm being goaded and lied to, maybe taunted, and my thoughts continue to go back to what Tara Grimm warned. Kathleen would feign a disconnection from her daughter when in fact the two of them are close.

"You seem to have a lot of details," I remark instead. "I'm sure the two of you have kept in touch."

"No way in hell. I'm not about to keep in touch," Kathleen says, shaking her head. "There's nothing good that would come of it with all the trouble she's in. What I don't need is any more trouble. What I know I found out from the news. We have supervised access to the Internet in the computer lab, and a selection of periodicals and newspapers in the library. I was working in the library before they moved me here."

"That sounds like a good place for you."

"Warden Grimm doesn't think you rehabilitate people by depriving them of information so they live in a news vacuum," she says, as if the warden might be listening.

"If we don't know what's going on in the world, how can we ever live in it again? Of course, this isn't rehab." She indicates Bravo Pod. "This is a warehouse, a graveyard, a place to rot." She doesn't seem to care who might be listening now. "What is it you want to know from me? You wouldn't be here if you didn't want something. Doesn't matter who asked first, supposedly. That was lawyers anyway." Kathleen stares at me like a snake about to strike. "I don't believe you're simply being nice."

"I'm wondering when you finally met your daughter for the first time," I reply.

"She was born April eighteenth, 1979, and the first time I met her she'd just turned twenty-two." Kathleen begins to recite the history as if she's scripted it in advance, and there's a chill around her now, less of an attempt to be friendly. "I remember it wasn't long after Nine-Eleven. January of 2002, and she said the terrorist attack was partly why she wanted to find me. That and the death of those people in California who she ended up with after getting passed around like a hot potato. Life is short. Dawn said that a number of times when she was with me the first time we met, and that she'd been thinking about me for as long as she could remember, wondering who I was and what I looked like.

"She said she realized she couldn't have peace until she found her real mother," Kathleen continues. "So she found me. Right here at GPFW, but not for the offense I'm currently serving time for. Drug-related charges back then. I was out for a while again and then back in again and feeling really low about it, about as much in despair as I'd ever been, because it was so damn hopeless and unfair. If you don't have money for lawyers or aren't notorious for doing something really horrible, nobody cares. You get warehoused, and here I was warehoused again and one day out of the blue, I'll never forget my surprise, I get a request that a young lady named Dawn Kincaid wants to come all the way from California to visit me."

"Did you know that was the name of the daughter you gave up for adoption?" I'm no longer careful what I ask.

"I had no idea. Of course, I assumed whoever adopts a baby would give it whatever name they decide on. I guess the first family who took Dawn were the Kincaids, whoever they were."

"Did you name her Dawn, or did they?"

"Of course I didn't name her. Like I said, never held her, never saw her. I was right here when I went into labor prematurely, right here at the GPFW in my cell and they rushed me over to Savannah Community Hospital. After it was over, I was right back in my cell like it never happened. It's not like I got any sort of follow-up."

"It was your choice to give her up for adoption?"

"What other choice was there?" she exclaims. "You give away your children because you're locked up like an animal and that's the way it goes. Think about the damn circumstances."

She glares at me, and I say nothing.

"Talk about being conceived in sin and the sins of the

parents being passed on," she says sarcastically. "It's a wonder anybody would want children born under circumstances like that. What the hell was I supposed to do, give them to Jack?"

"Give *them* to Jack?"

She looks bewildered for a moment and on the verge of tears, and she says, "He was twelve going on nothing. What the hell was he going to do with Dawn or me or anything? It wouldn't have been legally allowed and it should have been. We would have been all right, him and me. Of course, I always wondered about the life out there that he and I created, but my assumption was who would want a mother like me? So you can imagine my reaction twenty-two years later when I get this communication from someone named Dawn Kincaid. I didn't believe it at first, thought maybe it was a trick, that this person in graduate school was doing research, writing a paper. I thought, *How will I know for a fact this person really is my baby?* But all I had to do was lay eyes on her, she looked so much like Jack, at least the way I remembered him from the early years. It was eerie, as if he'd come back as a girl and appeared before me like a vision."

"You mentioned she'd somehow figured out who her real mother was. What about her father?" I ask. "When you met her that first time, did she already know about Jack?"

No one has been able to find this piece of the puzzle, not even Benton and his colleagues at the FBI, at Homeland Security, and the local police departments involved in the cases. We know that for months prior to Jack's murder, Dawn Kincaid was living in an old sea captain's house he was renovating in Salem. We now know he'd been in contact with her for at least several years, but there's been no forthcoming information to tell us how long ago the two of them were connected or why they connected or the extent of this connection.

I have searched my memory, going back to my earliest days in Richmond when Jack was my forensic pathology fellow. I've yet to recall anything he might have said or indicated to me about an illegitimate daughter or the woman who bore her. I was aware he had been abused by a staff member at some type of special ranch when he was a boy, but that was the extent of the information I had. He and I didn't talk about it, and I should have drawn him out. I should have tried harder at a time in his life when it might have helped, and even as this thought passes through my mind, a deeper part of me is convinced nothing would have helped. Jack didn't want to be helped and didn't think he needed it.

"She knew about him because I told her," Kathleen is saying. "I was honest with her. I told her everything I could about who her real parents were and showed her pictures I had of him from a long time ago and some more recent ones he'd sent. He and I kept in touch over the years. In the early days, we wrote letters."

I remember going through Jack's personal effects after his death. I don't recall seeing or hearing about any letters from Kathleen Lawler.

"Later it was e-mail for a while, which is probably

the hardest deprivation for me now," she says angrily. "E-mail's free and it's instant and I don't need people sending me stationery and stamps. Detritus and hand-me-downs, shit people don't want, and we're supposed to be grateful."

Benton and his FBI colleagues have read e-mails from more than a decade ago that have been described to me as flirty and juvenile and heavily seasoned with vulgarity. It isn't as hard for me to comprehend as one might imagine. I suspect Kathleen was Jack's first love. He probably was infatuated with her at the time of her arrest for sexual battery, and over the years, it was the stunted and damaged part of their psyches that related to each other through letters or e-mail that eventually stopped. Nothing else has been recovered that might indicate Jack communicated with Kathleen since about the time I left Virginia and he did, too. But that doesn't mean he wasn't in touch with his biological daughter, Dawn Kincaid, and in fact, he had to have been. It's just a matter of when. Maybe five years ago, if she took that picture of him.

"Mail's so damn slow," Kathleen continues complaining. "I mail something and someone in the free world mails something back, and I sit in my cell, waiting for days or longer. E-mail's instant, but Internet access isn't allowed in Bravo Pod," she reminds me resentfully. "And I can't have my dogs. I can't do training or have a greyhound in my cell. I was in the middle of training Trail Blazer and now I can't have him." She gets choked up.

"I'm so used to the company of having one of those precious dogs with me and I go from that to this, to something not much better than solitary confinement. I can't work on *Inklings*. Can't do a goddamn thing I used to."

"The magazine the prison publishes," I recall.

"I'm the editor," she says. "I was," she adds bitterly.

5

"Inklings, as in Tolkien, C. S. Lewis, the name of their group," Kathleen explains. "They'd meet at a pub in Oxford and talk about art and ideas, not that I get to talk about art and ideas very often, like most of these women give a shit. All they care about is flaunting themselves, getting their names out, getting attention and recognition. Anything to break the boredom and give a little hope that maybe you can still make something of yourself."

"Is *Inklings* the only publication here?" I ask.

"The only show in town." Her pride is obvious, but it's not about any literary achievement she might enjoy. It's about power. "There isn't much to look forward to. Special treats to eat, and I'm a regular test kitchen for treats, not that any of it is something I'd touch in the free world. And the publication of *Inklings*. I lived and breathed for that magazine. Warden Grimm is generous as long as you play by the rules. She's been really good to me, but I don't want to be in PC and don't need to be. She needs to move me back to the other side," she says, as if Tara Grimm is listening.

Kathleen has real power at the GPFW. Or she did. She got to decide who was recognized and who was rejected, who became famous among the inmates and who remained in obscurity. I wonder if this might have something to do with why certain inmates are after her, assuming what I've been told is true. I wonder what the real reason is for her being moved as I think of what Tara Grimm said about the family murdered in Savannah on January 6, 2002, and Jaime Berger's recent visits to Bravo Pod.

"I was an English major in college, wanted to be a professional poet but instead went into social work, got my master's in that," Kathleen tells me. "*Inklings* was my idea, and Warden Grimm let me do it."

January 2002 was when Dawn Kincaid came to Savannah and met Kathleen for the first time, or so Kathleen claims. Possibly Dawn was here in Savannah when the doctor and his family were murdered. Hacked and stabbed to death, a category of violence Benton describes as personal, hands-on, often accompanied by a sexual component. The perpetrator is aroused and stimulated by the physical act of penetrating a victim's body with a blade or, in the recent case of the boy in Salem, penetrating the skull with iron nails.

"We have our editorial meetings in the library to review submissions and go over the layout with the design team." Kathleen is talking about her magazine. "While I have the final say about what gets published, Warden Grimm approves everything, then each person whose original piece is selected gets her picture on the cover. It's a really big deal and can cause hard feelings."

"What's happening to your magazine now?" I ask, as I wonder if Lola Daggette might have known Dawn Kincaid and is aware that Kathleen is Dawn's mother.

"Of course they're not letting me do it," Kathleen says resentfully. "Someone else obviously is. I was working in the library, like I said, but I can't do that, either. That's how I funded my commissary account. Twenty-four dollars a month, and buying a treat now and then, paper, stamps, and it doesn't take long. Who's going to send me money from the outside when what I've got runs out? Who do I have to help? How am I supposed to buy a damn bottle of shampoo so I can wash my hair?"

I don't answer. She'll get nothing from me.

"The rules are the same for everyone in Bravo Pod, whether you're PC or a mass murderer. I guess that's the price you pay for being kept safe," she says, and I'm struck by how harsh she looks, as if something hideous inside her is working its way out. "Except I'm not safe. I've been stuck right here with danger right over my damn head."

"What danger is over your head?" I ask.

"I don't know why they'd do that to me. They need to move me back."

"What danger is over your head?" I ask again.

"It's Lola who's behind all this," she says, and the circle is complete.

Jaime Berger has been coming to the GPFW to talk to Lola Daggette, who's connected to Kathleen Lawler, who's connected to me. I don't let on that I know who Lola Daggette is as I continue to entertain the possibility that she is somehow connected to Dawn. I don't know how or why, but all of us are in the circle.

"She wanted to get me moved over here so I'd be near her," Kathleen says angrily. "We don't have a separate pod for death row. Lola's the only one on it right now. The last woman was Barrie Lou Rivers, the one who killed all those people in Atlanta by mixing arsenic in their tuna-fish sandwiches."

The Deli Devil. I'm familiar with the case, but I don't show it.

"Same people every day getting the same tuna special and she smiled at them, just as nice as she could be, as they got sicker and sicker," Kathleen goes on. "Right before she was supposed to die by lethal injection, she choked to death on a tuna sandwich in her cell. What I call one of life's black ironies."

"Death row is upstairs?"

"Just a maximum-security cell like any other, no different from the cell I'm in now." Kathleen is getting louder and more upset. "Lola's upstairs and I'm down here, one floor below her. So she's not yelling at me directly or passing kites directly. But her words get around."

"What words have you been hearing?"

"Threats. I know she's making them."

I don't point out the obvious, that Lola Daggette is locked up twenty-three hours a day just as Kathleen is, and it's not possible for the two of them to have physical contact. I don't see how Lola can hurt anyone.

"She knew if she got people riled up and placed me in danger, they sure as hell would move me to the same damn pod she's in. Which is exactly what they did," she says in a scathing tone. "Lola wants me nearby," Kathleen adds, and I don't believe Lola Daggette somehow willed Kathleen to Bravo Pod.

Tara Grimm did.

"Have you had similar problems with other inmates in the past?" I ask. "Problems that necessitated moving you?"

"You mean moving me to Bravo Pod?" Kathleen raises her voice. "Hell, no. I've never been in segregation before because why would I be? They need to let me out. I need to go back to my life."

Officer Macon walks past the windows of the visitation room. I'm aware of him looking in at us, and I avoid looking back as I think of the poem Kathleen sent and the prison's literary magazine that she edited until several weeks ago. I wonder how often she published herself and passed over others. I glance at my watch. Our hour is almost up.

"Well, it's nice of you to bring me this picture of Jack." Kathleen holds the photograph at arm's length and narrows her eyes. "I hope your trial goes all right."

The way she says it catches my attention, but I don't react.

"Trials aren't a picnic. Course, I usually just plead guilty in exchange for the lightest sentence I can get. Save the taxpayers money. Have had a few suspended sentences because I was honest enough to just say yup, I did it, sorry about that. If you don't have a reputation to protect, just plead guilty. Better than getting a jury of your peers," she snarls, "who want to make an example out of you."

She isn't thinking about Dawn Kincaid, who will never plead guilty to anything. A sensation begins in the pit of my stomach.

"Now, you do have a reputation, Dr. Kay Scarpetta. You have a reputation as big as the great outdoors, don't you? So it's not all that simple for you, is it?" She smiles coldly, and her eyes are flat. "I sure am glad we finally met so I could see what all the fuss was about."

"I don't know what fuss you're referring to."

"I got sick as hell of hearing about you. I guess you haven't read the letters."

I don't answer her about the letters she and Jack supposedly wrote to each other. Letters I've never seen.

"I can tell you haven't read them." Kathleen is nodding and grinning, and I can see the gaping spaces where she's missing teeth. "You really don't know, do you? It makes sense you didn't. I have to wonder if you would have had any contact with me if you knew. Well, maybe you would but maybe you wouldn't be so smug. Maybe you wouldn't think you're so high and mighty."

I sit quietly. Perfectly composed. Nothing shows. Not curiosity. Not the anger I feel.

"Before e-mail, we wrote real letters on paper," she says. "He always wrote to me on lined notebook paper like he was still a schoolboy. This would have been in the early nineties, and Jack was working for you in Richmond and miserable as hell all the time. He used to write that what you needed was to be fucked but good. That you were a frustrated crazy bitch and if someone just went ahead and fucked you good maybe it would improve your disposition. Apparently he and that homicide detective you worked with all the time back then used to joke about it in the morgue and at crime scenes. They'd joke you'd been in the cooler too long and with too many dead bodies and somebody needed to warm you up. Someone needed to show you what it was like to be with a man whose dick could still get stiff."

Pete Marino was a homicide detective in Richmond when I was chief, and I realize why I've not seen any such letters. The FBI would have them. Benton's the criminal intelligence analyst, the forensic psychologist assisting the Boston field office, and I know for a fact he's read the e-mails that Kathleen and Jack exchanged. Benton has given me an overview of what is in them, and I have no doubt he would have read any letters written on paper, too. He wouldn't want me to see what Kathleen Lawler has just described. He wouldn't want me to know about cruel comments Marino made, about him mocking me behind my back. Benton would shield me from anything that hurtful, arguing that there is nothing to be gained from it. I am steady and calm. I won't react. I won't give Kathleen Lawler the satisfaction.

"So here we are at last. Finally, I'm looking at you," she says. "The big chief. The big boss. The legendary Dr. Scarpetta."

"I suppose you're somewhat of a legend to me, too," I say with no affect.

"He loved me more than he ever loved you."

"I have no reason to doubt he did."

"I was the love of his life."

"I have no reason to doubt you were."

"He resented the fucking hell out of you," she says, and the calmer I am the nastier she is. "He used to say you have no idea how hard you are on people and maybe if you ever looked in the mirror you'd understand why you don't have any friends. He used to call you *Dr. Right* and he was *Dr. Wrong*. And the cops were *Detective Wrong* or *Officer Wrong*. Everybody wrong except you. *Wrong, Jack. You have to do it this way. Wrong, Jack!*" she continues, unable to disguise her delight. "Always telling him what to do and how to do it right. *Like the entire fucking world is a crime scene or a court case,* he used to complain to me."

"At times he resented me. It wasn't a secret," I reply reasonably.

"Well, he sure as hell did."

"No one's ever accused me of being easy to work for."

"People like you don't get where they are by being easy. They step on people and have to kick them out of the way or belittle them for the fun of it."

"That's one thing I don't do. It's a shame if he indicated otherwise."

"He always blamed you when things didn't go well."

"He often did."

"What he never did even once was blame me."

"Do you blame him for what's happened to you?" I ask.

"He might have been twelve, but he wasn't a boy. He sure as hell wasn't, take it from me. He started it. Following me around. Trumping up excuses to talk to me, to touch me, telling me how he felt, how smitten he was. Things happen."

Yes, things happen, I think. *Even when they absolutely shouldn't.*

"It just broke his heart when they hauled me off in handcuffs, and then later, when he had to look at me in court, it just about killed him," she says, and her hostility toward me has vanished as suddenly as it appeared. "They separated us, all right, busted us apart, but not our souls. We still had our souls. Jack did admire you. As tedious as it was hearing about it, he did have respect for you. I know he did. The thing about Jack, though, was he never felt just one thing about anybody. If he loved you, he hated you. If he respected you, he disrespected you. If he wanted to be with you, he'd run away. If he found you, he'd lose you. And now he's gone."

She looks down at her hands in her lap, and her shackles scrape and clank against the floor as she moves her feet and begins to shake. Her face is red, and she's about to cry.

"I had to get that out. I know it wasn't nice." She doesn't look at me.

"I understand."

"I hope you won't cut me off because of it. I'd like to keep hearing from you."

"It's all right to get things out."

"I didn't know how I would feel about it after some time has passed, about him being dead," she says, staring down. "I almost can't comprehend it. It's not like he was part of the life I have now, but he was my past. He's the reason I'm here. And now the reason is gone but I'm not."

"I'm sorry," I say.

"It feels so vacant. That's the word that keeps coming into my mind. Vacant. Like a big vacant lot windswept and barren."

"I know it's painful."

"If people had just left us alone." She lifts her eyes, and they are bloodshot and swimming with tears. "We didn't hurt each other. If they'd just left us alone, none of this would have happened. Who were we hurting? It's everyone else who was hurtful."

I say nothing. There is nothing to say.

"Well, I hope the rest of your time in Savannah is productive." It sounds very odd, the way she puts it.

Officer Macon walks past the glass windows on either side of the steel door again, making sure everything is okay, and while Kathleen doesn't look at him, I can tell he is on her radar.

"I'm glad you came and we had a chance to talk. I'm

glad your lawyer and all the lawyers opened that door for us, and I appreciate any pictures or anything else you're kind enough to give me," she adds, and it sounds strange, as if she means something other than what she's saying, something other than what I know, and she waits for Officer Macon to vanish from our view again.

Reaching inside the collar of her white uniform shirt, she withdraws something from her bra. She scoots a tightly folded piece of paper across the table to me.

6

Water drips from live oak trees and palmettos at the edge of the parking lot, and I smell rain and the sweet perfume of flowering shrubs, their petals littering the earth like bright confetti. The air is thick and hot, and the sun glowers intermittently through roiling dark clouds to the west, and I climb back into the cargo van, marveling that nobody stopped me.

As Officer Macon escorted me out of Bravo Pod and along a sidewalk still wet from the storm, he gave no indication that anything was out of line or even out of the ordinary, but I didn't believe him. I couldn't imagine he or someone, perhaps the warden herself, wasn't aware that Kathleen Lawler had slipped me a communication I'm not supposed to have. Back at the checkpoint, where my hand was scanned under a UV light, revealing the password *snow* stamped on my skin, nothing was said beyond Officer Macon's thanking me for coming, as if my visiting the Georgia Prison for Women was some sort of favor to the place. I told him Kathleen was afraid for her safety, and he smiled and said the inmates love to tell "tall tales," and that the very reason she'd been moved was to ensure her safety. I said good-bye and left.

I'm about to conclude that my original suspicion is correct. My conversation with Kathleen might have been audio-recorded, but she and I were not captured by a video camera. Otherwise, when she silently flicked the kite across the table to me, it would have been observed by corrections officers, at the very least. Most certainly I would have been marched back to the warden's ivy-infested office, where I would have been forced to surrender the folded piece of paper that I'm aware of in my back pocket as if it is a rock or something hot. It also occurs to me that Kathleen wouldn't have sneaked anything to me had she worried about being caught, and I have the growing suspicion she is part of a manipulation more treacherous than anything I might have imagined. Although I'm not ready to decide she just got the best of me, I realize she might have.

Cranking the engine, I remove what Kathleen gave to me as I scan the parking lot, making sure no one is nearby and watching. I'm aware of the mesh-covered narrow windows in the blue metal-roofed pods, of the columned redbrick administration building I just left. Steam rises from wet pavement and is carried on the heavy, warm air through my open window, and in a far corner of the crowded lot I notice a black Mercedes wagon reminiscent of a hearse, and a woman sitting inside it with the engine off, talking on a cell phone. It's hot and muggy to be inside a car with no air-conditioning running, but her windows are cracked. She doesn't seem to be paying any attention to me. I'm uneasy and unsettled, and by this point I believe I have reason to be.

Ever since Benton dropped me off at Logan early this morning, I've had the sensation that I'm being monitored or tampered with, yet I'm aware of no tangible evidence that might prove it. But the feeling has gotten stronger because of other odd things. This ridiculous van I never reserved, dirty and smelly, its glove box crammed full of Bojangles' napkins and charter-boat brochures. When I tried repeatedly to call Bryce to complain, leaving him the pointed message that I can't believe a high-end concierge rental company would have something like this in their fleet, he never called back. I've had no communications from him all day, as if my chief of staff is avoiding me. Then there's strange information I've been given. And now this.

I smooth open a piece of white paper that was folded into a diamond shape no bigger than a throat lozenge. Written in blue ballpoint ink is a phone number that is vaguely familiar at first, and then I'm jolted by recognition. "USE PAY PHONE," the note says in tiny block printing, and there is nothing else, just that underlined directive and Jaime Berger's cell phone number. The late afternoon is darker, rain starting again, tapping the

metal roof of the van, and I turn on the windshield wipers. They leave greasy arches as they slowly, loudly sweep
across the glass, and I retrieve my shoulder bag from
under the seat. I watch the black Mercedes wagon drive
out of the lot, noticing a Navy Diver bumper sticker on
the back as I get a strange feeling. Then I realize why.

My bag has been gone through. Am I sure? I think so.
Yes, I'm certain, I decide, as I reconstruct what I did
when I first arrived several hours earlier. I sent Benton a
text message and zipped my phone into the rear pocket
of my bag, where I always keep my wallet, my credentials,
my keys, and other valuables. Now my phone is in the
side compartment. How simple and safe to search the
van while I was inside the prison. Officers had my keys,
and I was locked up in Bravo Pod, talking to Kathleen,
but I can't think of anything important that someone
might have found. My iPhone and iPad are password-
protected, so no one could have gotten into those, and I
can't think of anything else that would matter. What
might someone have been looking for? Perhaps case files,
it occurs to me. Or, more likely, something that might
indicate I came here today for reasons other than what I
told Tara Grimm. I unlock my phone.

My first impulse is to call my niece, Lucy, and bluntly
ask her if she's been in touch with Jaime Berger. It's possible Lucy has information that might give me a hint
about what is going on, about what I've just walked into,
but I can't bring myself to do it. Lucy hasn't talked about
Jaime since all of us were together last, some six months
ago, during the holidays, and she has yet to admit they've

broken up, when I know they must have. My niece wouldn't have moved from New York to Boston if there hadn't been a personal reason.

It wasn't about money. Lucy doesn't need money. It wasn't about her wanting to bring her extraordinary computer expertise to the Cambridge Forensic Center, which just began taking cases last year. She doesn't need to work for me or the CFC. Her decision to relocate her entire existence most likely was about fearing a loss she believed was inevitable, and she did what she's always done so well. She aggressively avoided pain and dodged rejection. She probably ended the relationship before Jaime had the chance, and by the time Lucy did so, she'd already set up a new life for herself in Boston. My niece has a habit of telling you she's leaving after she's already gone.

I drive away from the GPFW, going out the same way I came in, past the nursery and the salvage yard, wondering where I'm going to find a pay phone. There isn't one on every corner these days, and I'm not sure I should call Jaime or anyone else. Benton worried that I was being set up, and I'm about to conclude he is right. By whom and for what reason? Maybe by Dawn Kincaid's defense team. Maybe by something far more sinister. Dawn Kincaid tried to murder me and failed, so now she wants to finish the job. The thought gusts through my mind like an arctic blast, and my head is beginning to pound as if my hangover is back.

You should get as far from here as possible. It's too late to fly out of the Savannah–Hilton Head Airport, but I could drive to Atlanta, where I'm sure I can get a flight to Boston tonight. In this damn cargo van? I envision myself broken down on the roadside near a swamp in the middle of nowhere and decide my wisest course is to stay in Savannah as planned. *Don't do anything rash. Be deliberate and logical,* I tell myself, as I drive in the rain, the van chugging and misfiring, slowing down and speeding up on its own while its worn-out wiper blades smear the glass with loud rubbery swipes. My head is aching like a bad tooth, and I'm out of Advil, having taken the last of it earlier today when I was traveling.

I roar past a truck dealership and an auto body shop, and every place I pass feels isolated and impenetrable and ominous, as if the world is in a lockdown. I've not noticed another car in miles and have the same eerie feeling I get right before something bad happens. A stillness, a shifting of reality, a sense of foreboding that always precedes a tragic announcement, a brutal case coming in, a horror of a scene in the room just ahead. My thoughts find their way back to Lola Daggette.

I don't remember much about the murders of the Savannah doctor and his family, only that they were savage and that there are still lingering questions to this day about whether there was one perpetrator or two, or if whoever is to blame had some connection to the victims. I remember I was staying in a hotel in Greenwich, Connecticut, when I first heard about the family murdered "in their sleep," as it was described all over the news. January 6, 2002. It was a time when I was between just about everything one could be between. Careers, relationships, residences, and the world prior to 9/11 and the one we've been left with since. It was a terrible phase, really, about as destabilized and depressing as any I can recall, and I was watching the evening news and eating dinner in my room when I heard about slayings in Savannah believed to have been committed by a teenage girl. I remember her young face repeatedly shown on the TV screen, and the victims' Federal-style brick mansion, its portico festooned with yellow crime scene tape.

Lola Daggette.

I remember she was smiling into television cameras at her arraignment and waving at people in the courtroom as if she didn't have a clue about the trouble she was in, and I was struck by the silver braces on her teeth and the teenage blemishes on her plump cheeks. She seemed like a harmless kid dazed by the attention and drama but enjoying it, and I was reminded that people rarely look like what they do. No matter how often I'm confronted by examples of that fact, I'm still surprised and chilled by how easy it is to make judgments based on appearances. Most of the time we're wrong.

I slow down and chug off the road into the parking lot of the first open businesses I've seen around here: a True Value hardware, a pharmacy, and a guns-and-ammo store where there are several pickup trucks and SUVs, and a pay phone next to an ATM. Of course, there would be a pay phone and an ATM at a business where the sign in front is a body diagram inside a red circle with a slash across, and the logo: *Don't be a victim. Buy a gun.* Through plate glass I see a wall of rifles and shotguns, and a showcase where several men are congregated, and to the left of the front door, a black pay phone is cradled inside a stainless-steel box attached to the wall.

Reaching for my briefcase, I get out my iPad as rain falls steadily, drumming the metal roof, and I flip off the monotonous wiper blades and headlights but leave the windows cracked and the engine running. Clicking on the browser, I log on to the Internet and search Lola Daggette's name and read a story published in the *Atlanta Journal-Constitution* last November:

SAVANNAH KILLER
LOSES FINAL APPEAL

A woman convicted and sentenced to death almost nine years ago for the grisly slayings of a Savannah doctor, his wife, and their two young children was denied an emergency stay today by the Georgia Supreme Court, clearing the way for the execution.

Lola Daggette was convicted of breaking into Dr. Clarence Jordan's three-story mansion in Savannah's historic district during the early-morning hours of January 6, 2002. According to the prosecutor and police, she attacked the thirty-five-year-old physician and his thirty-year-old wife, Gloria, in bed, stabbing and slashing them repeatedly with a knife before proceeding down the hallway to their twin son and daughter's room. It is believed that five-year-old Brenda was awakened by her brother's screams and tried to escape by running down the stairs. Her pajama-clad body was found near the front door. Like her parents and her brother, Josh, she had been stabbed and cut so savagely, she was almost decapitated.

Several hours after the homicides were committed, eighteen-year-old Lola Daggette returned to a nonsecure halfway house, where she was enrolled in a residential program for substance abuse. A staff member discovered Daggette in the bathroom, rinsing bloody clothing. DNA later connected her to the murders.

With the high court's action today, all of Daggette's state and federal appeals and habeas corpus issues have been exhausted, and her execution by lethal injection at the Georgia Prison for Women is expected to take place in the spring.

In other articles I skim, her defense counsel claimed she had an accomplice and it was this person who actually committed the homicides. Lola Daggette never entered the Jordan mansion but was to wait outside while her accomplice committed a burglary, her lawyers said. The sole basis for the defense was the alleged existence of an accomplice who has never been physically described or identified, someone who borrowed a set of Lola's clothing and afterward instructed her to dispose of it or clean it, possibly with the intention of setting her up to be charged with the crimes. Lola never took the stand, and I can see why a jury would have convened less than three hours before finding her guilty.

She was set to die this past April but was granted a stay after a botched execution resulted in a second dose of deadly chemicals and it took twice the usual time for the condemned to die. As a result, a federal judge blocked the executions of Lola Daggette and five male inmates at Coastal State Prison, asserting that he needed an opportunity to decide whether Georgia's lethal injection procedures place the condemned at risk of a prolonged and painful death, thus constituting punishment that was cruel and unusual. Georgia executions are supposed to resume this October, with Lola Daggette's believed to be scheduled first.

I sit in the van in the rain, baffled. If Lola Daggette didn't commit the murders but knows who did, why would she protect the real killer all these years? Months away from her execution and she's still not talking? Or maybe she is. Jaime Berger has been in Savannah. She's interviewed Lola Daggette. Possibly she's interviewed Kathleen Lawler, with whom she may have made promises of an early release, but how is any of this the jurisdiction of a Manhattan assistant DA, unless the Jordan homicides and possibly Dawn Kincaid somehow connect to a sex crime in New York City?

More to the point, if Jaime has any interest in Kathleen and her diabolical daughter, Dawn, why wouldn't

Jaime have contacted me? Apparently she just did, I'm reminded, as I look at the tiny piece of creased paper on the seat next to me, and I then think of the violent events of this past February, when I was almost killed. There was no break in Jaime's silence. She didn't call. She didn't send an e-mail. She didn't check on me. While we were never close friends, her seeming indifference was painful and surprising.

Returning the iPad to my briefcase, I retrieve my Visa card from my wallet and climb out of the van, the rain falling in big, cool drops on my bare head. I pick up the receiver of the pay phone and enter zero and the number Kathleen Lawler wrote on the kite. I swipe my credit card, and the call goes through. Jaime Berger answers on the second ring.

7

It's Kay Scarpetta—" I start to say, and she cuts me off in her crisp, strong voice.

"You're still staying the night, I hope."

"Excuse me?" She must think I'm someone else. "Jaime? It's Kay—"

"Your hotel is within walking distance of me." Jaime Berger sounds as if she's in a hurry, not rude but impersonal and brusque and not about to let me get in a word. "Check in first, and we'll have a bite to eat."

It's obvious she doesn't want to talk, that maybe she's not alone. This is absurd. You don't agree to meet someone when you don't know what it's about, I tell myself.

"Where?" I ask.

Jaime gives me an address that is several blocks off

Savannah's riverfront. "I'll look forward to it," she adds. "See you shortly."

I call Lucy next as a man in cutoff jeans and a baseball cap climbs out of a dusty gold Suburban. He doesn't give me a glance as he walks in my direction and slides a wallet out of his back pocket.

"I need to ask you something," I say immediately when my niece answers, and it's an effort not to sound frustrated. "You know it's never my intention to pry or interfere with your personal life."

"That's not a question," Lucy says.

"I hesitated to call you about this, but now I really must. It doesn't seem to be a secret that I'm down here. Do you understand what I'm getting at?" I turn my back to the man in the baseball cap as he gets cash out of the ATM next to me.

"Maybe you could be a little less mysterious. It sounds like you're inside a metal drum."

"I'm using a pay phone outside a gun store. And it's raining."

"What the hell are you doing at a gun store? What's wrong?"

"Jaime," I then say. "Nothing's wrong. That I know of."

After a long pause, my niece asks, "What's happened?"

I can tell by her hesitation and the tone of her voice that she isn't going to have information for me. She doesn't know that Jaime is in Savannah. Lucy isn't the reason Jaime somehow knows I'm here and why and where I'm staying.

"I'm just making sure you didn't perhaps mention to her that I was coming down to Savannah," I reply.

"Why would I do that? What's going on?"

"I'm not sure what's going on. In fact, a more accurate answer is I don't know. But you haven't talked to her recently."

"No."

"Any reason Marino would have?"

"Why would he? What damn reason would he have to contact her?" Lucy says, as if it would be a massive betrayal for Marino, who used to work for Jaime, to talk to her about anything. "To have some friendly chat and divulge private information about what you're doing? No way. Wouldn't make sense," she adds, and her jealousy is palpable.

It doesn't matter how attractive and formidable my niece is, she doesn't believe she will ever be the most important person to anyone. I used to call her my green-eyed monster because she has the greenest eyes I've ever seen and can be monstrously immature, insecure, and jealous. She's not to be trifled with when she gets that way. Hacking into computers is as effortless as opening a cupboard for her, and she's not bothered by spying or paying people back for what she perceives as crimes against her or someone she loves.

"I certainly hope he wouldn't divulge information to her or anyone," I reply, and I wish the man in the baseball cap would finish up at the ATM. It occurs to me he might be listening to my conversation. "Well, if Marino's said something," I add, "I'll find out soon enough."

I can hear Lucy typing on a keyboard. "We'll just see. I'm in his e-mail. No. Doesn't look like anything to or from her."

Lucy is the CFC's systems administrator and can get into any electronic communications or files on the server, including mine. She can get into virtually anything she wants, period.

"Not recently," she then says, and I imagine her executing searches, scrolling through Marino's e-mails. "Don't see anything for this year."

She's indicating she sees no evidence that Marino has e-mailed Jaime since she and Lucy broke up. But that doesn't mean Marino and Jaime haven't had contact by phone or some other means. He's not naïve. He knows Lucy can look at anything on the CFC computer. He also knows that even if she didn't have legal access, she'd look anyway, if that's what she feels like doing. If Marino's been in contact with Jaime and hasn't mentioned it to me, it's going to bother me considerably.

"Would you mind asking him about it?" I say to Lucy as I rub my temples, my head throbbing.

She does mind. I can hear her resistance when she says, "Sure. I can talk to him, but he's still on vacation."

"Then interrupt his fishing trip, please."

I hang up as the man in the baseball cap disappears inside the gun store, and I decide he wasn't paying attention to me, that I'm of no interest and am acting slightly paranoid. I follow the sidewalk past the hardware store, noticing what appears to be the same black Mercedes wagon with the Navy Diver bumper sticker parked in front of Monck's Pharmacy. Small and overstocked, with no other customers in sight, it is reminiscent of a country store with aisles of home-care supplies such as walking aids, vascular stockings, and seat-lift chairs. Friendly signs posted everywhere promise customized medications and same-day delivery *right to your doorstep,* and I scan shelves for pain relievers as I try to come up with any possible reason why Jaime Berger might have an interest in Lola Daggette.

What I don't doubt is that Jaime is relentless. If Lola Daggette has information that is important for some reason, Jaime will do everything she can to make sure the convicted killer doesn't take it to the grave. I can think of no other explanation for Jaime's visiting the GPFW, but what I can't fathom is how I factor in and why. *Well, you're about to find out,* I tell myself, as I carry a bottle of Advil gelcaps to the counter, where no one is working. *In a couple of hours you'll know what there is to know.* I decide water would be a good idea and return to the refrigerated section, selecting an iced tea instead, and I return to the counter and I wait.

An older man in a lab coat is busy counting pills in back, filling prescriptions, and I don't see anyone else, and I wait. I open the Advil and take three gelcaps, washing them down with the iced tea as my impatience grows.

"Excuse me," I announce myself.

The pharmacist barely glances at me and calls out to someone behind him, "Robbi, can you get the register?"

When no one answers, he stops what he's doing and comes to the counter.

"I sure am sorry. I didn't realize I'm the only one here. Guess everybody's out making deliveries, or maybe it's break time again. Who knows?" He smiles at me as he takes my Visa card. "Will there be anything else?"

It has stopped raining when I return to the van, and I notice that the black Mercedes wagon is gone. The sun breaks through the clouds as I drive away, and the wet pavement is bright in the sunlight. Then the old city comes into view, low brick and stone buildings spreading out to the Savannah River, and in the distance, silhouetted against the churning sky, is the familiar cable-stayed Talmadge Memorial Bridge, which would take me into South Carolina, were that my destination. I imagine splendid haunts such as Hilton Head and Charleston, envisioning the oceanfront condo Benton used to have in Sea Pines, and the historic carriage house with its lush garden that once was mine.

So much of my past is rooted in the Deep South, and my mood is nostalgic and edgy as I reach the gray granite Customhouse and the gold-domed City Hall, then my hotel, a stolid Hyatt Regency on the river, where tugs and tour boats are moored. On the opposite shore is the posh Westin Resort, and farther down, cranes look like gigantic praying mantises perched above shipyards and warehouses, the water flat and the gray-green of old glass.

I climb out of the van and apologize to a valet who

looks very Caribbean in his white jacket and black Bermuda shorts. I warn him about my cranky, undependable rental vehicle and feel obliged to let him know it wasn't what I reserved and that it wanders all over the road and the brakes are bad, while I grab my overnight bag and other belongings. A hot breeze stirs live oaks, magnolias, and palms, and traffic bumping over brick pavers sounds like the rain, which has completely stopped, the sky patched with hints of blue as the sun sinks and shadows spread. This part of the world, where I've been so many times before, should be a welcome respite and a rich indulgence. Instead it feels unsafe. It feels like something to fear. I wish Benton were here. I wish I hadn't come, that I had listened to him. I must find Jaime Berger without delay.

The lobby is typical of most Hyatts I've stayed in, an expansive atrium surrounded by rooms on six floors, and as I ride the glass elevator up, I replay the exchange I just had with the clerk at the front desk, a young woman who claimed my reservation had been canceled hours earlier. When I said that wasn't possible, she replied that she had taken the call herself not long after she started her shift at noon. A man called and canceled. Whoever it was had my reservation number and the correct information and was very apologetic.

I asked the clerk if whoever did this was from my office in Cambridge, and she said she thought so. I asked if his name was Bryce Clark, and she wasn't sure, and then I suggested it probably was my office calling to confirm,

not to cancel, and there had been a misunderstanding.
No, she shook her head. Absolutely not. The clerk said
the person called to cancel with the explanation that Dr.
Scarpetta was very disappointed she couldn't make it to
Savannah because it's one of her favorite cities, and he
hoped there would be no charge for the room even
though he was canceling at the last minute. Supposedly I'd missed my connection in Atlanta and therefore
couldn't possibly get here in time for the appointment I
had. The man was quite chatty, the clerk said, convincing
me it was my extroverted chief of staff, Bryce, who has
yet to call me back.

The canceled room is like the cargo van, like the note
from Kathleen Lawler and the pay phone, like everything
else that's happened today, and I tell myself I'll know
what it's all about soon enough. I unlock my door and
enter a room overlooking the river as a container ship as
tall as the hotel silently glides past, headed out to sea,
and I try to reach Benton, but he's not answering. I send
him a text message letting him know I'm heading out for
a meeting, and I give him the address Jaime gave me,
because someone I trust needs to know where I'll be. But
I tell him nothing else, not who I'm going to see or that
I'm uneasy and suspicious of just about everyone. Unpacking my overnight bag, I deliberate about changing
my clothes and decide not to bother.

Jaime Berger is on a mission in the Lowcountry, and
apparently she put Kathleen Lawler up to the task of arranging a meeting with me while I'm here. Indeed, Jaime
may have used her to lure me here to begin with. But no

matter how much I dissect the information I have, it all seems far-fetched, and I can't stop sorting through it in hopes it will make sense. But it seems impossibly illogical. If Jaime is behind my coming to the GPFW today and knows I'm spending the night in this hotel, then why would she need an inmate to sneak a cell phone number to me? Why wouldn't Jaime simply call me herself? My cell phone number hasn't changed. Hers hasn't, either. She has my e-mail address.

She could have reached me directly any number of ways, and why a pay phone? What was that about? The cargo van, my canceled reservation, and I think about what Tara Grimm said to me. *Coincidences.* I'm not someone who believes in them, and she's right, at least about the events of late. There are too many coincidences for them to be random and meaningless. They add up to something, but I really can't imagine what, and I may as well stop driving myself crazy about it. I brush my teeth and wash my face, in the mood for a long hot shower or bath that I don't have time for right now.

I study myself in the mirror over the bathroom sink and decide I look wilted by heat and rain, by hours spent in a prison and driving a malfunctioning van with no air-conditioning, and this isn't the way I want Jaime to see me. I can't completely define the way she makes me feel, but I recognize ambivalence and self-consciousness, a certain discomfort that has never gone away in all the years I've known her. It's irrational, but I can't seem to help it. To watch Lucy so openly adore her was indescribable.

I remember the first time they met more than a decade ago, how animated Lucy was, how riveted she was to Jaime's every word and gesture. Lucy couldn't take her eyes off her, and when it finally became what it was meant to become many years later, I was amazed and pleased. I was startled and unnerved. Most of all, I didn't trust it. Lucy was going to get hurt, I thought all along. She was going to get as badly hurt as she's ever been in her life, I feared. No woman she's ever been with can compare to Jaime, who is close to my age and undeniably powerful and compelling. She's rich. She's brilliant. She's beautiful.

I scrutinize my short blond hair and muss it with a dab of gel, staring at the face staring back at me. The overhead light is unkind, creating shadows that accentuate my strong features, deepening the fine lines at the corners of my eyes and the shallow folds from my nose to my mouth. I look shopworn. I look older. Jaime's going to sum me up in a glance by saying that what I've been going through has taken its toll. Almost being murdered has left its mark. Stress is toxic. It kills cells. It causes your hair to fall out. Extreme stress interferes with sleep and you never look rested. I don't look awful, really. It's the lighting in here, and I think of Kathleen Lawler's complaints about bad lighting and bad mirrors as I uncomfortably recall recent comments Benton has made.

I'm starting to look more like my mother, he mentioned the other day when he came up behind me and put his arms around me as I was getting dressed. He said it was the style of my hair, maybe because it's a little shorter, and he meant it as a compliment, but I didn't take it as one. I don't want to look like my mother, because I don't want to be anything like my mother, not anything like my only sibling, Dorothy, either, both of them still in Miami and always complaining about one thing or another. The heat, the neighbors, the neighbors' dogs, the feral cats, politics, crime, the economy, and, of course, me. I'm a bad daughter, a bad sister, and a bad aunt to Lucy. I never come to visit and rarely call. I've forgotten my Italian heritage, my mother said to me recently, as if growing up in an Italian neighborhood in Miami somehow makes me a native of the Old Country.

Outside the hotel, the sun has dipped behind stone and brick buildings along Bay Street, and the air is still hot but not nearly as humid. A bell in City Hall tolls, its rich metallic peal sounding the half hour as I follow steep granite steps down to River Street, walking behind and below the hotel. Through lighted arched windows on the lower level I see a ballroom being set up for some event, and then the river is before me. It has turned a deep indigo blue in the waning light of the approaching night, and the sky is clearing, the moon huge and egg-shaped as it rises, and streets and sidewalks are thick with tourists arriving for sunset cruises and the restaurants and shops. Old men sell stiff yellow flowers woven of sweetgrass, the air fragrant with the vanilla scent of the long, thin leaves, and I hear the distant sentimental notes of a Native American flute.

I'm vividly aware of everything I pass. I notice every person, but I don't look directly at anyone. *Who else knows I'm here? Who else cares, and why?* I walk with purpose I don't really feel, wishing I could duck inside one of the fine restaurants and forget about Jaime Berger and what she might want from me. I wish I could forget Kathleen Lawler and her hideous biological daughter and the horror of what happened to Jack Fielding, which was worse than death. He degenerated into something unrecognizable in those six months I was at Dover Air Force Base getting board-certified in radiologic pathology so we could begin doing CT scans or virtual autopsies at my new headquarters in Cambridge. I'd given Jack the opportunity of a lifetime, trusting him to run the place while I was gone, and he did. Right into the ground.

It might have been the drugs he was on, his daughter turning him into a crazed beast, and some of what he did may have been for money. What I won't say to anyone is that Jack is better off dead and I'm grateful I won't have to confront him and finally banish him for good. I can't imagine what he was thinking unless he just didn't care, but he spared both of us the vilest and most brutal showdown, and that's exactly what it would have been. A face-off that was a lifetime in coming, and one he would lose decisively. He had to have known that when I got home I would discover every bad thing he was doing, every loathsome violation, that I would uncover every immoral and selfish act. Jack Fielding knew he was done. He knew I would not have forgiven him. I would not have taken him back or protected him this time. When Dawn Kincaid killed him, he was already dead.

And in an odd way, realizing all this has given me an unexpected satisfaction and a little more self-respect. I have changed, and it's for the better. You really can't love unconditionally. People can burn and beat love out of you. They really can kill it, and it's not your fault you don't feel it anymore, and how liberating it is to finally realize that. Love isn't for better or for worse, through thick or thin. It damn well shouldn't be. Were Jack still alive, I would not love him. When I examined his dead body in the cellar of his Salem house, I did not feel love for him. He was stiff and cold beneath my hands, unyielding and stubborn, holding on to his dirty secrets in death the same way he did in life, and a part of me was glad he was gone. I was relieved. I was grateful. *Thank you for the freedom, Jack. Thank you for being gone forever so I don't feel obliged to waste any more of my life on you.*

I wander for a while to clear him out of my head, to steel myself, to wipe my eyes and hope they aren't red. Turning on Houston Street away from the river as the City Hall bell rings nine times, I move deeper into the historic district, taking a right on East Broughton and stopping on Abercorn in front of the Owens-Thomas House, a two-century-old mansion of limestone and Ionic columns that is a museum now. Around it are other gracious antebellum buildings and homes, and I'm reminded of the three-story old brick house I saw on the news nine years ago. I wonder where the Jordans lived and if it might be near here, and did the killer or killers target the family in advance, or were they random victims of opportunity? Most people in this area have burglar alarms, and it nags at me that the Jordans' must not have been armed, not that everybody bothers, even wealthy people, who should know better.

But if you were planning on breaking into an expensive house during early-morning hours when the family was asleep, wouldn't your first assumption be that there was an alarm and it was set? I noticed in articles I scanned while parked at the gun store that Clarence Jordan was out the Saturday afternoon of January 5, volunteering at a local men's emergency shelter, and returned home around seven-thirty that evening. No mention was made of the alarm and why he didn't bother to set it when he came in for the night, but it doesn't appear he did. The system couldn't have been armed when the break-in occurred at some point after midnight the following morning.

The killer—supposedly Lola Daggette—smashed the glass out of the first-story kitchen door, reached inside, flipped open the lock, and walked in. Assuming the alarm system didn't have glass-break or motion sensors, it would have had contacts, and even if the perpetrator knew the code, the instant the door was opened, the chime would have sounded, beeping or chirping until the system was disabled. It's hard to imagine four people would sleep through that. Maybe Jaime has the answer. Maybe Lola Daggette has told her what really happened and I'm about to find out why I'm here and what I have to do with it.

I stand on the sidewalk in darkness that is uneven in the glow of tall iron lamps, and I try my lawyer, Leonard

Brazzo. He is fond of steak houses, and when he answers his cell phone he tells me he's at the Palm and it's mobbed.

"Let me step outside," his voice sounds in my wireless earpiece. "Okay, better," he adds, and I hear cars honking. "How did it go? How was she?" He means Kathleen Lawler.

"She mentioned something about letters Jack wrote to her," I reply. "I don't recall any letters being found, and I didn't see such a thing when I was looking through his personal effects at his house in Salem. But it's possible no one mentioned letters to me," I say, as I stare at Jaime Berger's white-brick building across the street, eight stories, with large sashed windows.

He resented the fucking hell out of you.

"Got no idea," Leonard replies. "But why would Jack have letters he wrote to her?"

"I don't know."

"Unless she returned them to him at some point? Sorry about the wind. Hope you can hear."

"I'm just telling you what she said."

"The FBI," he says. "It wouldn't surprise me if they got a court order to search her cell or wherever she might have personal belongings stored, looking for letters or any other type of communication to or from or about Jack Fielding or Dawn Kincaid."

"And we wouldn't necessarily know about that," I reply.

"No. The police, DOJ, wouldn't be obliged to share any letters with us. Saying they exist."

Of course they wouldn't be obliged to share. I'm not the one on trial for murder or attempted murder, and that's the aggravating irony. During the discovery phase, Dawn Kincaid and her legal team have a right to all evidence the prosecution has obtained, including any mocking letters Jack might have written to Kathleen Lawler about me. But I wouldn't be told about them or learn of their content until they're produced in court and used against me. Victims have no rights while they're being victimized and few rights during the slow, tedious grind of the criminal justice process. The injuries don't heal but continue to be inflicted, by lawyers, by the media, by jurors, by witnesses who testify that someone like me had it coming or caused it.

He used to say you have no idea how hard you are on people . . . a bitch who needed to be fucked . . .

"Are you worried about what the letters might say?" Leonard is asking me.

"They don't appear to paint me favorably, if what I've been told is true. That will be helpful to her."

It will be helpful to Dawn Kincaid, I'm indicating without saying her name out loud, as I stand on a sidewalk in the dark, people and cars going by, headlights hurting my eyes. The more I'm disparaged, the less credible I become and the less sympathy jurors will have for me.

"Let's deal with any letters if they present themselves." Leonard says not to get worked up about something that hasn't happened.

"I also was curious if Jaime Berger might have been in touch with you," I get to that point.

"The prosecutor?"

"The very same."

"No, she hasn't been in touch. Why would she?"

"Curtis Roberts"—the lawyer Tara Grimm mentioned to me—"what can you tell me about him?"

"He's a volunteer lawyer with the Georgia Innocence Project, works with a firm in Atlanta."

"So he's representing Kathleen Lawler pro bono."

"Apparently."

"Why would the Innocence Project be interested in her? Is there a legitimate question about her conviction for DUI manslaughter?" I ask.

"I just know he called on her behalf."

I decide to ask nothing further as I think about Kathleen Lawler's note and her instructions for me to find a pay phone. *Why?* If that was Jaime's direction, then it suggests she might be concerned about my talking on my cell phone. I tell Leonard Brazzo I'll go into more detail later and to enjoy his dinner. I end the call and cross the street to face whatever I'm about to face. I wonder which windows are Jaime's and if she is watching for me and what it must be like to stare out at a world that no longer includes Lucy. I wouldn't want to miss my niece. I wouldn't want the misery of knowing her and then not having her anymore.

The building isn't full-service, not even a doorman, and I push the intercom button for apartment 8SE and the electronic lock buzzes loudly and clicks free, as if the person letting me in knows who I am without asking. For the second time this day I scan for surveillance cameras, spotting one in a white metal casing that blends with the white bricks in a corner over the door. It occurs to me that if Jaime sees me in a monitor, then it's likely the closed-circuit camera was installed by her and includes infrared capabilities, so it will work in the dark.

I see no indication that the building itself has security, nothing but electronic locks and an intercom system, and my curiosity builds. Savannah isn't merely a getaway—not if Jaime has gone to the trouble to install an advanced security system. As I'm opening the door I sense something behind me, and I turn around, startled, as a person wearing a flashing helmet climbs off a bicycle and leans it against a lamppost at the end of the walkway, near the street.

"Jaime Berger?" asks this person, a woman, I realize, and she takes off her backpack and opens it, pulling out a large white bag.

"That's not me," I reply, as she walks toward me carrying a take-out bag with the name of a restaurant on it.

She presses the buzzer and announces into the intercom, "Delivery for Jaime Berger."

As I hold the door open, I mention to her, "That's all right. I'm going up. I can take it. How much?"

"Two tekka maki, two unagi maki, two California maki, two seaweed salads. Already on her credit card." She hands me the bag, and I give her a ten-dollar tip. "Her usual Thursday delivery. Have a nice night."

I shut the door behind me and take the elevator to the top floor, where I follow an empty carpeted hallway to a unit in the southeast corner. Ringing the bell, I look up into the lens of another camera as the heavy oak door opens, and anything I might have said is eclipsed by my astonishment.

"Doc," Pete Marino says. "Don't be pissed."

8

He invites me in as if it's his apartment, and the seriousness of his eyes behind his unstylish wire-rim glasses and the hard set of his mouth completely unnerve me at first.

"Jaime should be back any minute." He shuts the door.

My shocked response just as suddenly turns to anger as I take him in from the top of his shiny shaved head and big weathered face to the rubber-soled canvas shoes he wears with no socks. I note his Hawaiian shirt and the drape of it over shoulders that seem more massive and a belly that seems flatter than I remember. Baggy green fishing shorts with cargo pockets hang low on his hips, and he's darkly tanned except for under his chin, where the sun has spared him. He's been out in a boat or on a beach, out somewhere in the summer weather, his skin bronzed with a ruddy hue. Even his bare pate and the tops of his ears are the color of cognac, but he is pale around his eyes. He's been wearing sunglasses and no cap, and I envision the white cargo van and the charter-boat brochures in the glove box. I think of the fast-food napkins.

Marino craves Bojangles' and Popeyes fried chicken and biscuits, and often complains that fried food isn't a "food group" in New England like it is in the South. There were the comments he made not long ago about preowned gas-guzzling trucks and boats selling for a song, and how much he misses warm weather, and I recall being somewhat bothered by his last-minute notice when he stopped by my office earlier this month. He said he'd been offered an opportunity for some great vacation package. He wanted to go fishing, and his calendar was clear. His last day on duty for the CFC was June 15.

Marino vanished in the middle of this month, and other things happened almost simultaneously. Kathleen Lawler's e-mails to me stopped. She was transferred to Bravo Pod. Suddenly she wanted me to visit the GPFW, to talk to me about Jack Fielding. Leonard Brazzo thought it was a good idea for me to agree, and then I discovered Jaime Berger is here. Now that I have the luxury of look-ing back, it's plain what occurred. Marino lied to me.

"She's picking up dinner," he says, taking the bag of take-out sushi from me. "Real food. I don't eat fish bait."

I notice a desk, a small table, and two chairs arranged near the far wall, with two laptops and a printer, and books and legal pads, and on the floor stacks of expansion file folders.

"The three of us talking in a restaurant isn't exactly a good idea," he adds, setting the take-out bag on the kitchen counter.

"I wouldn't know if it's a good idea or not, since I have no idea why you're here. Or, more to the point, why I am," I reply.

"You want something to drink?"

"Not now."

I move past the closed-circuit monitor mounted on the wall, past a coatrack, and for an instant I smell cigarettes.

"I don't blame you for wondering what the hell," Marino says, and paper rattles as he opens the bag. "I probably should stick this in the fridge. Don't be pissed, Doc. . . ."

"Don't tell me what to be. Are you smoking again?"

"Hell, no."

"I smell cigarettes. Someone was smoking in the rental van I didn't reserve, which also stinks like dead fish and stale fast food and has suspicious brochures in the glove box. I hope you're not smoking again, for God's sake."

"No way I'd get hooked on cigarettes after all I went through to quit."

"Who is Captain Link Michaels?" I refer to one of the brochures in the glove box. *Year-round fishing with Captain Link Michaels,* I quote.

"A charter boat out of Beaufort. A nice guy. Been out with him a few times."

"You weren't wearing a cap, probably not sunblock, either. What about skin cancer?"

"I don't have it anymore." He self-consciously touches the top of his ruddy bald head where he had several basal cell carcinomas removed some months ago.

"Just because spots have been removed doesn't mean you don't wear sunblock. You should always wear a hat."

"Blew off when we had the boat full throttle. I got a little burned." He touches the top of his head again.

"I guess we don't need to run the plate of that van I've been driving today. I guess we know it won't come back to Lowcountry Concierge Connection," I then say. "Who was smoking in it, if not you?"

"You weren't followed here, that's what matters," he says. "No one was going to follow you in the van. I forgot to clean out the glove box. Should have known you'd look."

"The kid who dropped it off to me, who was that? Because I don't believe he really works for some VIP rental-car company called Lowcountry Concierge Connection. Is that your rental van, and you got some charter-boat captain's kid to drop it off to me?"

"It's not a rental," Marino says.

"Well, I guess I know why Bryce hasn't returned my phone calls today. I have a feeling he got influenced, not that it hasn't happened before when you sneak around behind my back and get him to cooperate by telling him you have my best interests in mind. Did you instruct him to cancel my hotel room, too?"

"It doesn't matter, as long as it's turned out okay."

"Good God, Marino," I mutter. "Why would you have Bryce cancel my room? What the hell is the matter with you? What if they hadn't had another room available?"

"I knew they would."

"I could have been killed in that damn van. It's not drivable."

"It was fine the other day." He frowns. "What was it doing? I wouldn't put you in something that's not safe. And I would have known if you broke down."

"*Not safe* is an understatement," I reply. "Speeds up, slows down, lurching all over the road as if it's having a grand mal seizure."

"We had a lot of rain last night, a huge storm in South Carolina, even worse than here. It rained like hell, and it was sitting out. It needs a new hood seal."

"South Carolina?"

"Maybe the spark plugs got wet. Then maybe they got even more wet when you had it parked out there at the prison, and maybe Joey hit potholes or something and the tires are out of alignment. A nice kid but dumb as a box of hair. He should have called me if it was driving like shit. Well, I'm sorry about that. Yeah, I got a little place I just started renting. In Charleston, a condo near the aquarium, with a pier and boat slips, an easy drive or motorcycle ride from here. I was going to tell you about it, but things have happened."

I look around and try to make sense of what things Marino might mean. *What has happened? What on earth?*

"I had to make sure you weren't followed, Doc," he then says. "Let's be honest, Benton knows your plans and has your itinerary because Bryce copies him on the e-mails. They're on the CFC computer."

What he's saying is the rental car Bryce reserved for me is on my itinerary but a malfunctioning cargo van with a bad hood seal wouldn't be, and my room at the Hyatt is moot because it was canceled. But I'm not sure what Marino is implying about Benton.

"Put it this way," Marino says, "there's a Toyota Camry sitting in the lot at Lowcountry Concierge Connection with the name Dr. Kay Scarpetta on it. If anybody was hanging around, waiting for you to get in it because maybe they got access to your itinerary, your e-mails, or found out your schedule some other way, you would have been a no-show. And if they called your hotel, they would have found out you'd canceled your room because you missed your connection in Atlanta."

"Why would Benton have me followed?"

"Maybe he wouldn't. But maybe someone would see the itinerary that went from your e-mail to his. Maybe he knows the possibility or likelihood of that happening, and that's why he didn't want you coming down here."

"How do you know he didn't want me coming down here?"

"Because he wouldn't."

I don't reply or look Marino in the eye. Instead I look around. I take in the details of Jaime's charming loft of exposed old brick, pine floors, and high white plaster ceilings with rough oak beams, very much to my liking but definitely not to hers. The living area, simply furnished with a leather couch, a matching armchair, and a slate coffee table, flows into a large kitchen with a stone peninsula and the stainless-steel appliances of an industrious cook, which Berger most decidedly isn't.

There is no art, and I happen to know that she is a collector. I see no evidence of anything personal beyond what's on the desk and floor against the far wall under a big window filled with the night, the moon distant now, small and bone-white. I don't see any furniture or rugs that might be hers, and I know her taste. Contemporary and minimalist, predominantly high-end Italian and Scandinavian, a lot of light woods, such as maple and birch. Jaime's taste is uncomplicated because her life is its antithesis, and I'm reminded of how much she disliked Lucy's loft in Greenwich Village, a fabulous building that once was a candle factory. I remember being offended when Jaime used to refer to it as "Lucy's drafty old barn."

"She's renting this," I say to Marino. "Why?" I sit on the brown leather couch that is a reproduction, not at all Jaime's style. "And how do you fit into the equation? How do I fit into it? Why are you convinced someone would follow me, given the chance? You could have called me if you were so worried. What is it? Are you thinking of changing jobs? Or have you gone back to work for Jaime and forgot to let me know."

"I'm not exactly changing jobs, Doc."

"Not exactly? Well, she's pulled you into something. You should know that about her by now."

Jaime Berger is calculating, almost frighteningly so, and Marino is no match for her. He wasn't when he was an investigator with NYPD and was assigned to her office, and he's no match for her now and never will be. Whatever reason she's given him for his being here and maneuvering me into what feels like nothing less than a calculated machination, it isn't the whole truth or even close.

"You are working for her de facto because you're here at her bidding," I add. "You're certainly not working for me when you swap my car and cancel my hotel and scheme with her behind my back."

"I'm working for you but helping her, too. I haven't walked off the job, Doc," he says, with surprising gentleness for Marino. "I wouldn't do something shitty like that to you."

I don't reply that he has done plenty of shitty things to me over the twenty-plus years I've known him and worked with him, and I can't help thinking about what Kathleen Lawler said. Every other minute it enters my mind. Jack Fielding wrote to her in the early nineties, wrote to her on lined notebook paper, like a schoolboy— an immature, sophomoric, mean-spirited schoolboy who resented me. He and Marino thought I needed to be warmed up, humanized, fucked but good, and for an instant the Marino standing before me is the Marino from back then.

I envision him inside his dark blue unmarked Crown

Vic, with all of its antennas and emergency lights and crumpled fast-food bags, its overflowing ashtray, the air shellacked with a stale stench of cigarettes that air fresheners hanging from the rearview mirror couldn't begin to crack. I remember the defiance in his eyes, the way he blatantly stared, making sure he reminded me that I might be the first female chief medical examiner of Virginia, but I was tits and ass to him. I remember going home at the end of each day in the Capital of the Confederacy, where I certainly didn't belong.

"Doc?"

Richmond. Where I knew no one.

"What is it?"

I remember how alone I was.

"Hey. Are you okay?"

I focus on the Marino who has lived some twenty years since then, towering above me, as bald as a baseball and weathered by the sun.

"And if Kathleen Lawler had declined to play whatever this game is?" I say to him. "What if she hadn't given me the piece of paper with Jaime's phone number on it? What then?"

"I worried about that." He walks over to a window and stares out at the night. "But Jaime knew for a fact Kathleen would give you the note," he says, with his back to me, as he looks out and down, possibly looking for Jaime.

"She knew it for a fact. I see," I reply. "I'm not happy about this."

"I know you're not, but there are reasons." He wanders closer to me and stops. "Jaime couldn't reach out to you directly at this stage of things. The safe thing was to have you make the first call and do it in a way that couldn't be detected."

"Is this a legal strategy, or is she protecting herself for some reason?"

"There can't be a trail of Jaime initiating this meeting, of her reaching out to you at this point, plain and simple," he says. "You'll hook up with her tomorrow, officially, at the ME's office in the course of doing business, but you were never here. Not here and not now."

"Let me make sure I've got this straight. I'm supposed to pretend I'm not here now and that I didn't see Jaime tonight."

"Exactly."

"I'm supposed to go along with whatever lie the two of you have concocted."

"It's necessary and for your own good."

"I have no plans for hooking up with anyone and have no idea what business you're referring to." But I have a feeling I do know, as I think of the autopsy records of the slain Jordan family and any of the evidence from those cases stored at the local medical examiner's office and crime labs. "I'm leaving in the morning," I add, as my attention returns to the expansion files stacked on the floor by the desk. Each has a different-colored gusset and is labeled with initials or abbreviations that I don't recognize.

"I'll be picking you up at eight a.m." Marino is standing in the middle of the room as if he doesn't know what to do with himself, and his large physical presence seems to shrink everything around him.

"Maybe it would be helpful if you'd tell me what I'm meeting about."

"It's hard to talk to you when you're this pissed." He stares down at me, and when I'm sitting and he's not, I don't like it.

"Last I checked, you worked for me, not Jaime. Your loyalty is supposed to be to me, not to her or anyone else." I sound angry, but what I am is hurt. "I wish you'd sit down."

"If I'd said I want to help out Jaime, that I want to do some things a little different from the way I've been doing them, you would have told me no." Leather creaks loudly as he settles in the deep armchair.

"I don't know what you're referring to or how you could know what I might say." I feel he's accusing me of being difficult.

"You don't have the slightest idea what all is going on, because nobody's in a position to outright tell you." He leans forward, his big arms on his bare knees, which are the size of small hubcaps. "Some people want you destroyed."

"I think it's been established that there are—" I start to say, but he won't let me talk.

"Nope." He shakes his bald head, and stubble on his tan, heavy jaw looks like sand. "You may think you know, but you don't. Maybe Dawn Kincaid can't touch you while she's locked up in the cuckoo's nest, but there are other ways and other people. She has plans to bring you down."

"I can't imagine how she would communicate illegal or violent intentions without the staff at Butler knowing, without the police knowing, without the FBI knowing," I say logically, coolly, trying to get the emotion and heat out of my mood, trying not to feel wounded to my core about what Jack and Marino joked about twenty years ago, about how they really felt about me, how they ridiculed and isolated me.

"That's easy." His eyes are locked on mine. "Her scum-bucket lawyers, for starters. They can communicate with her in private the same way Jaime has with Kathleen Lawler. If you're worried about being monitored or recorded, you communicate in writing. You pass notes. You write it on a legal pad, and your client reads it and doesn't say anything."

"I seriously doubt Dawn Kincaid's lawyers have hired a hit man, if that's what you're suggesting."

"I don't know if they'd hire a hit man," he considers. "But they want you destroyed and in prison. You're in a lot of danger any way you slice it."

I can tell he completely believes what he just said, and I wonder how much of it came from Jaime. *What has she contrived and why?*

"I suspect I was at graver risk driving that van of yours than being taken out by a hit man," I retort. "What if I'd broken down out in the middle of nowhere?"

"I would have known if you were broke down. I know

exactly where you were all day, right down to the gun store one-point-four miles north of Dean Forest Road. I have a GPS tracking device on my van and can see where it is on a Google map."

"This is ridiculous. Who orchestrated all this, and what's the real reason?" I ask. "Because I don't believe it was your idea. Jaime's down here talking to Lola Daggette? What could that possibly have to do with me? Or with you? What is it she really wants?"

"About two months ago, Jaime called the CFC," he says. "I happened to be in Bryce's office and got on the phone with her, and she said she was following up on information relating to Lola Daggette, who happens to be in the same prison as Kathleen Lawler. All Jaime was interested in, supposedly, was if I happened to know anything about Lola Daggette, if there was any reason her name has come up during the Dawn Kincaid investigation—"

"And you never passed this on to me," I interrupt him.

"She asked to talk to me, not you," he said, as if Jaime Berger is the director of the CFC, or maybe Marino is. "It didn't take me long to figure out that her calling wasn't what it appeared to be. For one thing, caller ID didn't come up as the DA's office. It came up as *unknown*. She was calling from her apartment in the middle of the day, which I thought was unusual. Then she said, 'Things are so deep I need to decompress before I come up for air.' When I used to work for her, that was our code, meaning she needed to talk to me in private and not over the phone. So I went straight to South Station and took the Acela to New York."

Marino's not apologetic, he's so sure of what he's doing and saying. He has no qualms about what he's withheld from me for two months because the skillful, shrewd Jaime Berger has moved him around like a plastic pawn. She knew exactly what she was doing when she called him and spoke in code.

"It just amazes me," he then says, "that you live in the same damn house as the FBI and you don't know your phones are being tapped."

He settles deeper in the leather chair and crosses his thick legs, and I can see remnants of a past strength in them that had to be formidable. I remember photographs I've seen of him when he was a boxer. A heavyweight and a brute, nothing civilized about him. *How many people are walking around with concussive head injuries because of him, how many people did he brain-damage, how many faces did he smash?*

"They're going through your e-mail," he says, as I notice pale scars on his big knees and wonder how he got them. "They may be tracking you, tailing you."

I get up from the couch.

"You know how it works." His voice follows me into Jaime Berger's well-appointed kitchen, which looks un-used. "They obtain a court order to spy on you and then let you know after the fact."

9

I don't offer him anything to drink. I offer him nothing as I open the refrigerator, scanning glass shelves. Wine, seltzer, Diet Coke. Greek yogurt. Wasabi and pickled ginger and low-salt soy sauce.

Opening cabinets, I find little inside them, just the rudimentary dishes and cookware one might expect in a furnished rental. A salt-and-pepper set but no other spices, a fifth of Johnnie Walker Blue. I help myself to a bottle of water in the pantry, where there are more diet drinks, and an assortment of vitamins, analgesics, and digestive aids, and I recognize the desolate patterns of a life that's stopped. I know what is in the cupboards, pantries, and refrigerators of people who are terrified of loss. Jaime hasn't gotten over Lucy.

"How the hell does he keep something like this from

you?" Marino won't shut up about Benton. "I wouldn't have. I don't give a shit about protocol. If I knew the feds were after you, I'd tell you, give you a friggin' heads-up, which is exactly what I'm doing while he sits around and is the good Bureau boy, playing by the rules, not doing a damn thing while his own damn agency investigates his wife. Just like he didn't do a damn thing the night it happened. Sitting in front of the fire having a drink while you wander outside in the damn dark by yourself."

"It wasn't like that."

"He knew Dawn Kincaid and maybe others were on the loose, and he lets you go outside alone at night."

"That's not what happened."

"It's a miracle you aren't dead. I blame him, damn it. In a blink it could have all been over with because Benton couldn't bother."

I walk back to the couch.

"I won't forgive him." As if it is for Marino to forgive, and I wonder what Jaime has managed to stir up in him about Benton.

How much has she encouraged the jealousy that is always there, ready to lunge or strike with the slightest provocation.

"He didn't want you to come down here, but he didn't volunteer to come with you, now, did he?" Marino says loudly and hotly, and I think about the letters, about how insecure and selfish he can be.

When I was first appointed the chief medical examiner of Virginia and Marino was Richmond's star detective, he couldn't have been more unhelpful and unkind. He did what he could to run me off the job until he realized he was better served by having me as an ally and a friend. Maybe that's what really motivates him, after all. My authority and the way I've always taken care of him. Better to have me on his side. Better to have a good job, especially when good jobs are few and far between and he's not getting any younger. If I fired him, he'd be lucky to get hired as a damn Pinkerton guard, I think furiously, and then instantly I feel beaten up inside and on the verge of tears.

"I wouldn't have wanted Benton to come to Savannah with me, and he certainly couldn't have gone into the prison. That wouldn't have been possible," I reply, as I drink water from the bottle. "And even if what you're saying is true and the FBI is investigating me for some ridiculous unfounded reason, Benton wouldn't know."

I sit back down on the leather couch.

"They wouldn't tell him," I reply logically, repeating myself as I think of Kathleen Lawler's comments about my reputation and that unlike her, I have one to lose.

I remember being alerted by what seemed an allusion, as if she were warning me and taking pleasure in the thought that some misfortune might be in store for me. I think about the letters, about what she says is in them, and I'm stunned by how hurt I feel. After twenty-something years, it shouldn't matter, but it does.

"How can he work in criminal intelligence for the friggin' Bureau of Investigation and not know?" Marino says adamantly, and at times like this I know how much he dislikes Benton.

Marino will never accept that Benton and I are married, that I possibly could be happy, that my seemingly aloof husband has dimension and appeal that Marino will never comprehend.

"Let's start with how you would know such a thing," I reply.

"Because the Feds have issued a preservation order to the CFC so nothing is deleted from our server," he answers. "What that tells me is they've been in it for a while. They're snooping through your e-mails, maybe through other things in there, too."

"Why don't I know about a court order issued to my office?" I think of the highly sensitive information on the CFC server, some of it classified as secret or even top secret by the Department of Defense.

"Shit," Marino says. "How can you be so calm about it? Did you hear what I just told you? The FBI is investigating you. You're a target."

"I most certainly would know if I'm a target. I'd be on the verge of indictment for a federal crime, and they'd interview me. They'd put me in front of a grand jury. They would have been in touch with Leonard Brazzo by now. Why has no one told me about a court order?" I repeat.

"Because you're not supposed to know about it. I'm not supposed to know about it, either."

"Is Lucy aware of this?"

"She's the IT person, so she's the one who got the notice. It's up to her to make sure no electronic communications are deleted."

Obviously Lucy told Marino. But she didn't tell me.

"We don't delete anything anyway, and a preservation order doesn't mean anything's been looked at." Scare tactics, I think. Marino's not a lawyer, and Jaime has goaded him into overdrive for some reason that serves her purposes.

"You act like it's nothing." His face is incredulous.

"In the first place, my case is being tried in federal court," I reply. "Of course, the Feds, the FBI, might be interested in any electronic records, especially Jack's records, since we know he got in deep with a number of illegal activities and dangerous people while I was at Dover, not the least of which was his involvement with his daughter, Dawn Kincaid. The FBI already has been looking at his communications, at anything they can find, and they haven't finished yet. So I would expect a preservation order. But it's not needed, and what might I delete anyway? An itinerary for a trip to Georgia? I'm surprised Lucy has managed to keep this to herself."

"All of us could be charged with obstruction of justice," he says.

"And I'm sure Jaime's put that worry in your head, too. Has she also talked with Lucy about it?"

"She doesn't talk to Lucy or even about her." He confirms my belief that Jaime and Lucy aren't in touch. "I told Lucy and Bryce they'd be the ones who sent you to jail if they didn't watch themselves and started telling you things you're not supposed to know."

"I appreciate your encouraging them to keep me out of jail."

"It's not funny."

"It certainly isn't. I don't like the implication that if I were given information, I'd do something illegal in response, such as deleting records. I'm always under scrutiny, Marino. Every damn day of my life. What has Jaime said to you that's gotten you so agitated and paranoid?"

"They're interrogating people about you. Back in April, two FBI agents came to her apartment."

I feel betrayed, not by the FBI or Benton or even Jaime but by Marino. The letters. I never knew he used to deride me, belittle me to the man I mentored, to my protégé, Jack. I was just getting started, and Marino was poisoning my staff behind my back.

"They wanted to question her about your character because she knows you personally and has a history with you, going back to our Richmond days," Marino is saying, but what I'm hearing is what Kathleen Lawler said about the letters. "They wanted to corner her before she disappeared into the private sector," he adds. "And maybe there was a grudge, too. Politics. Her problems with NYPD . . ."

"Yes, my character." It boils out of me before I can stop it. "Because I'm such awful person to work for. So difficult. Someone who can relate to people only if they're dead."

"What . . . ?"

"Maybe I'm about to get indicted for being difficult. An awful human being who makes people miserable and ruins them. Maybe I should go to jail for that."

"What the hell is wrong with you?" He stares at me. "What are you talking about?"

"The letters Jack used to write to Kathleen Lawler," I reply. "I guess no one's wanted to show them to me. Because of what you and Jack said about me back in our Richmond days. Comments he made and ones you made that he repeated in letters he wrote to Kathleen."

"I don't know anything about any letters." Marino is sitting forward in his chair, a blank expression on his face. "No way there were any letters in his house that were to or from Kathleen Lawler. I got no idea what she might have from him, assuming it's true he wrote to her. But I doubt it."

"Why would you doubt it?" I exclaim, unable to stop myself.

"Jack never stayed single very long, and not one of his wives or girlfriends would have been very happy to know he was exchanging letters with the woman who molested him when he was a kid."

"They e-mailed each other. We know that for a fact."

"His wives or girlfriends weren't going into his e-mail, my guess is," Marino says. "But letters arriving in the mailbox, letters tucked in drawers or other places, that's a risk I can't imagine Jack would take."

"Don't try to make me feel better."

"I'm saying I never saw any letters and that he hid any shit about Kathleen Lawler," Marino says. "All the years I knew him he never mentioned her or what happened to him at that ranch. And I don't know what all I said back then in the early days. To be honest, some of it probably wasn't nice. Sometimes I was a jerk in the beginning, when you first took over as chief, and you shouldn't listen to bullshit from some piece-of-shit convict. Whether what she said is true or not, Kathleen Lawler wanted to hurt you, and she did."

I don't say anything as we stare at each other.

"I don't know what's taking Jaime so long." He abruptly gets up and looks out the window again. "I don't know why you're so pissed at me, unless it's because you're really pissed at Jack. Fucking son of a bitch. Well, you should be pissed at him. Goddamn worthless lying piece of shit. After all you did for him. Damn good thing Dawn Kincaid got him first, or maybe I would have."

He continues to stare out the window with his back to me, and I sit quietly. The mood has passed like a violent storm that erupted out of nowhere, and I'm struck by what Marino said a moment ago about Jaime Berger. When I finally speak to his big, broad back, I ask if he meant it literally when he said Jaime has disappeared into the private sector.

"Yeah," he says, without turning around. "Literally."

She isn't with the Manhattan DA's office anymore, he tells me. She resigned. She quit. Like a lot of sharpshooting prosecutors, she's switched to the other side. Almost all of them do it eventually, vacate low-paying thankless jobs in drab government offices turgid with bureaucracy, finally fed up with the never-ending parade of tragedies, parasites, remorseless thugs, and cheaters passing through. Bad people doing bad things to bad people. Despite public perception, victims aren't always innocent or even sympathetic, and Jaime used to comment that I was lucky my patients couldn't lie to me. It was a cold day in hell when a witness or a victim told her the truth. I think it's easier if they're dead, she said, and she was right on one count at least. It's much harder to lie when you're dead.

But I never thought Jaime would defect to the private sector. I don't believe her decision was driven by money as I listen to Marino describe her refusal of a retirement party or any sort of send-off, not even a luncheon or a cake or drinks at the local pub after work. She left silently, without fanfare, with virtually no notice, around the same time she called the CFC to ask about Lola Daggette, he says, and I know something has happened. Not just to Jaime but to Marino. I sense that both of their lives have been redirected somehow, and it disappoints me that I didn't know before this moment. It's very sad if neither one of them felt they could tell me.

Maybe I really am impossibly hard on people, and I hear Kathleen Lawler's cruel comments and see the triumphant expression on her face as she made them, as if she'd been waiting most of her life to make them. I'm raw. I realize just how raw I am, and it's because I know there's a grain of truth in what Kathleen said. I'm not easy. It's a fact I've never really had friends. Lucy, Benton, some former staff. And throughout it all, Marino. As bad as it's ever gotten, he's still here, and I don't want that to change.

"I have a feeling that's not all Jaime asked when she called the CFC," I say to him, and there is nothing accusatory in my tone. "I suspect it's not a coincidence that about the time she called the CFC and you took the train to New York, you also started talking about fishing and boats, about missing the South."

"We got along better when I didn't work for you." He turns around and wanders back to his chair. "I used to feel better about myself when I was called in as an expert, you know, a homicide detective, a sergeant detective with A Squad instead of working for your office, working for Jaime's office, now working for your office again. I'm an experienced homicide detective and trained in crime scene and death investigation. Shit, all I've done and seen? I don't want to play out the rest of my days stuck in a little cubicle somewhere, waiting to take orders, waiting for something to happen."

"You're quitting," I reply. "That's what you're trying to say."

"Not exactly."

"You deserve the life you want. You deserve it more than anyone I know. It disappoints me you would think you couldn't share what you've been feeling. That probably bothers me most."

"I don't want to quit."

"Sounds like you already have."

"I want to switch to being a private contractor," he says. "Jaime and me talked about it when I went to New York. You know, she's struck out on her own and she said I should think about it, that she could use my help on cases, and I know you can use my help. I don't want to be owned by anyone."

"I've never looked at it as my owning you."

"I'd like a little independence, a little self-respect. I know you can't relate to that. Why would someone like you ever lack in self-respect?"

"You'd be surprised," I reply.

"I want to have a little place on the water, to ride motorcycles, go fishing, and work for people who respect me," he says.

"Jaime's hired you as a consultant on the Lola Daggette case?"

"She's not paying me. I said I can't do that until I change my status with the CFC, and at some point I was going to talk to you about it," Marino says, as I hear the metal sound of a key in a lock and the door opens.

Jaime Berger walks in, and I smell savory meat. I smell french fries and truffles.

10

She sets two large blue paper bags on the stone peninsula in the kitchen and acts remarkably relaxed and cheerful for a New York prosecutor or even a former one who has set up a clandestine operation in coastal Georgia that requires security cameras and what I suspect is a handgun concealed in the brown cowhide hobo handbag slung over her shoulder.

Her dark hair is smartly styled, a little longer than I remember it, her features sharply defined and very pretty, and she is as lithe as a woman half her age in faded jeans and an untucked white shirt. She wears no jewelry and very little makeup, and while she might fool most people, she can't fool me. I see the shadow in her eyes. I detect the brittleness in her smile.

"I apologize, Kay," she says right off as she hangs her

unattractive heavy-looking pocketbook on the back of a bar stool, and I wonder if it's Marino's influence that possibly has her packing a gun.

Or is this a habit she acquired from Lucy, and it occurs to me that if Jaime is carrying a concealed weapon, she's likely doing so illegally. I don't know how she could have a license in Georgia, where she may rent an apartment but wouldn't qualify as a resident. Security cameras and a gun that isn't legal. Perhaps just the usual precautions, because she knows the same harsh realities I do about what can happen in life. Or it might be that Jaime has gotten fearful and unstable.

"I'd be absolutely livid if someone pulled something like this on me," she says, "but it's going to make more sense, if it doesn't already."

I think of getting up to hug her, but she's already involved with opening the take-out bags, which I interpret as her preferring to keep a safe distance from me. So I stay where I am on the couch and try not to feel anything about last Christmas in New York and the many times all of us were together before that or what Lucy would do if she could see where I am. I don't want to think about how she would react if she could see Jaime looking very pretty but with haunted eyes and a stiff smile, unpacking take-out food in an old loft that's reminiscent of the one Lucy had in Greenwich Village, a handbag nearby that might have a gun in it.

I'm nagged by a growing distrust that is fast reaching critical mass. Jaime's the sort of woman who is accustomed to getting what she wants, yet she gave up Lucy without a fight, and now I find out she's given up her career just as easily. *Because it suited her purposes for some reason,* it enters my thoughts like a judgment. I have to remind myself it doesn't matter. Nothing matters except my being here and why and if what I suspect will turn out to be true—that I'm being deceived and used by my niece's ex-lover.

"I'm sure you remember Il Pasticcio just a few blocks from here?" Jaime takes out foil-lined cardboard containers covered with plastic lids, and plastic quart containers of what might be soup, and the loft fills with aromas of herbs, shallots, and bacon. "Well, now it's the Broughton and Bull." She opens a drawer and starts collecting silverware and paper napkins. "They make an amazing pot pie with pearl onions. Braised rabbit. Shrimp bisque with poblano–green tomato oil. Seared scallops with bacon-wrapped jalapeños." She opens one container after another. "I thought I'd just let you help yourselves. Well, maybe it's easier if I serve," she reconsiders, glancing around as if expecting a dining-room table to appear, as if she's unfamiliar with the rented space she's in.

"I hope you got me the barbecue shrimp," Marino says from his chair.

"And fries," Berger says, as if she and Marino are comfortable companions. "And the mac-and-cheese with truffle oil."

"I'll pass." He makes a face.

"It's good to try new things."

"Forget truffles or truffle oil or whatever. I don't need to try anything that smells like ass." Marino retrieves a brown expansion file from the stack on the floor by the desk, a file labeled with a sticker that has *BLR* written on it in black Magic Marker.

"Would you like some help?" I ask Jaime, but I don't get up. I sense she doesn't want me in her space, or maybe it's simply that I'm the one feeling distant and untouchable.

"Please stay put. I can open bags and put food on plates. I'm not the cook you are, but I can at least do that."

"Your sushi's in the refrigerator," Marino says.

"My sushi? Okay, why not." She opens the refrigerator door and retrieves the containers Marino placed inside. "They have my credit card on file because I confess I'm addicted. At least three nights a week. I probably should worry about mercury. You still don't eat sushi, Kay?"

"I still don't. No, thank you."

"I think I'll serve the bisque in mugs, if nobody minds. How far did you get?" She looks at Marino. "Tell me where you left off."

"Far enough to know how much trouble it must have been for the two of you to make this evening possible," I answer for him.

"I really do apologize," Jaime again says, but she doesn't sound sorry.

She sounds very sure of her right to do exactly what she's done.

"Frankly, it's my prerogative to make certain you understand what's happening. I simply had to be extraordinarily careful how I did it." She glances up at me as she moves about in the kitchen. "I feel it's my moral responsibility to watch your back. Obviously I'll always err on the side of discretion and deemed it unwise to call you, e-mail you, or contact you directly. If asked I can truthfully say I didn't. You called me. But who will know that fact unless you decide to share it?"

"If I decide to share what? That an inmate slipped me a note and I drove off to find the nearest pay phone as if I'm in summer camp on a scavenger hunt?" I reply.

"I interviewed Kathleen yesterday and was reminded she was looking forward to seeing you today."

"Was reminded?" I say to her, as I look at Marino. "I'm sure you knew anyway. Curtis Roberts is probably an associate of yours. You know, the lawyer with the Georgia Innocence Project who called Leonard Brazzo."

"I can truthfully say you contacted me while you were in the area on your own business," Jaime repeats.

"Business you set up for me so you could get me here," I reply. "There's nothing truthful about any of this."

"Marino didn't brief you or divulge anything he shouldn't have," she continues to make her case. "He didn't pass along any invitations to you that might be unwise right now under the circumstances. No one passed on anything that might have negative consequences."

"Someone certainly did. That's why I'm sitting here," I answer.

"In a privileged conversation with a witness in a case

I'm working, I conveyed that I was hoping you would get in touch with me," she says, completely justified, at least in her mind.

"I seriously doubt much at the GPFW isn't monitored or recorded," I point out.

"I wrote a note on my legal pad asking Kathleen to give you my cell phone number and the instruction to call me on a pay phone," Jaime says. "She read the note as we sat at the table. Nothing was said out loud. Nothing was observed, and the legal pad left with me. Kathleen's happy to help me in any way possible."

"Because she's convinced she's going to get a reduced sentence, according to the warden," I comment.

"It would be a good idea for you to dispose of any notes anyone might have given you."

"From which I'm to conclude you were told not to talk to me and you're worried about the security of my communications," I get to the bottom line. "My office and home phones, my cell phone, my e-mail."

"Not exactly told not to talk," Jaime says. "Federal agents always encourage witnesses and other parties of interest not to communicate with the subject of an investigation. But I wasn't ordered not to talk to you, and as long as they don't know I did, and I prefer they don't, there shouldn't be any repercussions. And I think we've succeeded in that and are over that hurdle. Tomorrow's a different day and a different story, a different mission altogether. If they find out at some point we were together at Colin Dengate's office, it's of no consequence.

They can't stop us from working a case together while you happened to be in the area."

"Working a case," I repeat.

"Jerk-offs," Marino says, and he's come to like the FBI a lot less since he left law enforcement and no longer has the power to arrest anyone. His hostility also has to do with Benton.

"If one can avoid it, it's always best not to annoy the FBI," Berger adds, as she gets plates and mugs out of a cabinet. "If I annoy them, it doesn't help you. And some of this is about Farbman, about the problems he's caused and is capable of causing."

Dan Farbman is the deputy commissioner of public information for NYPD, and I'm aware that he and Jaime have crossed swords in the past. When I worked for the New York City Office of the Chief Medical Examiner a few years ago, I didn't get along with him all that well, either. But I don't know about anything recent or what Deputy Commissioner Farbman could have to do with any potential problems I might have with the Department of Justice. I say as much to Jaime. I tell her I don't see what Farbman could possibly have to do with me.

"What's happened in Massachusetts and Dawn Kincaid's subsequent arrest and indictments have nothing to do with NYPD or Farbman," I add, as I watch Marino sliding paperwork out of the file, flipping through it, and finding what looks like some sort of official form, lines of it highlighted in orange.

"Yours is a federal case," Jaime says to me. "An attack

on a medical examiner affiliated with the Department of Defense, and it's accepted that this attack was directed at a federal official and therefore is federal jurisdiction and will be tried in federal court. Which is a good thing. But it also makes you and your case of interest to the FBI."

"I'm well aware."

"The talk is that the commissioner may be the next director of the FBI, meaning Farbman thinks he'll go with him to be in charge of media relations. Were you aware of that?"

"I may have heard rumors."

"Unless I can block Farbman's appointment, which I fully intend to do. We don't need our national crime statistics and terrorist alerts tampered with next. He's not exactly a fan of mine."

"He never was."

"Now it's worse. I'd say our relationship is in critical condition—only I intend to be the one who survives," she says. "He won't forgive me for accusing him of lying about NYPD crime stats, accusing him of data cheating. And as you might recall, you had your run-ins with him, too, for the same reason." She arranges plates on the stone peninsula.

"I never actually accused him or anyone at NYPD of data cheating."

"Well, I have, and it's hard for me to imagine you're surprised that he's been doing it." She finds serving spoons in a drawer.

"He's always had a habit of presenting statistics and slanting stories in ways that are politically favorable. But

I hadn't heard he's been accused of data cheating," I reply.

"You really weren't aware."

"I wasn't," I repeat, and I get the feeling she's wondering if Lucy might have said something about this to me. When Jaime apparently confronted Farbman, she and Lucy were still together.

Marino sets paperwork on the coffee table, within my reach, and I pick up the photocopy of a document stamped *CONFIDENTIAL* by the Georgia Prison for Women:

Recommended Procedures for Execution by Lethal Drug Injection
  Materials
  Sodium Thiopental 5gr/2% Kit Sterile 50cc Syringe
  Pancuronium Bromide Injection (20mg) Simple Intravenous Line
  Potassium Chloride Injection, USP (40mEq) Sterile 20cc Syringe

This is followed by directions for the preparation of the drugs included with the "kit," instructions for mixing the solution and how to attach an intravenous line to an eighteen-gauge needle and a bag of saline to keep the line open. I'm struck by the informal, almost casual, tone of a document that is a step-by-step guide for how to kill someone.

Be sure to expel the air from the line so it will be ready for the injection. . . .

"I did the decent thing and complained directly to the commissioner instead of going to the media," Jaime continues to describe her conflict with Dan Farbman and NYPD.

Remember to check the prisoner immediately prior to the administration of any drugs to be sure the intracath is patent and there's no infiltration of the IV solution. . . .

"Unfortunately, the commissioner is pals with the mayor. It got ugly," Jaime explains. "I got ganged up against."

"And so the FBI decided to go into my e-mail and tap my phones because of your battle with Farbman? Because you've accused him of data cheating? And because some years ago I had a few run-ins with him, too?" I don't buy it.

Marino sets down another page, and I pick it up next, reading the highlighted paragraph:

Following the injection of the thiopental sodium into the system, it is "washed in" by normal saline. THIS STEP IS EXCEEDINGLY IMPORTANT. If the thiopental sodium remains within the IV and pancuronium bromide is injected, a precipitate will form and possibly clog the line.

"It's messy when you make enemies." Jaime doesn't answer my question as she removes chopsticks from their paper wrapper. "It's been messy enough in New York for me to leave the DA's office. My apartment's on the market. I'm thinking about alternative places to live."

"You've left your life in New York because of an acrimonious situation with Farbman? That's hard for me to imagine," I reply, as I look at more documents relating to Georgia's most infamous poisoner, the Deli Devil.

Between 1989 and 1996, Barrie Lou Rivers poisoned seventeen people, nine of them fatally, with arsenic she got from a pesticide company, all of her victims regular patrons of the deli she managed in an Atlanta skyscraper occupied by multiple companies and firms. Day after day, unsuspecting innocents lined up in the atrium at her deli counter for the tuna-fish special, which was quite the deal: sandwich, chips, a pickle, and a soda for $2.99. When her sadistic crimes were finally discovered, she told police she was tired of people "griping about their food and decided to give them something to gripe about, all right." She was sick and tired of "shitholes bossing me around like I'm Aunt Jemima."

"There are other nuances," Jaime Berger is saying as I read. "Unfortunately, of a personal nature. Some of what I was asked by the FBI agents who showed up at my door was most inappropriate. It was obvious they'd talked to Farbman first, and you can imagine his favorite point was about me. That you and I were almost family."

I scan the chain-of-custody form that accompanied the execution drugs scheduled for Barrie Lou Rivers, DOC #121195. The prescription was filled at three-twenty p.m. on the first day of March 2009. Kathleen Lawler told me that Barrie Lou Rivers choked on a tuna-fish sandwich in her cell. If that's true, she must have choked to death at some point after three-twenty p.m. on the day of her execution. The prescription for what was to be her lethal cocktail was filled but never administered, because she died before prison officials could strap her to the gurney. It occurs to me that her last meal may have been the same thing she served to her victims.

"You've been back and forth to the GPFW, interviewing Lola Daggette, whose appeals have run out," I say to Jaime. "I assume she's talking to you about something important or you wouldn't have transplanted yourself to Savannah. Your problems in New York aren't why you're here, I don't imagine."

"She's not been helpful," Jaime says. "You'd think she would be, but she's not as afraid of the needle as she is of *Payback*. The person she claims killed the Jordan family."

"Has she said she knows who *Payback* is?" I inquire.

"*Payback* is the devil," Jaime says. "Some evil ghost that planted bloody clothes in Lola's room."

"Her execution is set for this fall, and she's still saying such things?"

"October thirty-first. Halloween," Jaime says. "I suspect the judge who delayed her execution and then reset it is letting everyone know what he really thinks of Lola Daggette, wants to make sure she's given a trick, not a treat, four months from now. Emotions still run high about that case. A lot of people are eager for her to get what they perceive she deserves. They want her to die as painfully as possible. You know, wait just a little too long after administering the sodium pentothal. Forget to expel air from the line. Hope it gets clogged."

Marino places a stack of color printouts on the table, autopsy photographs, and I pick them up.

"Sodium thiopental is fast-acting and can wear off just as quickly, as I'm sure you know," Jaime continues. "If you screw up the timing when injecting the remaining drugs, and what we're really talking about is the neuromuscular blocking agent pancuronium bromide? If you wait too long? The sodium thiopental, the anesthesia, begins to wear off. A blocked line and prison officials have to put in a new one, and the efficacy of the sodium thiopental has dissipated by the time all that's been done.

"You may look asleep, but your brain has come to," she says. "You can't open your eyes, talk, or make a sound as you lie on the gurney with restraints holding you down, but you're conscious and aware that you can't breathe. The long-acting pancuronium bromide has paralyzed the muscles in your chest, and you asphyxiate. No one watching has any idea that you're anything but peacefully asleep as your face turns blue and you suffocate. One minute, two minutes, three minutes, maybe longer, as you die a silent, agonizing death."

The autopsy of Barrie Lou Rivers was performed by Colin Dengate, and I have a good idea how he might feel about someone who poisoned innocent victims by lacing their deli sandwiches with arsenic.

"Except the warden knows." Jaime retrieves a bottle of wine and a Diet Coke from the refrigerator and shuts the door with her hip. "The executioner knows. The anonymous doctor in his hood and goggles knows and can damn well see your panic as he monitors your racing heart before you finally flatline. But then, some of these very people presiding over judicial homicides, the death squad, want the condemned to suffer. Their secret mission is to cause as much pain and to terrorize as much as possible without lawyers, judges, the public knowing. This sort of thing has been going on for centuries. The executioner's ax blade is dull or off the mark and requires a few extra blows. The hanging doesn't go well because the noose slips and the person strangles slowly, twisting at the end of a rope in front of a jeering crowd."

As I listen to what sounds like one of Jaime Berger's classic opening arguments in court, I know that most people who count in this part of the world, including certain judges and politicians and most of all Colin Dengate, would be unmoved by her. I have a pretty good idea how Colin feels not only about what happened to the Jordan family but about what should happen to Lola Daggette. Yes, emotions run high, especially those of my feisty Irish colleague who heads the Georgia Bureau of Investigation's Coastal Regional Crime Lab in Savannah. Jaime Berger coming down to the Lowcountry wouldn't impress him and might just feel like an invasion. I suspect he's not inclined to give her the time of day.

"As you're well aware, Kay, I don't believe that a form of euthanizing begun in Nazi Germany to eliminate undesirables is one we should emulate in the United States. And it shouldn't be legal," she says, as she arranges sushi and seaweed salad on a plate. "Doctors are prohibited from playing any role in executions, including pronouncing death, and the lethal-injection drugs are increasingly difficult to obtain. There's a shortage because of the stigma for U.S. manufacturers to make them, and some states have been forced to import the drugs, making the source and quality of them questionable. The drugs shouldn't be legally available to prison officials, and none of this stops anything. Doctors participate and pharmacists fill the prescriptions and prisons get their drugs. Regardless of one's beliefs or moral convictions, Lola didn't kill the Jordans. She didn't kill Clarence, Gloria, Josh, and Brenda. In fact, she never met them. She was never inside their house."

I glance up at Marino as I study copies of photographs. Last I knew, he was in favor of capital punishment. An eye for an eye. A taste of their own medicine.

"I think Lola Daggette was a screwed-up person, a drug addict with a temper, but she didn't kill anyone or help do it," he says to me. "It's more likely she was set up by the person she calls *Payback*. She probably thought it was friggin' fun."

"Who thought it was fun?"

"The one who really did it. She got her hands on some kid who's in a halfway house and basically retarded." Marino looks at Jaime. "IQ's what? Seventy? I think that's legally retarded," he adds.

"*She?*" I ask.

"Lola's innocent of the crimes she was tried for and convicted of," Jaime says. "I'm not as clear as I need to be about what happened the early morning of January sixth, 2002, but I do have new evidence to prove it wasn't Lola who was inside the Jordans' house. What I can't know is what went on from a forensic standpoint, because I'm not that kind of expert. The injuries, for example. All inflicted by the same weapon, and if so, what was this weapon? What do the bloodstain patterns really mean? How long had the Jordans been dead when the next-door neighbor went out with his dog and happened to notice the glass was broken in the back door and then no one answered the bell or the phone?"

"Colin is that kind of expert," I remark.

"I have a very nice Oregon pinot," Jaime says. "If that's all right with you."

She pulls the cork out of the bottle of wine as I study photographs of Barrie Lou Rivers on the stainless-steel autopsy table, her shoulders propped up by a polypropylene block, her head hanging back, her long gray hair stringy and bloody. The skin of her chest has been reflected up to above the larynx and the vocal cords, and there is nothing lodged in her airway. Close-ups of the small triangular vocal cord opening show it is unobstructed and clear.

Whether it's an object as small as a peanut or a grape or a large bolus of meat, nothing can get below the level of the vocal cords when someone is choking, and Colin was appropriately careful to make sure he checked for aspirated food before he did anything else. He also deemed the case important enough to stay late or return to his lab after hours and perform the postmortem ex-

amination immediately. The time and date of the autopsy are listed on the protocol as nine-seventeen p.m.,
March 1.

I go through more photographs, looking for anything
that might verify what Kathleen Lawler told me about
Barrie Lou Rivers's death in custody. I ask Marino for
rescue-squad run sheets or statements made by the guards
on duty, for the autopsy report, and he shuffles through
the file and hands over whatever there is. I get confirmation that Barrie Lou Rivers likely ate a tuna-fish sandwich
on rye bread with pickles not long before she died. Her
gastric contents are consistent with this: two hundred
milliliters of undigested food, what appear to be fishlike
particles, pickles, bread, and caraway seeds.

But there's nothing to support Kathleen's claims that
Barrie Lou Rivers choked to death. Apparently nobody
attempted a Heimlich maneuver, so it doesn't seem possible that a bolus of sandwich or anything she might have
been choking on was ejected, thus explaining why it
wasn't found during the autopsy. There's no official document that mentions food aspiration or choking, but I
know Colin looked for it. I can tell he did by the autopsy
photographs.

Then I read a call sheet that includes handwritten
notes he made at eight-oh-seven p.m. The suggestion
that choking was the cause of death was made by Tara
Grimm. "Barrie Lou seemed to be having a hard time
breathing," the warden apparently said to Colin over
the phone while the body was in transit, en route to the
morgue. She didn't witness this herself, she said, but it

was reported to her that Barrie Lou "was struggling for breath and seemed distressed." The guards thought it was anxiety, Tara Grimm told Colin. "It wasn't too long before she was to be taken into the death chamber and prepped, and Barrie Lou was prone to emotional fits and anxiety. Now I'm wondering if she might have choked on her last meal."

Colin wrote these remarks on the call sheet, and he dutifully checked for food aspiration when he made his first incision on Barrie Lou Rivers's body less than an hour after he was on the phone with the warden, who did not attend the autopsy. Official witnesses listed on the protocol as having been present include a morgue assistant, a death investigator, and a representative from the GPFW, Officer M. P. Macon. The same prison guard who was my escort earlier today.

11

The cause of death listed on the preliminary autopsy report is undetermined and the manner is the same. *Undetermined* and *Undetermined*. In forensic pathology this is a no-hitter, a game tied at zero inning after inning and finally called because of rain or dark or who knows what, but in the end it doesn't count.

Every death should count, and I am not a good sport when I can't find an answer. I know there always is one. But now and then forensic pathologists like Colin Dengate and me are forced to accept we've failed. The dead won't tell us what we need to know, and we have no choice but to come up with what is most plausible medically even if we don't quite believe it. We release the body and personal effects so those left behind can tidy up legal affairs, collect insurance, arrange funerals, and go on living. Or in the case of Barrie Lou Rivers, she was signed out and buried in a potter's field because nobody claimed her or gave a damn.

Eventually Colin amended the autopsy report to a sudden cardiac death due to myocardial infarction with a manner of natural, and this is what is on her death certificate as well. It was a default diagnosis based on an equivocal amount of coronary artery disease. Sixty percent of the left anterior descending artery. Twenty percent of the right at one centimeter from the ostium. The circumflex coronary artery was clear. She was awaiting her execution, and at some point after a last meal of a tuna-fish sandwich on rye, potato chips, and Pepsi cola, witnesses claimed she suffered shortness of breath, sweating, weakness, extreme fatigue—symptoms that were interpreted as a panic attack precipitated by her impending execution. A panic attack is consistent with the undigested food Colin found when he opened the stomach during the autopsy. Extreme stress or fear, and the digestion completely quits.

By all accounts, it appears she was dead from a massive heart attack at seven-fifteen p.m., or not quite two hours before she was scheduled to die by lethal injection. As I continue to review her case, Jaime talks from the kitchen while she arranges each of our meals on her rental unit's white plates. She's talking about the Jordan family. She wants their injuries and any other artifacts and crime scene information interpreted as precisely and as irrefutably as possible. She needs my help.

"Colin should be able to tell you about their injuries and everything else," I remind her. "He went to the crime scene and did the autopsies. He's a very competent forensic pathologist. Have you tried to discuss the case with him?"

"One perpetrator. Lola Daggette. Case closed," Marino replies. "That's what everybody around here's got to say about it."

As Jaime gets out wineglasses I recall Colin's demeanor during the case presentation he gave at the NAME meeting in Los Angeles years ago. He was personally outraged by the savage deaths of Dr. Clarence Jordan and his wife, Gloria, and visibly upset over their two little children, Brenda and Josh. Colin's opinion then was that only one person had committed those crimes—the teenage girl who was washing the victims' blood out of her clothing in a halfway-house bathroom within hours of the homicides. Any subsequent stories and rumors about Lola Daggette's mysterious accomplice were a defense attorney's fiction, I remember him saying.

"I've been to his lab only once, several weeks ago," Jaime says. "He didn't come out of his office to meet me, and when I went in to speak to him, he didn't get up from his desk."

"You can't force him to be friendly, but I can't imagine him deliberately impairing an attorney's ability to get needed information," I reply, and what I really want to say is that Jaime is Jaime, and what's worse, she's a New Yorker, one of those northern aggressors who comes to a small southern city and assumes everyone is backward, bigoted, dishonest, and somewhat stupid.

I suspect her attitude is obvious when she deals with Colin, who grew up in these parts and is steeped in local tradition, whether it is participating in Civil War reenactments or Irish parades on Saint Patrick's Day.

"He's bound by statute to give you anything that could be exculpatory," I add.

"He didn't volunteer anything."

"He doesn't have to volunteer anything."

"He thinks I'm just looking for someone to support an alternate theory."

"He very well might think that, because that's exactly what you're doing," I reply. "You're doing the same thing any good defense attorney does. What I haven't been told is how or why it is you're involved. You left the DA's office and suddenly you're in the opposite camp, representing Lola Daggette. And what is your interest in Barrie Lou Rivers?"

"Cruel and unusual punishment." Jaime pours wine. "Barrie Lou was so terrified as she awaited her execution in a holding cell, she died of a heart attack. Whose idea was it to serve her a last meal that was identical to what she poisoned her victims with? Was it hers? If so, why? To show remorse, or a contemptuous lack of it?"

"There's no forensic analysis that will answer that," I reply.

"I seriously doubt she picked the menu," Jaime makes her point. "I suspect the objective was to taunt her with what awaited her when she was strapped on that gurney, to terrorize her about what the death squad had in store for her and how much they were looking forward to her getting what she deserved. Barrie Lou had a panic attack, all right. She was literally scared to death."

"I don't know if it's true she was tormented, and I don't think you can know it, either, unless someone who was involved admits to such a thing. And I'm curious about why you're suddenly so interested," I tell her frankly. "I'm puzzled by why you're suddenly up to your elbows in defending the very sort of people you used to lock up and throw away the key."

"Not suddenly. I've been having discussions for a while. My troubles with Farbman and just my having my fill . . . well, it goes back longer than you might think. I alerted Joe at the end of last year that I was looking into other prospects, that I was interested in wrongful convictions."

"Good ole Joe *Nail 'em* Nale," Marino quips, as he flips a page of another report. "I wish I was a fly on the wall when you told him that," he says to Jaime.

Joseph Nale is the district attorney of Manhattan, Jaime's former boss, and not the sort to be favorably inclined toward any individual or organization dedicated to exonerating people wrongfully convicted of crimes. Most prosecutors, if they're honest about it, aren't fond of lawyers who make it their mission to fight the injustices caused by other lawyers and those they recruited as experts.

"I informed him I'd also been talking with some attorneys I know who work with the Innocence Project," Jaime continues to explain.

"The one here in Georgia?" I ask.

"The national organization in New York. But I'm acquainted with Curtis Roberts, and I did ask him to do a favor."

"So Leonard Brazzo wouldn't know you were behind the invitation for me to meet with Kathleen Lawler. So I wouldn't know," I presume.

"I'm having dialogues with firms and in the process of narrowing it down," Jaime says, as if she didn't hear me. "Much of it depends on where I want to live."

"I'm sure what happens in the Lola Daggette case will have some bearing on which law firm you pick," I say, not so subtly.

"Obviously a large one that also has offices in the South and Southwest," she replies, as she hands me a glass of wine and gives Marino a Diet Coke. "Red states are fond of executing people, although I don't intend to have my home base in Alabama or Texas. But to answer your question about how I came to be involved in Lola Daggette's wrongful conviction, she wrote a number of letters to the Innocence Project and a number of groups and lawyers who take on cases like hers pro bono. The letters were badly written, let me add, and were shelved until this past November, when an emergency stay of execution was denied by the Georgia Supreme Court, inspiring a legal review by various public policy organizations. Then earlier this year there was a botched execution here in Georgia that has caused a lot of concern about whether it was deliberately cruel.

"I was asked if I were interested in Lola Daggette's case, as there seemed to be some utility in having a woman involved, I was told," Jaime continues. "Lola's not known to cooperate with men, and in fact is incapable of trusting a man because of the extreme abuse she suffered as a child at the hands of her stepfather. I said I would take a look. At the time, there was no reason to think there might be any link to you. I started reviewing Lola's case before Dawn Kincaid attacked you."

"I'm not seeing a link to Lola Daggette beyond her being in the same prison as Dawn Kincaid's biological mother," I reply. "Although if Dawn's mother, Kathleen Lawler, is to be believed, Lola seems to have some sort of connection to Kathleen. An adversarial one."

"Most of these cases reviewed by national litigation and public policy organizations involve people incarcerated in Georgia, Virginia, Florida, the red states." Jaime ignores what I just said. "Many of these people are given life sentences or sentenced to death because of flawed forensics, misidentification, coerced confessions. And there aren't many women on death row. Currently, Lola is the only woman on death row in Georgia, only one of fifty-six nationwide. And there aren't many women attorneys with my degree of experience and track record taking on these cases."

"That's not an answer to my question." I won't let her

get away with her self-serving rhetoric. "What it does further explain is your interest in having a presence in certain locales and why it might be wise to take a job with a big firm that has offices everywhere."

"I have no dining-room table, I'm sure you've noticed, so we'll make ourselves comfortable in the living room. Stay where you are, and I'll serve." Jaime carries in our food, and her deep blue eyes meet mine. "I'm glad you got here safely, Kay. I regret any inconvenience or confusion."

What she means is she regrets any lies. She regrets finding it necessary to manipulate me into showing up to help her with a case that will make a name for her in criminal defense law if she succeeds in freeing Georgia's most notorious killer, who happens to be the only woman in the state on death row. I don't want to think there is no altruism involved, but I'm certain I smell ambition and other motivating factors. This isn't completely about Jaime's wanting to right a wrong, maybe not even mostly about it. She wants power. She wants to rise from the ashes after being forced out of office in New York City, and she wants sufficient influence to crush enemies such as Farbman and probably a long list of others.

"I shouldn't drink Diet Coke," Marino says, as he begins to eat. "Believe it or not, artificial sweeteners can make you fat."

"I was determined to convey two things to you," Jaime says to me, as she sits down on the couch with her plate of sushi. "You'd better watch yourself, because you and I both know it's all about the case. It's never purely about justice when cops, the FBI, sink their teeth into something. It's the case. First, last, and always. Quotas, headlines, and promotions." She reaches for her glass of wine.

"I appreciate the forewarning," I reply. "But I don't need your help."

"Well, you do. And I need yours."

"White sugar and fake sugar." Marino glances up at me as he eats, the spoon loudly clacking against the side of the mug. "I stay away."

"I have a feeling you've alienated Colin." I state the obvious to Jaime. "He can be stubborn but is very good at what he does. He's well respected by his peers, by law enforcement. He's also a southern gentleman, and an Irish one at that, through and through. You have to know how to work with people like him."

"I'm not used to being a pariah." She is facile with chopsticks. "In fact, you might say I've gotten spoiled. Nothing more welcome in an ME's office or a detective squad than a prosecutor. It's jolting to find I've suddenly turned into the enemy." She takes a bite of pickled ginger and a spicy tuna roll.

"You've not turned into the enemy. You've turned into a defense attorney, and I don't think it's fair to assume that those of us committed to seeking truth are only on the side of the prosecution."

"Colin is offended that I intend to get Lola off death row and out of prison," she says. "He has no interest in my contention that Barrie Lou Rivers is a compelling argument for the GPFW going out of its way to make

executions exceedingly cruel. To inflict pain and suffering, and that's what they'll do to Lola, who was barely of
legal age when she was locked up in that place. It's all the
more barbaric and outrageous because she's innocent.
Colin feels I'm questioning him."

"And you are. But we're used to being questioned."

"He doesn't like it."

"Maybe he doesn't like the way you're doing it."

"I could use a good coach." She smiles, but her eyes
don't.

"I'm grateful you felt morally obligated to tell me
that someone might be spreading lies about me, trying
to get me in trouble with the Feds," I tell her pointedly.
"But this isn't quid pro quo."

"I don't guess you got any Sharp's hidden anywhere,"
Marino says to Jaime, and he's already devoured his
shrimp bisque and half his french fries, invested in his
dinner as if he hasn't eaten all day.

Jaime dips another roll into wasabi and says to him,
"I should have thought to pick up something nonalcoholic, I'm sorry." Then to me she says, "I was determined
to tell you exactly what's going on before you find out
in a way that's legally and professionally not to your
advantage, and the safest way to do this was to talk behind the scenes during the course of other normal things
going on."

"You told an inmate to slip me your cell phone number and instruct me to use a pay phone. I'm not sure that
anything thus far constitutes normal things going on." I
try one of the scallops.

"Yes, I did give Kathleen that instruction."

"And if she tells someone?"

"Who would she tell?"

"One of the guards. Another inmate. Her lawyer. Inmates do nothing but talk, given the chance."

"I don't know who would give a shit." Marino is working on his barbecue shrimp, his napkin making a scratchy sound as he wipes his mouth. "It's not people at the prison you got to worry about," he says to me, as he opens another take-out packet of catsup. "It's the FBI you got to worry about. It wouldn't be a good thing if they knew Jaime's informing you of everything they're doing so they've lost the element of surprise by the time they finally show up to question you. I got to do something about my van. Maybe pick up a six-pack of Sharp's while I'm at it."

Marino's right that the FBI wouldn't like it if it were known that I've been forewarned. But it's too late. The element of surprise is gone for good, even if I'm not clear on exactly what I'm accused of, but the likely scenario is that Dawn Kincaid and her legal counsel are making some sort of false case against me that is at least remotely credible. It's not the first time, and it won't be the last, that I'm baselessly accused of misdeeds and violations and any manner of disreputable acts, whether it is falsifying death records or lab results or mislabeling evidence. In my business, someone always goes away unhappy. It is a fifty percent statistical probability that one side or the other is going to be extremely upset.

"Next time remind me," Jaime says to Marino. "And

I'll make sure I pick up whatever your favorite is. Sharp's, Buckler, Beck's. There's that market on Drayton, not too far from here. They should have nonalcoholic beer. I'm sorry I didn't think of it earlier."

"No one drinks the watered-down shit I do, so why would anybody think about it?" He gets up, the leather crackling again, as if the big chair is upholstered in parchment. "If you could give me the valet ticket for my van," he says to me. "The more I think about it, it might be the alternator's going bad. Thing is finding a mechanic at this hour." He looks at his watch, then at Jaime. "I'd better head out."

I dig the valet ticket out of my shoulder bag and give it to him. Marino goes to the door and opens it, and the alarm chime makes a loud chirp, like a smoke alarm with a low-battery warning. I think of the Jordans' house again, wondering if it's true they didn't have the burglar alarm armed that night, and if so, why not? Were they simply cavalier and trusting? I wonder if it's possible the killer knew the alarm wasn't going to be an issue or was simply lucky.

"If you tell me when you're ready to leave, I'll come get you," Marino says to me. "Either in the van if it's running okay or I'll grab a cab. I'm staying at the Hyatt tonight, too. We're on the same floor."

There's no point in asking how he knows what floor I'm on.

"I've got a go-bag for you," he adds. "Some field clothes and other stuff put together since I know you weren't planning on staying another day or two. Is it okay if I put it in your room?"

"Why not," I reply.

"If you have an extra key, it would be easier."

I get up again and give him that, too. Then he's gone, leaving Jaime and me alone, and I suspect that's the point rather than the urgency of needing a six-pack of nonalcoholic beer or getting his van fixed after hours, when automotive-repair services likely are closed. Jaime probably instructed him to be on his way after he ate, or maybe she gave him some other signal I missed, and I can only assume that whenever it was Marino left the Boston area for his alleged vacation, he carried a go-bag for me. There can't be any doubt that my sitting in Jaime's apartment this moment was carefully planned.

Pushing off her blue leather slip-ons, she gets up from the couch, her stocking feet quiet on old pine flooring as she heads to the kitchen for the bottle of wine. She lets me know she has a very nice Scotch if I'd like something stronger.

"Not for me," I reply, anticipating what tomorrow will bring.

"I think stronger might be better."

"No, thank you. But help yourself."

I watch her open a cabinet and find the Johnnie Walker Blue.

"What could the FBI or anyone possibly think they have on me?" I ask her.

"I believe in dealing proactively," she replies, as if I

asked a different question. "I never take anything for granted."

She unscrews the metal cap from a blended Scotch so fine that it's hard for me to imagine she bought it to drink alone. Possibly she thought she'd sit up half the night with me and get me to lower my defenses and agree to whatever she wants.

"Perception can be a lethal weapon," she adds. "Which may be their point."

"Whose point?" I ask, because I'm not sure that the person making a point isn't Jaime.

12

A generous pour, neat with no ice, and she returns from the kitchen, the bottle of wine in one hand, her glass of Scotch in the other.

"Dawn Kincaid's point. Her lawyers' point," Jaime says. "According to them, what happened to Dawn was self-defense. But not your self-defense. Hers."

"It's not hard to predict what she's going to claim," I reply. "That it was Jack who hacked to death Wally Jamison last Halloween and next hammered nails into six-year-old Mark Bishop's head before going on to kill MIT grad student Eli Saltz, and finally committing suicide with his own gun. My deranged deputy chief who's no longer around to defend himself did it all."

"And then you, his deranged boss, attacked Dawn

Kincaid." Jaime sits back down, and I smell peat and burnt fruit as she sets her drink on the table.

"I'm not surprised she might conjure up a fabrication like that. I'd like to hear the part about her being on my property and ambushing me inside my garage at night after disabling the motion-sensor light in the driveway."

"She showed up at your Cambridge home to get her dog," Jaime answers. "You had her rescued greyhound, Sock, and she wanted him back."

"Please." I feel a rush of irritation.

"You'd removed the injection knife from Jack's cellar earlier that day while working the crime scene. . . ."

"The knife was gone long before I got there," I interrupt, with increasing impatience. "Police will tell you they found its empty hard case and canisters of CO_2 and that was all."

"Police want her successfully prosecuted, don't they?" She refills my wineglass. "They're prejudiced against Dawn Kincaid, aren't they? And the case against her is complicated by your FBI husband being involved. That's not exactly impartial and objective, is it?"

"Are you implying Benton may have removed the injection knife from the scene or knows I did and would lie about such a thing? That either one of us would tamper with evidence or obstruct justice in any way?" I confront her, and it's difficult knowing which side she's on, but it doesn't feel like mine.

"We're not talking about me or what I might imply," Jaime says. "We're talking about what Dawn will say."

"I'm not sure I understand why you might know what she will say."

"She'll claim that while you awaited her expected arrival on your property that night, you made sure you put body armor on," Jaime replies. "You made sure the Maglite you carried with you didn't work and loosened the bulb in the motion-sensor light by the garage so you could later claim you couldn't see what happened. You claimed you swung the heavy metal flashlight blindly in the dark, a reflex when you supposedly were attacked, when in fact it was you who ambushed Dawn."

"It was an old flashlight, and I didn't test it before walking out of the house. I should have. And it certainly wasn't me who loosened the bulb in the motion-sensor light." I'm having a hard time disguising my annoyance.

"You were ready and waiting for her when she appeared to pick up Sock." Jaime resettles herself more comfortably on the couch, placing a pillow in her lap and resting her arms on top of it.

"And it makes sense she would contact me and ask if she can drop by to get her dog when the police, the Feds, everybody, is looking for her?" I remark. "Who's going to believe anything so illogical?"

"She'll say she wasn't aware the police were looking for her. She'll say she wouldn't have imagined anyone was looking for her, since she didn't do anything wrong."

Jaime reaches for her drink. The expensive Scotch is burnished gold in a cheap glass, and she's beginning to sound a little drunk.

"She'll say her beloved rescued greyhound, trained by her mother and entrusted to her care, was at her father's house in Salem," Jaime continues. "Dawn will say you took the dog home with you, stole him, and she wanted him back. She'll say you attacked her and she managed to get the knife away from you, but in the process badly cut her hand, losing part of a finger and suffering nerve and tendon damage, and then you struck her in the head with the heavy metal flashlight. She'll say that if Benton hadn't appeared in the garage when he did, you would have finished the job. She'd be dead."

"She'll say all this, or has she already said it?" I put down my plate and look at her, and my appetite has tucked itself into a tight place, out of reach and done for the night. I couldn't swallow another bite if I tried.

If I didn't know better, I'd think that Jaime Berger is Dawn Kincaid's counsel and has lured me to Savannah to tell me that. But I know it isn't true.

"She'll say it, and she has said it," Jaime replies, grasping seaweed salad in the tips of her chopsticks. "She's said it to her lawyers, and she's said it in letters to Kathleen Lawler. Inmates can write to other inmates when they're family. Dawn is clever enough to have begun addressing Kathleen as Mom. *Dear Mom,* she writes, signing them *your loving daughter,*" she says, as if she's seen these letters, and maybe she has.

"Has Kathleen written to her as well?" I inquire.

"She says she hasn't, but she's not telling the truth," Jaime says. "I'm sure you don't want to hear it, Kay, but

Dawn Kincaid is playing quite the role. A brilliant scientist who has lost the use of a hand and is suffering mental and emotional problems due to trauma and a concussion, which is being described as a significant head injury with lasting ill effects."

"Malingering."

"Pretty, charming, and now suffering dissociative states. Delusions and impaired cognition, which is why she was transferred to Butler."

"Deliberate pretense."

"Her lawyers attribute all of it to you, and you might expect a civil suit filed next," Jaime says. "And your contact with her mother today and any communications in the past, in my opinion, have been unwise. It only serves to make your behavior more questionable."

"Contact that you've orchestrated." I remind her that I'm no fool. "I'm here because of you." She wanted me in a weakened position.

"No one twisted your arm to come here."

"No one needed to," I reply. "You knew I would, so you set me up for it."

"Well, I certainly thought you might come, and I recommend you have no further contact with Kathleen. Not any type at all," Jaime instructs me, as if she's now my lawyer. "While I think a criminal case against you is a stretch, I worry about litigation," she goes on painting inflammatory scenarios.

"If a burglar injures himself while ransacking your house, he sues," I reply. "Everybody sues. Litigation is the new national industry and has become the inevitable aftermath of virtually any criminal act. First someone tries to rob, rape, or kill you. Or maybe they succeed. Then they sue you or your estate for good measure."

"I'm not trying to aggravate or scare you or put you in a compromising situation." She places her chopsticks and napkin on her empty plate.

"Of course you are."

"You think I'm bluffing."

"I didn't say that."

"When the FBI came by my apartment, Kay, they wanted to know if I'd ever observed instability, violence, any traits in you that might have given me concern. Are you truthful? Do you abuse alcohol or drugs? Isn't it true you've been known to brag that you could get away with the perfect murder?"

"Of course I've never bragged about such a thing. And what happened in my garage was far from perfect."

"Then you're admitting you intended to murder Dawn Kincaid."

"I'm admitting that if I thought I was going to be attacked, I would have armed myself with more than a flashlight I found in a kitchen drawer. I'm admitting that the entire event wouldn't have happened had I been paying attention, if I'd not been so distracted and sleep-deprived."

"The FBI wanted to know if I was aware of your relationship with Jack Fielding," Jaime tells me. "Had the two of you ever been lovers, and might you have been possessive or unnaturally attached to him or felt spurned by him and given to jealous rages?"

She takes another sip of Scotch, and I'm tempted to get up and help myself. But it wouldn't be smart. I can't afford to make myself more vulnerable to her than I already am or to be foggy tomorrow.

"And they brought up this fanciful story about self-defense?" I ask.

"No. They wouldn't do anything as generous as that. The FBI is extremely skilled at getting information and not inclined to return the favor. They wouldn't tell me why they were asking about you."

"This isn't quid pro quo," I again say.

"I should think you'd want to help someone who is about to be executed for a crime she didn't commit," Jaime replies. "Maybe, in light of the situation you find yourself in, you can relate more than ever to being falsely accused of killing someone or attempting to," she adds with emphasis.

"I don't need to be falsely accused of a crime in order to have a sense of right and wrong," I answer.

"Lola will die in a horrific way," she says. "They won't make it painless or merciful. Dr. Clarence Jordan was from old Savannah money, a good Christian, a moral man, generous to a fault. Known for giving free medical care to people in need or volunteering in the ER, the soup kitchen, the food bank on Thanksgiving, on Christmas Eve. A saint, according to some."

I suppose it's possible a man of great faith, a saint,

might not bother setting his burglar alarm. I wonder if he installed the alarm system himself, or did a previous owner of his historic home?

"Do you know details of the alarm system in the Jordan house?" I ask.

"It doesn't appear to have been set the early morning of the murders."

"Does that bother you?"

"The question continues to interest me. Why wasn't it set?"

"Lola's offered no explanation?"

"She wasn't the one who broke in," Jaime reminds me. "I have no credible explanation."

"Has anybody tried to determine if it was habit of the Jordans not to set the alarm?"

"There's no one alive to state as fact what their habits might have been," Jaime says. "But I've had Marino looking into it, among other things."

"If the alarm was active and connected by a telephone line to an alarm company, there should be records of whether it was routinely armed and disarmed," I reply. "There should be a record of false alarms, trouble on the line, anything that might indicate the Jordan family was using it and paying a monthly bill."

"A very good point, and one that isn't satisfactorily addressed in the records I've reviewed," Jaime answers. "Or through interviews."

"Have you talked to the investigator?"

"GBI Special Agent Billy Long retired five years ago and says his reports and records speak for themselves."

"You talked to him yourself?"

"Marino did. According to Investigator Long, the alarm wasn't set that night and the assumption was that the Jordans were trusting and not particularly security-conscious," Jaime says. "And that they were tired of false alarms."

"So they stopped setting it entirely, even at night? That seems a bit extreme."

"Careless but maybe understandable," she replies. "Two five-year-olds, and you can imagine what happens. They open doors and the alarm goes off. After the police show up a few times, you get tired of it and get complacent about setting it. You have a deadbolt that requires a key and are more worried about small children being locked in if there's a fire. So you give in to the very bad habit of leaving the key in the deadbolt lock, making it possible for an intruder to break out the glass and reach in and open the door from the inside."

"And these explanations for the Jordans' seeming carelessness are based on what?" I ask.

"Based on Special Agent Long's assumptions at the time," Jaime says, as I dig myself deeper into a case that I shouldn't want any part of.

Because I've been tricked.

Jaime Berger pulled a number of stunts to make sure I'm sitting in this very living room and having this very conversation.

"Unfortunately, assumptions are easy to make when you believe a case is already solved," I say.

"Yes. They had the Jordans' DNA on bloody clothing

that Lola Daggette was washing in the bathroom of her halfway house," Jaime agrees.

"I can see why the GBI, why the prosecutor, wouldn't have been unduly caught up in the details of the alarm system," I remark.

"I'm curious about why you're caught up in these details." She reaches for her glass.

"An intruder knowing or not knowing whether the alarm was set tells us something about this person." I get in deeper, as Jaime knew I would. "Do you happen to know if the keypad was visible from outside the door? Could an intruder have looked through the glass and seen the alarm was or wasn't set?"

"It's not easy to tell from the photographs. But I think it's possible someone could have looked through the glass and seen the light on the keypad was either green or red, indicating the status of the alarm."

"These details are important," I explain. "They tell us something about the mind-set of the killer. Was the Jordan house random? Was it luck of the draw? Did someone break out the glass of the kitchen door and unlock it, deciding, if an alarm went off, to run like hell? Or did this individual have reason to know there was a good chance the alarm wasn't going to be set? Or could the person see it wasn't set? I assume the Jordan house still exists?"

"The kitchen has been remodeled. I'm not sure what else has been, but there's an outbuilding in back that didn't used to be there. The original kitchen door is gone, replaced by a solid one. The alarm company used by the current owner is Southern Alarm. There are signs posted on the property and stickers on the windows."

"I bet there are."

"We've found nothing that might indicate what the facts are about the Jordans' alarm system except that the company was Southern Cross Security."

"Never heard of it."

"A small local company that specialized in installations in historic buildings where the main priority was not to damage original woodwork, that sort of thing." Jaime takes another sip of her drink. "It went bankrupt several years ago when the economy tanked and real estate values went into the toilet, especially for grand old homes from the past. A lot of these mansions are now condos or office spaces."

"This is what Marino found out?"

"I'm wondering why it matters who found it out."

"I ask because he's an experienced and thorough investigator. Information he gets as a rule is reliable."

She studies me as if what I just said isn't true. She's checking to see if I'm jealous. She expects I'm unhappy that Marino is here because of her and planning to resign from his full-time position at the CFC. Maybe she's experiencing a secret satisfaction that she's stolen Marino from me, but jealousy is not what I'm feeling. I'm unhappy about her influence on him, and not for any reason she might divine. I don't trust her with his well-being or with the well-being of anyone.

"Did you ask Colin Dengate if he knew anything about the alarm system?" I ask her. "Did you ask if he might have heard the investigators discussing why the alarm wasn't set?"

"Any matters relating to the police investigation he doesn't share with me," she says. "He directs me to the source, which is proper but not helpful. Not even cooperative, if we're honest about it. He's allowed to talk and voice his opinions but chooses not to with me."

"Does he talk to Marino?"

"I wouldn't have Marino approach him directly. That wouldn't be appropriate. Colin should talk to me. Or you."

A mistake, I think. Marino is the very sort of rough-around-the-edges no-nonsense cop that Colin Dengate would feel quite comfortable with.

"What kind of doctor was Clarence Jordan?" I ask, as if what happened to him has become my responsibility.

"Had a very successful family practice on Washington Avenue. You don't murder someone like Clarence Jordan, and you don't kill his wife." Jaime's eyes are steady on me as she talks and drinks. "You certainly don't kill his beautiful little children. People aren't going to want to accept that Lola is innocent. Around here, she's Jack the Ripper."

"Your method for inviting me to help you as an expert isn't exactly what I'm accustomed to," I finally say.

"There's more than one thing going on. By getting you down here, I'm helping both of us."

"Not sure I see that. What I do see is you know how

to work Marino. Or, better put, you still know how to work him," I remark.

"You're a person of interest in a federal investigation, Kay. I wouldn't trivialize that fact."

"It's also pro forma, and you know that better than most," I say. "In light of who I am, and especially because of my affiliation with the Department of Defense, any allegation has to be looked into. If I'm accused of being the Easter Bunny, it has to be checked."

"You wouldn't want it in the news that you're being accused of anything at all. Certainly not accused of attacking someone and maiming that person. Wouldn't be pleasant to wake up to that headline."

"I hope you're not threatening me. Because that comment sounds like one a defense attorney might make," I reply.

"Good God, no. Why would I threaten you?"

"I think it's obvious why you might."

"Of course I'm not threatening you. In fact, I'm in a position to help you," she says. "I might be the only person in a position to do so."

I don't know what she's talking about. I don't see how Jaime Berger can help me, but I don't ask.

"A lot of people might be sympathetic to Dawn Kincaid," she says. "In my opinion, you might be better off if your attempted murder case never sees a jury."

"So she can get away with it? I fail to see how that's helpful."

"Does it matter which case she's punished for, as long as she is?"

"She'll be tried on cases other than mine. For homicide. Four counts of it." I assume this is what she's alluding to.

"A shame she has the scapegoat of Jack Fielding for those homicides, the Mensa Murders." She stares thoughtfully at what's left of her Scotch. "Blame those sadistic crimes on a dead man who was a bodybuilder, an unstable and aggressive forensic expert who was involved in a number of activities that will offend your average juror."

I am silent.

"If the worst happens and the murder cases don't go well, that rather much leaves you hanging out to dry. If Dawn manages to successfully blame the murders on Jack, you have no case, in my professional opinion," Jaime says, and now she's the prosecutor talking. "If jurors believe Jack was the killer, then it will appear you attacked an innocent woman who happened to show up on your property to retrieve her dog. If nothing else, you're going to get sued and it's going to be expensive and ugly." She's the defense attorney again.

"It wouldn't be good if the belief is that Jack was the killer," I admit.

"What would help your case is a silver bullet, don't you agree?" She smiles at me as if ours is a pleasant conversation.

"Yes. We always hope for silver bullets. I'm not sure they exist, except in folklore."

"It just so happens they can exist," Jaime says. "And we happen to have one."

13

S he lets me know happily, confidently, that DNA results from recent retesting of evidence connects Dawn Kincaid to the Jordan murders.

"Swabs and samples taken in the Jordan house, including blood from the handle of a knife, samples that came back as unknown at the time of the murders, are a match," Jaime explains, as I check my iPhone for messages and deny her the reaction she expects from me.

Gratitude. Relief. What can I do to thank you, Jaime? Anything you want. You just name it.

"Dawn Kincaid was definitely there," Jaime states, as if there can be no doubt. "She definitely was inside the Jordan house at the time of the murders. She left pubic hair and urine in the toilet. She left skin cells and blood under the fingernails of five-year-old Brenda, who apparently clawed the hell out of her."

She gives me a moment to feel the weight of what she's just said, pausing for effect as I think about another matter entirely.

You okay? Where are you? Benton has just text-messaged me. *Who or what the hell is Anna Copper LLC?*

"I guess I can understand your interest in Kathleen Lawler," I say to Jaime, as I answer Benton with a question mark.

I don't know what he means. I've never heard of Anna Copper LLC.

"I'm sure Kathleen hopes there's a deal to be had if she cooperates with you," I say to Jaime. "Maybe you can finagle a reduced sentence or influence a pardon board."

"She's been very cooperative," Jaime answers. "And yes, she wants her life back. She would do just about anything."

"Does she know about the DNA? That new test results point at her biological daughter?"

"No."

"How can you be so sure? I get the feeling the GPFW is keenly interested in everything said and done in there."

"I've been careful."

"Did Lola Daggette have injuries when the police arrested her shortly after the murders?" I inquire. "Was she checked for injuries? For abrasions, for scratches or bruises? Was she given a forensic physical examination?"

"Not that I know of. But there were no obvious injuries, and that should have been a clue," Jaime says, and she's right. "There was no question Brenda struggled with her assailant and scratched this person badly enough to draw blood. So it should have been problematic for the police that Lola had no scratches."

"If she had no injuries, then it should have been a clue," I agree. "And if the DNA of this biological evidence recovered from underneath Brenda's fingernails didn't match Lola's DNA, that should have been another clue. A very big clue, and a very big problem."

"Yes, it should have suggested that Lola didn't do it."

"Or that she didn't do it alone."

"It's called people having their minds as closed as a steel vault," Jaime says. "People around here wanted these murders solved. They needed them solved for their own peace and safety, and to feel order and sanity had been restored to their lovely little city."

"Unfortunately, that happens. Especially in extremely emotional, high-profile cases."

"It was Dawn who killed the Jordan family and got clawed and scratched and made a sandwich and used the downstairs toilet," Jaime summarizes. "And ironically, the reason I know this for a fact is because of what happened to you in Massachusetts. Dawn's DNA profile was entered into CODIS after her arrest for your attempted murder, and when I had DNA from the Jordan crime scene retested and entered into CODIS, we got a hit. It's a shock, I realize that. It's stunning."

"Maybe not a shock." I refuse to give Jaime that. "Kathleen Lawler indicated Dawn might have been in Savannah when the Jordan murders were committed.

January of 2002, she said to me, when I was talking to her today. Supposedly that was the first time the two of them met. Do you think Kathleen might have any idea what her daughter did?"

"I can't imagine it. Why would Dawn confess such a thing unless she was hoping to get caught," Jaime answers. "This is such a tremendous break in more than one case. We know for a fact that Dawn Kincaid was here in Savannah. She had to be. It won't matter if she continues her lies about what happened at your house on February tenth. If she had any credibility, it's about to be gone."

"So I should be doubly motivated to help you make your case," I say.

"Justice, Kay. On more than one front."

"When did you get the DNA results?"

"About a month ago."

"No news about it, as far as my case is concerned, or I'd know," I comment. "I haven't heard a word. But that doesn't mean other people don't know."

"Neither Dawn nor her counsel knows her DNA's been connected to the Jordan case, to multiple homicides committed nine years ago," Jaime says, with confidence I don't feel.

"What lab did you use?" I ask.

"Two different independent ones in Atlanta and Fairfield, Ohio."

"And no one knows," I say skeptically. "The FBI doesn't know? I'm assuming the attorney general of Georgia allowed the retesting?"

"Yes."

"And the AG doesn't know the results?"

"He and other key people understand the importance of not releasing information until the case has been prepared. And I'm still in the early stages of that."

"One of the biggest threats to any investigation is leaks," I remind her of a fact that would have been obvious to her not so long ago.

She is full of herself. Or maybe she's desperate.

"And it seems to me in this particular case, the threat level would be very high for leaks," I add. "Extraordinarily high, in fact. There are a lot of people who have a personal interest in the Jordan case, including powerful people in Georgia's state government who might be embarrassed that a New York lawyer came down here and discovered one of their most notorious murder cases had been mishandled and a teenager was sentenced to death for a crime she didn't commit."

"I didn't just fall off the turnip truck."

"No, but maybe you're being idealistic. You're excited about this case, understandably, but I wouldn't be much help to you if I didn't point out that you very likely aren't flying under the radar or operating under a mantle of secrecy." Tara Grimm is on my mind, and I wonder if she's aware of the new test results.

She knows retesting was ordered. *Who told her that?*

"So you're willing to help me. I'm delighted to hear it," Jaime says, but she doesn't look delighted.

She looks tired and haunted, her eyes getting sleepy and not as bright as I remember them from times past.

She seems uncomfortable in her own skin, constantly shifting her position on the couch, tucking her feet under her and placing them back on the floor. Restless and fidgety and drinking too much.

"I'm helping you now by reminding you there may be people who know about the new DNA results and might try to interfere or already be interfering," I say to her. "The DNA evidence you retested was entered into the FBI Laboratory's Combined DNA Index System and got a hit in the Arrestee Index, and next Dawn Kincaid's identification was confirmed. Therefore, you can't say with certainty that the FBI isn't aware that Dawn Kincaid, who is of intense interest to them, might be linked to nine-year-old murders in Savannah. If the attorney general knows, it's possible the governor does, and the governor seems quite invested in having Lola Daggette executed. When I talked to Tara Grimm, it was clear to me that she knew about evidence retesting and that there might be, and I quote, 'a jailbreak' at the GPFW."

"They record everything in there," Jaime replies matter-of-factly, as if she's not at all concerned about what I just said. "I knew damn well when I sat in that contact visit room in Bravo Pod that every word was being recorded, which is why I resorted to writing notes on my legal pad when it was critical that what I communicated remain confidential. Kathleen is motivated to be careful what she talks about, but I admit Lola is another matter. She's very limited intellectually and has poor impulse control. She's given to boasting and flaunting herself, will do almost anything for attention. While she knows we've retested evidence, I've not told her the results."

"I'm just wondering if she knows them anyway. It might explain her hostility toward Kathleen, the mother of the person whose crimes Lola has spent the last nine years paying for," I suggest.

"My bigger worry is this hitting the media before I'm ready," Jaime says.

"I don't think that should be your biggest worry. I notice you've installed a security camera, an alarm system." I don't add that she might be carrying a gun. "Maybe you should be worried about your professional and personal safety," I add.

"And I imagine you would have a first-rate security system and camera surveillance if you were working down here. Or someone would do it for you," she adds, and I wonder if she's referring to Lucy. "As soon as I have more forensic facts and am completely sure of my case, I'll file a petition to vacate Lola's capital-murder convictions. I'll redirect prejudice to the facts. I'll redirect a lust for revenge to hard science, and hopefully you're going to help me."

She pauses as if expecting me to tell her I will, but I don't offer that assurance.

"There was never any evidence to link Lola to those crimes except for the bloody clothing Dawn Kincaid obviously instructed her to dispose of or to clean or maybe planted in her room to frame her," Jaime says. "But I need details. I intend to be fully armed when I go forward."

"How did Lola and Dawn know each other? Or do we know if they did?" I inquire, as Benton text-messages me again.

Where are you? Not answering in your hotel room.

I'm safe, I text-message him back.

Call when you can. (Anna Copper has a tarnished rep.)

I answer him for the third time with a question mark as Jaime says, "Let me interject that I'm not violating privilege. Lola has given me permission to discuss the details with you."

"Why? Besides the fact she likely would do whatever you said."

"Your influence would be taken seriously by the courts," Jaime answers. "What we lack is a recognized and reputable forensic expert who will stick his or her neck out."

She means Colin Dengate isn't going to stick his neck out. Or at least that is what she believes.

"It's not a popular position to take in light of the outrage over these murders," she adds. "Public sentiment is nothing less than hateful, even after all these years. The beauty in proving Dawn Kincaid murdered the Jordan family is it also helps you," she makes that point again.

She's trying to bribe me into doing the right thing, and maybe that's what is offending me most.

"If Dawn Kincaid slaughtered an entire family in their sleep, she's certainly capable of committing the crimes in Massachusetts, and no one is going to believe a word she says about you," Jaime concludes an argument that isn't necessary or complimentary in what it implies.

"Has Lola mentioned Dawn Kincaid? Has she admitted or insinuated that Dawn is the mysterious accomplice she refers to as *Payback*?" I ask.

"No." Jaime cradles her drink and looks at me from the corner of the couch, where she is restless and getting drunker. "She says she doesn't have any idea. She woke up in her room at the halfway house the morning of January sixth and discovered articles of her own clothing on the floor, clothing that was covered with blood. Terrified she would get in trouble, she tried to wash them."

"Do you believe that?"

"Lola's afraid. That I do believe. She is terrified of this person she continues to refer to as *Payback*."

"Terrified of a person or a devil or a monster? Maybe something she's imagined?"

"I think it's possible Lola met Dawn on the street and got enticed by an opportunity for money or drugs. It's possible Lola didn't know the real name of this person who got her mixed up in something that resulted in her being set up and framed."

"She would have been in the halfway house at the time Dawn came to Savannah and the murders were committed." I remind her that someone remanded to a halfway house because of drug charges might not be permitted to wander the streets with impunity.

"An uncontrolled halfway house," Jaime says. "The residents were allowed to come and go with permission. Lola was in and out, supposedly looking for a job, supposedly dropping by a nursing home in Savannah to visit her ailing grandmother. She had plenty of opportunities to meet someone like Dawn, who probably used an alias, or perhaps she offered the nickname *Payback*, and that may very well be the only name Lola ever knew. Disguising her identity would make the most sense when you think about what Dawn intended to do. But it's irrelevant. DNA doesn't lie. DNA doesn't care about aliases."

"Have you asked Lola if the name Dawn Kincaid might be familiar? Might be a name she's repressed out of fear?"

"She wouldn't admit it—assuming she remembers. But I have asked her if the name Dawn Kincaid means anything, and she says no. I've been very careful. I haven't mentioned the DNA results," Jaime repeats.

"She's that afraid of whoever *Payback* is. Even after nine years."

"She says she hears *Payback*'s voice," Jaime answers. "She hears *Payback* describing the terrible things she'll do if Lola ever crosses her. Now Lola doesn't have to talk or tell us who *Payback* is," Jaime says, and I can't help entertaining the possibility that *Payback* is made up.

A scary fantasy in the head of an emotionally damaged young woman with an IQ of seventy who is scheduled to be executed on Halloween.

"The DNA is the only voice we need to hear," Jaime says. "And Dawn Kincaid is safely locked up and will stay locked up."

"She knows Dawn Kincaid is locked up and will stay

locked up? That at some point she'll be going to trial?" I want to make sure.

"She knows that Dawn has been charged with multiple counts of homicide in Massachusetts," Jaime confirms. "It's been in the news, and I've mentioned it. It's not a secret at the GPFW that Kathleen Lawler's daughter is at Butler and facing trial."

"I'm sure you've talked about Dawn with Kathleen."

"I've interviewed Kathleen, as you know. Of course we've talked about her daughter."

"Dawn's locked up, and yet Lola is still too afraid to talk." It doesn't make sense to me, no matter what Jaime explains.

If Lola's been on death row for the better part of a decade for crimes she didn't commit and the real killer, Dawn Kincaid, is locked up in Massachusetts, why is Lola still terrified of her, and why is Kathleen Lawler terrified of Lola? Something is wrong about all of this.

"Fear is a powerful emotion," Jaime says confidently, beginning to slur her words, "and Lola's had a very long time to be afraid of this person on the outside, of Dawn, who is alive and well and unimaginably cruel. You've seen what she's capable of. She was only twenty-two years old when she slaughtered the Jordans in their own beds. Because she felt like it. Because it was a blood sport. Because it was fun. And then made herself a sandwich and drank a few beers and set up a troubled and intellectually impaired eighteen-year-old girl to take the blame."

"You could have just asked me, Jaime," I say to her. "The rest of it wasn't necessary. You didn't need to manipulate me or entice me, and it concerns me that you might think you need to bribe me. I can fight my battles with the FBI or anyone else, and I think after all we've been through, you should have known I'd help if you asked."

"You would have come to Savannah and been my forensic expert in the Lola Daggette case?" She looks at her glass as if considering a refill. "You would have intervened with your redneck colleague Colin Dengate, who's given me a lot of yes-no answers, and that's about all? You would have taken him on?"

"Colin's not a redneck," I answer. "He's just very convicted in his opinions and beliefs."

"I didn't know how you'd feel about it," she replies, and she isn't referring to my questioning Colin Dengate's findings.

Jaime's thinking about being *almost family*. She's wondering if what happened between Lucy and her would obviate my being helpful or even civilized.

"Lucy doesn't seem to know you're here," I answer the question Jaime should have asked. "She got somewhat upset when I called her after Kathleen gave me your cell phone number this afternoon. I asked Lucy if she'd told you I was coming to Savannah, if that's how you knew. She said no. She indicated she's not talked to you."

"We haven't talked in six months." Jaime stares past me, and her voice is tight and edgy.

"You don't have to tell me what happened."

"I told her I never wanted to see her again, and not to contact me for any reason," she says coldly.

"You don't have to explain," I repeat.

"Obviously she hasn't told you why."

"She moved to Boston and you were no longer around or mentioned. That seems to be the extent of what she's explained to anyone," I reply.

"Well, it's not anything she did intentionally to cause what should have been damn predictable if she'd given it a second thought." Jaime gets up, headed back to the kitchen and the bottle. "I'm sure she didn't mean to hurt me. But that doesn't alter the fact that she managed to destroy everything I've built and seemed to have less insight about the damage she caused than even Greg did."

Greg is Jaime's ex-husband.

"At least he understood the demands of my career," Jaime says from the kitchen as she pours Scotch into her glass. "As a lawyer and a mature and reasonable human being, he knows exactly how things work and that there are certain rules and realities one can't disregard simply because one assumes they don't apply. Through it all, Greg was at least discreet, smart, even professional, if one can use the word *professional* about behavior in a relationship or during the dissolution of one." She returns to the couch and settles back into her corner. "And he was never so reckless as to do something in the name of helping me that would ensure my ruination."

"You don't have to tell me what Lucy did. Or what you perceive she did," I say quietly, carefully, so I don't show what I really feel.

"Why do you think I know about Farbman's data cheating?" Jaime meets my eyes, and hers are dark like open wounds, her pupils large. "Just why do you think I might know it as a fact, not simply suspecting it based on statistics that don't quite ring true?"

I don't answer her, because I'm already imagining what she's about to say.

"Lucy somehow hacked into the Real Time Crime Center, into whatever server or mainframe or data warehouse she had to get into." Jaime's voice catches. For an instant I see her devastation over a loss she refuses to admit. "While I can appreciate her feelings about Farbman, about all of the complaints she heard ad nauseam behind closed doors in the privacy of our intimate times together, it wasn't exactly my expectation that she would take it upon herself to hack into the NYPD computer system so she could help me prove a point."

"And you know without a doubt that she did such a thing."

"I suppose I should blame myself." She stares past me again. "The fatal error I made was to succumb to her vigilantism, her complete lack of boundaries, and let's face it, her sociopathy. I of all people know what the hell she's like. For God's sake, you and I both know. What I've had to extricate her from, which is how I got tangled up with her to begin with . . ."

"Tangled up?"

"Because you asked me to help." She sips her drink. "Poland, and what she did over there. Jesus God. How would you like to have a relationship with someone you can't know everything about? Someone who's . . . Well, I'm not going to say it."

"Killed people?"

"I know more than I wish I did. I've always known more about her than I wish I did."

I wonder what's changed Jaime Berger. She didn't used to be so self-absorbed, so quick to place blame on everyone but herself.

"How often do you think I've told her 'Not another word'? I don't want to hear it. I'm an officer of the court. How could I be so stupid?" she says awkwardly, as if her tongue's not working right. "Maybe because of my loathing of Farbman. He wanted to be rid of me for years, but what I didn't realize is he's not the only one who felt that way. When Lucy gave me the information and I knew exactly what data Farbman had falsified, I went to the commissioner, who, of course, demanded proof."

"Which you couldn't exactly give."

"I didn't think he'd ask for it."

"Why wouldn't he?"

"Emotions. Being caught up in them and making an irreparable miscalculation. I became the accused. I was the one compromised. Nothing was said directly. It didn't need to be. All certain people had to do was drop Lucy's name into the discussion at strategic points. They knew. A forensic computer expert considered somewhat of a rogue, fired by the FBI, by ATF, in her earlier life. Everybody knows what she's capable of, and I can't control what you tell Lucy. But I don't advise . . ." she starts to say.

"It's best you don't advise me about anything to do with her," I reply.

"I didn't expect you to agree with—"

"It's not for me to agree or disagree," I cut her off, as I get up from the couch and begin collecting dishes. "You had your relationship with Lucy, and mine is different, has always been different, will always be different. If what you've told me is what really happened, it was terrible judgment, an outrageously stupid and self-destructive thing for her to do." I carry dishes into the kitchen. "I should let you get some rest. You look tired."

"Interesting you would say it that way." She clumsily sets wineglasses and the empty bottle by the sink. "*Self-destructive*. And here I was thinking that I was the one who got destroyed."

I turn on hot water and find an almost empty bottle of dishwashing soap under the sink. I look for a sponge, and Jaime says she forgot to buy one as she leans against the stone peninsula, watching me clean up after a meal she did nothing to provide beyond making a phone call and walking a few blocks to the restaurant to make sure she wasn't in the apartment when I arrived. So Marino could set the stage for her. So she could make a grand entrance. So she could continue to direct what she has scripted.

"Unfortunately, I'm not good at banishing people,"

I remark, as I wash dishes with soap and my bare hands. "Maybe when they're finally dead and I decide it's a damn good thing because I've had enough, and I tell myself it's damn good they're gone. But it's probably not true. I probably don't mean it. I'm probably quite flawed that way. Maybe you could find a dish towel in this unlived-in rented apartment of yours and help me dry."

"I need to get those, too." She reaches for a roll of paper towels instead.

"We'll just leave them to air-dry in the rack," I decide.

I stuff empty take-out containers into a trash bag. I cover the pungent mac-and-cheese and tuck it inside the empty refrigerator, and decide that Marino's right about truffles. I've never liked them, either.

"I didn't know what else to do." Jaime's not talking about cleaning up after dinner or her getaway place down here in the Lowcountry. She's talking about Lucy. "How do you love a liability?"

"Who are you talking to?"

"You're her family. It's not the same. I'm afraid I'm going to have a terrible headache in the morning. I don't feel so good."

"Obviously it's not the same. I love her no matter what, even when it's not convenient or helpful to my politically correct image." I return to the couch, grabbing my shoulder bag, so angry I'm afraid of what I might do next. "And who the hell isn't a liability?"

"It's like loving an amazing horse that will break your neck someday."

"And who goaded it?" I walk back into the kitchen. "Who spurred it into acting dangerously?"

"You don't really think I asked her to do something like that?" She looks at me sleepily.

"Of course not." I enter Marino's number into my phone. "I'm sure you didn't ask her to hack into NYPD's computer any more than you asked me to come to Savannah."

14

Marino's van chugs and backfires somewhere from the dark direction of the river many blocks from here, and I emerge from the deep shadows of a live oak tree, where I've been waiting because I couldn't be with Jaime Berger a moment longer.

"I'm going to have to get off the phone." So far I've managed to keep the anger out of my tone and not sound judgmental as I talk with my niece. "I'll call you back when I'm in my room in about an hour or so. I want to make a stop first."

"I can call the hotel phone, if you don't want to use your cell," Lucy says.

"I'm already using it. I've been using it." I don't

elaborate on what I think of Jaime and her self-serving ideas of pay phones and FBI eavesdropping.

"You shouldn't have any of this on your mind at all," Lucy says. "It's not about you. It's not your problem. And I don't view it as my problem anymore."

"You don't get over something like this as if it never happened," I reply, looking in the direction of Marino, of what there can be no doubt is his van, which isn't fixed.

On the wooded square across the street, the Owens-Thomas House hulks against the night, pale English stucco with tall white columns and a serpentine-shaped portico. The shapes of old trees stir and iron lamps glow, and for an instant I catch something moving, but as I stare in that direction, I find nothing. My imagination. I'm tired and stressed. I'm unnerved.

"I still worry about who knows or might find out. You're right about that," Lucy says, as I step closer to the street, looking up and down it and into the square, seeing no one. "When I first found out about the protective order issued to the CFC, that's what I thought it was about. They were after me for hacking. I've been careful. They'd probably like nothing better than to get me into trouble because of old shit with the FBI, with ATF."

"Nobody's after you, Lucy. It's time you put that out of your mind."

"It depends on what Jaime's said to certain people and what she continues saying and how she twists the facts. What she told you isn't what happened, not exactly. She's made it a whole lot worse than it was," she says. "It's like she's obsessed with turning me into a bad person so she feels justified in what she did. So everyone will understand why she ended it."

"Yes, I'd say it's exactly like that." I watch for the van, which I can hear but not yet see, on Abercorn now and getting closer as I try to contain my complete disrespect for someone I suspect my niece still loves.

"Which is the real reason why I left New York. I knew there was talk about the security breach even if I wasn't outright accused. No way I could continue doing forensic computer work there."

"The way she treated you is what hurt you most and why you left New York, left absolutely everything you'd built for yourself," I disagree calmly, quietly. "I don't believe for a minute you started all over again in Boston because of rumors."

I look back at Jaime's building, at her windows lit up. I can see her silhouette moving past the drawn draperies in what I assume is the master bedroom.

"I just wish you'd told me. I don't know why you didn't," I add.

"I thought you wouldn't want me at the CFC. You wouldn't want me as your IT person or want me around."

"That I would banish you the way she did?" I say before I can stop myself. "Jaime asked you to commit a violation when she knew how vulnerable you were to her. . . . Well, I don't mean to sound like this."

Lucy doesn't say anything, and I watch Jaime Berger's silhouette moving back and forth past the lighted window. It occurs to me she might have a security camera monitor in her bedroom and she's checking it. She might be watching me, or maybe she's distressed because I spoke my mind and walked out as if I might never come back. I think of the old saying that people don't change. But Jaime has. She's reverted back to an earlier vintage of herself that's gone bad like wine not properly stored. Living a lie again, but now she's impossible to take. I find her completely unpalatable.

"Anyway, I know about it now," I tell Lucy. "And it doesn't change anything with me."

"But it's important you believe it's not the way she's described."

"I don't care." Right now, I really don't.

"All I did was verify a few numbers by looking at electronic records of the original complaints and the way they were coded, but I shouldn't have."

No, she shouldn't have, but what Jaime did was worse. It was calculating and cold. It couldn't have been more unkind. She abused the power she had over Lucy and betrayed her, and as I get off the phone I wonder who Jaime will manipulate and manage to compromise next. Lucy and Marino, and I suppose I should include myself on the list. I'm in Savannah, immersed in a case I knew virtually nothing about until a few hours ago, and I look up at her apartment again. I watch her silhouette move past the lighted window in back. She seems to be pacing.

It is almost one a.m., and the van gleams ghostly white in uneven lamplight, loudly heading in my direction like some demon-possessed machine out of a horror film, slowing down and speeding up, lurching and shuttering. Obviously Marino didn't find a mechanic after he left Jaime's apartment several hours ago, and by now I'm convinced he deliberately left me alone with her for a reason that has nothing to do with anything I might want or need. Brakes screech when he slows to a stop in front of the apartment building, and the passenger door squeaks as I open it, the interior light out because Marino always disables it in any vehicle he's in so he's not an easy target or *a fish in a barrel,* as he describes it. I notice bags on the backseat.

"Do a little shopping?" I ask, and I hear the tenseness in my tone.

"I picked up some water and other stuff so we'd have it in our rooms. What happened?"

"Nothing I feel good about. Why did you leave me alone with her? Was that your instruction?"

"I thought I said I'd call you when I got here," he reminds me. "How long you been standing outside?"

I fasten my shoulder harness, and the door squeaks again as I pull it shut. "I needed to get some air. This thing sounds terrible. In the agonal stages of a drawn-out tortured death. Good Lord."

"I thought I told you it's not a good thing to be wandering around by yourself. Especially this time of night."

"As you can see, I didn't wander far."

"She wanted time alone with you. I thought you'd want it, too."

"Please don't think for me," I reply. "I'd like to take a detour, take a look at the Jordan house, if this thing can make it without breaking down completely. I don't believe wet spark plugs are the problem."

"Pretty sure it's the alternator," he says. "Maybe loose plug wires, too. The distributor cap might be dirty. I found a mechanic who's going to help me out."

I stare up at Jaime's apartment, and she has returned to her living room, where the shades are up. I can see her clearly as she stands before a window watching us drive off, and she has changed into something maroon, possibly a bathrobe.

"It's kind of creepy, isn't it?" Marino says, as we head south, the dark shapes of trees and shrubs moving in the hot wind. "I asked Jaime if she picked her apartment because it's close to where it happened. She says she didn't, but it's like two minutes from here."

"She's obsessed. The case of a lifetime," I comment. "Only I'm not really sure what case she's working. The one in Savannah or her own."

We roar past grand old houses with windows and gardens lit up, their façades a variety of textures and designs. Italianate, colonial, Federal, and stucco, brick, wood, and ballast stone. Then the right side of the street opens up into what looks like a small park surrounded by a wrought-iron fence, and as we get closer I can make out gravestones and crypts and white crisscrossing paths dimly illuminated by incandescent lamps. On the cemetery's southern edge is East Perry Lane, where there are large old homes on spacious lots thick with trees, and I recognize the Federal-style mansion from photographs I found earlier today when I read stories online about Lola Daggette while I was parked in front of the gun store.

The hot night air carries the sweet perfume of oleander as I survey three stories of Savannah gray brick with double-hung windows symmetrically placed and a grand central portico flanked by soaring white columns. The roof is red tile, with three imposing chimneys, and off to one side is an attached stone carport with archways that used to be open and now are glassed in. We park directly in front of a property I can't imagine owning, I don't care how handsome it is. I wouldn't live in any place where people were murdered.

"I don't want to sit here long, because the neighbors have a hair trigger about suspicious strangers and suspicious cars, as you might expect," Marino says. "But if you look to the right, almost at the back of the house, just behind the carport is the kitchen door where the killer broke in. Well, you can't see it from here, but that's where it is. And that big villa to the right belonged to the neighbor who went out with his dog the morning of January sixth and noticed the glass busted out of the Jordans' kitchen door and a lot of lights on for so early in the morning. Based on what I've been able to reconstruct, the neighbor, a guy named Lenny Casper, woke up around four a.m., when his poodle started yapping. Casper says the dog was upset and wouldn't settle down, so he figured it needed to go out."

"Have you talked to this neighbor yourself?"

"On the phone. He also was interviewed by the media

at the time, and what he says now is pretty much the same thing he said back then." Marino looks past me, out my open window, at the Italianate house he's talking about. "Around four-thirty his poodle was doing his business right there where those palm trees and bushes are."

He points at the up-lit landscaping of palms and oleander, and trellises of yellow jasmine that separate the two properties.

"And he happened to notice the broken glass in the Jordans' kitchen door," Marino says. "He told me the kitchen lights and a lot of lights in upstairs rooms were on, and his first concern was someone had tried to break in and maybe that's what woke up his dog. So he went back inside his house and called the Jordans, who didn't answer the phone. Next he called the police, and they rolled up around five, found the kitchen door unlocked, the alarm off, and the little girl's body at the bottom of the stairs, near the entryway."

I take in the former Jordan property, at what I estimate is an acre of wooded yard illuminated by post-mounted lanterns that cast large, thick shadows. The driveway is granite gravel edged in brick, and slate stepping-stones lead from it past the carport to a kitchen door that I couldn't possibly see without getting out of the van and trespassing.

"He moved to Memphis not long after the murders," Marino then says. "Neighbors on both sides moved, and based on what I hear, what happened really hurt real estate values. Fact is, hardly anybody within blocks on either side who was living here at the time still lives here now. From what I understand, the Jordan house is one of the most popular stops on ghost tours, especially since it happens to be right across the street from Savannah's most famous cemetery, where a lot of the tours begin and end, at Abercorn and Oglethorpe, at the entrance we just went past a minute ago."

Marino reaches in back, and paper rattles as he pulls out two bottles of water.

"Here." He hands me one. "I feel like all I've done all day is sweat. You know, foot tours," he resumes talking about Savannah's haunted attractions and the crowds they draw. "Some of them candlelit at night, and you can imagine how old it would get if you live here, either in this house or nearby, and all these tourists are gawking while some guide goes on and on about the family murdered here. Hate to think what it's like now, with it all over the news that Lola Daggette's execution has been reset. Everybody around here has the Jordan murders on their minds again."

"Have you been here during the day?" I ask.

"Not inside." He takes a noisy swallow of water. "I'm not sure going inside would tell you anything nine years after the fact, and the house has been bought and sold a number of times, lived in by different people and probably changed a lot. Besides, I think it's pretty obvious what happened. Dawn Kincaid busted the glass out of the door back there, reached in and unlocked it easy as pie. I guess Jaime told you the key was in the deadbolt, which is one of the stupidest things people do. Installing a deadbolt near glass panes or windows and then leaving the key in it. You know, take your choice. Get trapped if there's a fire or make it easy for someone to break in and kill you in your sleep."

"Jaime also said you've been looking into the question of why the alarm wasn't set. Who installed it? Did the Jordans routinely use it? She says that they stopped setting it because of false alarms."

"That's the story."

"I can tell you one thing from where we are on the street right now," I add. "You can't see the kitchen door. If you were walking or driving by, you wouldn't know from casual observation that there's a kitchen door or any door on the right side of the house. It's out of sight because of the carport."

"But you can see flagstones leading to something in the back that might be a door," Marino says.

"Or the flagstones lead to the backyard. You'd have to look to know." I twist the cap off my bottle of water. "What's important is the kitchen door isn't visible from the street, which would suggest to me that whoever broke in nine years ago either knew about the side entrance back there and it had glass panes and a deadbolt that required a key that often was left in the lock, or this person had gathered intelligence on some earlier occasion."

"Dawn Kincaid sure as hell's the type to gather intelligence," Marino says. "She probably knew a rich doctor lived here. She probably cased the place."

"And it was just her good fortune the key was in the lock and the alarm wasn't set?"

"Maybe."

"Do we know anything about where she stayed when she was in Savannah nine years ago, or how long she was in this area?"

"Only that fall classes at Berkeley ended on December seventh and the spring semester began January fifteenth," Marino says. "She definitely completed her fall semester there and was enrolled in classes for the spring."

"So she might have spent her holiday break in this area," I decide. "She may have been here for several weeks before she visited her mother for the first time."

"During which time she might have met Lola Daggette," Marino suggests.

"Or become aware of her," I reply. "I'm not at all convinced they knew each other. Maybe Lola knows who Dawn Kincaid is now, because of the Massachusetts cases and whatever Jaime or perhaps someone else has said to her. Lola may even know that Dawn had something to do with the Jordan murders, because I don't care what Jaime says. You can't know what's been leaked about the new DNA test results. But regardless of what Lola knows right this minute, we can't assume she connects Dawn Kincaid with anybody from nine years ago when the Jordan murders occurred, at least anybody she knew by name. Do you know what courses Dawn was taking at the time?"

"I just know it had to do with nanotechnology."

"The department of materials science and engineering, most likely." I stare at a mansion where four people were murdered in their sleep, as it's been described, and I continue to be perplexed.

Why wouldn't they set the alarm? Why would they leave a key in the deadbolt lock, especially during the holiday season, when burglaries and other property crimes typically are on the rise?

"Were the Jordans known for being careless or cavalier?" I ask. "Were they hopelessly idealistic and naïve? If nothing else, people who live in historic homes in historic neighborhoods usually are extremely careful about securing their property and their privacy. They keep their gates locked and their alarm systems armed. If nothing else, they don't want tourists wandering into their gardens or up onto their verandas."

"I know. That part bothers the hell out of me," Marino says.

His dark shape inside the dark van leans closer to me as he looks out at a mansion that wouldn't appear remotely foreboding if one didn't know what happened there nine years earlier at around this same time in the morning. After midnight. Possibly between one and four a.m., I've read.

"There's a big difference between 2002 and now in terms of security awareness. Especially here in Savannah," Marino continues. "I can guarantee you that people who might have been slack about not setting their alarms or leaving keys in locks probably don't do it anymore. Everybody worries more about crime, and they sure as hell have it on their minds that an entire family was murdered in their own beds inside their million-dollar mansion. I know people do stupid things, we see it all the time, but it strikes me as unusual that Clarence Jordan was known for having family money and was gone a lot because of all the volunteer work he did, especially during the holidays. Thanksgiving, Christmas, New Year's were his busiest times helping out in clinics, ERs, homeless shelters, soup kitchens. You would think he might have been a little bit worried about the safety of his wife and two little kids."

"We don't know that he wasn't."

"It appears he went to bed that night and the alarm wasn't set," Marino repeats the detail that continues to tug at my attention.

"What about the alarm company records?"

"They've been out of business since the fall of 2008."

A light blinks on upstairs in a window of the Jordans' former house.

"I talked to the former owner of Southern Cross Security, Darryl Simons," Marino says, "and according to him, he doesn't have the old records anymore. He says they were on computers he donated to charity after he went out of business. In other words, the records were deleted or thrown out three years ago."

"Any reasonably reputable businessperson holds on to records for at least seven years in case of a tax audit, if for no other reason," I reply. "And he's telling you he didn't have backups?"

"Busted," Marino says, as the porch lights blink on next.

We drive off loudly and conspicuously as the front door opens and a muscular man in pajama bottoms steps out on the porch, staring after us.

"You can understand why this guy Darryl Simons doesn't want people calling about the Jordans' alarm system," Marino says, as the van bucks and roars. "If it had been armed and working, they wouldn't be dead."

"So why wasn't it armed and working?" I ask. "Did he say if it was installed by Dr. Jordan? Or perhaps by the previous owner of the home?"

"He didn't remember."

"Right. Hard to remember something like that in a case where four people were murdered."

"He doesn't want to remember it," Marino says. "Kind of like being the one who built the *Titanic*. Who wants credit? Have amnesia and ditch the records. He wasn't happy to get my call."

"We need to find out what happened to his company computers, where they were donated. Maybe they still exist somewhere or he has disks in a safe," I suggest. "It would be helpful to see his monthly statements. It would be very helpful to see a log. You would think that investigators might have looked into this at the time. What exactly did Investigator Long tell you? Jaime says you talked to him."

"Did she mention he's old as dirt and had a stroke since then?"

The van backfires. It sounds like a gun going off as

we struggle past movie theaters, cafés, and ice cream and sub and bicycle shops near the College of Art and Design.

"Two thousand two wasn't all that long ago," I say to Marino. "These aren't even cold cases by my definition. Cool, lukewarm, but not cold. We're not talking about unsolved murders that are fifty years old. There should be plenty of documentation and plenty of people with good recall in a case as big and infamous as this one."

"Investigator Long said whatever happened is in his reports," Marino says. "I said, 'Well, that doesn't seem to include anything about the Jordans' burglar alarm.' He claims they'd had trouble with false alarms and quit setting it."

"If he knew that, he must have talked to the alarm company," I answer, as we wind around Reynolds Square, dark and wooded with benches and a statue of John Wesley preaching, near an old building once used as a hospital for malaria patients.

"Yeah, he must have, but he doesn't remember."

"People forget. They have strokes. And they have no interest in reopening an investigation that might prove them wrong."

"I agree. We should see the log," Marino says.

"There must have been quite a number of people around here who'd had alarm systems installed by Southern Cross Security. What happened to those customers?"

"Obviously some other company took over their accounts."

"And maybe that company has the original records. Maybe even a hard drive or computer backups," I suggest.

"That's a good idea."

"Lucy might be able to help you. She's pretty good when it comes to electronic records that supposedly have vanished into thin air."

"Except Jaime won't want her help."

"I wasn't suggesting she help Jaime. I'm suggesting Lucy help us. And Benton might have some interesting insights to offer. I think we could use any informed opinions we can get, because the evidence seems to be pointing in different directions. It's a good thing we're not very far away, because this thing sounds as if it will quit any second or seize up or explode," I add, as the van stutters and shudders north toward the river.

Most of the restaurants and breweries we pass are closed, the sidewalks deserted, and then the Hyatt is just ahead on our right, huge and lit up, illuminating an entire city block.

"It's feeling like we're being stonewalled," Marino says. "People forgetting or records that are gone."

"What Jaime is doing in Savannah is recent, and the alarm company went out of business and supposedly got rid of its records at least three years ago," I reply. "So it doesn't sound like you're getting stonewalled, at least not on that front, because of what's happening with the case now."

"Well, it sure seems like there might be something else certain parties don't want anybody snooping into."

"You don't know that for sure, either," I reply. "It's typical that once people have been through the ordeal of a homicide investigation and a trial and all the publicity that goes with it, a lot of them want to be left alone. Especially in cases as gruesome as these."

"I guess it's easier if Lola Daggette gets the needle and then it's all over with," Marino says.

"For some people, that would be easier and emotionally satisfying." Then I ask, "Who is Anna Copper?"

"I sure as hell don't know why Jaime would mention that to you," Marino replies, as we loudly creep to a halt in front of the hotel.

"I'm wondering who or what Anna Copper or Anna Copper LLC is," I ask again.

"A limited liability company she's been using of late when she doesn't want her name on something."

"Such as the apartment she's rented here in Savannah."

"I'm really surprised she would mention it to you. I would figure she'd assume you're the last person who'd appreciate hearing about that LLC," Marino says.

A valet cautiously approaches the driver's window, as if he's not sure what to make of the chugging, backfiring van or if he wants to park it.

"It's better I drive this thing into the garage myself," Marino tells him.

"I'm sorry, sir, but no one is allowed to drive anything in there. Only authorized personnel can access underground parking."

"Well, you don't want to be driving this. How about I park it right over there by that big palm tree and I'll get it first thing in the morning so I can take it in for repairs."

"Are you a guest here?"

"A regular VIP. I left the Bugatti at home. Too much luggage."

"We're not really supposed to—"

"It's about to die. You don't want it dying with you in it."

The van chugs and moves in fits and starts as Marino parks off to one side of the brick drive. "Anna Copper is an LLC that Lucy created about a year ago, I guess," he says. "It was her idea, and she didn't exactly do it for a nice reason. It happened after she and Jaime had a disagreement. Well, by then they'd probably been having a lot of them."

"Is it Lucy's LLC or Jaime's?" I ask, as he turns off the engine and we sit in the silent dark. The air blowing through our open windows is still very warm for almost two a.m.

"Jaime's. Lucy basically created a smoke screen for Jaime to hide behind. It was supposed to be funny in a mean sort of way. Lucy went on one of these Internet legal sites, and next thing you know, Anna Copper LLC was filed, and when she got the paperwork in the mail, she wrapped it up in a big fancy box with a bow and gave it to Jaime."

"This is according to Jaime? Or did Lucy tell you?"

"Lucy did. It was a while back when she told me, around the time she moved to Boston. So I was surprised when I realized Jaime is actually using that LLC."

"And the reason you found out?"

"Paperwork, a billing address. When I was helping set up her security system I had to know certain information," Marino says, as we get out of his van. "That's the name she's using on everything down here, and I admit it's a little unusual—at least, I think it is. She's a damn lawyer. It wouldn't take her five minutes to create a new LLC. Why would she use one that has certain memories associated with it? Why not forget the past and move on?"

"Because she can't."

Jaime can't give up Lucy, or at least the idea of Lucy, and I wonder if Benton is thinking the same thing. When he text-messaged me that Anna Copper's "rep is tarnished," I wonder if he was referring to Jaime. If so, he must have run a check on her apartment building and come across a resident named Anna Copper LLC, and then run another check and realized who it was. He likely wouldn't accept it as an accident of fate that Jaime has resurfaced in our lives, and he might know something about the trouble she got into that caused her to abandon her life in New York.

We walk through the bright lobby, where at this hour there is a solitary clerk at the desk, only a few people in the bar. When we reach the glass elevator, Marino taps the button several times, as if it will make the doors open faster.

"Shit," he says. "I left the damn groceries in the van."

"Did Lucy ever tell you what Anna Copper means? Where she got the name?"

"All I remember is it had something to do with Groucho Marx," he says. "You want me to drop off some water for you?"

"No, thanks." I'm getting into the tub. I'm making phone calls. I don't want Marino stopping by my room.

I board the elevator and tell him I'll see him in the morning.

15

It was still hot when the sun came up, and by eight a.m. I'm sweltering in black field clothes and black ankle-high boots as I sit on a bench in front of the hotel, drinking a venti iced coffee I got at a nearby Starbucks.

The bell in the City Hall tower rings in the first day of July, deep, melodious peals echoing in brassy reverberations as I watch a cabdriver watching me. Rawboned and weathered, with pants hitched up and a beard as scruffy as Spanish moss, he reminds me of characters I've seen in Civil War photographs. I imagine he hasn't migrated far from the birthplace of his ancestors and still shares traits in common with them, like so many people I notice in cities and towns insulated from the outside world.

I'm reminded of what Kathleen Lawler said about genetics. No matter what we strive to become in life, we're still who and what the forces of biology shape us to be. Hers is a fatalistic explanation, but she's not completely wrong, and as I recall her comments about predetermination and DNA, I have a feeling she wasn't referring only to herself. She was also alluding to her daughter. Kathleen was warning me, perhaps attempting to intimidate me, about Dawn Kincaid, with whom she claims to have no contact, yet according to a number of sources, it simply isn't true. Kathleen knows more than she's letting on, has secrets she keeps that likely are related to why Tara Grimm moved her into segregation at the same time I was lured down here. I believe Jaime Berger has caused real trouble.

She doesn't know what she's dealing with, because she isn't as rationally motivated or as in touch with herself as she believes. While her selfish reasoning may very well have been precipitated by her clashes with New York police and politicians, most of what drives her is related to my niece, and now none of us have ended up in a good place, certainly not a safe one. Not Benton, not Marino, not Lucy, not me, and least of all Jaime, although she might not see it or believe it if I pointed it out. She's completely deluded herself, and I'm along for the ride and reminded of what an old Diener used to tell me during my Richmond days:

You have to live where you wake up, even if somebody else dreamed you there.

When I woke up this morning after very little sleep, I

realized I can't afford to waver in my resolve. Too much is at stake, and I don't trust Jaime's analysis of most matters or have faith in her approach, but I will do what I can to help. I'm involved not because I volunteered. I was drafted, practically abducted, and that's of no consequence anymore. My sense of urgency isn't about Lola Daggette or Dawn Kincaid and her mother, Kathleen Lawler.

It's not about nine-year-old murders or the recent ones in Massachusetts, although these cases and those involved in them are critically important, and I will make investigative sense of them as best I can. What overrides all of it is Jaime's meddling with the people closest to me. I feel she has endangered Lucy, Marino, and Benton. She has threatened our relationships, which have always been intricate and complicated, held in place by fragile threads. The network that we are is sturdy only when each of us is.

These people Jaime trifles with are my family, my only family, really. I don't count my mother or my sister, I'm sorry to confess. I can't rely on them, and frankly wouldn't think of entrusting myself to their care, not even on their better days, the few they have. There was a time when I was happy to widen my inner circle to include Jaime, but what I won't permit is for her to range about on the perimeter and dislodge the rest of us from our moorings or change who we are to one another. She abandoned Lucy in a way that was cold and unfair, and now Jaime seems determined to redefine Marino's career, his very identity. In short order, she has managed to inflame his jealousy of Benton again and imply that my husband has betrayed me and is indifferent to my safety and happiness.

Even if there weren't old murders connected to recent ones that seem to share the common denominator of Savannah, I wouldn't leave right now. I extended my hotel reservation and booked a room for Lucy, who took off in her helicopter with Benton at dawn. I said I needed their help. I told them I usually don't ask, but I want them here. Marino's white cargo van turns into the hotel's brick driveway, still loud but at least not bucking and shaking, and I get up from the bench. I walk toward the cabdriver with the scruffy beard and smile at him as I drop my Starbucks cup into the trash.

"Good morning," I greet him, as he continues to stare.

"You mind me asking who you're with?" He eyes me up and down, leaning against his blue taxicab parked beneath the same palm tree where Marino left his crippled van some seven hours earlier.

"Military medical research." I give the taxi driver the same meaningless answer I've offered other people this morning who wondered aloud why I'm wearing black cargo pants, a long-sleeved black tactical shirt with the CFC shield embroidered in gold on it, and boots.

The go-bag I found in my room when I walked in at close to two a.m. had all of the essentials I might need on the road working a case but nothing suited for the civilian world, certainly not one located in the subtropics. I recognize Marino's handiwork. In fact, I have no doubt he packed the go-bag himself, removing items from my office closet and bathroom and also my locker in the morgue changing room. As I've continued reconstructing these past several months and especially the two weeks since he's been gone I recall being puzzled when certain items seemed to be missing. I thought I had more uniform shirts. I was sure I had more cargo pants. I could have sworn I had two pairs of boots, not just one. The contents of the go-bag suggest that from Marino's point of view, I'm going to spend my time down here in labs or a medical examiner's office, or more to the point, with him.

Had Bryce packed for me, and that's the usual routine when an emergency rushes me out of town or I'm stranded somewhere, he would have included a suit bag with blazers, blouses, and slacks generously padded and wrapped with tissue paper so nothing gets wrinkled. He would have picked out shoes, socks, workout clothes, and toiletries, his choices made with far more thoughtfulness and flair than if I'd packed myself, and most likely he would have stopped by my house. Bryce doesn't hesitate to help himself to anything he anticipates I might need, including lingerie, which is of no personal interest to him beyond his occasional comments about various labels and fabrics, and which detergents and dryer sheets he prefers. But he would not have sent me off to Georgia in the summer with three sets of cold-weather field clothes, three pairs of men's white socks, a flak jacket, boots, one deodorant, and an insect repellent.

"I didn't know if you ate yet," Marino says, as I open

the van's door, and right away I notice the interior is much cleaner than it was when I was in it last. I smell citrus-scented air freshener and butter and deep-fried steak and eggs. "They got a Bojangles' a couple miles from here near Hunter Army Airfield, which gave me an excuse to do a test run. The van's good as new."

"With the minor exception of air-conditioning." I buckle up and notice the bulging bag on the floor between our seats as I roll the window down all the way.

"Would need to get a new compressor for that, but the hell with it. I mean, you wouldn't believe the deal I got on this thing, and you sort of get used to not having air. Like the old days. When I was growing up, a lot of cars didn't have it."

"Or shoulder harnesses or air bags or antilock brakes or navigational systems," I reply.

"I got you a plain egg biscuit, but there's a few steak, egg, and cheese ones, too, if you're hungry," he says. "And there's water in a cooler." He pokes a thumb toward the backseat. "No olive oil at Bojangles', so you just have to make do. I know how you feel about butter."

"I love butter, which is why I stay away from it."

"Jesus. I don't know what the hell it is about craving fat. But I just go with it now. I'm learning not to fight some things. If you don't fight them, they don't fight you back."

"Butter fights me back when I try to button my pants. You must have stayed up all night. When did you find time to get this thing fixed and give it a bath?" I ask.

"Like I said, I found a mechanic, got his home number off the Internet. He met me at his shop at five this morning. We swapped out the alternator, balanced the tires, cleaned out the wheel wells, tightened the plug wires, and I replaced the wiper blades while we were at it, and cleaned it up a little," he says, as we drive along West Bay, past restaurants and shops of stucco, brick, and granite, the street lined with live oaks, magnolias, and crepe myrtles.

Marino is dressed for the field, but he was sensible in what he selected for himself, the CFC summer uniform of khaki cargo pants and beige polo shirt in a lightweight cotton blend, and he wears tactical nylon mesh and suede trainers instead of boots. A baseball cap protects the top of his bald head and the tip of his sunburned nose, and he has on dark glasses and sunblock that is watery white in the deep creases of his sweaty neck.

"I appreciate your thinking to pack my field clothes," I say to him. "I'm wondering when you did that."

"Before I left."

"That much I deduced on my own."

"I should have brought you the khakis. You must be hot as hell. I don't know what I was thinking."

"Probably that you would take what you could find when you rummaged, and it's been a bit too chilly in Massachusetts for warm-weather uniforms, since we've had an unusually cold spring. My khakis are in a closet at my house. If you had asked Bryce . . ."

"Yeah, I know. But I didn't want him involved. The more involved he gets, the harder it is for him to keep his mouth shut, and he makes such a big thing out of whatever it is. He would have turned packing into a fashion show and sent me down here with a steamer trunk."

"You packed for me before you left," I repeat. "And when might that have been, exactly?"

"I pulled a few things together the last time I was in the office. I don't know, the fourteenth or fifteenth, not that I was positive what would happen when I got down here."

He turns onto US-17, heading south, the air blowing through our open windows as hot as an oven.

"I think you were absolutely positive what would happen," I correct him. "Why don't we just come clean about it?"

I open the glove box for extra napkins and spread them in my lap before retrieving our breakfast from the bag between our seats.

"It would be helpful if you'd admit that when you decided to take a last-minute vacation, you knew you were coming down here to assist Jaime," I say to him. "You also knew I soon would follow without the benefit of the real reason why and would arrive with little more than the clothes on my back."

"I've tried to make you understand why you couldn't know in advance."

"Yes, you've tried, and I'm sure you're convinced of your reasoning even if I'm not. In fact, I shouldn't call it your reasoning. It's Jaime's reasoning."

"I don't know why you don't care if the FBI's spying on you."

"I don't believe it. And if they are, they must be bored. Now, which one of these am I opening for you?" I examine warm biscuits in yellow wrappers slick with butter.

"They're all the same except yours."

"Okay, I think I can figure out mine, since it's half the weight of the others." I open more napkins and drape them over Marino's thigh. "I would like a little clarity. And not about the FBI but about you."

"Don't get pissed again."

"I'm asking for clarity, not a disagreement or a fight. Had you already rented your apartment in Charleston before Jaime called the CFC two months ago and you took the train to New York to have a secret meeting with her?"

"I'd been thinking about it."

"That's not what I asked."

I unwrap a chicken-fried steak, egg, and cheese biscuit, and he takes it in his huge hand and a third of it is gone in one bite, buttery crumbs snowing down on his napkin-covered lap.

"I'd been looking into it," he says, as he chews. "I'd been checking out rentals in the Charleston area for a while, more of a pipe dream, really, until I talked to Jaime. She told me about her work in the Lola Daggette case and that she could use my help, and I'm thinking this is kind of amazing, sort of like it was meant to be. It's the same part of the world where I was just looking for something to rent. But it makes sense when you realize that most places with good fishing and motorcycle riding also have the death penalty. Anyway, I decided she was right. It might be smart to become a private contractor."

"Her suggestion. Of course."

"Well, she's smart as hell, and it made sense. You know, I can pick and choose my hours a little better, pick and choose where I want to be, earn a little more money, maybe." He takes another bite of his biscuit. "I told myself it's now or never. This is your chance. If you don't try to make things turn out the way you want right now when it's under your nose, you probably won't get asked twice."

"Did Jaime go into detail about what happened to her in New York? About why she quit?" I ask.

"I guess she told you what Lucy did."

"I thought you said she hadn't mentioned Lucy to you." I open my egg biscuit, and although I usually don't eat fast food and certainly don't share Marino's addiction to all things fried, suddenly I'm starved.

"She didn't, exactly," Marino says, and we are on the Veterans Parkway now, making very good time through long stretches of forests, the sky huge and a whitish blue that augurs a scorching day. "All she mentioned was the Real Time Crime Center, that its security was compromised and Jaime basically got blamed. No one officially accused her, but she said comments were being made about how coincidental it was that here she is claiming NYPD is skewing crime stats at the same time their computer system is broke into and it just so happens she's in a relationship with a well-known computer hack."

"That's not the story Lucy tells," I reply. "She says it wasn't the Real Time Crime Center. It was one precinct where they allegedly were bumping down felony grand larcenies to misdemeanors and changing burglaries to criminal-mischief complaints."

"That's bad enough."

"I don't know exactly what she got into or how, but yes, it's bad enough. And I'm sorry if that's how Lucy is described, as a well-known computer hack. If that's what people think of her."

"Well, shit, Doc, she's always going to do it," Marino says. "If she can get into something, she's going to get into it, and there isn't much she can't get into. I know you know that by now, so why pretend it's ever going to change? Maybe I'd be the same way if I was like her, do what's needed to get what you want because you can. *Legal* is just moguls on a black-diamond slope. Something you go over and around, and the more of them and the more difficult they are, the more Lucy likes it."

I look out my open window at tawny marshes and snaking estuaries and creeks, the hot air blowing in the rotten-egg smell of pluff mud.

"Not that Lucy really gives a shit what anybody thinks of her." Paper crinkles as he wads up his biscuit wrapper.

"I'm sure she'd like you to believe she doesn't give a shit. She cares about a lot of things more than you might think she does. Including Jaime." I take a bite of my biscuit. "I know I'm going to regret it, but this is pretty good."

"I'd better have another one in case we don't get lunch."

"You look like you've lost weight, and I don't know how."

"I only eat when my body's hungry instead of when I am," he says. "It took me half my life to figure it out. It's like I wait until I'm hungry at a cellular level, if you know what I mean."

"I don't have a clue." I hand him another biscuit.

"It really works. No shit. The goal is not to think. When you need food, your cells will let you know, and then you take care of it. I don't think about meals anymore." He talks with his mouth full. "I don't plan on having this or that or not having this or that or feel I have to eat at a certain time of day. I let my cells tell me and go with it. I've lost fifteen pounds in five weeks, and I'm toying with the idea of writing a book about it. *Don't Think You're Fat, Just Eat.* A play on words. I'm not really telling people not to think they're fat. I'm telling them not to think about it at all. I believe people would go for it. I probably could dictate it and get someone to type it up."

"I'm worried you're smoking again."

"I don't know why the hell you keep saying that."

"Someone's been smoking in your van."

"I think it smells pretty good in here."

"It didn't smell pretty good yesterday."

"A couple fishing buddies of mine. Something about driving with the windows wide open when it's hot as hell. People feel like lighting up."

"Maybe you could be a bit more evasive," I reply.

"What's all this shit about cigarettes? Like suddenly you're the smoking police."

"You remember what Rose went through." I remind him of my secretary Rose's miserable death from lung cancer.

"Rose didn't smoke, not even once her whole life. She didn't have any bad habits and still got cancer, and maybe that's why. I've decided if you try too hard, everything gets worse, so what's the point in depriving yourself so you can die prematurely in good health? I wish she was still around. It's not the same. Damn, I hate missing people. I still walk in your office and think she's going to be there with that old IBM typewriter and an attitude. Some people should never be gone, and those that should hang around forever."

"You recently were diagnosed with basal cell carcinoma and had several lesions removed. The last thing you need is to start smoking again."

"Smoking doesn't cause skin cancer," he says.

"It triples your chances."

"Okay. So now and then I bum a cigarette when someone else is lighting up. It's no big deal."

"*Don't Smoke Cigarettes Anymore. Just Bum Them.* Maybe that's another book you can write. People probably would buy that, too."

"The shit Lucy worries about will never be proved."

He goes back to that because he doesn't want to be lectured. "Nobody's been accused or is going to be. Jaime's gone for good from the DA's office, and that's what people like Farbman wanted, plain and simple. He must feel like he won the lottery."

"Jaime certainly doesn't feel that way, despite her protests to the contrary."

"She seems pretty happy with what she's doing now."

"I don't believe it."

"She just doesn't like how it happened, because she was forced. How would you feel if someone ran you off from your career after all you did to get there?"

"I'd like to believe I wouldn't entice someone I supposedly love to do something destructive because I wanted out of the relationship," I answer.

"Yeah, but breaking up with Lucy doesn't have anything to do with Jaime getting run out of the DA's office."

"It has everything to do with it. Jaime uncreated herself," I reply. "She didn't like what she saw, and she smashed it, destroyed it, so she could start all over. But that doesn't work. It never does. You can't rebuild yourself on the foundation of a lie. You helped her with the security and camera system. Is she carrying a gun now, too?"

"I've given her a couple of shooting lessons at an indoor range here."

"Whose idea?"

"Hers."

"Most New Yorkers don't carry guns. It's not part of

their culture. It's not a natural default. Why does she suddenly think she needs a gun?"

"Maybe from being down here, where she doesn't exactly belong, and let's face it, anything related to Dawn Kincaid is scary. I think what she's doing now has spooked her, and she got used to guns from Lucy, who's always armed. She probably takes her Glock into the friggin' shower. Maybe Jaime got used to guns because of living with them."

"Just like she got used to having an LLC called Anna Copper that started out as a somewhat spiteful joke because Lucy was hurt? Yes, Groucho Marx, who was heavily invested in Anaconda Copper, a mining company that tanked during the Great Depression and is blamed for polluting the environment. You don't see what's going on here, do you?"

"I don't know. Maybe I do."

"You invest in something that seems hugely valuable but is toxic, and you lose everything. It almost does you in."

"You ever listen to those old radio programs of his? *You Bet Your Life*. You know, what color is the White House or who's buried in Grant's tomb, that sort of thing. He was pretty funny. You shouldn't worry about Jaime's shit."

"I should worry about her shit, and so should you. It's one thing to offer objective assistance in a case, and it's another to be drawn into an agenda, especially a vindictive one, a highly personal one, a dysfunctional one. Jaime has all the incentive imaginable to make some big point, to re-create herself with a vengeance. There are other factors as well. I think you know what I'm referring to."

Marino makes loud crumpling noises as he digs into the Bojangles' bag, pulling out more napkins, as we cross a bridge that spans the Little Ogeechee River.

"I just hope you're careful," I continue, lecturing him again. "I'm not going to interfere if you choose to consult with other people, if you change your professional status with the CFC, but you need to be very cautious when it comes to Jaime. Do you understand why it might be difficult for you to be completely clearheaded about her?"

He wipes his mouth and fingers as we pass over Forest River now, where shrimp boats are moored and seagulls are congregated on a long wooden pier.

"It's dangerous when people are propelled by powerful motivations they aren't aware of. That's all I need to say." I don't expect him to understand or to be persuaded.

Jaime feeds his ego in a way I don't, because I refuse to manipulate him. I don't charm and flatter him into doing what I want. I'm blunt and honest, and for the most part it annoys him.

"Listen," he says. "I'm not stupid. I know she's got other things going on and Lucy complicated everything. She's so damn wide open, and I remember her coming into the DA's office, acting like what was going on between them not only wasn't a secret, it was something to brag about."

Just ahead is the Savannah Mall, where I ate a seafood lunch with Colin Dengate last time I was here, and I try to remember when that was. Maybe three years ago, when I was still in Charleston and he was battling a spate of hate crimes in coastal Georgia.

"It shouldn't have needed to be a secret," I reply. "In fact, it should have been something to brag about if two people love each other."

"Well, let's be honest," Marino says. "Not everybody feels the way you do. The two of them getting together isn't the typical fairy-tale couple. It's not like they're Prince William and Kate. It's not like everybody celebrated Jaime and Lucy. Just my opinion, but I think Jaime wanted out of it because it was causing her big problems. All that shit on the Internet, like suddenly she'd been voted off some reality show. Dyke DA, Lesbo Law. It was ugly, and she bailed, and now she's sorry, even if she won't admit it."

"I'm interested in why you think she's sorry."

We're on a narrow two-lane road called Middle Ground Drive, winding through a state-owned tract of land thick with underbrush and pines, not a sign of human habitation. The Georgia Bureau of Investigation keeps the location for their medical examiner's office and forensic labs as isolated as possible for a reason.

"Shit. You think she's happy with the life she's picked?" Marino says. "I'm talking personally."

"I'd rather hear what you think."

"After they broke up, Jaime started dating men, including that guy from NBC, Baker Thomas."

"Did she tell you that?"

"I still got friends at NYPD. When I went to see Jaime a couple of months back, I hooked up with a few of them and heard stuff. Point is, you think she could be more obvious? Going out with a TV correspondent who's considered one of New York's most eligible bachelors. Even though I got my theory about him. It's not an accident he's never been married. Lucy used to see him in the Village in the kind of bars Bryce would like."

The Coastal Regional Crime Laboratory is tucked in trees and surrounded by a high privacy fence topped by anti-climb spikes. A metal gate bars the entrance, and to the left of it is a camera mounted on top of an intercom.

"What time is Jaime supposed to meet us?" I ask.

"She thought it would be good to give you a chance to look through the cases first."

"You've talked to her today?"

"Not yet. But that's the plan."

"I see. I go through them first, and she doesn't need to show up until it suits her, if she bothers at all."

"Depends on what you find. I'm supposed to call her. Damn, this place has almost as much security as we do."

"Hate crimes," I comment. "Years and years of them, going back to when the lab was first built. Colin's been quite vocal about it. One case in particular that was all over the news when we had the office in Charleston. You might remember it."

Marino slows down and eases the van up to the intercom.

"Lanier County, Georgia. African American named Roger Mosbly, a retired schoolteacher engaged to a white woman," I continue. "He was driving home late at night, and as he pulled into his driveway, two white men stepped out in front of his car."

Marino reaches his arm out the window. He presses the intercom button, and it buzzes loudly.

"They beat him to death with bottles and a baseball bat, and there was pressure behind the scenes for Colin to help the defense make their case that it was a fair fight," I say. "Road rage. Mosbly started it, even though the defendants had no injuries and he had an abundance of abrasions and bruises to show they tried to drag him out of his car while he still had his seat belt on."

"White supremacist Nazi asswipes," Marino says.

"Threats were made because Colin told the truth, and shortly before the trial, the lab's front windows were shot out one night. After that, the fence went up."

"Doesn't sound like the kind of guy who would want someone executed for a crime they didn't commit." Marino presses the intercom button again.

"If he were that kind of person, his place wouldn't need all this security." I don't add that Jaime Berger has misjudged Colin Dengate, that she has misrepresented him. I don't remind Marino yet again that this lawyer he thinks it would be wonderful to work with has self-serving agendas and really isn't honest or kind.

A woman's voice sounds through the speaker: "May I help you?"

"Dr. Scarpetta and Investigator Marino here to see Dr. Dengate," he announces, as I check my iPhone for messages.

Benton and Lucy just landed in Millville, New Jersey, for fuel, Lucy wrote eleven minutes ago. They're making terrible time, with strong winds gusting out of the southwest, right on their nose, and there's a message from Benton that is disturbing:

D.K. no longer at Butler. Will let you know more when I do. Advise caution.

A loud humming as the metal gate slowly slides open on a track across asphalt, and I see the stucco-and-brick lab building, one story but sprawling. Parked in the front lot are white SUVs with the GBI gold-and-blue crest on their doors, and the white Land Rover with an Army-green canvas roof that Colin Dengate has driven for as long as I've known him.

"You going to tell Dr. Dengate about the new DNA results?" Marino asks, and I'm thinking about what Benton just wrote. That's all I can think about.

Flags hang limply from poles, not a breath of air stirring, and the walkway is lined with red-flowering bottlebrush shrubs that hummingbirds love, sprinklers watering them, nozzles spraying at the edge of the grass. We park in a visitor's space in front of ground-level reflective windows that are bullet- and shatter-resistant and designed to withstand the force of a terrorist blast, and the only thing on my mind is that Dawn Kincaid has escaped from Butler State Hospital for the Criminally Insane.

If it's true, someone else will die. Maybe more than one person. I'm sure of it. She is shockingly clever. She is sadistic, and has managed to get what she wants all of her blighted predatory life, and no one has stopped her. No one ever has, including me. I slowed her down, but I certainly didn't stop her, and the only reason I'm still here is luck. A mist from the sprinklers touches my face, and I remember the mist of her blood. I remember the taste of salt and iron inside my mouth, on my teeth, on my tongue. A bloody fog on my face, in my eyes, in my hair. Tara Grimm suggested that Kathleen Lawler might be getting out of prison early. It enters my mind that Dawn Kincaid is planning to come down here.

"Hey? You look like you seen a ghost."

I realize Marino is talking to me.

"I'm sorry," I reply, as I slide open the van's back door.

"You going to tell him about the DNA?" he asks again.

"No, absolutely not. It's not for me to tell. I'd rather review the cases as if I know nothing. I intend to keep an open mind." I retrieve dripping bottles of water from the cooler. "I don't know when you put ice in this thing," I add. "But if you want to brew tea, we probably could."

"At least it's wet." He takes a bottle from me.

"I'll be right in. I need to make a phone call." I step into the hot shade of a tree and call Benton, hoping he and Lucy haven't taken off yet.

"I'm glad you're still there," I say with feeling when he answers. "Sorry about the wind. I'm sorry I asked you to come to Savannah and it's proving to be such an ordeal."

"The wind is the least of my worries. It's just slow. You all right?"

"Not dressed for this weather."

"Getting a shot of coffee while Lucy pays for fuel. Christ, it's hot as hell in New Jersey, too."

"What's happened?"

"I don't have anything official and probably shouldn't get you worried when it might not be a problem. But I know what she's like and capable of, and so do you. She managed to convince guards and other personnel at Butler that she needed to go to the hospital, to the ER."

"For what?"

"She has asthma."

"If she didn't before, I'm sure she does now," I say, with a flare of anger.

"Jack had it, and in all fairness, asthma can be inherited."

"Malingering and more manipulations." I don't feel like being fair.

"She was transported by ambulance around seven this morning. A contact of mine at Butler who's not involved in her case and has no direct information heard about it and left me a message about half an hour ago. I'm really glad you're a thousand miles away, but be careful. This makes me nervous. I don't trust it."

"Understandable, considering who we're talking about." Sweat is running down my chest and my back, the air stagnant and thick like steam. "She's still in custody, right?"

"I assume so, but I don't have details."

"You assume it?"

"Kay, all I know is they've transported her to MGH, and this happened very recently. It's not like we can go barging in questioning her when she's in the middle of an alleged medical problem. She has her rights."

"Of course she does. More than the rest of us."

"Knowing her capabilities and skill at manipulating, of course I'm concerned this is a ploy, a scheme," Benton says.

"They can't possibly have a clue what they've got on their hands." I mean that Massachusetts General Hospital can't.

"If nothing else, this may be another ruse on the part of her lawyers to garner sympathy or imply she's being mistreated or to add to this bullshit about the damage you've caused to her mental health, her physical health. Asthma's made worse by stress."

"The damage I've caused?" I think about what Jaime said last night.

"The obvious case she's making."

"I didn't know you thought she had a case."

"I'm saying she's making one. I didn't say she has one or that I think she does. You sound really upset."

"If you knew she was trumping up a case against me," I reply, "it would have been helpful if you'd told me."

I feel shaky inside as I remember Marino's accusation

that my own husband knows I'm under investigation. How could he live in the same house with me and know such a thing, and why did he let me walk out alone that night, as if Benton doesn't care. As if I mean nothing to him. As if he doesn't love me. *Marino and his jealousy*, I remind myself.

"We'll talk more about this when I get there," Benton says. "But if you didn't know her defense is going to blame everything on you, then you're the only person who didn't know. Lucy's walking out to the helicopter, so I need to go. I'll call when we land next."

He tells me he loves me, and I get off the phone. Heat is a shimmering wall rising from blacktop as sprinklers spray, water sweeping in waves and splashing on foliage. I walk to the entrance of the lab building, then into a lobby of comfortable blue cloth chairs and couches, and an area rug with a Persian Serapi design in beige and rose, and potted palms, and prints of aspen trees and gardens arranged on off-white walls. An elderly woman sits alone in a corner, staring blankly out a window, in this tasteful place where no one wants to be, and I try Jaime Berger.

The hell with pay phones and pretending we haven't talked. I don't give a damn who's listening, and I don't believe her anyway. Her cell phone rings and goes to voicemail.

"Jaime, it's Kay," I leave a message. "There's been a development up north that I can't help but suspect you know about." I hear the accusation in my tone, as if whatever has happened somehow is her fault, and maybe it is.

Dawn Kincaid is up to something because she knows about the DNA, I'm sure she does, and Jaime is being naïve or is into denial to think otherwise. A number of people who can cause trouble might know, for that matter. I don't believe it's the secret Jaime assumes it is. She has started something terribly dangerous.

"Call me when you get this," I tell her in a tone that conveys I mean it. "If I don't answer, try Colin's office and ask someone to find me."

16

Colin Dengate has graying red hair he wears in a buzz cut, and a closely clipped mustache smudges his upper lip like rust. He is built like a bullet, with no fat to spare, and, like a lot of MEs I know, has a sense of humor that can border on silliness.

As he leads me deeper into his headquarters I walk past a skeleton dressed for Mardi Gras and beneath hanging mobiles of bones, bats, spiders, and ghouls that shiver and spin slowly in cool air blowing out of vents. A ringtone of spooky music and a witch's cackle announces Colin's wife, who can't find the key to their daughter's bicycle lock, and he suggests using bolt cutters. The eerie pulsing of a *Star Trek* Tricorder as we head down a hall is a GBI investigator named Sammy Chang letting Colin know he's clearing the scene of a motor-vehicle fatality on Harry Truman Parkway and the body is en route.

"And when it's me?" I wonder what ringtone Colin would assign.

"You never call," he says. "But let me think. Maybe Grateful Dead. 'Never Trust a Woman' is a good one. Heard them on tour a couple times in my glory days. They don't make music like they used to. I'm not sure they make people like they used to."

I left Marino in the break room, where he was getting coffee and flirting with a toxicologist named Suze who has a tattoo on her biceps depicting a grinning winged skull. Colin wants a word with me alone. He's been friendly so far, despite the reason I'm here.

"Can I get you a coffee, a Vitaminwater?" We enter his corner office overlooking the loading dock behind his building, where a big truck has just pulled up. "Coconut water's good in this weather. Replaces potassium, and I keep a stash in my personal fridge. And certain bottled waters have electrolytes, and that's helpful in this heat. What would you like? Anything?"

His Georgia drawl isn't as drawn out as most. For this part of the world, he talks fast and with a great deal of energy. I drink from the bottle of warm water I retrieved from Marino's ice chest. Maybe it's my imagination, but I smell dead fish again.

"It's been a while since I've dealt with Florida or Charleston summer weather," I tell him. "And Marino's van doesn't have air-conditioning."

"I don't know why you're dressed that way, unless you're asking for hyperthermia." He surveys my black ensemble. "I usually stick with scrubs." Which is what he has on now, cotton ones the color of crème de menthe. "They're nice and cool. I don't wear anything black this time of year unless it's a bad mood."

"A long story I doubt you have time for. Actually, a cold water would be good."

"A surprising thing about air-conditioning in cars?" He opens a small refrigerator behind his ergonomic chair, retrieves two waters, and hands me one. "Not everybody in this part of the world has it. My Land Rover, for example. A 1983 I've completely restored since I saw you last." He settles behind his piled-up desk in an office overwhelmed by memorabilia. "New aluminum flooring, new seats, new Gear Gators and windscreen. Stripped the roof frame and powder-coated it black. You name it, but didn't bother with air-conditioning. Driving it makes me feel the way I did when I was a young buck fresh out of med school. Windows wide open, and you sweat."

"Ensuring not everybody wants to ride with you."

"An additional benefit."

I move my chair closer, the two of us separated by a big maple desk crowded with Ball jars of cartridge cases, large-caliber tarnished brass shells sitting upright like rockets, a Secret Service ashtray filled with minié balls and Confederate uniform buttons, tiny toy dinosaurs and spaceships, animal bones that I suspect were mistaken for human, a model of the CSS *H. L. Hunley* submarine, which vanished from Charleston's outer harbor during the Civil War and was discovered and raised about a decade ago. I couldn't begin to catalog or explain all the eccentric mementos crowding every surface and crammed on bookcases and tightly arranged on his walls except that I have no doubt all of it has stories and meaning, and I suspect some items might be toys from when his children were small.

"That right there is a commendation from the CIA." He catches me looking around and indicates a handsome shadow box displaying a gold Agency Seal Medal mounted on the wall to the left of me. The elaborate accompanying certificate cites a significant contribution to the CIA's intelligence efforts but includes no name of the recipient or even a date.

"About five years back," he explains, "I worked a case involving an airplane crash in a swamp around here. Some intelligence folks, although I had no idea until suddenly the CIA and some of your Armed Forces MEs showed up. Had to do with the nuclear sub base at Kings Bay, and that's all I'm at liberty to say, and if you know about it, I'm sure you're not at liberty to say anything, either. Anyway, it was a big ordeal, spy stuff, and at some point afterward I got summoned to Langley for an awards ceremony. Now, let me tell you, that was squirrelly. Didn't know who the hell anybody was, and they never said who the medal was for or what the hell I did to earn it except to stay out of the way and keep my mouth shut."

His greenish-hazel eyes read me carefully as I take another swallow of cold water.

"I'm not sure why you've involved yourself in the Jordan murders, Kay." He finally gets around to why I'm sitting across from him. "I got a call just the other day from your friend Berger to inform me you were coming in to review the cases. Now, my first thought"—he opens a desk drawer—"is why you wouldn't call me yourself." He offers me a small box of slippery-elm throat lozenges. "You ever had these?"

I take one because my mouth and throat are parched.

"Best thing since sliced bread if you've got to give a talk or testify. Popular with professional singers, which is how I know about them." He takes the box back from me and pops a lozenge into his mouth.

"I didn't call you, Colin, because I wasn't aware I was scheduled to see you until last night." I talk around the lozenge, which has a slightly rough texture and pleasant maple flavor.

He frowns as if what I just said is impossible, and his chair creaks as he leans back in it, not taking his eyes off me, the throat lozenge a small lump in the side of his cheek.

"I came to Savannah because I had an appointment at the Georgia Prison for Women to talk to an inmate named Kathleen Lawler," I start to explain, as I wonder where to begin.

Already, he's nodding. "Berger told me," he says. "She said you were coming down here to meet with an inmate at the GPFW, which is all the more reason I didn't understand why you didn't call me yourself to at least say hi and maybe let's have lunch."

"Jaime told you I was coming," I repeat, as I wonder what she has said to him and others, and how much of it was tailored to suit her purposes. "I'm sorry I didn't call and suggest lunch. But I really thought I would be in and out."

"She's called here enough," he says, about Jaime. "Everybody in the front office knows who the hell she is." The lozenge slips from one cheek to the other as if there is a small animal moving around inside his mouth. "Good stuff, huh? Also a demulcent. Tried ones before, more than I can shake a stick at, that purport to be a demulcent but aren't. These work, really soothe the mucous membrane. Sodium- and gluten-free. No preservatives and importantly, no menthol. That's the misnomer out there. That menthol is the cure-all for the throat, when in fact what it does is cause temporary loss of the vocal cords." He savors the lozenge, looking up at the ceiling as if he's a sommelier tasting a complex grand cru. "I've started singing in a barbershop quartet," he adds, as if that explains everything.

"In summary, I was to be here in Savannah very briefly for another reason and was informed last night that an appointment was made for me to come to your office. I gather you aren't being cooperative in a way that suits her," I say to him. "I told her you're slightly stubborn and not a redneck."

"Well, I am a redneck," he says. "But I think I'm understanding why you didn't call me yourself, and that makes me feel better, because I did feel a little dissed. Maybe that's stupid, but I did, it was so out of the blue hearing from her and not you. Regardless of anything personal, I think I get what's going on more than you might imagine. Jaime Berger is somewhat histrionic, and it fits her script if I'm the redneck bigoted medical examiner in Savannah who stonewalls her because I'm intent on Lola Daggette getting the needle. You know, kill 'em all and let God sort 'em out. That's the way everybody thinks south of the Mason-Dixon Line. And west of it."

"Jaime says you didn't come out to greet her when she was here. That you ignored her."

"I sure as hell didn't greet her, because I was talking on the phone to a poor woman who didn't want to be told that her husband's death was a suicide." His eyes narrow, and he gets louder and more indignant. "That his gun didn't accidentally go off while he was outside drinking beer and mending his crab pots. And just because he hugged her and seemed to be in an unusually good mood and said he loved her before he went outside that night didn't mean he didn't have suicidal thoughts, and I deeply regretted that what I filled in on the autopsy report and his death certificate means she won't get his life insurance. I'm right in the middle of having to tell someone shit like that when Berger shows up here dressed like Wall Street. Then she's hovering in my damn doorway while the woman is crying uncontrollably on the other end and I sure as hell wasn't going to hang up on her and offer some pushy New York attorney coffee."

"I can see you have no feelings about her," I say wryly.

"I've got the Jordan cases for you, including photographs of the crime scene, which I think you'll find helpful. I'll let you look and get your own impressions, and then I'm happy to discuss anything you want."

"There's a perception you are convinced that Lola Daggette committed the murders and did so alone. As I recall from your presentation of this case during the NAME meeting in Los Angeles, you seem pretty firm in your opinion."

"I'm on the side of truth, Kay. Just like you."

"I must admit I find it unusual that DNA supposedly from blood and skin under Brenda Jordan's fingernails wasn't a match for Lola Daggette. And it didn't match a family member. An unknown DNA profile, in other words."

"*Supposedly* being the operative word."

"I might conclude from the DNA that it's possible more than one assailant or intruder was involved," I add.

"I don't interpret the lab reports or decide what they mean."

"I'm just curious if you have an opinion about it, Colin."

"Brenda Jordan's hands were incredibly bloody," he says. "Yes, an unknown DNA profile was related to my swabbing under her nails when I did the autopsies, but I don't know what that means. It could have been from an unrelated source. Her own blood was under her nails. Her brother's DNA was under her nails."

"Her brother's?"

"He was in the bed next to hers, and I'm guessing his blood was transferred to Brenda's body, to her hands, when the killer attacked her, probably after murdering Josh first. Or maybe the killer stabbed Brenda first. Maybe the killer thought she was dead and started on the brother, and Brenda wasn't dead and tried to run. I don't know exactly what happened and probably never will. Like I said, I don't interpret lab reports or decide what they mean."

"I feel compelled to emphasize that an unknown donor of DNA at that scene should have caused the police to consider more than one assailant might have been involved."

"In the first place, the scene wasn't contained all that well, and a lot of people ended up in the house who shouldn't have been there."

"And these people who shouldn't have been there touched the bodies?"

"Well, not that, thank God. The cops know better than to let anyone near my bodies or they'll have hell to pay from me. But more to the point, at the time it just wasn't accepted as a possibility that someone other than Lola Daggette was involved."

"Why?"

"She was in a halfway house to deal with anger management and her problems with drugs. Within hours after the murders, she was discovered washing clothing that was stained with the Jordans' blood. And she was local. I remember there was some talk at the time that she might have read or heard about Dr. Jordan in the news and realized he had a lot of money, was a successful doctor from an old Savannah family that had made a fortune from cotton. His mansion was an easy walk from the halfway house, where she'd been for more than a month when the murders occurred. She'd had plenty of time to gather intelligence, including figuring out that the family didn't always bother with the alarm system."

"Because they'd had a number of false alarms."

"Kids," he says. "A big problem with alarm systems is kids accidentally setting them off."

"What seems to be nothing more than conjecture," I point out. "It's also conjectured that burglary wasn't the motive."

"No evidence of it, but who knows? An entire family dead. If something was missing, who's going to say?"

"Was the house ransacked?"

"It wasn't. But again, if everyone is dead, who's to say if something was looked through or moved?"

"So the DNA results didn't concern you at the time. I don't mean to keep pushing you on this. But the results bother me."

"Push all you want. Just doing my job. I've got no dog in the fight," he says. "The DNA was commingled. As you well know, it's not always simple to decide what sample the result is from. Was the unknown DNA from blood or skin cells or from something else, and when was it left? It could have been from a source that has nothing to do with the case. A recent guest in the house. Someone Brenda had been in contact with earlier in the day. You know what they say. Don't put your case in a lab-coat pocket. DNA doesn't mean crap if you don't know how it got there and when. In fact, it's my theory

that the more sensitive the testing gets, the less it's going to mean. Just because someone breathed in a room
doesn't mean that person killed anyone. Well, don't get
me started. You didn't come all this way to hear my phi-
losophizing and sounding like a Luddite."

"But no DNA profile at the crime scene or associated
with the bodies was Lola Daggette's."

"That's right. And it's not up to me to decide who's
guilty and who's not, or even to care. I just report my
findings, and the rest is up to the judge and jury," he
says. "Why don't you take a look at what I've left for
you, and then we'll chat."

"I understand Jaime discussed Barrie Lou Rivers with
you, too. I'm wondering if I might take a look at her case
while I'm at it."

"Jaime Berger's got copies. She put in her requests
for records, I don't know, at least two months ago."

"If it's not too much trouble, I always prefer originals
when I can get them."

"That record's not paper because it's more recent. You
know, GBI's gone all paperless. I can have it printed, or
you can look on a computer."

"Electronic is fine. Whatever's easiest."

"A strange one, I'll give you that," he says. "But don't
ask me to be going down the road of cruel and unusual.
I know what Berger's spin on that one is, too, and how
it's all a nice neat puzzle she's piecing together. Not *nice*,
what am I saying? Meant to shock and repulse. It's like
she's already rehearsing for the press conference, think-

ing of the inflammatory points she might make about how the condemned are tortured to death in Georgia."

"It's uncommon for someone awaiting execution to die suddenly in the holding cell outside the death chamber," I remind him. "Especially since the person is supposed to be under surveillance every second."

"And let's be honest, Kay, she probably wasn't watched every second," he says. "I'm guessing she started feeling bad after eating. Maybe it was assumed to be indigestion at first, when in fact she was suffering the classic symptoms of a heart attack. And by the time the guards were sufficiently alarmed to call for medical assistance, it was too late."

"This occurred very close to the time when she was supposed to be brought into the death chamber and prepped," I reply. "Seems there would have been medical personnel on hand, including the physician who was to assist in the execution. One might expect that a doctor or at least someone from the death squad trained in CPR would have been nearby and able to respond quickly."

"That might very well have been the irony of the century. A member of the death squad or the executioner himself resuscitates her long enough to kill her." Colin gets up from his desk and hands me the box of lozenges. "In case you want more. I buy them by the truckload."

"I assume it's all right if Marino looks."

"He works with you and you trust him, I got no problem. You'll have one of my path techs with you at all times."

Colin has to have someone in the room with me, not only for his protection but also for mine. He must be able to swear under oath that I couldn't have planted a document in a file or taken something away with me.

"I'm also interested in clothing that you and the GBI might still have," I add, as he walks me back down the hall, past offices of other forensic pathologists, the forensic anthropology and histology labs, past the break room, restrooms, and then the conference room is to our right.

"I assume you're referring to the clothing Lola Daggette was washing in her bathroom at her halfway house? Or what the victims had on when they were murdered?"

"All of it," I answer.

"Including what was submitted as evidence in the trial."

"Everything."

"I suppose I could take you to the house if you wanted."

"I've seen it from the outside."

"Possibly it could be arranged for you to go through it. I don't know who lives there, and I doubt they'd be thrilled."

"Not necessary at the moment, but I'll let you know after I go through the cases."

"I can set up a scope if you want to look at the original slides. Actually, Mandy can take care of that, Mandy O'Toole, who will be in there with you. Or we can do recuts, create a second set of slides, because, of course, I still have the tissue sections. If we do recuts, however, we're creating new evidence. But whatever answers any questions you have."

"Let me see what they are first."

"The clothing is stored in various places. But most is in our labs. I don't let anything get very far from my sight."

"I'm sure you don't."

"Don't know if the two of you have met," he says, as I notice a woman in blue scrubs and a lab coat just inside the conference-room doorway.

Mandy O'Toole steps out and shakes my hand. Around forty, I estimate, she's tall and all legs like a colt and has long black hair tied back. She is attractive in an unusual way, her features asymmetrical, her eyes cobalt blue, giving her an appearance that is off-putting but compelling. Colin salutes me with his index finger and leaves me alone with her inside a modest-size room with a cherry-finish table surrounded by eight black leather chairs with tufted cushions. Abnormally thick windows set in sturdy aluminum frames overlook a parking lot enclosed by a tall chain-link fence, and beyond, a dark green pine forest stretches endlessly into the pale sky.

17

Jaime Berger's not with you?" Mandy O'Toole moves to the far end of the table and takes a chair where there are a Vitaminwater and a BlackBerry with earphones.

"I believe she may be coming in later," I reply.

"Now, that's somebody with no off switch, and I guess that's good if you do what she does. You know, everybody's fair game." Colin's pathology technician begins talking about Jaime, as if I asked. "I ran into her in the ladies' room when she came here a couple weeks ago and I'm washing my hands and she starts in about Barrie Lou Rivers's adrenaline level. Did I notice anything histologically that might hint at a surge of adrenaline indicating stress and panic, like if she was being abused the night of her execution. And I said histology wouldn't show something like that, because you can't see adrenaline microscopically. That would require a special biochemical study."

"Which was probably ordered, knowing Colin," I comment.

"That's him, all right. No stone unturned. Blood, vitreous, cerebrospinal fluid, and I think that was the lab result Ms. Berger might have come across. Barrie Lou Rivers did have a moderately elevated level of adrenaline. But people are way too quick to read something into findings like that, don't you agree?"

"People often are quick to read all sorts of things into findings that don't necessarily mean what they assume they do," I reply.

"Well, if someone's suffering a catastrophic event like a heart attack or they're choking on food, they certainly might panic and dump a lot of adrenaline antemortem," she says, her blue stare unwavering. "I mean, if I was choking to death, I'm sure I'd have a lot of adrenaline pumping. Nothing to make a person more panic-stricken than not being able to breathe. Gee, it's an awful thought."

"Yes, it is."

I wonder again what Jaime Berger has been circulating about me. She told Colin I visited Kathleen Lawler at the GPFW yesterday. What else has Jaime been saying? Why is Mandy O'Toole looking so intently at me?

"I used to watch you when you had that show on

CNN," she then says, and I realize the possible explanation for her interest. "I'm sorry you quit, because I thought it was really good. At least you offered some common sense about forensics and not all this screaming and sensationalism like some of the other shows. It must be cool to have your own show. If you ever have another one and need someone to talk about histology . . ."

"That's very kind, but what I'm doing these days isn't necessarily compatible with having a TV show."

"Well, I'd jump at it if I was asked. But nobody wants to watch tissue processing. I guess the coolest part is removing the specimens from the body—you know, what you get to do. Although finding the perfect fixative and knowing which one to use with what is kind of exciting."

"How long have you worked with Colin?"

"Since 2003. The same year the GBI started becoming paperless. So you're lucky or not with the Jordan cases, depending on how you look at it. Everything now is electronic, but it wasn't back then in January 2002. I don't know about you, but I still like paper. There's always that one thing someone decided not to scan, except when it's Colin. He's crazy obsessive-compulsive. He doesn't care if it's a paper napkin that got mixed in with the paperwork, it goes into the file. He's always saying the devil's in the details."

"And he's right," I reply.

"I should have been an investigator. I keep asking him to send me to a death-investigation school like the one at the New York City OCME, where you used to be, but it's all about money. And there's not any." She reaches for the BlackBerry and earphones on the table. "I should let you get to work. Let me know if you need anything."

I remove the top case file from the stack of four on the end of the table closest to the door, and a quick look affirms what I might have hoped for but certainly didn't expect. Colin has offered me collegial respect and professional courtesy, and quite a lot more than that. By law he's required to disclose only those records he directly generated, such as the medical examiner's report of initial investigation, preliminary and final autopsy reports, autopsy photographs, and lab and special studies requests.

He could be stingy with his personal notes and call sheets if he's of a mind to be, and conveniently overlook almost any documents he chooses, forcing me to ask for them and possibly to butt heads with him. Worse, he could treat me like a member of the public or the media, compelling me to write an official letter of request that will have to be approved and responded to with an invoice for the services and costs involved. Payment would have to be received before the documents can be mailed, and by the time all is said and done, I would be back in Cambridge and it would be the middle of July or later.

"Suze did the tox on Barrie Lou Rivers." Marino's big voice precedes him as he enters the conference room and stares at Mandy O'Toole sitting at the far end of the table. "Didn't know anybody else was in here," he adds, and I can always tell when he likes what he's looking at.

She takes off her earphones and says to him, "Hi. I'm Mandy."

"Yeah? What do you do?"

"Path tech and more."

"I'm Marino." He takes a chair next to me. "You can call me Pete. I'm an investigator and more. I guess you're the watchdog."

"Don't mind me. I'm listening to music and catching up on e-mail." She puts her earphones back on. "You can say anything you want. I'm just the wallpaper."

"Yeah, I know all about wallpaper," Marino says. "Can't tell you how many cases get blown because of wallpaper leaking information."

I barely listen to them as I take a survey of what Colin Dengate has made available, and I'm appreciative and relieved. I almost want to find him to thank him, and in part it might be a reaction to my being deceived and mishandled by Jaime Berger, and how demeaning and upsetting that feels. Colin easily could have resorted to any number of maneuvers and ploys to make reviewing anything inconvenient if not impossible. But he didn't.

Regardless of any personal opinion he might have about Lola Daggette's guilt, he's not trying to force on others what he perceives as justice. Based on the girth of the files he's left for me to peruse, he's doing quite the opposite. He hasn't vetted much, if anything, including records one might argue he shouldn't disclose, and that thought leads to others. He wouldn't be this generous without getting the approval of Chatham County District Attorney Tucker Ridley, and I wouldn't have expected Ridley to budge an inch beyond his legal obligations as mandated by the state's open-records act. I could have been offered nothing more than the most basic medical examiner reports when what I'm most interested in is the rest of it.

Police, incident and arrest reports, even criminal or medical histories or witness statements—it could be absolutely anything that might find its way into a decedent's case record because the detective happened to hand over copies to the medical examiner, and if the ME is like me, every scrap of paper, every electronic file, is preserved. All such documents I assumed would be excluded. When Colin walked me to this conference room, I anticipated finding very little to review and within the hour wandering back down the hall to his office so he could fill in the blanks if he was so inclined.

"Anything that goes on around here, I know about it anyway." Mandy has taken off her earphones again.

"That right?" Marino blatantly flirts. "What do you know about Barrie Lou Rivers? Any rumors about her floating around? You involved in her case?"

"I did the histology, was in and out of the autopsy room collecting tissue sections while Colin was doing her post."

"You must have come in after hours," Marino says, as if he's investigating Mandy O'Toole for something. "And you weren't listed as an official witness. Some prison guard named Macon and a couple other people. I don't remember seeing your name."

"That's because I wasn't an official witness."

I rearrange my chair to face a view of tall, spindly pines and buzzards floating high above them like black kites, and I decide it could be argued that the Jordan case is no longer active and all direct litigation is final. This might explain why the district attorney made a calculated decision not to impede me in any way. When an investigation is terminated, its documents are subject to disclosure, and as I follow my reasoning a little further, it occurs to me that Tucker Ridley might very well be done with Lola Daggette. Despite Jaime's retesting of evidence, in Tucker Ridley's mind and maybe in Colin Dengate's, the investigation was terminated when Lola Daggette's appeals were exhausted and the governor refused to commute her sentence to life.

"He always this difficult?" Mandy says, and I realize she's talking to me about Marino.

"Only if he likes you," I reply, as I think about public perception.

For the sake of it alone, the district attorney isn't going to get in the way of someone of my rank and reputation, so he's opened up the country store and invited me to help myself. Why? Because it doesn't matter anymore. As far as Tucker Ridley is concerned, Lola Daggette has an appointment with death on Halloween. He has no reason to believe she won't show up. Or maybe the opposite is true, I consider.

Maybe the new DNA results have been leaked and it doesn't matter what I look at because Lola's sentence will be vacated soon, and maybe my other fear is legitimate, too. Dawn Kincaid knows she's about to face new murder charges in Georgia, where, unlike Massachusetts, she could get the death penalty. So she's orchestrating something, possibly an escape from a Boston hospital that can't possibly offer the level of security a forensic facility like Butler has.

"I'm just trying to figure out who was around when her body came in," Marino continues to badger Mandy O'Toole. "Because the case bugs me. You ask me, there's something not right about it. It's a little unusual for a histologist to be working at nine o'clock at night, and that's bugging me, too."

"The night Barrie Lou Rivers died, I was working late in my lab, on deadline for a journal article about types of fixatives," she says.

"I thought that's what old people use to keep their dentures glued in."

"The advantages of glutaraldehyde for electron microscopy, and the problems of mercurials."

"I don't like mercurial people, either. They're a pain in the ass."

"Disposing of the tissue is problematic, since mercury is a heavy metal." She's toying with him, too. "You know, maybe better to use Bouin's solution if what you're after is nuclear detail. Course, when I work with Bouin's I end up with yellow fingers for a while if I forget and touch something without gloves."

"Bet that's hard to explain on a date."

"When Colin got the call from the prison I was still

here, right down the hall," she gets back to that, "and I told him I'd hang out and get his table set up, help in any way needed. But I wasn't a witness."

"What about rumors," Marino again says. "What was the word about what happened to her?"

"Originally it was thought that Barrie Lou Rivers choked on her last meal. But no evidence of that. No rumors I've heard in recent memory. Nobody was talking about the case anymore until Jaime Berger started looking into it. I would offer water, coffee, but I can't leave the room. You want something, just tell me and I'll make a call." She directs this at me. "If you want something," she says, smiling at Marino as she puts her headphones back on, "get it yourself."

"Suze mentioned one thing kind of interesting about Barrie Lou Rivers's CO level," Marino tells me, as his attention continues drifting back to Mandy. "It was like eight percent. She says normal's maybe six at most."

"I don't know if it's interesting or not," I reply, as I go through the transcript of a clemency hearing for Lola Daggette in which Colin Dengate testified, and also GBI investigator Billy Long. "I'll have to look at her case. Not an unusual level for a smoker."

"You can't smoke in prisons anymore. None I know of. Not for years."

"Yes, and drugs, alcohol, cash, cell phones, and weapons aren't allowed in prisons, either," I reply, as I review the factual history of what happened in the early-morning hours of January 6, 2002. "Guards could have given her a cigarette. Rules get broken depending on who has power."

"But smoking could explain her CO, and if so, why would someone give her a cigarette?"

"We certainly can't know if anybody did. But it's true that carbon monoxide and nicotine from cigarettes put a strain on the heart, which is further exasperated by the narrowing of the arteries from heart disease, which is why I keep reminding you not to smoke." I slide pages in Marino's direction as I finish with them. "Her heart's already working hard if she's stressed, and then an exposure to smoke and her heart works even harder."

"So maybe that's why she had the heart attack," he persists.

"It could have been a contributing factor, assuming someone gave her a cigarette or cigarettes while she was awaiting execution," I comment, as I read about Liberty Halfway House, a nonsecure, not-for-profit treatment program for girls located on East Liberty Street, just blocks from Colonial Park Cemetery, very close to the Jordan house, maybe a fifteen-minute walk from it, I estimate.

At approximately six-forty-five the morning of January 6, a Liberty Halfway House volunteer on the health-care staff had begun making rounds of the residential facility to collect urine specimens for a random drug screening. When she arrived at Lola Daggette's room and knocked on the door, there was no answer. The volunteer entered and heard the sound of running water.

The bathroom door was shut, and after knocking and calling out Lola's name and getting no response, the volunteer became concerned and walked in.

She discovered Lola naked on the floor of the shower stall with hot water running. The volunteer testified that Lola was frightened and excited and was using shampoo to wash items of clothing that appeared to be very bloody. The volunteer asked Lola if she had hurt herself, and she said no and demanded to be left alone. She claimed she was doing laundry because she didn't have access to a washing machine and to "just leave the fucking cup by the sink and I'll pee in it in a minute."

At this point, according to the transcript, the volunteer turned off the hot water and ordered Lola to step out of the shower. On the tile floor were "a pair of tan corduroy pants, women's size four, a blue turtleneck sweater, women's size four, and a dark red Atlanta Braves Windbreaker, size medium, all of them extremely bloody, and the water on the shower floor was pinkish-red from all the blood," the volunteer testified, and when she asked Lola whose clothing it was, she replied that it was what she'd had on when she was "checked in" five weeks earlier and was issued uniforms. "They were what I was wearing on the street, and since then they've been in my closet," Lola explained to the volunteer.

Questioned about how blood could have gotten on the clothing, at first Lola said she didn't know. Then she offered, "It's that time of the month" and claimed she'd had an accident in her sleep, the volunteer testified. "I got the distinct impression she was making things up as

I was standing there, but Lola was known for that at the LHH. She was always talking big and saying whatever would impress someone or keep her out of trouble. She'll say and do pretty much anything for attention and to protect herself or get a favor and never seems to realize how it's perceived or any possible consequences.

"Unfortunately, she's like the boy who cried wolf around here, and it couldn't have been more obvious the blood could not have come from her having her period," the volunteer said under oath in the hearing. "It wouldn't make sense for menstrual blood to be on the thighs, knees, and cuffs of a pair of pants and on the front and sleeves of a sweater and a jacket. Quite a lot of it hadn't washed off yet, because there was so much of it, and my first thought was wherever it came from, the person must have hemorrhaged, assuming it was human blood, of course.

"I also don't know why Lola would sleep in street clothes, which the wards aren't supposed to wear while they are in residence." The volunteer continued a testimony that was damning. "They wear them when they get here and when they're released. The rest of the time they wear uniforms, and it didn't make sense why Lola would have been wearing the clothing in bed. Nothing she said made sense to me, and when I told her that, she kept changing her story.

"She said she'd found the bloody clothes in a plastic bag in her bathroom. I asked to see the plastic bag, and she changed her story again and said there was no bag. She said she'd gotten up to use the bathroom and the clothes were on the floor, in there, in the bathroom, just inside, to the left of the door. I asked if the blood was wet or dry, and she said it was sticky in spots and other stains were dry. She claimed she didn't know how the bloody clothes got there but was scared and tried to wash them because she didn't want to be blamed for something."

The volunteer reminded Lola that what she was suggesting would mean someone had gone into her closet and removed the clothing, gotten it bloody somehow, then reentered her room while she was asleep and left the clothing in the bathroom. Who would do such a thing, and why didn't Lola wake up? The person who did it "is quiet like a haint and is the devil," Lola reportedly said to the volunteer. "It's payback for something I done before I got stuck in here, maybe someone I used to get drugs from, I don't know," she said, and she got angry and began to yell.

"You can't tell no one! You can just fucking throw them out but can't tell no one! I don't want to go to jail! I swear I didn't do nothing, I swear to God I didn't!" the volunteer testified Lola said, and the more I read, the more I understand why no one at the time considered any suspect other than Lola Daggette.

18

Marino does little more than glance at what I slide over to him, handling the pages with a casualness and lack of curiosity that makes me suspect he's studied them before.

"You're familiar with this transcript?" I ask.

"Jaime's got it in the records she's been collecting. But she didn't get it from him." He means she didn't get it from Colin Dengate.

"I wouldn't have expected him to turn this over, because it wasn't generated by him. She would have to get it from Chatham County Superior Court."

"She figured he'd let you look at everything."

"Apparently she figured right. But what I'm seeing so far doesn't exactly help her case."

"Nope," he says. "Makes Lola Daggette look guilty as

hell. No big surprise she got convicted. You can see how it happened."

"I'm confused about the uniforms," I add. "Jaime mentioned that Lola was in and out of Liberty House on job interviews, visiting her grandmother in a nursing home, that Lola could come and go rather much as she pleased as long as she had permission and was present and accounted for when they did a bed check at night, I assume. What did she wear when she went out?"

"The way I understand it, the uniforms looked like regular street clothes, like jeans and a denim shirt. That's what the wards—and they called them wards—wore all the time."

"You're talking in past tense." I take a sip of the water Colin gave me in his office, my black field clothes damp from sweat, the air-conditioning chilly.

"Lola Daggette wasn't good for business, especially a place that depended on private donations," Marino says. "Rich people in Savannah weren't exactly eager to write checks to Liberty House anymore after Lola was convicted of murdering Clarence Jordan and his family. Especially since one of the things he was known for was helping out in shelters, clinics, helping people who had problems, people who had nothing and couldn't afford going to the doctor."

"Did he ever help out at Liberty House?" I get up to adjust the temperature in the room.

"Not that I know of."

"Liberty House is gone, I assume. Let me know if you

get too warm in here." I sit back down, noting that Mandy O'Toole is ignoring us, or appears to be.

"A homeless shelter for women run by the Salvation Army. Nobody from the old days there anymore, and it doesn't look the same, either," Marino says. "You read this stuff, and what goes through your mind is Lola Daggette wasn't smart enough to kill anyone and get away with it."

"She didn't get away with it. But we don't know that she killed anyone."

"The devil wore her clothing and then left it in her bathroom after the fact," he says. "And she won't tell anybody who the devil is except the name *Payback*?"

"Seems she started thinking about *Payback* when she was caught in the bathroom literally red-handed, washing the bloody clothing," I reply, arranging more paperwork in front of me. "Someone was paying her back, someone from her drug days on the street. Seems she might have been thinking that she was set up, and maybe *Payback* is how she began to refer to whoever is responsible."

"You really think she had nothing to do with it and doesn't know who did?"

"I don't know what I think. Not exactly, not yet."

"Well, I sure as hell know how it sounds," Marino says. "Sounds the same now as it did at the time. Makes no friggin' sense. Plus, you'll see when you get to the DNA part that it's everybody's. Lola's clothes have the blood of the entire Jordan family on them, so I'm telling

Jaime from day one, I don't know how you explain that away."

"It gets explained away by Jaime the same way it was by Lola's original defense team. Lola's DNA wasn't recovered from the Jordan house or from their bodies or whatever clothing they had on when they were killed," I reply, as I come to a section in the transcript that includes photographs. "Her DNA was recovered from the clothing she was washing in the shower, and nowhere else. Only from the corduroys, sweater, and Windbreaker, but so was the DNA of the victims. To a jury, that's quite incriminating, although scientifically it raises questions." I don't say what questions.

Not in front of Mandy O'Toole, who gives no sign she can hear us or is interested as she types on her BlackBerry with headphones on, purportedly listening to music.

"She's naked in the shower, washing the clothing," Marino says. "Seems like she'd leave her DNA on it just from that. She's touching everything. And her DNA probably was on the clothing to begin with, since they were the street clothes she had on when she first arrived at Liberty House."

"Correct. So no matter where the clothing came from, she'd certainly contaminated it with her own DNA by the time she was ordered out of the shower," I agree. "That her DNA was recovered from her own clothing isn't necessarily significant. Now, if another individual's DNA was recovered in addition to Lola's, that would have been a different story," I add, as I think of Dawn Kincaid, whom I'm not going to mention. "If another individual had worn her clothing, and that person's DNA was recovered from the pants, sweater, and Windbreaker left on the bathroom floor?" I'm careful what I say as I probe for information.

I won't take the chance that Mandy O'Toole might overhear any allusions to new DNA results. According to Jaime, Colin Dengate doesn't know. Scarcely anybody does, and I don't understand how she can feel so sure of that, unless it's what she wants to believe and her wish is her reality. In my opinion she should have filed a motion to vacate Lola's sentence weeks ago. Then the truth would be known and there would be nothing to leak. It would have been safer for the case but not safer for Jaime. She couldn't have hoodwinked me into coming to Savannah if I'd known about her new career and her big case down here.

She wasn't off the mark last night when she doubted I would have volunteered to be her forensic expert if I'd had time to think about it, if she'd been up front with me instead of lying and manipulating and setting me up to be sitting where I am right this minute. The more I've mulled over everything that's happened, the more certain I am that I would have said no. I would have referred her to someone else, but not because I would have worried about Colin's response to my reviewing his findings and possibly second-guessing him. I would have been worried about how Lucy would react. I would have felt that anything I did with Jaime would be tainted by an unpleasant past and would be a bad idea for almost every reason imaginable.

"Well, if someone borrowed Lola's clothes so this person could commit multiple murders, why wasn't that person's DNA recovered from the pants, sweater, the Windbreaker?" This is Marino's way of confirming that neither Dawn Kincaid's nor any other individual's DNA was recovered from Lola's clothing.

"Washing with hot soapy water could have eradicated another donor's DNA if we're talking sweat and skin cells. Maybe not blood, but it depends on how much, and if it was a small amount, perhaps from being scratched by a child, the blood might have been washed off in the shower," I contemplate out loud. "Especially in early 2002, when the testing wasn't nearly as sensitive as it is today. Did anybody look at Lola Daggette's shoes?"

"What shoes are you talking about?"

"She must have had shoes. Were they issued by Liberty House?"

"I don't think the wards were issued shoes. Only jeans and denim shirts. But I really don't know," Marino answers me, as he continues looking at Mandy O'Toole, who isn't looking at him. "Nobody's ever said anything about shoes that I'm aware of."

"Someone should have looked for blood on her shoes. I see nothing here to indicate Lola was cleaning a pair of shoes in the shower. Or undergarments, for that matter. If clothing is saturated, the blood soaks through onto panties, undershirts, bras, socks. But she was washing only the pants, sweater, and jacket."

"You and shoes," Marino says.

"Because they're really important."

Shoes are happy to tell me where a person's feet were at the time of a terminal event. At a homicide scene. On the brake pedal or accelerator. On a dusty windowsill or balcony before the person jumped or was pushed or fell. On the body of a victim who was stomped and kicked, or in one case I had, in wet cement when a murderer fled the scene through a construction site. Shoes, boots, sandals, all types of footwear have tread patterns and unique flaws that leave their mark, and they deposit evidence and carry it away.

"Whoever killed the Jordans would have had blood on his or her shoes," I say. "Even if it was trace amounts, something would have been there."

"Like I said, I haven't heard anything about shoes."

"Unless Colin has them in the lab, stored with the other evidence, it's too late now," I reply, as I look through photographs included in Lola Daggette's bid for clemency last fall.

The first few pages are portraits and candid shots intended to humanize the victims and inflame the governor of Georgia, Zebulon Manfred, who ultimately denied clemency to Lola Daggette. He is quoted in a photocopied newspaper article included in the transcript as stating that efforts to spare her life are based on evidence already heard and rejected by a jury of her peers and the appeals courts. "We can ruminate about this heartless act of human depravity until the cows come home," he said in a public statement, "and it all comes back to the same horror acted out by Lola Daggette, who was in a mood to massacre an entire family on the early

Sunday morning of January sixth, 2002. And she did. With no motive whatsoever except that she felt like it."

I can only imagine the governor's outrage when he looked at a studio portrait of the Jordan family during the last Christmas season of their lives, just weeks before their brutal deaths. Clarence Jordan, with his shy smile and kind gray eyes, was dressed festively in a dark green suit and tartan plaid vest, his wife, Gloria, sitting next to him, a plain-looking young woman with dark brown hair parted down the middle, demure in green velvet and ruffles. Their five-year-old twins are seated on either side of their parents, towheads with rosy cheeks and big blue eyes, Josh dressed exactly like his father, Brenda like her mother. There are more photos, and I flip through them, getting the point all too well as they draw whoever is looking at them deeper into the nightmare that begins on page seventeen of the transcript.

A child's bloody bare arm dangles off a blood-soaked bed. The wallpaper is Winnie-the-Pooh and the sheets have a western pattern of lassos, cowboy hats, and cacti, all of it spattered with elongated drops of cast-off blood, and drips and large dark stains, and what appear to me to be wipe marks. Dawn Kincaid enters my mind without my inviting her, and I see her inside that dark bedroom, pausing during her frenzied attack, using the sheets and bedspread to clean off her hands and the weapon. I feel her lust and rage and hear her breathing hard and fast as her heart hammers and she stabs and slashes, and I wonder why she would slaughter two children, two five-year-olds.

Twins, a boy and a girl who looked almost exactly alike at that young age, pretty blue-eyed blonds. Had she met them before? Had she watched them in the past, perhaps while gathering intelligence about their house and the family's habits? How did she know about Josh and Brenda and whose room they were in, or did she? What is the psychology of her going after them in what I interpret as an enraged attack? Who was she really killing when she went after them while they were asleep in their own beds?

It wasn't necessary. It wasn't needed or expeditious or motivated by a certain goal, such as stealing. Maybe the parents, but not young children who couldn't defend themselves and possibly couldn't identify anyone. There could have been no sensible reason, only a highly personalized driving force, and I feel Dawn Kincaid's hatefulness, her victims' blood the language of a fury that she reveled in. I believe she didn't go after them randomly or impulsively any more than her coming after me was a whim. It was thought out. She intended to leave the entire Jordan family dead. Including the children. *Why?*

Taking from them what she never had, it enters my mind. Robbing them of their safe home and parents who held them and took care of them and didn't give them away, and I try not to fill the scene in my mind with images of her, of the woman who would come after me nine years later. Blood on the bedroom floor becomes blood inside my garage, and I feel the warm mist on my face. I smell its iron smell. I taste its iron-salty taste, and I will Dawn Kincaid to leave me. I force her out of my thoughts and banish her from my psyche as I follow the bloody trail into the hallway.

Partial footwear prints, drips, smears, and streaks along the fir wood floor. Small handprints and swipes made by bloody clothing and bloody hair low on the white plaster wall at the level of the banister, and then a pinpoint constellation, as if the person was struck, and larger drops in an arterial pattern that spattered and ran down the white wall, a fatal injury that could not be survived longer than several minutes. The carotid was severed or partially severed, probably from behind, the killer in pursuit, and then the arterial spatters are gone, as if evaporated. More drips and a confusion of patterns on the stairs leading to a large puddle beginning to co-agulate under a small body curled in a fetal position in the entryway, near the front door. Tousled blond hair and pink SpongeBob pajamas.

The kitchen has a black-and-white tile floor that looks like a checkerboard with bloody partial footwear prints, and in the white sink is a residue of blood and two bloody dish towels wadded up. On the counter is a fine china plate, and on it a half-eaten sandwich, bloody smudges and smears everywhere, and nearby a block of yellow cheese and a packet of boiled ham that is opened. A close-up of a knife handle reveals what looks like more smudges of blood, and I'm aware of Marino getting out of his chair. I'm aware of a rapid high-pitched pulsing.

White bread, jars of mustard and mayonnaise left out, and two empty bottles of Sam Adams, and next the guest bath, blood drips and footwear prints all over gray marble. Formal peach linen hand towels, bloody and bunched up by the sink, a bottle of lavender-scented hand soap turned on its side, bloody fingerprints visible on it. A bar of soap sits in a puddle of bloody water in a dish shaped like a shell, and then the toilet that wasn't flushed, and I shuffle through documents, looking for reports from the fingerprints examination. *Lab reports, where are they? Did Colin include them?*

I find them. Fingerprint analysis reports issued by the GBI. The bloody prints on the bottle of hand soap and a kitchen knife were from the same individual but were never identified. There was no hit in the Integrated Automated Fingerprint Identification System, but there should have been when Dawn Kincaid's fingerprints were taken after her arrest nine years later, this past February. The unidentified prints from the bottle of hand soap and the knife handle in the Jordan case should still be in the IAFIS database, so why wasn't there a hit when Dawn's prints were entered? Two different DNA labs have linked her to the murders, but the prints aren't hers?

"Something's not right about all this," I mutter, as I flip through more pages, looking at more photographs.

A narrow staircase at the back of the house and terra-cotta tile flooring in a glassed-in sunporch, and blood droplets and a scale for measurement. A labeled white plastic six-inch ruler was placed next to each dark stain, seven close-up photographs of droplets spaced out along the brick-colored tile flooring, the drops round with minimally scalloped edges, each more than a millimeter in diameter. Low- to medium-velocity impact spatter with an angle of approximately ninety degrees, each drop surrounded by much tinier ones. The blood broke apart upon impact because the surface of the floor is smooth, flat, and hard.

I follow the blood outside into the yard, into a garden planted in the footprint of what appears to be an outbuilding from an earlier century, crumbled stone walls exposed and incorporated into the landscaping, and a caved-in area of earth filled in with plantings, what is left of a root cellar, it occurs to me. Statuary is graying, some of it tinted green with mildew, an Apollo planter, an angel holding a bouquet, a boy with a lantern, and a girl with a bird. Dried bloody droplets darkly speckle blades of grass and the leaves of japonicas, tea olives, and English boxwoods, then more dark droplets, these closer together and angled on rockery, what might be a rock garden for flowers in the spring. I'm careful with my conclusions. I'm careful not to read too much into what I'm seeing.

More than a few bloodstains are required to establish a pattern, but this isn't cast-off blood. It isn't back or forward spatter. It wasn't tracked into the sunporch or out into the yard and garden by bloody footwear. I don't believe it dripped from bloody clothing or from a bloody weapon or that an assailant with scratches from a child's fingernails bled this much. The seven droplets on the terra-cotta tile floor are round and some eighteen inches apart, and one of them is smeared as if it might have been stepped on.

I envision someone dripping blood as he or she walks through the sunporch, heading for the back door that leads out to the yard, and into the garden, or maybe the person headed the other way. Maybe someone bleeding was walking into the house, not out of it, and there is no reference to this important evidence in anything I've seen so far. Jaime didn't mention it last night. Marino hasn't mentioned it, and suddenly I'm aware of people talking. I look up and focus on where I am. Marino is standing in the open doorway with Mandy O'Toole. Behind them, Colin Dengate has a peculiar look on his face as he holds his phone to his ear.

". . . Are they hearing you? Because I don't want you to keep calling me about it so I have to repeat myself. Tell them for me I don't give a shit what they want to do. They're not to touch a damn thing . . . Well, hello? Exactly. You don't know that one of them, one of the guards didn't . . . We always have to include that into the equation, not to mention they don't know crap about how to work a scene," Colin is saying, and he must be talking to GBI investigator Sammy Chang, whose ringtone is a *Star Trek* Tricorder, the strange electronic pulsing I heard minutes ago.

"Okay, good . . . Sure, yes. Within the hour . . . Yes, she told me that." Colin's eyes fix on me as if I'm the person who might have told him whatever he refers to. "I understand. I'm going to ask her . . . And no. For the record, for the third time, the warden's not to set foot in there," he says, as I get out of my chair.

Colin ends the call and says to me, "Kathleen Lawler. I think you should come. Since you were there, it might be helpful."

"Since I was where?" But I know.

He turns to Mandy O'Toole. "Get my gear and see if Dr. Gillan can take care of the motor-vehicle fatality coming in. Maybe you can give him a hand. The victim's poor mother has been waiting in the lobby all damn morning, so maybe you can check on her while you're at it. I was going to but can't now. See if she needs water, a soda or something. Damn state trooper told her to come straight here to ID him. Well, based on what I've been told, he sure as hell isn't viewable."

19

Colin Dengate shifts his old Land Rover into fourth gear, and the big engine roars as if it's ravenous. We speed along a narrow strip of pavement hidden by impenetrable woods, the road bending sharply through shaded pines and straightening out into an open flat terrain of apartment buildings and blazing sun, the Coastal Regional Crime Laboratory as hidden from civilization as the Bat Cave.

Hot wind buffets the olive-green canvas roof, making a loud drumming sound as Colin passes along information that is suspiciously detailed when one considers that Kathleen Lawler was alone the final hours of her life. While other inmates might have heard her, they couldn't see her when she died inside her cell, most likely from a heart attack, Officer M. P. Macon suggested to Investigator Sammy Chang before Chang could get there. By the time Chang was called, the prison had Kathleen's death figured out, one of those sad random events probably related to Lowcountry summer weather. Heat stroke. A heart attack. High cholesterol. Kathleen never had taken care of herself worth shit, Chang was told.

According to Officer Macon, Kathleen reported nothing unusual earlier in the day, wasn't ill or out of sorts when her breakfast tray of powdered eggs, grits, white toast, an orange, and a half pint of milk was passed through the drawer of her cell door at five-forty a.m. In fact, she seemed cheerful and chatty, reported the corrections officer who delivered her meal and later was questioned by Officer Macon.

"He told Sammy that she was asking what it would take to get a Texas omelet with hash browns. She was joking around," Colin says. "Apparently of late she'd become more obsessed than usual with food, and it's Sammy's impression from what's been said to him that she might have been assuming she wasn't going to be at the GPFW much longer. Maybe she was fantasizing about her favorite things to eat because she was anticipating having whatever she wanted, and I've seen this syndrome before. People block out what they've been deprived of until they believe it's within their reach. Then that's all they think about. Food. Sex. Alcohol. Drugs."

"Probably all of the above, in her case," Marino's loud voice sounds from the backseat.

"I think Kathleen was under the impression a deal was in the works if she was cooperative," I say to Colin, as I write a text message to Benton. "Her sentence was going to be reduced and she was on her way back to the free world."

I explain to Benton that he and Lucy might not be able to reach us when they land in Savannah, that I'm on my way to a death scene, and I tell him whose. I ask him to let me know as soon as possible if there is anything new with Dawn Kincaid and her alleged asthma attack.

"Has anyone bothered to mention to Jaime Berger that she has shit for clout with prosecutors and judges around here?" Colin looks in the rearview mirror, directing this to Marino.

"I can't hear too good in this wind tunnel," he answers loudly.

"Well, I don't think you want the windows up," Colin yells.

"Whether Jaime has clout or not around here, I wouldn't underestimate the power of organized protest, especially these days, because of the Internet," I remind Colin of the damage Jaime Berger can do. "She's perfectly capable of mounting a campaign of social and political pressure, similar to what happened in Mississippi recently when civil- and human-rights groups pressured the governor into suspending the sentences of those two sisters who'd gotten life sentences for robbery."

"Damn ridiculous," Colin says in disgust. "Who the hell gets life for robbery?"

"I can't hear a damn thing back here." Marino is perched on the edge of the bench seat, leaning forward and sweating.

"You need to buckle up," I say over the hot wind rushing in through open windows, the engine loud and growling, as if the Land Rover wants to claw across a desert or up a rocky slope and is bored and restive with the tameness of a paved highway.

We are making good time, on 204 East now, passing the Savannah Mall, heading toward Forest River and the Little Ogeechee, and marshland and endless miles of scrub trees. The sun is directly overhead, the glare as intense as a flashgun, blindingly bright as it beats down on the square nose of the white Land Rover and the windshields of other traffic.

"My point," I say to Colin, "is Jaime's perfectly capable of going to the media and making Georgia look like a stronghold of bigoted barbarians. In fact, she'd enjoy it. And I doubt Tucker Ridley or Governor Manfred wants that."

"Doesn't matter now," Colin says. "It's moot."

He's right, it is, at least in Kathleen Lawler's case. She won't be getting a suspended sentence or even a reduced one, and she'll never taste free-world food again.

"At eight this morning she was escorted to a recreation cage for her hour of exercise," Colin says, and he explains that he was told the one hour allowed for exercise is set early in the morning during the summer.

Supposedly Kathleen walked inside the cage more slowly than usual, resting frequently as she complained about how hot it was. She was tired, and the humidity made it difficult to breathe, and when she was returned to her cell at a few minutes past nine she complained to other inmates that the heat had worn her out and she should have stayed inside. For the next two hours, Kathleen continued to complain on and off that she wasn't feeling well. She was exhausted. She found it difficult to move, and she was having a hard time catching her breath.

She worried that breakfast hadn't agreed with her and she shouldn't have been walking around in the heat and humidity that was bad enough to kill a horse, as she reportedly put it. At around noon she said she was having chest pains and hoped she wasn't having a heart attack, and then Kathleen wasn't talking anymore and inmates in other cells nearby began shouting for help. Kathleen's cell door was unlocked at approximately twelve-fifteen. She was discovered slumped over on her bed and could not be resuscitated.

"I agree it's strange she said what she did to you," Colin remarks, weaving around traffic as if responding to a scene where it's not too late to save someone. "But there's no way an inmate on death row could have gotten to her."

He's referring to Kathleen Lawler's claim that she was moved to Bravo Pod because of Lola Daggette and that Kathleen was afraid of her.

"I'm simply repeating what she told me," I reply. "I didn't necessarily take her seriously at the time. I didn't see how it was possible for Lola Daggette to, quote, 'get' her, but Kathleen seemed to believe Lola intended to harm her."

"Bizarre timing, and I've certainly seen my share of

it," Colin says. "Cases where the decedent had some sort of premonition or prediction that didn't make sense to anybody. Then next thing you know, boop. The person's dead."

Certainly I've had family members tell me that their loved one had a dream or a feeling that presaged his or her death. Something told the person not to get on the plane or into the car or not to take a certain exit or go hunting that day or out for a hike or a run. It's nothing new to hear such stories or even to be told that a victim issued warnings and instructions about an imminent violent end and who would be to blame. But I can't get Kathleen Lawler's comments out of my head or push aside my suspicion that I'm not the only one who heard them.

If our conversation was covertly recorded, then there are others who are privy to Kathleen's complaints about how outrageous and unfair it was to move her to a cell where danger was directly overhead, as she described it not even twenty-four hours ago.

"She also commented on the isolation of Bravo Pod and that the guards could do something bad to her and there would be no one to witness it," I tell Colin. "She worried that by being moved into segregation she'd been made vulnerable. She seemed sincere, not necessarily rational but as if she believed it. In other words, I didn't get the sense she was saying it for effect."

"That's the problem with inmates, especially those who've spent most of their lives locked up. They're believable. They're so manipulative it's not manipulation anymore, at least not to them," Colin says. "And they're always saying someone's going to get them, mistreat them, hurt them, kill them. And of course, they're not guilty and don't deserve to be in prison."

When we turn off Dean Forest Road, passing the same strip mall where I used a pay phone the day before, I ask about the blood droplets in the photographs I was in the midst of reviewing when Sammy Chang called. Is either Colin or Marino aware there was blood in the Jordans' sunporch, in their backyard and their garden? Someone was bleeding, and it's possible this person was leaving the house, perhaps exiting the property through the garden and a stand of trees that led to East Liberty Street. Or perhaps the person was injured in the backyard and dripped blood while returning to the house. Blood that wasn't cleaned up, I add, which makes me wonder if it was left at the time of the murders.

"A steady drip," I explain. "Someone bleeding from an upright position while moving, possibly walking in or out of the house. For example, if someone cut his or her hand and was holding it up. Or a cut to the head or a nosebleed."

"It's curious you'd mention a cut hand," Colin replies.

"I don't think I know about this." Marino is loud in my ear again.

"I would imagine the bloodstains I'm talking about were swabbed for DNA," I add.

"I don't know about blood on a porch or in the yard," Marino says. "I don't think Jaime's got those photos."

"Off the record?" Colin says, as we retrace my steps

from the day before, the GPFW minutes away. "Because you need to get this from the actual DNA reports. But it's never been believed those bloodstains have anything to do with the murders. You're doing what I did back then—getting caught up in something that ended up meaning nothing."

"The photos were taken when the crime scene was processed," I assume.

"By Investigator Long, and are part of the case file but weren't submitted as evidence during the trial," Colin says. "They were determined to be unrelated. I don't know if you saw the photos of Gloria Jordan."

"Not yet."

"When you do, you'll note she has a cut on her left thumb, between the first and second knuckle. A fresh cut but more like a defensive injury, which baffled me at first because there weren't any other defense injuries. She was stabbed in the neck, chest, and back twenty-seven times, and her throat was cut. She was killed in bed, and there's no indication she struggled or even knew what was happening. As it turns out, the DNA of the blood drips on the porch was Gloria Jordan's. When I found that out, it occurred to me that she might have cut her thumb earlier and it had nothing to do with her murder. This sort of thing happens more often than not these days. Old blood, sweat, saliva that has nothing to do with the crime you're investigating. On clothing, inside vehicles, in a bathroom, on the stairs, on the driveway, on a computer keyboard."

"Was her cut thumb bloody when you examined the

body?" Marino asks, as we drive past the salvage yard with its mangled heaps of wrecked cars and trucks.

"Jesus. There was blood everywhere," Colin answered. "Her hands were like this." He takes his hands off the wheel and tucks them under his neck. "Maybe a reflex to move them to her throat after it was cut or to tuck up in a fetal position as she died. Or they might have been positioned like that by the killer, who I believe spent some time staging the bodies, making a mockery of them. Point is, her hands were covered with blood."

"Anything in the bathroom to make you think she might have cut herself earlier?" Marino asks.

"No. But one of their neighbors said in a statement that Mrs. Jordan was out in the garden the afternoon before the murders, presumably doing winter pruning," Colin continues, as I envision the dormant garden behind the Jordans' house, the branch stubs, water sprouts, and sucker growth I noted in photographs I just saw.

Gloria Jordan wasn't much of a gardener, or she hadn't gotten very far with her pruning when she cut her thumb and had to stop.

"The guy next door who had a poodle?" Marino asks. "Lenny Casper, the neighbor who called the police the morning of the murders after noticing the busted glass in the kitchen door?"

"Yes, I believe that's the name. As I recall, he could see the Jordans' backyard from several of his windows, and he noticed Mrs. Jordan working in her garden earlier that day, during the afternoon. The theory that makes the most sense is she cut herself while pruning. The blood drips were left by her when she came back in from the garden after she cut her thumb. My guess is she was holding her hand up and it dripped in the pattern you observed in the scene photographs. She walked back into the house and dripped blood on the floor of the sun-porch, and a few drops were found in the hallway in the area of the guest bath."

"That's possible," I suppose dubiously.

"It was a vital wound," he adds. "You'll see that in photos and the histology. She had a blood pressure, she had tissue response, when it was inflicted."

"Maybe so," I reply, but I have my doubts. "Why no Band-Aid? No dressing of any kind?"

"I don't know. I thought it was a little odd. But people do odd things. In fact, they do them more often than not."

"Maybe she wanted the air to get at it," Marino shouts. "Some people do that."

"She was married to a doctor, who likely knew that infection is the most common complication of an open wound," I reply. "In fact, if she'd not had a tetanus shot in recent memory and cut herself on a garden tool, that should have been in the equation, too."

"There's just no other logical explanation for the blood on the sunporch and in the garden," Colin says. "It's definitely hers. So obviously something happened that caused her to bleed, and it's not related to her being stabbed to death, most likely in her sleep. She and her husband both had anxiolytics, sedatives, on board. Clo-nazepam. In other words, Klonopin, which is used to re-

lieve anxiety or panic or as a muscle relaxant. Some
people use it as a sleep aid," he explains, for Marino's
benefit. "The hope is the Jordans never knew what hit
them."

"Was it your theory at the time that her husband
was killed first?" I ask.

"It's not possible to know the order they were killed,
but logic would suggest the killer would get him first,
then her, then the children."

"Her husband's stabbed to death right next to her and
it didn't wake her up? Must have been a lot of clonazepam," I comment.

"I'm guessing it happened incredibly fast. A blitz attack," he says.

"What about her shoes? If she was bleeding while
walking back inside the house earlier in the day, it's likely
she dripped blood on whatever shoes she was wearing in
the garden. Anybody think to check for bloody shoes?"

"I think you got a shoe fetish," Marino says, to the
back of my head.

"Since she had only a nightgown on and was barefoot
when she was murdered," Colin replies, "shoes weren't
something anybody was interested in."

"And at some point earlier she left blood on the sunporch floor and in the hallway?" I ask, as we pass the
greenhouse with its diapered shrubs and potted trees in
front. "It was there for the rest of the day and night, and
no one cleaned it up?"

"They probably didn't use the sunporch much in
the winter, and the tile was dark red. The flooring in the

hallway was dark hardwood. She might not have noticed or probably just forgot," he says. "I do know for a fact the DNA is hers. It was her blood," he emphasizes. "I think you'll agree she wasn't dripping blood downstairs and outside in the early-morning hours when the murders took place. There is every reason to believe she never got out of bed."

"I agree it doesn't seem possible she was bleeding on the sunporch and in her backyard, and then climbed back in bed to be stabbed multiple times while an intruder was inside her house murdering her entire family," I reply, as I'm reminded of the obvious pitfalls of ending an investigation before it's begun because everyone involved believes the killer has been caught.

When Lola Daggette was discovered washing bloody clothing in her shower at the halfway house, assumptions were easy, and what difference did it make if they were wrong? Blood on the sunporch floor or a cut on Gloria Jordan's thumb or the burglar alarm not being set or unidentified fingerprints didn't matter anymore. Lola's farfetched lies and fantastic alibis, and the case was over, the killer tried and convicted and on death row. There are no more questions when people already have the answers.

20

We gather crime scene cases and personal-protection equipment from the back of the Land Rover and follow the concrete walkway through blooming shrubs and flower beds, their colorful blossoms washed out by the glare. Inside the checkpoint of the white-columned brick building, Officer Macon and the warden are waiting for us.

"An unhappy time, I'm afraid," Tara Grimm greets us, and today her demeanor matches her name.

She is unsmiling, her dark eyes unfriendly when they fix on me, her mouth firmly set. In frumpy contrast to her elegant black dress from the day before, she wears a pastel blue skirt suit, a loud flower-printed blouse with a looping bow tie, and toeless flats.

"I guess you're with Dr. Dengate," she says to me, and

I sense disappointment. I detect hostility. "I thought you'd gone back to Boston."

She assumed I was far north of here or at least on my way, and I can see in her eyes and the expression on her face that her mind is making rapid recalculations, as if my presence somehow changes what might happen next.

"This is my chief of investigative operations," I introduce her to Marino.

"And you happened to be in Savannah for what reason?" She doesn't even try to be gracious.

"Fishing."

"Fishing for what?" she asks.

"Mostly I get croakers," Marino says.

If she gets his unseemly pun, she doesn't let on. "Well, we're very grateful for your time and attention," she says to Colin, as Officer Macon and two other uniformed guards inspect our crime scene cases and equipment.

When they turn their attention to the personal-protective clothing, Colin orders them to halt.

"Now, you can't be touching that," he says. "Unless you want your DNA on everything, and I'm guessing you don't, since we don't know for a fact what killed this lady."

"Just let them on through." The warden's lilting voice has the iron ring of a military commander. "You come with me," she orders Officer Macon, "and we'll escort them over to Bravo Pod."

"Sammy Chang with the GBI should be there," Colin says.

"Yes, I believe that's his name, the agent with the GBI who's been going through the cell. Now, how do you want to do this?" she addresses Colin in a different voice altogether, as if I'm not here, as if our mission is a casual one.

"Do what, exactly?" The first steel door slides open and slams shut behind us with a jarring clang. Then the next door opens and shuts. Officer Macon is ten feet ahead of us, communicating over his radio with central control.

"We can arrange transport to your facility," she suggests.

"I think to keep things clean and simple, we'll take care of that," Colin answers. "One of our vans is on the way."

The hallway the warden leads us along creates the illusion of a labyrinth, each corner, locked door, and connecting corridor reflected in the large convex mirrors mounted high on the walls, everything gray concrete and green steel. We emerge back into the sultry afternoon, with its oppressive heat, and women in gray silently drift about the prison yard like shades, moving in groups between buildings, pulling weeds by hand along walkways, congregated beneath a cluster of mimosa trees, three greyhounds squatting or lying in the grass, panting.

Inmates watch our passage with no expression on their faces, and I feel sure the news has reached every pod that Kathleen Lawler is dead. A well-known member of their community who allegedly was forced into protective custody because it was feared one or many of them might hurt her lasted in maximum security barely two weeks.

"They're not kept out long," Tara finally speaks to me, as Officer Macon opens the gate leading into Bravo Pod, and I realize she means the dogs. "In this weather, they stay in most of the day except for when they have to potty."

I imagine what an ordeal it must be in a prison when one of the rescued greyhounds signals it's time.

"Of course, they're fairly well acclimated to heat, with their long snouts and lean builds. They have no under-coats, and you can imagine the heat at the racetrack. So they do fine here, but we're careful," she continues, as if I might have accused her of animal abuse.

Keys jangle from a long chain attached to Officer Macon's belt as he unlocks the door to Bravo Pod and we step inside that dreary world of solid gray. I can almost feel a heightened alert as we pass by the second level's mirrored glass tower, where guards invisibly watch and control the interior doors. Instead of turning left toward the visitation rooms where I was yesterday, we are led to the right, past the stainless-steel kitchen, which is de-serted, then the laundry room with its rows of industrial maximum-load machines.

Through another heavy door we enter an open empty area with stools and tables bolted to the concrete floor, and one level up is a catwalk and behind it the maximum-security cells with green metal doors, each with a face peering out of the small pane of glass. Female inmates stare down at us with unwavering intensity, and the kicking begins as if on cue. They pound their feet against their metal doors, and the thudding rings in a shocking din, as if the very gates of hell are slamming.

"Holy shit," Marino says.

Tara Grimm stands perfectly still, looking up, and her eyes move along the catwalk and fix on a cell directly above the door we just came in. The face looking out is pale and indistinguishable from my vantage point one floor down, but I can make out the long brown hair, the wide stare, the unsmiling mouth, as a hand enters the glass and she gives the warden the finger.

"Lola," Tara says, holding Lola Daggette's stare as the terrible racket continues to pound and bang. "The ever gentle, harmless, and innocent Lola," she says, with an edge. "So now you've met. The wrongfully convicted Lola, who some think belongs back in society."

We move on, passing a door with covered glass, then a cart of library books parked near an unfinished puzzle of Las Vegas, pieces sorted in small piles on a metal table-top. Officer Macon unlocks another door with his jingling keys, and the instant we're through it, the kicking stops, returning an absolute silence. Ahead are six doors on each side, sequestered from the rest of the pod, some with empty white plastic trash bags hanging from shiny steel locks, and the faces in the windows range from young to old, and the tense energy in them reminds me of an animal about to lunge, about to bound away like something wild that is terrified. They want out. They want to know what happened. I feel fear and anger. I can almost smell it.

Officer Macon leads us to a cell at the far end, the only one with an empty window and the door ajar, and Marino begins to hand out the protective clothing as we set crime scene cases and camera equipment on the floor. Inside Kathleen Lawler's cell—a space smaller than a horse stall—GBI crime scene investigator Sammy Chang is perusing a notepad he's apparently removed from books and other notepads arranged on two gray-painted metal shelves. His gloved fingers flip pages and he's covered from head to toe in white Tyvek, what Marino calls *overkill clothes,* having come from an era when the most investigators bothered with was surgical gloves and a swipe of Vicks up their nose.

Chang's dark eyes wander from Marino to me, and he looks at Colin as he says, "Got pictures of pretty much everything in here. Not sure what more we can realistically do because of access."

What he implies is the guards and other prison personnel have access to Kathleen's cell, and countless other inmates have been detained in it over time as well. Dusting for prints and other routine forensic procedures typically done in a suspicious-death case probably aren't going to be helpful because the scene is contaminated. Deaths in custody are similar to domestic homicides, both complicated by prints and DNA meaning very little if the killer had regular access to the home or location where the death occurred.

Chang is careful what he communicates. He doesn't want to suggest openly that if someone who works at the prison is responsible for Kathleen Lawler's death, we're probably not going to figure that out by processing her cell the way we would a typical crime scene. He's not going to say in front of Officer Macon and Tara Grimm that his main purpose since he got here has been to secure Kathleen's cell and make certain nobody—including the two of them—tampers with potential evidence. Of course, by the time he arrived, it really would have been too late to protect the integrity of anything. We don't know for a fact how long Kathleen was dead in her cell before the GBI and Colin's office were notified.

"Haven't touched the body," Chang tells Colin. "She was like this when I got here at thirteen hundred hours. According to the information I have, she'd been dead about an hour when I got here. But the times I've been given for events are a little murky."

Kathleen Lawler is on top of the rumpled gray blanket and dingy sheet of a narrow steel bed attached to the wall like a shelf beneath a slit of a window covered with metal mesh. Half on her back and half on her side, her eyes are barely open, her mouth agape, and her legs are draped over the edge of the thin mattress. The pants of her white uniform are shoved up above her knees, and her white shirt is bunched up around her breasts, perhaps disarrayed by resuscitative efforts that failed. Or she might have been thrashing about before she died, rearranging her position in a frantic attempt to get comfortable, to relieve whatever symptoms she was suffering from.

"Was CPR attempted?" I ask Tara Grimm.

"Of course, every effort was made. But she was already gone. Whatever happened, it was very fast."

As Marino, Colin, and I put on white coveralls, I notice an inmate staring through the glass window of the cell across from Kathleen's. She has a matronly face, a sunken mouth, and a helmet of tightly curled gray hair, and as I look at her she looks back at me and begins to talk in a muffled loud voice through her locked steel door.

"Fast? The hell it was fast!" she starts in. "I was hollering for thirty damn minutes before anyone showed up! *Thirty damn minutes!* She's over there strangling, I mean, I could hear it, and I'm hollering and nobody comes. She's gasping, 'I can't breathe, I can't breathe, I'm going blind, somebody help me, please!' *Thirty damn minutes!* Then she got quiet. She's not answering me anymore, and I start hollering at the top of my lungs for somebody to come. . . ."

In three swift steps Tara Grimm is before the inmate's door, rapping the glass with her knuckles. "Quiet down, Ellenora." The way the warden says it makes me think that Ellenora is volunteering this information for the first time. Tara Grimm seems genuinely taken aback and angry. "Let these people do what they need to do, and we'll let you out and you can tell them exactly what you observed," she says to the inmate.

"Thirty minutes at least! Why did it take so long?

I guess if a body knows they're dying in here, that's just too damn bad. If it's a fire or a flood or I'm choking on a chicken bone, too damn bad," Ellenora says to me.

"You need to quiet down, Ellenora. We'll get to you soon enough, and you can tell them what you observed."

"Tell them what I observed? I didn't observe a thing. I couldn't see her. I already told you and all of them I didn't see nothing."

"That's right," Tara Grimm says coolly, condescendingly. "Your original statement was you didn't observe anything. Are you changing your mind?"

"Because I couldn't! I couldn't observe nothing! It's not like she was standing up and looking out the window. I couldn't see her, and that made it awful, just hearing her pleading and suffering and groaning. Making these bloodcurdling sounds like an animal suffering. A body could die in here, and who's going to come! It's not like we got a panic button we can push! They let her die in her cell," she says to me. "They let her just die in there!" Her wide eyes stare at me.

"We'll have to move you to a secure unit if you don't stop," Tara warns her, and I can tell she doesn't know quite what to do.

She wasn't expecting this display, and it occurs to me that the inmate named Ellenora is cagey like a lot of inmates. She behaved herself when she was questioned by prison officials the first time, because she wanted a chance to do exactly what she's doing now, to make a scene when we arrived. Had she erupted earlier, I suspect she would already have been moved to a secure unit, no doubt a euphemism for solitary confinement or a cell where psychiatric patients are restrained.

Colin's booties make a sliding sound as he walks into Kathleen Lawler's cell, and Marino opens crime scene cases on the polished concrete floor. He checks out the cameras as I lean against the wall, steadying myself to work shoe covers over my big black boots with their big tread. As I pull on examination gloves, I feel the inmate's stare. I feel what's in it, the high voltage of fear, of near hysteria, and Tara Grimm knocks on the window again as if to shut her up in advance. Ellenora's frightened face in the tiny pane of glass flinches as the warden's knuckles suddenly are there, rapping.

"What makes you think she couldn't breathe?" Tara Grimm asks loudly, for our benefit.

"I'm sure she couldn't, because she said so," Ellenora replies from behind her barrier. "And she was aching and feeling puny. So tired she could hardly move, and she was gasping. She hollered, *'I can't breathe. I don't know what's happening to me.'*"

"Usually when someone can't breathe they can't talk. I'm wondering if you misunderstood. If you can't breathe, you can't holler, especially through steel doors. You have to have a lungful of air to holler," Tara says to her so I will hear it.

"She said she couldn't talk! She was having trouble talking! Like her throat was swelled up!" Ellenora exclaims.

"Well, now, if you tell someone you can't talk, that's a contradiction, isn't it?"

"It's what she said! I swear to God Almighty!"

"Saying I can't talk would be like running for help because I can't stand up."

"I swear to God Almighty and Jesus Christ it's what she said!"

"It doesn't make sense," Tara Grimm tells her ward on the other side of the thick steel door. "And you need to calm down, Ellenora, and lower your voice. When I ask you questions, you need to answer what I ask and not yell and make a fuss."

"What I'm saying is the truth, and I can't help if it's upsetting!" Ellenora gets more excited. "She was begging for help! It was the most awful thing I ever did hear! *'I can't see. I can't talk. I'm dying! Oh, fuck, oh, God! I can't stand this!'*"

"That's enough, Ellenora."

"What she said exactly. Gasping and begging, *'Please help me!'* It was terror, pure terror, her begging, *'Oh, fuck, I don't know what's happening! Oh, please, someone help me!'*"

Tara knocks the glass again. "Enough of that language, Ellenora."

"It's what she said, not me. It's not me saying it. She said, *'Fucking help me, please! I must've got hold of something!'*"

"I'm wondering if she might have had allergies, food allergies, insects," the warden says to me. "Possibly to wasps, bees, allergies she never told anyone about. Might she have gotten stung by something when she was outside exercising? It's just a thought. There's certainly a lot of yellow jackets when it's hot and muggy like this and everything's in bloom."

"Anaphylactic reactions to insect stings or after an exposure to shellfish, peanuts, whatever the person is allergic to, usually are very swift," I reply. "It doesn't sound as if this death was swift. It took longer than minutes."

"She was feeling bad for at least an hour and a half!" Ellenora yells. "Why did they take so damn long?"

"Did you hear her get sick?" I look at Ellenora through the thick pane of glass. "Did it sound like she might have vomited or had diarrhea?"

"I don't know if she got sick or not, but she said she had a sour stomach. I didn't hear her get sick. I didn't hear her toilet flush or nothing. She was yelling about being poisoned!"

"So now she's been poisoned," Tara says, cutting her eyes at me as if to remind me to consider the source.

Ellenora's face is agitated, her eyes wild. "She said, *'I've been poisoned! Lola did it! Lola did it! It's that shit I ate!'*"

"That's quite enough. Now, stop it," Tara says, as I walk inside Kathleen Lawler's cell. "You watch that mouth of yours," I hear Tara say behind my back. "We have people here."

21

In the polished-steel mirror that Kathleen Lawler complained about when I was with her yesterday afternoon, Investigator Sammy Chang's reflection walks behind me and stops in the doorway of the cell.

"I'll be right here, giving you some room," he lets me know.

The toilet and sink are combined into a stainless-steel unit with no movable parts except buttons for flushing and turning tap water on and off. I don't see or smell anything that might indicate Kathleen Lawler was sick before she died, but I note a very faint electrical odor.

"Do you smell something odd?" I ask Chang.

"I don't think so."

"Something electrical but not exactly. An unpleasant peculiar odor."

"No. I don't think I smelled anything at all while I was looking around. Wouldn't be the TV." He indicates the small television encased in transparent plastic on a shelf.

"I don't believe that could be it," I reply, noticing water stains in the steel sink and a vague chalky residue.

I lean closer, and the odor is stronger.

"Acrid, like something shorting out, like a blow-dryer that overheats." I do my best to describe it. "A battery smell. Sort of."

"A battery?" He frowns. "No batteries I saw. No blow-dryer."

He walks over to the sink and bends close. "Well, maybe," he says. "Yeah, maybe something. I don't have the best nose."

"I think it would be a good idea to swab whatever this is in the sink," I tell him. "Your trace-evidence lab has SEM/EDX? We should take a look at the morphology at high magnification, see if it's some sort of particulate that was in a solution and figure out what it is. Metals, some other material. If it's a chemical, a drug, something that won't be picked up by X-ray spectroscopy? Don't know what other detectors the GBI's scanning electron microscope might have, but if possible, I'd ask for EDX, FTIR to get the molecular fingerprint of whatever this is."

"We've been thinking of getting one of those hand-held FTIRs, you know, like HazMat uses."

"A very good idea these days, when you're faced with the possibility of explosives, weapons of mass destruction, nerve and blistering agents, white powders. It would also be a good idea to charm whoever is in charge of your trace lab and get this analysis done quickly, as in now. They could do it in a matter of hours if they move it to the head of the line. I don't like the symptoms described." I talk quietly and choose my words carefully, because I don't know who's listening.

But I have no doubt someone is.

"I can be pretty charming." Chang is small and slender, with short black hair, deadpan, almost monotone, but his dark eyes are friendly.

"Good," I answer. "A little charm right now would be welcome."

"You think she might have been sick in here?"

"That's not what I'm smelling," I reply. "But that doesn't mean she wasn't queasy, which is what her neighbor Ellenora described. A sour stomach."

The most obvious consideration on the differential diagnosis is going to be what's already being suggested by those who aren't qualified to do so and certainly aren't objective. Kathleen Lawler was vulnerable to a sudden cardiac death precipitated by physical exertion in conditions that were risky for a woman her age who has never taken good care of herself. She was dressed in a synthetic-blend uniform with long pants and long sleeves, and I estimate it is close to a hundred degrees outside, the humidity at least sixty percent and climbing. Stress makes everything worse, and Kathleen certainly seemed stressed and upset about being moved into segregation, and I won't be surprised if we discover she had heart disease from a lifetime of unhealthy eating and drug and alcohol abuse.

"What about trash," I say to Chang. "I noticed white trash bags on some of the doors, but I don't see one in here. Empty or full."

"Good question." He meets my eyes, and we exchange an understanding.

If there was a trash bag or any trash in here earlier, it was gone by the time he arrived.

"Do you mind if I look around?" I ask him. "I won't touch anything without your permission."

"Except for anything you want me to collect, I'm done in here. So help yourself." His gloved hands open the plastic packaging of sterile applicators as he moves past me to the sink.

"I'll tell you as I get to whatever it is," I inform him anyway, because legally the scene is his. Only the body and any associated biological or trace evidence are Colin Dengate's, and I'm nothing more than an invited guest, an outside expert who needs permission. Unless a case is the jurisdiction of the Armed Forces Medical Examiners—in other words, the Department of Defense—I have no statutory authority outside of Massachusetts. I will ask before I do the smallest thing.

Built into the wall opposite the toilet are the two gray metal shelves arranged with books and notepads, and an assortment of clear plastic containers that are supposed to prevent the concealment of contraband. I open each and recognize the scents of cocoa butter, Noxzema, balsam shampoo, mint mouthwash, and peppermint tooth-

paste. In a plastic soap dish is a thick white cake of
Ivory soap, in a plastic tube a toothbrush, and in another
plastic bottle what looks like hair gel. I note a small plastic comb, a hairbrush without a handle, and large-size
foam rollers, perhaps from a time when Kathleen Lawler's
hair was longer.

There are novels, poetry, and inspirational books, and
transparent plastic baskets full of mail, notepads, and
writing tablets. I see no evidence of a shakedown, nothing to suggest a squad has rifled through Kathleen's
belongings, but I wouldn't expect obvious signs of disturbance. If her property was gone through before
Chang got here, the purpose wasn't to search for mari-
juana or a shank or anything else prohibited by the
prison. The purpose would have been something else
that at the moment I can't fathom. What might a prison
official have been looking for? I don't know, but there
isn't a legitimate reason for someone to have removed her
trash bag before the GBI got here, and my bad feeling is
getting worse.

"If it's all right with you, I'd like to look." I indicate
the contents of the baskets, informing Chang of my
every move.

"Sure." He swabs the steel sink. "Yeah, there's sort of
an odor, you're right. And whatever it is, it's gray. A milky
gray." He tucks the applicators into a plastic collection
tube and labels the blue screw cap with a Sharpie.

Each notepad is ruled and has a glued top and a cardboard back, probably purchased from the commissary,
where spiral notebooks would not be sold because wire

could be fashioned into a weapon. The pages contain poetry and prose interspersed with doodles and sketches, but most are filled with journal entries that are dated. It appears Kathleen was a faithful and expansive diarist, and I'm immediately struck by the absence of anything current. As I flip through each notepad, I determine that she was consistent about making detailed daily entries dating from some three years ago, when she was returned to the GPFW for DUI manslaughter. But there is nothing after this past June 3, when she filled the notepad's last page front and back in her distinctive hand:

June 3 Friday

Rain thrashes a world I've lost and last night when the wind hit the steel mesh on my window just right it sounded like a bending saw. Discordant then screaming like steel cables straining. Like some monstrous beast made of metal. Like a warning. I lay here listening to loud metal groans and reverberations and I thought, "Something is coming."

In the chow hall at supper a couple of hours ago I could feel it. I can't describe what it was. Not tangible like a stare or a comment, just something I sensed. But definitely I could tell. Something brewing.

All of them eating mystery-meat hash and not looking at me, as if I wasn't there, like there's a secret they keep. I didn't speak to them. I didn't see them. I know when not to acknowledge anyone, and they know when I know it. Everybody knows everything in here.

I keep thinking it's about food and attention. People will kill over food, even bad food, and they'll kill over credit, even undeserved and stupid credit. I published those recipes in Inklings and didn't give credit because it sure as hell wasn't earned or remotely merited, and it wasn't my choice anyway. I don't have the final say and I did worry I'd get the blame. A little bit of blame goes a long way in here. I don't know what else to figure. My magazine just came out and suddenly there's a shift.

One microwave in the unit shared by sixty of us, and we all do the same damn things in Mama's Test Kitchen, as the other inmates refer to me and my culinary creativity. Or they used to. Maybe they won't anymore, even if the treats are my idea. Treats always have been all about me and my inventiveness. Who else would think of it when there's not a damn thing to work with besides crap and more crap?

Crap we get from the commissary. Crap we get in the chow hall. Beef and cheese sticks, tortillas and butter pats I taught them to turn into potstickers. Pop-Tarts, vanilla-cream cookies and strawberry Kool-Aid to make strawberry cake. Yes, everybody does it when it's treat time because I was doing it first.

I don't care who submitted what. The recipes are mine! Who taught who the art of scraping vanilla cream out of cookies and whipping it up with Kool-Aid to make pink icing? Who showed them the art of dissolving Pop-Tarts and crumbled cookies in water (reconstituting and reinventing, as I repeatedly explain) and cooking it in the microwave until the center bounces back at a touch?

The Julia Childs of the slammer, that's who. It was me. NOT YOU! I've done it all along because I've lived here longer than most of you are goddamn old, and my recipes are so legendary they've become like a quote or a cliché or a proverb with an origin long forgotten and therefore up for grabs in your small, ignorant minds. "A good man is hard to find" wasn't Flannery O'Connor's idea, it was the title of a song. And "a house divided against itself cannot stand" wasn't Lincoln, it was Jesus. Nobody remembers where anything came from and they help themselves. They steal.

I did what I was told and published the recipes—my recipes—and gave no credit to anyone, including me, that's the fucking irony. I'm the one cheated. All of you pouting, sulking, eating your slop in cold silence when I'm around as if you've been wronged. There's no room at your table when I get there because the seat is saved.

Don't think I don't know the source. Lemmings led into the sea.

Lights out in five. And again the darkness comes.

Mindful of eyes and ears beyond the open door of the cell, I say nothing about what I've just read. I do not comment that at least one notepad seems to be missing, possibly a diary, maybe more than one that Kathleen had been keeping since June 3, and, more important, since she was moved to Bravo Pod. I don't believe she abruptly stopped writing, certainly not after she was transferred into segregation.

During the past two weeks, I would have expected her

to have written more, not less, having little to do twenty-three hours a day except to sit inside this tiny cell with no view and its terrible television reception, cut off from other inmates and her job in the library, and no longer having a magazine or e-mail access. What might she have recorded in writings that someone doesn't want us to read? But I don't ask, and I don't mention how struck I am by her metaphor of lemmings led into the sea.

Are lemmings other inmates, and if so, who has led them? I envision Lola Daggette giving Tara Grimm the finger a few minutes ago, and it very well may have been Lola who instigated the kicking of the cell doors. Full of bravado and hostility and with no impulse control and a low IQ, she was someone Kathleen feared. But Lola Daggette isn't the reason Kathleen is dead on her bed. Lola's not the reason inmates in the general population of medium security started shunning Kathleen in the chow hall, either. How would inmates in other pods have a clue what Lola Daggette thinks or says, or whether she has a problem with someone? She is as isolated and confined in her upstairs cell as Kathleen was in this one.

I suspect Kathleen was referring to someone else, and I'm reminded of Tara Grimm's explanation that Kathleen had to be moved into protective custody because word got out that she was a convicted child molester. What word? What got out? Information the warden could blame on others, something that was on TV, caught by another inmate, by someone, she wasn't sure who, and I didn't believe her when she offered this explanation in her office yesterday, and I don't believe her now.

I suspect I know who has been doing the influencing. Provoke inmates into being angered over something as petty as credit in a magazine, and nothing got published in *Inklings* that Tara Grimm didn't approve. She had the final say about recipes with no names attached, and inmates felt slighted and it's true that small slights can be huge, and Kathleen got moved. Maybe in her paranoid and agitated state she came up with the reason: Lola Daggette was behind an unprecedented loss of freedom that must have felt like punishment. Or perhaps a suggestion was made to Kathleen. Guards like Officer Macon may have informed her, taunted her, teased her into believing that Lola was making threats, and maybe she was. It doesn't matter. Lola didn't kill her.

I don't let on to Marino that anything is unusual when he rustles past me in white and places a digital thermometer on the foot of the bed to record the ambient temperature. He hands a second thermometer to Colin for the temperature of the body. Despite witness accounts that place the time of death at approximately twelve-fifteen p.m., we will calculate it ourselves based on postmortem changes. People make mistakes. They are shocked and traumatized, and get the details wrong. Some people lie. Maybe everybody at the GPFW does.

I look around some more, entertaining the possibility that a notepad for June will turn up in here somewhere as I scan gray walls taped with the handwritten poems and passages of prose Kathleen mentioned to me in e-mails. The poem titled "Fate" that she sent me is directly over the small steel ledge of a desk anchored to the wall. Near a steel stool bolted to the floor is another transparent plastic basket, this one large and stacked with undergarments, a uniform neatly folded, and packs of ramen noodles and two honey buns Kathleen must have gotten from the commissary. She told me she had no money because she no longer had her library job, yet she seems to have made purchases. Maybe they aren't recent. I'm reminded she's been in the segregation of Bravo Pod only two weeks. I poke the honey buns with my gloved finger. They don't feel stale.

At the bottom of the plastic basket are copies of *Inklings*, several dozen of them, including the one for June that Kathleen referred to in the journal entry I just read. On the magazine's front cover are artistic renderings of the contributors, Andy Warhol–like portraits of each woman who is famous for a month because something she wrote will be read by inmates at the GPFW and whoever else has access to the magazine. On the back cover are credits for the staff: the art director, the design team, and, of course, the editor, Kathleen Lawler, with special thanks to Warden Tara Grimm for her support of the arts, "for her humanity and enlightenment."

"She's still quite warm." Colin is squatting next to the steel bed and holding up the thermometer. "Ninety-four-point-six."

"It's seventy-three in here," Marino says, as his thick gloved fingers hold up the thermometer that was on the foot of the bed. He looks at his watch. "At two-nineteen."

"Allegedly dead two hours and she's cooled around

four degrees," I observe. "A little rapid but within normal limits." That's the best I can say.

"Well, she's clothed and it's relatively warm in here," Colin agrees. "All we're going to get is a ballpark."

He's implying that if Kathleen has been dead thirty minutes longer or even an hour longer than we've been led to believe by those giving us information, we aren't going to know by postmortem indicators such as her temperature or rigor mortis.

"Rigor's barely starting in her fingers." Colin manipulates the fingers of Kathleen's left hand. "Livor's not apparent yet."

"I wonder if she could have gotten overheated outside in the cage," Marino says, looking around at the writings taped to the walls, taking in every inch of the cell. "Maybe she got heat exhaustion. That can happen, right? You come back inside, but you've already got a problem."

"If she'd died of hyperthermia," Colin says, as he stands up, "her core temperature would be higher than this. It would be higher than normal even after several hours, and her rigor likely would have sped up and be disproportional to her livor. Also, her symptoms as described by the inmate in the cell across from this one are inconsistent with a prolonged exposure to excessive heat. Cardiac arrest? Now, that's quite possible. And that certainly can happen following strenuous activities on a hot day."

"All she did was walk in the cage. And she rested every lap or two," Marino repeats what's been said.

"The definition of *strenuous* is different for different people," Colin replies. "Someone who is sedentary inside a cell most of the time? She goes outdoors and it's very hot and humid, and she loses too much fluid. Blood volume decreases, and that causes stress to the heart."

"She was drinking water while she was outside," Marino says.

"But was she drinking enough water? Was she drinking enough water inside her cell? I doubt it. On an average day the average person loses about ten cups of water. On an extremely hot, humid day, you can lose three gallons or more if you sweat enough," Colin says.

He walks out of the cell, and I ask Chang if he has any objections to my continuing to examine what's on the shelves and on the desk, and he indicates he doesn't. I retrieve a transparent plastic basket of mail as I'm again reminded of the letters Jack Fielding supposedly wrote, describing how difficult I am, how awful I am to work for. I look for any letters from him or from Dawn Kincaid and don't find them. I find nothing from anyone that might be important, except for a letter that appears to be from me. I stare in disbelief at the return address, at the CFC logo printed on a ten-by-thirteen-inch white envelope that Bryce orders in quantities of five thousand for the CFC:

Kay Scarpetta, MD, JD
COL USAF
Chief Medical Examiner and Director
Cambridge Forensic Center

The self-sealing flap has been slit open, probably by prison personnel who scan all incoming mail, and inside is a folded sheet with my office letterhead. The note is typed and supposedly signed by me in black ink:

June 26

Dear Kathleen,

I very much appreciate your e-mails to me about Jack and can only imagine your pain and it's impact during what must be an oppressive confinement since you've been moved into protective custody. I look forward to chatting with you on June 30 and sharing confidences about the very special man we had in common. He certainly was a powerful influence on both of our lives, and it is important to me that you believe I wanted only the best for him and would never have intentionally hurt him.

I look forward to meeting you finally after all these years and to our continued communications. As always, let me know if there is anything you need.

Regards,

Kay

22

I sense Marino's presence, and then he's next to me, looking at the letter I hold in my purple nitrile gloved hands, reading what it says. I meet his eyes and barely shake my head.

"What the hell?" he asks under his breath.

I answer by pointing out the typed words *it's impact*. The usage is improper. *It's* should be possessive, should be *its* and not a contraction. But Marino doesn't understand, and right now I'm not going to explain the inconsistencies or that the wording doesn't sound like me and that I wouldn't sign such a letter "Regards, Kay," as if Kathleen Lawler and I really were friends.

It's impossible to imagine my writing or saying to her that I would "never have intentionally hurt" Jack Fielding, as if to imply I might have hurt him unintentionally, and I think of what Jaime said last night. Kathleen's daughter, Dawn Kincaid, has been trumping up a case that I'm an unstable, violent person. But Dawn Kincaid could not have created this forged letter. It's not possible she could have done such a thing from Butler State Hospital, where she would have been confined when this letter was mailed.

I hold up the sheet of stationery to the light, directing Marino's attention to the absence of the CFC watermark, making sure he understands that the document is fake. Then I place the sheet of stationery on the desk and begin to do something he isn't likely to see very often. I take off my gloves and stuff them in a pocket of my white jumpsuit. I start taking photographs with my phone.

"You want the Nikon?" he asks, his face baffled. "A scale—"

"No," I interrupt him.

I don't want the thirty-five-millimeter camera or a close-up lens or a tripod or special lighting. I don't want a labeled six-inch ruler for a scale. I have a different reason for taking these pictures. I don't tell him anything else, but I do feel compelled to say something to Chang, who is watching all this intently from his station in the open doorway.

"I assume you have a questioned-documents lab?" I step closer to him.

"We do." He watches me type a text message to my chief of staff, Bryce.

"Samples of my office paper that are going to be sent

to your labs by FedEx priority overnight? Who will sign for them?"

"Me, I guess."

"Okay. Sammy Chang, GBI Investigative Division." I type as I talk. "I'm going to wager a bet that an examination will show significant differences between the CFC's authentic paper and this." I indicate what's on the desk. "The lack of a watermark, for example. I'm making sure my chief of staff sends the same letterhead, the same envelope, right away, and you can compare them yourself so you'll have irrefutable proof of what I'm describing."

"A watermark?"

"There's not one. Possibly a different paper that can be determined under magnification or by analyzing chemical additives. Maybe a slightly different font. I don't know. Well, big surprise. No signal in here. I'll resend it later."

The message and attached photographs to Bryce are saved as a draft, and I look past Chang and notice that the glass window in the cell across from us is empty. Ellenora isn't looking out anymore. She is silent.

"The prison obviously checks mail when it's delivered," I say to Chang. "In other words, someone checked this envelope when it was delivered. Scanned it or opened it in front of Kathleen, whatever the usual protocol is. Possible you can find out what else might have been inside the envelope? The postage of a dollar and seventy-six cents is more than needed for a single sheet of stationery and a large Tyvek envelope unless something else was in it. Of course, it's possible whoever sent it overpaid."

"So you didn't . . ." he starts to say, as he glances be-hind him.

"I absolutely didn't." I shake my head no. I did not write this letter. I did not mail it or whatever else might have been in the envelope. "Where is everybody?"

"They took her to a quiet place where Dr. Dengate can question her about what she observed. Of course, her story gets more elaborate each time." He's referring to Ellenora. "But Officer Macon's right here." He says it loudly enough for Officer Macon to hear him just fine.

"Maybe you can ask him about any mail Kathleen Lawler's gotten in the past few days." I refrain from add-ing that Chang shouldn't count on being told the truth about a letter or about anything at all that goes on in this place.

I put on fresh gloves and pick up the letter written on what looks like my own office stationery, holding it up to the light again, relieved there is no watermark and at the same time suspecting that whoever forged a letter from me doesn't seem to know that the CFC uses an inexpen-sive recycled twenty-five percent rag paper with a custom watermark to protect our correspondence and documents from this very threat. While it would be possible to create a reasonably good facsimile of my letterhead or any doc-ument I might generate, it is impossible to counterfeit such a thing and get away with it unless one has access to authentic CFC paper. It occurs to me that whoever sent this letter may not care whether the police, scientists, or even I am fooled. Possibly the only purpose of this faked letter was to fool Kathleen Lawler into believing it came from me.

I fold the letter in half, the way I found it, and return it to its large envelope, puzzled by the size, again wondering if something may have been included. If so, what else did I supposedly send to Kathleen Lawler? What else did she receive that she believed was from me? Who is impersonating me, and what is the ultimate goal? I recall Tara Grimm's oblique references yesterday to my being accessible, and then Kathleen mentioned my generosity. I found their comments perplexing, and I try to conjure up exactly what Kathleen said. Something about people like me giving a thought to people like her, about my supposedly paying attention to her, and at the time I assumed she was alluding to my coming to see her.

But what she really was saying was she appreciated my writing to her and perhaps sending her something. She would have received the forged letter before I saw her yesterday. It was postmarked in Savannah on June 26 at four-fifty-five p.m., mailed from a location, possibly a post office, with a 31401 zip code. Five days ago, a Sunday, I was home, and Lucy took Benton and me to a tequila bar that's become a favorite hangout of hers, Lolita Cocina. The waitstaff certainly could testify to the fact that I was there that night. I could not have been a thousand miles south in Savannah at four-fifty-five p.m. and in Boston's Back Bay by seven p.m., having dinner.

"Gonna grab a few things and find the little boys' room." Marino squeezes past me.

"I'll have to take you," I hear Officer Macon's voice as it occurs to me that someone could claim Marino mailed the letter for me. He was down here by June 26, or at least nearby in South Carolina.

My attention returns to Chang. He is standing in the open doorway, his dark eyes watching me.

"If you're fine with my checking a few more things, then I'll be done in here and can show you what I'd like collected," I say to him.

He looks at his watch. He looks behind him as Officer Macon escorts Marino to a men's room.

"Has the van gotten here?" I ask.

"Ready when you are."

"What about Colin?"

"I think he's depending on you to wind it up. There's nothing else he wants to do until we get her in."

"Fine. I'll bag her hands, photograph her, if that's all right."

"I've got plenty of photos."

"I'm sure you do. But as you can tell, I like to overdo things," I say to him.

"How about a real camera? And while you're overdo-ing things, there's also a locker box."

"A locker box?" I look around the cell to see what he might be talking about.

"Attached to the foot of the bed." He points. "Hid-den by the covers."

"I'd like to take a look."

"Knock yourself out."

"I'll be quick so you can get in and collect a few things that need to go to the labs. I'm sure you're ready to get out of here."

"Not me. I love prisons. Reminds me of my first marriage."

I resume examining what is on top of Kathleen's desk, a thin stack of cheap white paper and plain envelopes, a see-through Bic pen, a book of self-adhesive postage stamps, and a small tablet with the cover flipped back that seems to be an address book. I don't recognize any names, but I riffle through the pages, looking for Dawn Kincaid and Jack Fielding. I don't find them. In fact, most of the names have Georgia addresses, and when I come across one for Triple Q Ranch outside of Atlanta, I realize how old the address book is. Triple Q was where Kathleen was a therapist when she got involved with Jack in the mid- to late-seventies. More than thirty years old, at least, I think, as I continue turning pages. Whoever she's been writing recently most likely isn't in here, I decide. If she had a current address book, it appears to be missing.

"This should go in, too," I tell Investigator Chang.

"Yeah, I noticed it."

"Old."

"Exactly." He knows what I'm implying. "Course, she might not have any friends, anyone to write or call anymore."

"I was told she liked to write letters." I open the book of stamps, noting that six out of twenty are missing. "She worked in the library to fund her commissary account. And maybe got a few contributions now and then from family." I mean from Dawn Kincaid.

"Not from family in the past five months or after she was moved in here, not in maximum security."

"No," I agree Kathleen wasn't in a position to fund her account since she was moved to Bravo Pod, and certainly Dawn couldn't have been doing it from Butler, and before that, from the Cambridge jail. "It might be interesting to see how much money is left in that account and what she might have bought of late," I suggest.

"Good idea."

There is a pocket dictionary and a thesaurus, and two library books of poetry, Wordsworth and Keats, and next I go to the bed. I crouch at the foot of it, moving the blanket and sheet out of the way, and I'm mindful of Kathleen Lawler's legs draped over the side. My left shoulder brushes against her hip, and it is warm against me but not warm as in life. Minute by minute, she continues to cool.

I open the locker box, a single metal drawer filled with a hodgepodge of personal effects. Drawings and poetry, family photographs, including several of an exquisite little blond girl who got more gorgeous as she got older, and then suddenly was a temptress, overly made up, with a voluptuous body and dead eyes. I find the photograph of Jack Fielding that I gave to Kathleen yesterday, included with the others, as if he was her family. There are a few of him when he was young, perhaps ones he mailed to her in the early years, and the photographs are worn and torn at the edges, as if they have been handled frequently.

I don't find any other diaries, but there is a booklet of fifteen-cent stamps and also stationery with a festive border of party hats and balloons, which seems a strange choice for an inmate, possibly left over from someone who used it for invitations to a birthday celebration or some other fun event. The stationery isn't something that would be sold in a prison commissary, and I suppose it's also possible Kathleen has had it from a time that predates her being locked up for DUI manslaughter. Maybe that's the explanation for fifteen-cent stamps that feature a white sandy beach with a bright yellow-and-red umbrella beneath a vivid blue sky, a seagull flying overhead.

The last time I paid fifteen cents for a stamp was at least twenty years ago, so either she was saving them for a special reason or someone sent them to her, and I recall Kathleen mentioning to me the hardship of affording postage. The book originally contained twenty stamps, and the top pane of ten is missing. I pick up the thin stack of white copying paper from the desk and hold up a sheet of it to the light, finding no indentations that might have been made by writing on a sheet of paper that was on top. I try the party stationery next, holding up a sheet, tilting it in different directions as I make out indentations that are fairly deep and visible: the date, *June 27,* and the salutation, *Dear Daughter.*

". . . Yes, because I'd like to ask exactly what she did," I overhear Colin saying to Tara Grimm beyond the cell's open door. "You were told she walked around the cage for an hour, for the entire hour. Fine. I appreciate that, but like I said, I need to hear it from the officer who was present. Did she drink water? How much? How often did she rest? Did she complain of light-headedness, muscle weakness, headache, or nausea? Did she voice any complaints at all?"

"I asked all that and have passed it on to you word for word." Tara Grimm's quiet, melodious voice.

"I'm sorry, but not good enough. I need you to get the officer and bring her here or take us to her. I need to talk to her myself. I'd like to see the exercise cage. It would be good if we could do this now, so we can get the body to my office without further delay. . . ."

I make out some words but not others indented on the stationery. It won't be possible to determine exactly what Kathleen wrote in her letter on party paper until it can be examined in better conditions than a mesh-covered window and low-output recessed cell lighting that probably is manipulated by a key switch in the control room, preventing inmates from turning off their lights to ambush a guard coming in. I catch the shadow of what is written in a graceful hand that now is familiar:

> I know . . . a joke, right? . . . so I thought I'd share . . . from PNG . . . Kind of fits with everything else . . . trying to bribe me and win me over . . . How are you feeling . . . ?

PNG as in persona non grata? A person who isn't welcome or, in legal terms, someone, usually a foreign diplomat, who is censured by no longer being allowed to enter a certain country. I wonder to whom Kathleen was referring as I hear the papery sound of Marino walking back into the cell, and he sets down a rugged waterproof Pelican case next to the bed.

"I'm sure there's a hand lens somewhere," I say, as he snaps open stiff clasps. "A ten-X with LEDs, if possible. The lighting's not so great in here."

He finds an illuminated magnifier, which I turn on with a switch and begin to slowly move over the tops of Kathleen Lawler's pale hands. The smooth pinkish palms, her fingers and their pads, the wrinkles of her skin, the minutiae of her prints and faint bluish veins are ten times their normal size in the lighted lens. Her unpainted nails are slightly furrowed and clean, a few whitish fibers under them that could be from her uniform or the bedsheets, and a hint of something orange under the nail of her right thumb.

"If you could locate the fine forceps and a GSR kit for me. If Colin doesn't have one, I'm sure Investigator Chang will," I say to Marino, as I hold up the right hand by the second knuckle of the thumb, the body cooling but still limber, as in life.

Marino shuffles equipment around inside the case and says, "Got it."

Like a surgical assistant, he lays the tweezers in my nitrile-covered palm and then gives me a small metal stub with a circular carbon tape adhesive disk on top for lifting gunshot residue off the palmar and back surfaces of hands. I instruct him to hold the illuminated lens over the thumbnail as I use the tweezers to coax out the whitish fibers and minute flecks of a crumbled orange pasty substance, capturing them with the sticky stub, which I seal inside a small plastic evidence bag that I label and initial.

Crouching by the bed, I begin to look at the exposed flesh of the lower legs and the bare feet, holding the magnifier over an area on the top of the left foot where there is a cluster of bright red marks.

"Maybe she got bit by something," Marino says.

"I think she might have dripped something hot on herself," I reply. "First-degree burns that you might expect if you drip a hot liquid on your foot."

"I don't see how she could heat up anything in here." He leans close to the body, looking at the area of skin I'm talking about. "Could water from the sink do that?"

"You can run it and see. But I doubt it."

"It's okay to run it?"

"I swabbed the sink," Chang tells him from the open door. "You can run water if you want to see how hot it gets. Maybe she had something in here. Something electrical?" he suggests. "Possible she was electrocuted?"

"Right now a lot of things are possible," I reply.

"A blow-dryer, a curling iron, if someone brought one in for her to use," Chang suggests. "Would be against regulations, that's for sure. But it could account for the electrical smell."

"Where would she have plugged anything in?" I ask, seeing no electrical outlets, only an enclosed wall mount where the TV is connected.

"Something battery-operated could have exploded."
Marino turns water on in the sink. "If enough heat
builds up with anything that's got a battery, it can explode. But if that happened, she'd have more than just
those little spots on her foot. And you're sure they aren't
insect bites?" He holds his hand under running water,
waiting to see how hot it will get. "Because that might
make more sense, since she was outside and then started
feeling bad. I've had that happen. A damn yellow jacket
gets into my shoe or sock and keeps stinging until it
dies. Once I was going about sixty on my Harley and
rode through an entire swarm of honeybees. Getting
stung inside your helmet isn't a lot of fun."

"Some edema, some minor swelling. These look like
burns, very recent ones, confined to the outer layer of
skin, first-degree or possibly superficial second-degree. It
would have been painful," I describe.

"No way that did it." Marino turns off the water.
"Not hot at all. No better than lukewarm."

"Maybe you could ask if she might have burned her
foot somehow."

He steps past Chang, disappearing outside the cell.
"The Doc wants to know if she might have burned herself," I hear him say.

"If who did?" Colin's voice.

"If Kathleen Lawler did. Like if someone maybe gave
her a cup of really hot coffee or tea and she dripped it on
her foot."

"Why?" Colin asks.

"Impossible," Tara Grimm says. "Inmates in segregation have no access to microwave ovens. There are no microwave ovens in Bravo Pod, except in the kitchen, and she certainly had no access to the kitchen. It's impossible she could have gotten hold of something hot enough for her to get burned."

"Why are you asking?" Colin appears in the doorway, no longer in white Tyvek, and he's sweating and doesn't look happy.

"She has burns on her left foot," I reply. "Looks like something splashed or dripped on her."

"We'll take a closer look when we get her to the office." He walks out of sight again.

"Did she have her shoes and socks on when she was found?" I ask whoever is listening.

Tara Grimm appears in the doorway of the cell.

"Of course not," she says to me. "We wouldn't have removed her shoes and socks. She must have taken them off when she came in from exercise. We didn't do anything to her."

"Seems like putting on a sock, a shoe, over burns wouldn't have felt very good," I observe. "Was she limping during her hour of exercise? Did she mention any discomfort?"

"She complained about the heat and that she was tired."

"I'm wondering if she burned herself after she was returned to her cell. Did she take a shower when she came in from the exercise area?"

"I'll say it again. No, it's not possible," Tara says flatly, slowly, and with undisguised hostility. "There was nothing to burn herself with."

"Any chance she might have had something electrical in her cell at some point this morning?"

"Absolutely not. There are no accessible outlets in any of the cells in Bravo Pod. She couldn't have burned herself. You can ask fifty times, and I'll keep saying the same thing."

"Well, it appears she did burn herself. Her left foot," I reply.

"I don't know anything about burns. And she couldn't have. You must be mistaken." Tara stares hard at me. "There's nothing here she could have burned herself with," she repeats. "She probably has mosquito bites. Or stings."

"They're not bites or stings."

I palpate Kathleen's head. My purple-gloved fingers feel along the contours of her skull and down her neck, checking what I always check, using my sense of touch to discover the most subtle injury, such as a fracture or a spongy, boggy area that might indicate hemorrhage to soft tissue hidden by her hair. She is warm, and her head moves as I move my hands, her lips slightly parted as if she's asleep and might open her eyes wide at any moment and have something to say. I feel no injuries, nothing abnormal, and I tell Marino to give me the camera and a transparent six-inch scale.

I take photographs of the body, focusing on the hand where I removed the orange substance and white fibers from underneath the nails. I photograph the burns on the bare left foot and slip brown bags over it and each hand, securing them at the ankle and wrists with rubber bands to ensure nothing is added or lost during transport to the morgue. Tara Grimm watches everything I do, no longer subtle about it. She stands in the doorway with her hands on her hips, and I take more photographs. I take more than I need. I take my time as I get angrier.

23

Colin opens a back door of the Coastal Regional Crime Laboratory, and we step out into the heat and glare as thunder rumbles and a volatile sea of dark clouds rolls closer. It is a few minutes after four p.m., the wind gusting out of the southwest at about thirty knots, blowing Lucy's helicopter back into last week, she tells me over the phone.

"We had to land in Lumberton to refuel yet a third time after waiting out rain showers and bad viz in Rocky Mount," she says. "Endless boredom over pine trees and hog farms. Smoke everywhere from controlled burning. I think next time Benton might take the bus."

"Marino left for the airport a few minutes ago, and it looks like a big storm is getting close," I tell my niece, as I accompany Colin across a wide expanse of asphalt tarmac used for staff parking and deliveries, the air so thick with humidity I can almost see it.

"We'll be fine," Lucy says. "VFR all the way, and should be there in maybe an hour, an hour-fifteen, unless I end up vectoring around Gamecock Charlie and following the coast down from Myrtle Beach. The scenic route but slower."

Gamecock Charlie is a Military Operations Area airspace used for training and maneuvers that are neither publicized nor safe for nonparticipating or civilian aircraft that happen to be nearby. If an MOA is active, or "hot," it's wise to stay away.

"You know what I always say. Never be in a hurry to have a problem," I tell her.

"Well, I think it's hot, based on what I've been picking up on Milcom," Lucy goes on, referring to military communications or UHF monitoring. "I don't really want to get into the middle of intercepts, low-altitude tactics, aerobatics, whatever."

"I'd appreciate it if you wouldn't."

"Not to mention avoiding drones, some aircraft buzzing around that's remotely controlled by a computer in California. You ever notice how many military bases and restricted areas there are around here? That and deer stands. I don't guess you know what happened yet." She means what happened to Kathleen Lawler. "You don't sound very happy."

"We're getting ready to find out, hopefully."

"Usually you're more than hopeful."

"This isn't usual. We were given a hard time at the

prison, and I don't sound happy because I'm not." I envision Tara Grimm's face as she planted herself in the doorway of the cell, glaring at me, and then what happened after that with the guard who supervised Kathleen Lawler's hour of exercise.

According to Officer Slater, a big woman with a defiant air and resentful eyes, nothing out of the ordinary occurred this morning between eight and nine o'clock, when Kathleen was escorted out to walk "just like she's been doing" since she was transferred to Bravo Pod, she told us, after we were escorted to the exercise cage right before we left. I asked if there was any indication Kathleen might have felt unwell or uncomfortable.

Was she, for example, complaining of being tired or dizzy or having difficulty breathing? Any chance she might have been stung by an insect? Was she limping? Did she seem to be in pain? Did she mention anything at all about the way she felt this morning, and Officer Slater reported that Kathleen griped about the heat, repeating much of the same information we've been told multiple times now.

Kathleen would walk around the cage and periodically lean against the chain-link fencing, Officer Slater said. Kathleen did stoop down to retie one of her sneakers several times, we were told, and it could be that one of her feet was bothering her, but she didn't mention anything about burning herself. It wouldn't have been possible for her to burn herself in Bravo Pod, Officer Slater stated with unnecessary defensiveness, parroting what Tara Grimm had told us.

"So I don't know why you'd get a notion like that," Officer Slater said to me as she looked at the warden. Inmates don't have use of microwaves in Bravo Pod, and the water from the taps isn't hot enough to cause a burn. Now and then, Kathleen asked for a drink while inside the cage and said her throat was a little scratchy, maybe from pollen or dust or she was "trying to catch some- thing like the flu, and she might of mentioned she was feeling sleepy."

"What might Kathleen have meant by 'sleepy'?" I in- quired, and the officer seemed to be annoyed by that. "Well, sleepy," she repeated, as if she was sorry she said it and wanted to take it back. There's a difference between being sleepy and fatigued, I explained. Physical activity can make one fatigued, as can illness, I pointed out. But sleepiness by my definition indicates feeling drowsy, hav- ing difficulty keeping one's eyes open, and this can occur when someone is sleep-deprived but also when certain conditions such as low blood sugar are to blame.

Officer Slater's answer was to cut her eyes at Tara Grimm and say to Colin and me that Kathleen com- plained she wished she hadn't eaten so close to going outside in the heat and humidity. Eating a big meal might have given her indigestion, and maybe she was having heartburn, she wasn't sure, but Kathleen was al- ways complaining about the food at the GPFW, Officer Slater let us know.

Kathleen "fussed" about the food whether it was de- livered to her cell in Bravo Pod or when she was eating in the chow hall. She talked about food all the time, usually complaining it wasn't any good or there wasn't enough, "but it was always something she was unhappy about," Officer Slater said, and the inflection of her voice and the shifting of her eyes as she continued to talk gave me the same feeling I got when I was talking to Kathleen yesterday. Officer Slater was mindful of the warden and not the truth.

"What's Benton doing?" I ask Lucy.

"Talking to the Boston field office."

"Do we have an update?" I want to know about Dawn Kincaid.

"Not that I know of, but he looks intense out there on the ramp, where no one can hear him as usual. You want him?"

"I don't want to hold you up. We'll talk when I see you. I don't know who might be here." What I'm suggesting is she could run into Jaime Berger, who still hasn't bothered to return my phone call.

"Maybe it will be her problem," Lucy says.

"I'd rather it isn't anybody's problem. I'd rather you don't have an unpleasant encounter."

"Gotta pay for gas."

I smell creosote and Dumpsters baking in the sun as Colin and I reach the morgue, a windowless pale yellow cinder-block building flanked by HVACs and an industrial backup generator on one side and the bay on another. Beyond the back fence, tall pines sway in the wind, and in the distance, lightning shimmers in blooming black clouds and I can see veils of rain far off to the southwest, a bad storm heading this way from Florida.

The huge metal shutter door is rolled up, and we walk through an empty concrete space to another door that Colin unlocks with a key.

"We probably autopsy on average two per year, and then another five or six that we sign out after a view." He picks up where he left off when Lucy called, explaining the types of cases he typically gets from the GPFW.

"If I were you, I'd review all of them for however many years Tara Grimm has been the warden," I reply.

"Mostly we're talking cancer, chronic obstructive pulmonary disease, liver disease, congestive heart failure," Colin says. "Georgia's not exactly known for compassionate release if an inmate is terminally ill. That's all we need. Convicted felons getting out early because they're dying of cancer and they rob a bank or shoot someone."

"Unless the inmate died in hospice, in other words, a death that was beyond questioning, I'd go back and look," I suggest.

"I'm thinking."

"Any case that gave you even the slightest concern. I'd review it again."

"No concern at the time, to be perfectly honest, but you've got my hindsight kicking in. Shania Plames," he then says. "A really sad story. Suffered from postpartum psychiatric problems, depressed and delusional, and ended up killing her children, all three of them. Hanged them from a balcony railing. Her husband owned a tile company in Ludowici, was out of town on a fishing trip. Imagine coming home to that?"

He checks the big black log inside the receiving area

that has a floor scale, a walk-in refrigerator, and a small office with in-out boxes.

"Good, she's here." He means Kathleen Lawler is.

"Shania Plames was a sudden death at the GPFW," I suppose.

"On death row," he says. "About four years ago, she asphyxiated herself after she came in from the exercise cage one morning. Used a pair of her uniform pants, wrapped one leg around her neck, the other leg around her ankles, sort of hog-tying herself, and lay on her belly. The weight of her legs hanging over the edge of the bed put just enough pressure on her jugular to cut the oxygen off to her brain."

We follow a white tiled hallway past locker rooms, bathrooms, various storage rooms, and the decomp autopsy room, with its solitary table and double drawer refrigerator-freezer, and Colin continues to tell me it was an unusually creative way to kill oneself in an environment that is virtually suicide-proof, and he wasn't really sure if what Shania Plames had rigged up with her trousers would work but he wasn't about to try it. He gives me every detail he can recall about her and one other case, Rea Abernathy, who was, just last year, found with her head in the toilet bowl, the steel rim of it compressing her neck, her cause of death positional asphyxia.

"She didn't have a ligature mark, but one might expect the absence of that when what she'd allegedly used to strangle herself was a wide, relatively soft fabric," Colin says, about Shania Plames. "There were no injuries to the internal structures of the neck, and that wasn't unusual, either, in a suicidal hanging by partial suspension or ligature strangulation by positioning. No injuries or evidence that gave me anything to go on with Rea Abernathy, either."

As in the Barrie Lou Rivers case, his diagnoses were based mainly on the history, a process of elimination.

"Not at all the way I want to practice forensic medicine," Colin says darkly, as we enter an anteroom of deep steel sinks, red biohazard trash cans, hampers, and shelves of disposable protective clothing. "Frustrating as hell."

"Why was Rea Abernathy in prison?" I ask.

"Paid someone to drown her husband in the swimming pool. Was supposed to look like an accident and it didn't. He had a big contusion on the back of his head, a big intracranial hematoma. Dead before he hit the water. Plus, the guy she paid to do it was someone she was having an affair with."

"And what about her? She absolutely didn't drown in the toilet?"

"Wouldn't have been possible. Prison toilets are shallow and elongated, the water below the level of the bowl. Built to be suicide-resistant, like everything else inside the cell. You'd have to get your face way down inside it to drown or suffocate, and that's not going to happen unless someone holds you forcibly, and there was no sign of that, no injuries, like I said. The story was she was sick, was gagging. Or maybe was trying to throw up. There was a suggestion she might have had an eating disorder. And she passed out or had an arrhythmia."

"Assuming she was alive when she ended up in that position."

"I'm not in the business of assuming," Colin says unhappily. "But there was nothing else. Negative tox. Another diagnosis of exclusion."

"The symbolism," I point out. "Her husband supposedly drowns, and she dies with her head in a toilet and at a glance, at least to the uninitiated, might appear to have drowned. Shania Plames hangs her children and then herself." I remember what Tara Grimm said about not forgiving anyone who harms a child or an animal, and that life was a gift that could be given or taken away. "Barrie Lou Rivers poisons people with tuna-fish sandwiches, and that's what she ate for her last meal," I add.

We pull on splash-proof sleeves and fluid-resistant aprons, then shoe covers, and surgical caps and masks.

"I liked the old days better, when we didn't have to bother wearing all this shit," Colin says, and he sounds angry.

"It's not that we didn't need to." I cover my nose and mouth with a surgical mask. "We just didn't know any better." I put on a pair of safety glasses to protect my eyes.

"Well, there's more to worry about now, that's for sure," he says, and I can tell he feels terrible. "I keep waiting for some God-awful scourge we haven't heard of or dealt with before. Weaponizing chemicals and diseases. I don't give a damn what anybody says. Nobody's prepared for vast numbers of infectious or contaminated dead bodies."

"Technology can't fix what technology destroys, and if the worst happens, nobody's going to deal with it very well," I agree.

"That's something for you to say with the resources you've got. But the fact is, there's no cure for human nature," he says. "No putting the genie back into the damn bottle when it comes to what shitty people can do to one another these days."

"The genie was never in the bottle, Colin. I'm not sure there is a bottle."

We pass the open door of the X-ray room, and I catch a glimpse of a C-arm fluoroscope that I never use anymore. But advanced technologies such as computed tomography or magnetic resonance imaging with 3-D software wouldn't help us if we had it. Whatever killed Kathleen Lawler probably wouldn't be visible on a CT or MRI or any other type of scan, and I hope Sammy Chang already is receipting documents and swabs to the labs.

Inside the main autopsy room a muscular young man in soiled scrubs and a bloody plastic apron is suturing closed the body of what I assume is the motor-vehicle fatality from earlier today. The head is misshapen like a badly dented can, the face smashed beyond recognition, blood streaking flesh, all of it in stark contrast to sterile cold concrete and shiny metal, to the lack of color and texture typical of morgues.

I can't tell the victim's age, but his hair is quite black and he is lean and well built, as if he went to a lot of trouble to be physically fit. I smell the early hints of blood and cells breaking down, of biology giving itself up to decomposition as a long surgical needle glints in the overhead light with each sweep of white twine, and water dribbles into a sink, tap-tapping on steel. On the far side of the room, Kathleen Lawler is on a gurney, a body shape pouched in white.

"Do we know why we posted him instead of doing a view?" Colin asks the morgue assistant, who has a Marine Corps bulldog tattoo on the side of his neck and a crew cut. "Since he doesn't have much of a head left, almost looks like he got the wrong end of a shotgun? Seems like a view would have sufficed. What exactly was the question in this MV fatality that's now costing Georgia taxpayers?"

"If he had a heart attack first and that caused him to swerve into oncoming traffic during rush hour." He sutures in long sweeps and tugs that create a Y-shape of railroad tracks running from the sternum to the pelvis. "He had a history, had been hospitalized for chest pain last week."

"And what did we decide?"

"Hey, not me deciding. I don't get paid enough."

"Nobody around here gets paid enough," Colin says.

"The Mack truck smashed him to smithereens, and he died of cardiac arrest because his heart quit."

"What about respiratory arrest? George, I don't know if you've met Dr. Scarpetta." Colin is grim.

"Yeah, he definitely quit breathing. Nice to meet you.

I'm just giving him grief. Somebody has to." George winks at me as he sutures. "How many times a week do you tell med students rotating through here that cardiac and respiratory arrest aren't causes of death?" He mimics his boss. "You get shot ten times and your heart quits and you stop breathing, but that's not what killed you," he teases Colin, who's not laughing, not even smiling.

"I'll be finished up here in a few," George says more seriously. "You need me for the next one?"

He cuts the heavy twine with the sharp, curved tip of the long needle and jabs it into a block of Styrofoam.

"If not, I got supplies that came in this morning and I need to put them away, and I'd like to pressure-wash the bay real good. We're going to have to deal with the stock jars one of these days. I hate to keep reminding you. We don't want the damn shelves to collapse and formalin and pieces and parts everywhere. Out of room and out of money. That's the country-music song I'm going to write about this place," he says to me.

"You know how I am about throwing things out. Hang around for a bit. Dr. Scarpetta and I will get started and see how it goes." Colin's face is hard, and I can see the thoughts in his eyes.

He's wondering what he might have missed, wondering what all of us dread, those of us who take care of the dead. If we misdiagnose a patient, someone else might die. Carbon monoxide poisoning or a homicide, if we can catch it, we can prevent more of the same. It's rare we can save anyone, but we must work every investigation as if it's possible.

"You've got the stock jars in those old cases?" I ask about Barrie Lou Rivers, Shania Plames, and Rea Abernathy.

"Well, I didn't save their gastric, damn it. I should have frozen it."

"Why would you think to?"

"I didn't. I wouldn't have thought of it, had no reason to, but I wish I had."

"And how many times have people like us said that?" I try to make him feel better. "There's been some success in testing formalin-fixed tissue," I add. "Depending on what you're looking for."

"That's the thing. Screen for what?"

We cross a tan epoxy-sealed floor where three additional tables mounted on columns and attached to sinks are spaced beneath illuminated fresh-air hoods. Parked by each station is a trolley neatly arranged with surgical instruments, evidence tubes and containers, a cutting board, an electric oscillating saw that plugs into an overhead cord reel, and a bright red sharps container. Cabinets, light boxes, and ultraviolet air sanitizers are mounted on walls, and there are evidence drying cabinets, and countertops and metal folding chairs for doing paperwork.

"Not that I'm in charge, but first on my list is what she might have been exposed to," I say to Colin. "A grayish chalky residue that smelled like overheating electrical insulation. It would be extremely helpful to get an analysis ASAP of whatever was in her sink. It certainly didn't smell like anything indigenous to her cell. I'm not trying to tell you what to do, but if you've got any influence."

"Sammy's got enough influence for both of us, and trace, tool marks, documents, they all like a challenge. Everything these days is DNA, and not everything can be solved by damn DNA, but try telling prosecutors that, and especially the police. My guess is the folks in trace will get on it right away. I didn't smell whatever it is, but I'll take your word for it, and you can tell me what to do all you like. Offhand, I can't think of any poison that might smell like overheating electrical insulation."

"So what was it?" I ask. "What did she get hold of, and how? In the maximum security of Bravo Pod, it's not as if she could wander around in common areas and mingle with other inmates and get her hands on something she wasn't supposed to have."

"Obviously we have to worry about people who had access to her cell. Always my concern when it's a death in custody. Even under what may appear to be the most normal of circumstances, and this isn't in the normal category," he says. "Not anymore."

24

On a countertop are boxes of different-size gloves, and I get two pairs for each of us, and Colin unzips the body pouch. Plastic rustles as he opens it all the way.

I help him slide Kathleen Lawler onto the steel table, and he walks to bins mounted on a wall and begins to collect blank forms, securing them to a metal clipboard as I remove the rubber bands around her wrists and ankle. I remove the brown paper bags I placed over her hands and left foot earlier, and fold them and package them for the trace evidence lab, then I tear off a large sheet of white butcher paper from a dispenser on a counter and cover the autopsy table beside the one we're using.

Her body is considerably cooler but still limber and

easy to manipulate as we begin to undress it, and we place each article of clothing on the paper-covered table next to us. The button-up white uniform shirt with INMATE stamped on the back in large dark blue letters. The white trousers with a button fly and the blue initials GPFW down the sides of the legs. A bra. A pair of panties. I find a hand lens on a cart and turn on a surgical lamp, and under magnification I discover a faint area of orange smearing, as if Kathleen might have wiped her hand on her right pant leg. I retrieve a camera from a shelf and place a scale next to the stain, centering it under the light.

"I don't know where you get food testing done around here," I say to Colin. "This looks like cheese, but we should find out. I'm not going to swab it, will let trace take care of it. She had something orange under her right thumbnail, too. Might be the same thing, something she touched or ate not long before she died."

"GBI uses a private lab in Atlanta that analyzes food, cosmetics, consumer products, you name it," he says. "I wonder if inmates can buy these cheese sticks or cheese spread in the commissary."

"Definitely the yellowy-orange color of cheddar or a cheddar spread. I didn't see any cheese or cheese sticks in her cell, but that doesn't mean she didn't have something like that earlier. Of course, we'd know more if her trash hadn't disappeared. What about petechial hemorrhages of the eyes, the face, in the Plames case?" I return to the subject of Shania Plames's death as I return to the table bearing Kathleen Lawler's body.

"Nothing. But you don't always have that, either, in suicidal hangings with full vascular compression."

"Based on the rig you've described, the way her uniform trousers were tied around her neck and legs, I'm not sure I would expect the full vascular compression associated with full—not partial—suspension or with complete ligature strangulation."

"It was unusual," he agrees solemnly.

"Possibly staged?"

"Never entered my mind at the time."

"Why would it? I doubt it would have entered mine."

"I'm not going to say it couldn't have been staged," he continues. "But I would have expected evidence of a struggle, of some means of incapacitating her. Not so much as a bruise."

"I'm just wondering if it's possible she was already dead when she was tied up and placed in the position she was found."

"Right about now I'm wondering a lot of things," he says grimly.

I measure a tattoo on the lower-right abdomen, a Tinker Bell–like fairy that is six and a half inches from wing to wing. Based on the way the image is stretched, I estimate that Kathleen got the tattoo when she was thinner.

"And if she already was dead when she was positioned on her bed," I add, as I continue to think about Shania Plames, "the question is, dead from what?"

"Dead from what and with no indication of foul play or anything out of the ordinary." Colin pushes up the mask loose around his neck, covering his nose and mouth. "Something that doesn't show up on autopsy or on a tox screen."

"There are countless poisons that don't show up on a standard drug screen," I contemplate, as we hold the body on its side, checking the back. "Something fairly fast-acting, causing symptoms that remain largely unreported because either witnesses aren't reliable or the victim is isolated and out of sight or all of the above." I measure another tattoo, this one a unicorn. "And most important, something not survivable. The person doesn't live to tell. There are no failed attempts that anybody ever reports."

"None that we know of, at any rate," he says. "But we wouldn't know. If someone gets extremely ill in prison and survives, we're not going to find that out. We don't get near-deaths reported to us."

He presses his fingers against an arm, a lower leg, and makes a note of moderate blanching. He opens the eyelids and with a plastic ruler measures the pupils.

"Dilated equally, six millimeters," he says. "Theoretically, with opiates you can see constricted pupils postmortem. I never have. Other drugs cause dilation, but dead pupils are dilated anyway." He makes swift incisions with the scalpel from clavicle to clavicle and down the length of the body. "We'll PERK her. Work her up for sexual assault. Work her up for every damn thing we can possibly think of." He begins reflecting back tissue, guiding the scalpel with his right index finger and manipulating with his thumb as he holds forceps in his left hand.

"Which cabinet?" I ask, and he points a bloody gloved finger.

I find the Physical Evidence Recovery Kits and examine the body for sexual assault, swabbing every orifice and photographing, labeling each evidence bag.

"I'm going to swab the inside of her nose and mouth for toxicology while I'm at it," I let Colin know. "And submit hair."

He removes the breastplate of ribs and drops it in a plastic bucket by his feet as the morgue assistant, George, walks in with films. He attaches them to light boxes, and I walk over to have a look.

"An old fracture of her right tibia. Nothing recent. Typical arthritic changes." I move from one light box to the next, scanning bright white bones and the shadowy shapes of organs. "She does have a fair amount of food in her stomach. I wouldn't expect that if she ate at five-forty this morning and died at around noon, or some six hours later. Delayed gastric emptying." I return to the autopsy table and pick up a scalpel. "Something that's causing the digestion basically to quit. Barrie Lou Rivers's last meal was undigested. What about the other two?" I refer to Shania Plames and Rea Abernathy.

"I vaguely recall. And yes. Undigested food. Certainly in Barrie Lou Rivers's case, and I figured it was stress," Colin says. "I've seen it before in executions. The inmate eats his last meal and it's mostly undigested because of anxiety, of panic. Although go figure how any of them eat. If I was about to be executed, I don't think I would. Just give me a bottle of bourbon and a box of Cuban cigars."

I cut a slit in the stomach and empty its contents into a carton. "Well, she certainly didn't have what we were told was delivered to her cell early this morning."

"No eggs and grits?" Colin glances at what I'm looking at as he uses both hands to lift the liver out of the electronic scale's stainless-steel bowl. He picks up a long-handled, wide-bladed autopsy knife.

"Two hundred and eighty MLs, with pieces of what looks like chicken, pasta, something orange."

"Orange as in the fruit? Supposedly an orange was on the breakfast tray." He cuts sections of liver as if he's slicing bread.

"Not that kind of orange," I answer. "I'm not seeing evidence of fruit. Orange as in the color orange. Cheeselike, and the same color as the orange material I found under her thumbnail and on her trousers. Where might she have gotten chicken, pasta, and cheese this morning?"

"Moderate fatty changes in the liver but not bad, considering. But about one out of three livers are normal in alcoholics," he says, starting on the lungs. "You know what makes you an alcoholic. You drink more than your doctor. So they lied about what she ate this morning. Chicken and pasta? I got no idea." He grabs a lung out of the scale and wipes his bloody hands on a towel. "If they somehow killed her, wouldn't you think they'd be smart enough to know she's going to end up here and we can tell what she ate?" He jots down weights on the clipboard.

"Not everyone is that astute, especially if she really did eat between five-thirty and six this morning, when breakfast apparently is served in Bravo Pod." I label a carton for toxicology. "The assumption might have been that her food would be digested by the time she died. Under normal circumstances, it would have been."

"She's got some congestion, mild edema." He slices sections of a lung. "Engorgement of alveolar capillaries, pink foamy fluid in the alveolar spaces. Typical of acute respiratory failure."

"And typical in heart failure. Hers is surprisingly good." I begin cutting sections of her heart on the large cutting board. "Looks a little pale. No scarring. Vasculature widely patent. Valves, chordae tendineae, papillary muscles are without note," I dictate as I dissect. "Ventricular wall thicknesses, chamber diameters are appropriate. Exiting great vessels widely patent. No lesions in the myocardium."

"I sure wouldn't have guessed that." Colin wipes his hands again and writes it down. "Nothing to make us think an MI, then. All roads keep leading to toxicology."

"Not seeing anything at all to indicate an MI. You can check for histologic evidence, the theory that cardiac myocytes divide after myocardial infarction. But generally if I don't see anatomic evidence, I'm skeptical. And I'm seeing no evidence. Aorta has minimal atherosclerosis." I look up as the doors to the autopsy room swing open. "Nothing whatsoever to indicate she died from anything cardiac-related, in my opinion." I hear familiar voices as George walks back in.

I recognize Benton's calm, mellow baritone, and my mood is lifted by the sight of him in creased khaki pants and a green polo shirt, lean and handsome. His silver hair is slicked back, probably from sweating in a van with no air-conditioning, and it doesn't matter that we are in a stark autopsy room that smells like death or that my white gown and gloves are bloody and Kathleen Lawler is opened up, her sectioned organs in a bucket on the floor beneath the table.

I'm happy to see Benton, but our being in a morgue in the middle of an autopsy isn't why I don't want him close, and then Lucy appears, slender and foreboding in a black flight suit, her auburn hair loose around her shoulders and streaked rose gold in the overhead lights. Both of them stay where they are, on the other side of the room.

"You need to stay over there," I tell them anyway, and I sense from Benton's demeanor that something is wrong. "We don't know what she's been exposed to, but a tox death is first on our list. Where's Marino?"

"He didn't want to come in. Probably for the same reason you don't want us getting close," Benton says, and something absolutely is wrong.

I can see it on his face, in the tense way he is standing and the imperviousness of his face. His eyes are locked on mine, and he looks quietly agitated, the way he gets when he is intensely worried.

"Dawn Kincaid's in a coma," he then says.

An alarm begins to sound at the back of my thoughts.

"I got the latest update when we landed, and they're saying that she's brain-dead but they're not entirely sure." He projects his voice so Colin and I can hear him. "You know how that is. They're never really sure even when they are. Whatever's the cause, it's very suspicious," he adds, and I envision Jaime Berger's face last night right before I left her apartment.

She looked sleepy, and her pupils were dilated.

"But all indications are that the oxygen was cut off from her brain for too long," Benton says, as I hear Jaime's speech before I left her around one a.m., talking thickly and slurring her words. "By the time they got to her in her cell, she'd stopped breathing, and while they've kept her alive, she's gone."

I remember the take-out bag I carried into the apartment and where it came from, handed to me by a stranger, and I accepted it without thinking.

I start to say, "I thought she was fine. Just an asthma attack—"

"Limited information at the time, and this is being kept extremely hushed," Benton interrupts. "The initial thought was an asthma attack, but very quickly her symptoms became severe, and attending staff at Butler tried a single dose of epinephrine, assuming anaphylaxis, but there was no improvement. She couldn't talk or breathe. There's a concern she was poisoned somehow."

I envision the woman wearing the lighted helmet leaning her bicycle against the lamppost.

"No one can begin to imagine how she could have gotten hold of anything poisonous at Butler," Benton is saying from the other side of the room.

A delivery woman handing me the bag of sushi, and I vaguely recall something felt wrong but I ignored the feeling because so much felt wrong yesterday. Everything that happened from the time Benton drove me to the airport in Boston yesterday, the entire day felt wrong, and then the rest of it plays out in my memory. Jaime walking into her apartment after Marino and I had been talking for the better part of an hour. She didn't seem aware she had ordered sushi, and I didn't question it.

I put down the scalpel. "Has anybody talked to Jaime today? Because I haven't, and she's not called here."

Nobody answers.

"She was supposed to stop by the lab today. I left her a message, and she's not called back." I pull off my hair cover and the disposable gown. "What about Marino? Does anybody know if he's talked to her? He was going to call her."

"He tried while he was driving us here and didn't get an answer," Lucy says, and the look on her face indicates she realizes why I'm asking.

I throw my soiled clothing into the trash and peel off my gloves.

"Call nine-one-one, and maybe you can get hold of Sammy Chang, and he can meet us," I tell Colin. "Make sure they send an ambulance." I give him the address.

25

Two police cruisers and Sammy Chang's white SUV are parked in front of the eight-story brick building, but there are no emergency lights or flashers, no sign of tragedy or disaster. I don't hear sirens nearby or in the distance, just the sound of the cargo van's big engine and its new windshield wipers thudding. It is stuffy and stifling with the windows up, the blower circulating hot, humid air, the rain so heavy it sounds like a car wash. Thunder rumbles and cracks, the old city shrouded in fog.

Chang and two Savannah-Chatham Metropolitan officers are huddled out of the weather under the overhang at the top of the steps by the same front door that buzzed open for me as a delivery woman on a bicycle appeared seemingly out of nowhere like a phantom last night. Lucy, Benton, Marino, and I emerge from the van into the rain and wind, and I look around again for an ambulance, not seeing or hearing one, and I'm not happy, because I asked. As a precaution I want a rescue squad. To save time if there is time left and anything to save. Rain splashes on the steamy brick walkway, the sound of the downpour loud like clapping hands.

"Police. Anybody home? Police!" an officer announces, as he holds the intercom button. "Yeah, she's not answering." He steps back and looks around as rain falls harder. "We need to figure out another way. Every damn day now." He looks up at the moiling dark sky and billowing curtains of water. "As usual, left my slicker in the car."

"It won't last long. Will be over by the time we come back out," the other officer says.

"Well, I hope we don't get hail. I've already had one car messed up that way. Looked like someone went after it with a high-heel shoe."

"What's a New York prosecutor doing down here anyway? She on vacation? A lot of permanent residents in this building, but they leave in the summer, some of them renting their places by the week. She here short-term or what?"

"Did anybody call for an ambulance?" I ask loudly, as wind rocks giant live oak trees and Spanish moss whips like gray swags, like frayed dirty rags. "It would be a good idea to have an ambulance here," I add, as the two officers and Chang watch the four of us roll up on them with the urgency of the storm that is thundering closer, almost overhead, the hard rain sizzling on the walkway and the street and pouring off the gabled overhang.

"I'm wondering if there's a leasing office," one of the officers says. "They'll have a key."

"Not one in this building, I don't think."

"Most of these older places don't have one on site," Chang says.

"Or we can try some of the neighbors, maybe . . ."

Then Marino is pushing past everyone, almost shoving the uniformed officers out of the way, keys in hand.

"Whoa. Easy, partner. Who are you?"

I'm distractedly aware of Chang explaining who we are and why we're here as Marino unlocks the door, and I'm vaguely mindful of my sopping-wet black field clothes and boots. I comb back my dripping hair with my fingers as I hear *FBI* and *Boston* and *chief ME working with Dr. Dengate* while all of us head to the elevator, Lucy close behind me, her hand pressing against my back, pushing me and hanging on, and I feel what's in her touch. I feel the desperation in the pressure of her hand flat against my back, a gesture I've not felt in a very long time, what she used to do when she was a little girl, when she was being protective or was scared, when she didn't want to get separated from me in a crowd or for me to leave her.

I've told Lucy everything will be okay, because it will be somehow, but I don't believe it will be okay the way we hope, the way we wish, the way it should be in a perfect world. We don't know anything, I've reminded my niece, even though I have no hope. I just don't feel it. Jaime isn't answering her cell phone or apartment phone or e-mails or text messages. We haven't heard from her since Marino and I left her at around one o'clock this morning, but there could be a logical explanation, I've said to Lucy. While we have to take every action possible, that doesn't mean we are assuming the worst, I've reassured her repeatedly.

But I am assuming the worst. What I'm experiencing is painfully familiar, like a sad old friend, a grim companion who has been a depressing leitmotif on my life's journey, and my response is a feeling I know all too well, a sinking, a solidification, like concrete setting, like something settling heavily into a deep darkness, a bottomless lightless space, out of reach and over. It's what I sense right before I walk into a place where death quietly and finally waits for me to tend to it as only I can. I don't know what is going through Lucy's mind. Not this same feeling or premonition I'm having but something confusing and contradictory and volatile.

During the twenty-minute ride here she was logical and held together, but she is pale as if she is sick, and she looks both terrified and angry. I see the shadings and flares of her emotions in her intense green eyes, and I heard her internal chaos in a comment she made during the drive. She said that the last time she talked to Jaime was six months ago when Lucy accused her of getting into something for the wrong reason. *Getting into what?* I asked. *Getting into defending people and saving them by turning their lies into truth if that's what it takes, because that's what she's doing to herself. It's what she's comfortable with*, Lucy said. *It's as if Jaime managed to climb up a big mountain of truth only to fall over the other side of it*, Lucy said in the loud, hot van as the rain began, and her voice was double-edged with fear and rage. *I warned her because I could see it so plainly*, she said. *I told her exactly what she was doing, and she did it anyway.*

"You go ahead," Benton is saying to Marino.

She kept pushing it to the next dangerous level, Lucy said as we drove into the storm, her voice trembling slightly as if she was out of breath. *Why did she have to do this? Why!*

"She been having problems or something?" one of the cops asks Marino. "Personal problems, financial trouble, anything like that?"

"Nope."

"Bet she just went out somewhere, maybe sightseeing, and didn't tell anyone."

"That's not her," Lucy says. "No fucking way."

"And left her phone or the battery's dead. Know how many times that happens around here?"

"She doesn't fucking sightsee," Lucy says behind my back.

Marino wipes his wet face on his sleeve, his eyes darting around, the way he looks when he's extremely upset beneath his imperviousness, his rudeness. The elevator doors slide open, and all of us crowd inside except Benton and Lucy, as the police keep offering possibilities, trying to talk us out of our growing sense of urgency when they have no reason to talk us out of a damn thing.

"She's probably fine. I see it all the time. Someone visits from out of town, and if you don't hear from them? People get worried."

They are beat cops, and this is really nothing more than what's known on the street as a welfare check, maybe a more dramatic one than usual, with a bigger, more official posse showing up, but a welfare check nonetheless. The police do them daily, especially this time of year, when it's the height of tourist season, vacation time, and the schools are out. Someone calls 911 and insists the police check on the welfare of a friend, a family member who isn't answering the phone or hasn't been heard from for a while. In ninety-nine cases out of a hundred, it's nothing. In the one case when it's something, it isn't tragic. Rarely does it turn out that the person is dead.

"I'm going with you," Lucy says to me.

"I need to go in first."

"I have to go with you."

"Not now."

"I have to," Lucy insists, and Benton puts his arm around her, pulling her close to him in what's more than a comforting hug. He'll make sure she doesn't bolt for the stairs and try to force her way inside the apartment.

"I'll call as soon as I'm in," I promise Lucy in the narrowing space of the closing doors, and they shut completely and she is gone, and the ache inside my chest is indescribably awful.

The elevator of gleaming old wood and polished brass lurches as it lifts, and I explain to the police that no one has heard from Jaime Berger and she didn't come to

Savannah to sightsee. She's not here on vacation. It may be nothing, and I certainly hope it's nothing. But it's out of character for her, and she was expected to show up at some point at Dr. Dengate's office today, and she hasn't appeared and hasn't called. An ambulance should have been requested, and it would be a good idea to call for one now, and all the while I'm saying this I realize it's repetitive, it's perseverative, and the officers, both of them young, have their own theory about what is going on.

It's clear they assume that Marino lives with this out-of-town woman who's not answering her phone or contacting anyone. Why else would he have keys? Most likely this is a messy domestic situation that nobody wants to talk about. I reiterate that Jaime is a prominent prosecutor from New York, or actually a former one, and we have reasons to be worried about her safety.

"When did you see her last?" one of the officers asks Marino.

"Last night."

"And nothing was out of the ordinary?"

"Nope."

"Everybody getting along?"

"Yeah."

"You didn't have words?"

"Nope."

"Maybe a little disagreement?"

"Nope."

"Maybe a little fight?"

"Don't even start that shit with me."

"There are some unusual circumstances," Chang tells the officers, as the elevator bumps to a stop, and there is only so much Chang or any of us is going to explain.

We're not going to mention Kathleen Lawler or suggest that she may have been poisoned. I have no intention of volunteering information about Lola Daggette or the Mensa Murders, and I'm not going to share that Dawn Kincaid, who was locked up in a state hospital for the criminally insane, is brain-dead and perhaps was poisoned. I'm not going to comment right now that a woman on a bicycle showed up last night with sushi Jaime probably didn't order. I don't want to talk or explain or speculate or imagine. I'm frantic, and at the same time already know what awaits us, or fear I do, and we are out of the elevator, rushing down the hallway, to the end of it, where Marino unlocks the heavy oak door.

"Jaime?" his big voice booms as we enter the apartment, and I notice instantly that her burglar alarm isn't set. "Fuck!" Marino glances at the keypad by the door, noticing the same ominous detail, his tanned face flushed and slick with sweat, his CFC khakis a grayish tan from the rain. "She always sets it. Even when she's here. Hello! Jaime, you home? Shit."

The kitchen looks exactly as it did when I left last night, except for a bottle of antacid on the counter that I know wasn't there when I washed dishes and put food away, and her big brown handbag isn't on the back of the chair where I saw her hang it by its shoulder strap when she came in with the take-out food from the Broughton and Bull. Her bag is on the leather couch in the sitting area, its contents scattered over the coffee table, but we don't stop to see what might be missing or what she might have been digging for. Chang and I follow Marino's long stride down the hardwood hallway that leads to the master area in back.

Through the open doorway I see a sleigh bed and rumpled green and brown covers, and Jaime in a maroon bathrobe that is untied and disarrayed. She is face-down, with her hips twisted to one side, her arms and head hanging off the bed, her position inconsistent with someone who died in her sleep and similar to Kathleen Lawler's, as if their last moment was a struggle, an agonizing one. The bedside lamps are on, and the drapes are drawn.

"Shit," Marino says. "Jesus," he mutters, as I go to her and detect the odor of burnt fruit and peat. What smells like Scotch is spilled on the bedside table, and there is an overturned tumbler, and near it the empty base unit for a cordless phone.

I touch the side of her neck to check for a pulse. But she is cold, and rigor is well advanced, and I look up at Chang, then at one of the uniformed officers stepping inside the room.

"I'll be right back," Chang says to me. "Need to get some things out of the car," he adds, as he leaves.

The officer stares at the body draped over the right side of the bed. He moves closer as he slips his portable radio off his belt.

"You need to keep back and don't touch anything," Marino snaps at him, his eyes blazing.

"Hey, take it easy."

"You don't know shit," Marino erupts. "There's no fucking reason for you to be in here. You don't know shit, so get the hell out."

"Sir, you need to calm down."

"Sir? What? I'm a fucking knight? Don't call me 'sir.'"

"Take it easy," I say to Marino. "Please."

"Goddamn. I can't believe this. Jesus Christ. What the hell happened?"

"The more we can limit exposure, the better," I say to the officer. "We really don't know what we're dealing with here," I add, and he backs up several steps, staying by the doorway as Marino stares at the body and then looks away, his face deep red.

"You mean it could be something we could get, like something contagious?" the officer asks.

"I don't know, but it's best you don't get close or touch anything." I scan every visible part of her, seeing nothing that tells me anything, and the absence of anything tells me something. "Lucy and Benton shouldn't come in here," I tell Marino. "Lucy doesn't need to be exposed to this. She doesn't need to see this."

"Jesus. Shit!"

"Can you go out there and make sure she doesn't try to come in? Make sure the apartment door is shut and locked."

"Jesus. What the hell could have happened?" His voice shakes, and his eyes are bright and bloodshot.

"Please make sure the door is locked," I instruct Marino. "Make sure your partner stays out there so no one comes in who's not supposed to come in," I say to the officer, who has short red hair and deep blue eyes. "We can't do anything else, and we shouldn't touch anything. We have a suspicious death, and we need to treat this as a crime scene. I'm worried about poisoning, and we need to stop right now before anything is disturbed. I'd prefer you're not in here, because we don't know what we're dealing with," I repeat. "But I need you to stay right there. I need you to stay with me," I say to the officer, as Marino walks out, his footsteps loud on hardwood.

"What makes you think it's a crime scene?" The officer with red hair is looking around, but he doesn't move away from the doorway. He has no interest in getting near the body after what I just said. He has no interest in being inside this room. "Except for her purse out there. But if she let someone in who ended up robbing her, it must have been someone she knew, or how could he get in the door downstairs?"

"We don't know that anyone was in here."

"So something could be poisonous inside this apartment."

"Yes."

"Or maybe an overdose and she was digging in her purse for pills." The officer doesn't budge from his position in the doorway. "Maybe I should check her bathroom." He looks at a door that is ajar to the left of the bed, but he doesn't move an inch.

"It's best you don't, and I need you to stay with me." I enter Benton's number on my phone.

"I was on a scene last year. Woman OD'd on oxys, and it looked a lot like this. Nothing really out of place except for where she was digging around for drugs in drawers, in her purse. She was dead on the bed, kind of on top of the covers, sort of lying across the bed instead of in it. A real pretty girl trying to be a dancer who got hooked on oxys."

I press *call* as I stare at the master bath, but I don't go near it. Light seeps through the partially open doorway. The bedside lamps are on, and the light is on inside the bathroom. Jaime never went to bed last night, or if she did, she got up again at some point.

"They said accident, but my personal opinion was suicide. Boyfriend had just broke up with her, you know. She had a lot of problems," the officer is saying, and he may as well be talking to himself.

"Lucy can't come in here," I tell Benton the instant he answers, and he knows what that means and is silent. "I don't know what to suggest," I add, because I don't know what he should say to Lucy right now.

She's going to know the truth if she doesn't already. There is one question with only two possible answers. Jaime is dead inside this apartment or she's not, and Lucy already knows. Right this very minute it's occurring to her as Benton listens to what I'm telling him on the phone, as I describe what I'm seeing, and he's not doing anything to dispel what Lucy fears. A look, a smile, a gesture, or a word that would make it all go away, but he gives her nothing, and I imagine him staring straight ahead as he listens to me. Lucy realizes the worst, and I have no idea what to do about it, but I can't go out and deal with her at the moment. I have to deal with what's happened in here. I have to deal with Jaime. I have to deal with what might happen next.

I look at her body on the bed, her open robe tangled around her hips. She is nude underneath it, and I can't stand the idea of the redheaded officer in the doorway, of anybody else seeing her this way. But I can't touch her. I can't touch anything, and I stand near a window. I don't wander around or get any closer.

"Please stay with Lucy, and I'll get back to you as soon as I can," I'm saying to Benton over the phone. "If you can find a way to get her to the hotel, and I'll meet you there, that might be the best plan. It's not good for her to hang around, and you really can't do anything." I don't care that he's FBI. I don't care what he is or what powers he has. "Not here, not right now. Please just take care of her."

"Of course."

"I'll meet you back at the hotel."

"Okay."

I tell him that the room arrangements need to be changed. I want a suite with a kitchenette, if possible. I want rooms that can be connected, because I have a strong feeling about what will happen. I'm quite sure I know what we're going to need to do, and most of all, we need to be together.

"I'll handle it," Benton promises.

"All of us together," I say it again. "It's not negotiable. Maybe you can get a rental car or a Bureau car. We need a car. We can't just ride around in Marino's van. I don't know how long we're going to be here."

"I'm not sure about him." Benton is quiet and gives nothing away in his tone.

Without saying it, he is communicating that if Jaime has been murdered, Marino could have a problem with the police. They might consider him a suspect. He has keys to her building and her apartment. He probably knows her alarm code. He was closely associated with her, and the police already have asked if the two of them might have been arguing or fighting last night. In other words, the assumption is they were lovers.

"I'm not sure exactly what's happened, obviously," I say to Benton. "I know what I suspect, and I suspect it strongly, and will deal with it accordingly as best I can. As much as can be allowed."

I'm implying that I believe Jaime was murdered.

"But I'm not sure about him or either of us." I'm saying I've got a similar complication.

Marino won't be the only suspect. I carried in the take-out sushi last night. I might have delivered death to Jaime in a white paper bag.

"I'm here," I add. "I'll do whatever I can to help."

"Okay" is all Benton says, because Lucy is with him and he can't say much.

I end the call, alone in the bedroom with Jaime's dead body and a Savannah-Chatham officer whose nameplate reads *T. J. Harley*. He has remained in the doorway, looking at the body, looking around, having no informed idea what he needs to be looking for or if he should stay with me as I've requested or join his partner or call for a supervisor or a detective from the homicide unit. I can see myriad thoughts in his eyes.

"What's making you think it's suspicious besides her purse having been gone through?" he asks.

"We don't know that someone else did that," I reply. "She might have gone through it herself."

"For what besides pills?"

"We don't know that she's an overdose."

"She make it a habit to carry a lot of cash in her wallet?"

"I have no idea what's in her wallet or how much cash she carries routinely," I reply.

"If she does, that could be a motive."

"We don't know that anything's been stolen."

"Possible she was strangled or smothered?"

"No ligature mark or petechial hemorrhages," I answer. "Nothing to make me think that from what I'm seeing. But she needs to be carefully examined. She needs an autopsy. Right this moment, we don't know why she's dead."

"What do you know about her relationship with her friend?" He means Marino.

"He used to work for her when he was with NYPD and has been helping her very recently as a consultant. Understandably, he's upset."

"NYPD?"

"Investigations. He was assigned to the sex crimes unit, to her."

"So maybe something was going on with them," he decides.

"Maybe our first priority should be to find out if she placed an order for sushi last night," I reply. "Instead of assuming the obvious. That maybe it's someone close to her who maybe had something going on and maybe did something terrible."

"It usually is, though."

"Usually? I'd say often but not always or usually."

"Really, though." He's sure of himself. "You look in the backyard first."

"You look where the evidence takes you," I reply.

"You're joking about sushi, right?"

"No."

"Oh, I thought you were implying raw fish did it. Me? I won't touch the stuff. Especially now. Oil spills, radioactive water. I may quit eating fish. Even cooked."

"There will be take-out containers, a bag, a receipt in the trash. Leftovers in the refrigerator," I inform him. "Please make sure that neither you nor your partner touches anything. I advise you to stay out of the kitchen and let Investigator Chang handle it or Dr. Dengate. Or whoever they direct."

"Yeah, Sammy's the investigator, not me, and no way I'm messing with his scene. Not that I couldn't. I might put in for it one of these days because I think I'm a good fit. You know, attention to detail, that's the most important part, and I'm anal about detail. I've worked with him before, the OD I was just telling you about." Officer

Harley gets on his radio and transmits, "Could be an exposure. Don't touch anything in the kitchen or trash or anywhere."

"A what?" his partner's voice replies inside the bedroom.

"Just don't touch anything. Nothing at all."

"Ten-four."

I decide not to say anything else about sushi or my suspicions. I'm not going to describe my time with Jaime last night. I'll save it for Chang, for Colin, for whomever. I know Marino and I will have to give statements independently, possibly to a detective from Savannah's homicide unit, but not to Officer T. J. Harley, who is nice enough but naïve and much too invested in playing detective. Chang will make sure that Marino and I are questioned by the appropriate party, depending on who takes jurisdiction, and likely it will be a joint investigation. The GBI and the local police will work this together, and the FBI will be next. If Jaime's death is connected to what's happened in Massachusetts—specifically, the alleged poisoning of Dawn Kincaid—then the cases have crossed state lines and the FBI will become involved in what's going on in Savannah and possibly take charge just as it has up north.

I nudge aside the drawn drapery, looking down at the street in front, where Chang is getting his crime scene equipment out of his SUV. Rain pelts the building's roof as if small pebbles are hitting it, and lightning shimmers over the low skyline of homes and historic buildings and trees. Thunder sounds like a distant kettledrum or the artillery fire of a faraway war, cracking and splitting the air, and I know what I would do if Cambridge weren't a thousand miles from here.

I would direct that the truck, our mobile containment autopsy facility, be driven to Savannah right now. But the distance makes such a plan impractical if not impossible, because Colin Dengate isn't going to wait two days to do the autopsy, and he shouldn't. We don't want to wait. We mustn't wait. We need serum. We need tissue specimens. We need gastric contents. Of course, there is the Centers for Disease Control and Prevention, the CDC, in nearby Atlanta, but Colin probably won't wait for their truck, either, and we've been exposed and are okay. A number of people have been exposed and seem to be fine. I was inside Kathleen Lawler's prison cell. I touched her and breathed the air and smelled what was in her sink, and I've been exposed to her blood and gastric contents, to her inside and out. I don't feel sick. Marino, Colin, and Chang don't, either. There are no warning signs at all that we might be at risk.

Whatever killed Kathleen or Jaime or poisoned Dawn Kincaid, assuming it is all the same toxin, works relatively swiftly. It shuts down digestion and interferes with breathing. Something that paralyzes, I consider. In food or drink. And I remember the way Jaime looked before I left her around one o'clock this morning. Her eyelids were heavy. She was slurring her words and having difficulty speaking. Her pupils were dilated. I assumed she was intoxicated and drowsy, but the antacid on the kitchen counter suggests her stomach was bothering her, and that's the same complaint Kathleen had, if the woman in the cell across from her was telling the truth.

"You know they work all our crime scenes now since they've been getting training at that forensic academy in Knoxville where the Body Farm is . . ." Officer Harley says.

He is talking and I'm barely listening as I continue to look out at the stormy late afternoon, at trees thrashing in the wind, at headlights shining down Abercorn Street. Then the Land Rover comes into view.

"Every GBI investigator's been trained there, every single one, meaning we got the best-trained crime scene people probably in the entire United States," Officer Harley boasts, as if he has no feelings about the body on the bed, as if there is nothing extraordinarily monstrous about what has occurred.

Officer T. J. Harley didn't know Jaime Berger. He has no idea who she is or who any of us are or what we are to one another, and I feel something change in me as Colin parks and extinguishes the headlights. I feel a flat calm, a detachment, the way I get when something is too much and yet I must function and in fact function at the highest level. I know what I'm in for, only a fool wouldn't know that, and I slide my hands into the pockets of my cargo pants as I envision Jaime's silhouette passing behind the drawn drapes in this room late last night.

Marino and I were sitting in his van on the street below, and her shadow moved back and forth as if she were restlessly pacing. Then she got undressed. The clothes she was wearing when we were with her are on a chair by the dresser as if she dropped or tossed them, the way one does when drunk, upset, in a hurry, not feeling well. She put on the maroon robe she eventually would die in and was looking down at us from a window in the living room as we drove off, and I didn't know. I had no clue what had been done and the role I likely played in it.

26

I turn away from the window, and Jaime Berger's stiff unnatural position remains the same, draped over the side of the bed like a Dalí painting.

Her biological existence has ended, and flesh and blood have begun breaking down like a set being struck after a drama has been played out and is over. She is gone. Nothing can undo it. Now the rest of it must be dealt with, and that is what I know how to manage, and I'm strongly motivated to help. But there are serious complications.

"I'm not going to touch anything or do anything else unless appropriately instructed," I tell Officer Harley. "Dr. Dengate just pulled up, but I need you to stay right where you are. Or if I walk into any other area of the apartment, you need to be with me," I remind him again.

"I must be accompanied by you or Investigator Chang, and I need one of you able to swear to that."

"Yes, ma'am." He stares at me as if he's not quite sure what I might do that requires watching or swearing to.

"I was in here last night. Not in this room. But in this apartment, and it's likely I'm the last person to see her alive."

"That's the thing about this kind of work." He leans against the doorframe, his duty belt making scraping sounds against wood. "You never know who or what you're going to encounter. I've rolled up on scenes before and it turned out I knew the victim. Not that long ago, a guy killed on his motorcycle was someone I went to high school with. That was kind of weird."

My impulse is to move her body, to cover her, to reposition her so she isn't bent like a hairpin, her arms and head hanging over the edge of the bed. Her face and neck are suffused a deep purplish-red from blood settling due to gravity after her circulation quit, and her lips are parted, her upper teeth bared, one eye closed, the other open to a slit. Death has made a mockery of Jaime Berger's perfect beauty, contorting and distorting her obscenely and grotesquely, and I don't want Lucy to see her, not even a photograph, and I notice the overturned glass again and the empty phone charger. I get down on the floor to look and discover the handset several inches under the bed, as if Jaime might have been groping for it and knocked it off the table. I don't pick it up. I don't touch anything.

"I was in the living room and kitchen from around

nine o'clock last night until close to one a.m.," I inform Officer Harley. "I was in the guest bathroom once not long before I left. I handled a number of things while I was here. Paperwork. Items in the kitchen. I'll make sure Investigator Chang is aware."

"So you came down from Boston to meet up with her."

"No. I came to Savannah for another reason. She asked to see me while I was here." I'm not going to explain any more than that, not to a uniformed officer, a first responder who won't be investigating this case. "We have a long, rather complex history that I'll be happy to go over in detail with whoever I need to talk to when we get to that point. In the meantime, if you'll just stay nearby so I have a witness to what I do or don't do in here."

"Sure. Or you can wait outside if you'd rather . . . ?"

"I'm already inside this apartment, and I intend to help if I can," I say firmly.

Under ordinary circumstances I would have left already, but I refuse to consider what some in my profession might deem an act of self-preservation. I ignore the part of me that is arguing I should get out of here now. I shouldn't compromise myself further. No medical examiner would want to be in the position I find myself in, but if I can help determine what happened to Jaime, I feel morally obliged; in fact, I must. This isn't just about her. I can't save her. I am worried about others.

Homicidal poisonings are rare and greatly feared because there isn't always an intended victim, and even when there is, it might not be that person who dies. Barrie Lou Rivers apparently didn't care who ate her arsenic-laced tuna-fish sandwiches. Whatever cruel and coldly calculated point she intended to make didn't necessarily involve a specific individual, and take-out food from her deli could have ended up with anyone. Poison doesn't leave fingerprints or DNA. It almost never has a size or shape like a bullet or a blade, and it rarely leaves a track that can be measured like a wound. I've worked only a handful of homicidal poisonings in my career, and they were frustrating and terrifying. Stopping the perpetrator was a race against time.

Chang is back, setting his crime scene case on the bedroom floor. He gives me gloves as if we are partners, and I pull on two pairs. I slip my hands into my pockets as more footsteps sound in the hallway.

"The phone's under the bed." I indicate where, and then Colin walks in, dressed in street clothes, a plaid shirt and light gray slacks, his dark blue GBI Windbreaker and glasses speckled by rain.

He carries the same hard case he had with him at the prison earlier today, and he sets it on the floor and says to me, "What we got?"

"No obvious injuries, but I haven't examined her, and I shouldn't. Looks like she might have fumbled for the phone, perhaps knocking over her glass," I answer. "Scotch, I think. She was drinking Scotch when I left her very early this morning. The phone's under the bed."

"She pour the Scotch herself?" Chang bends over and holds up the bedcovers with a gloved hand.

"Yes. And the wine."

"Just want to know whose prints or DNA might be on what."

"You guys don't need to be in here now," Colin says to Officer Harley. "Thanks for your help, but the fewer people in here, the better, okay? Don't be eating or drinking anything in here, needless to say, and be careful what you touch. We've had several victims possibly exposed to something, and we don't know what it is."

Officer Harley says, "So you don't think it's drugs? I didn't notice pill bottles or anything, but I didn't open up any cabinets or drawers. I haven't looked around because I've been in here with her the whole time." He's letting them know he's kept an eye on me. "I can check out the bathroom, for example. I could check out the medicine cabinet, if you want."

"Like I said, I don't know what it is," Colin answers. "Could be drugs. Could be something else. Could be a damn ice bullet."

"There's not . . . ?"

"We really don't know what we're checking for." Colin scans the room. "And the fewer people, the better."

"There's really no such thing as an ice bullet. . . ."

"Not in this heat," Colin says.

"We can handle it from here," Chang tells the officer, "but it would be really good if one or both of you stay outside, keep the perimeter secure. We don't want anyone walking in. Hard to know who else might have keys, for example."

"When Marino and I had dinner with her last night, there was a sushi delivery," I begin to tell Colin and Chang, as I stay near the window, out of the way of photographs, out of the way of Colin opening his sturdy plastic scene case as he prepares to examine the body in situ. "It would be a very good idea to check with Savannah Sushi Fusion. If you're uncomfortable with my being here . . . ?" I will leave if that's what they want, regardless of my preference. "The reason is pretty glaring. I was with Kathleen Lawler late yesterday afternoon, and this morning she's dead. I was with Jaime last night, until about one a.m., and now she's dead."

"Well, unless you're going to confess to something," Colin says, as he pulls on gloves, "it's not crossing my mind you're the reason people are dead, and I'm just happy as hell that you're okay. And that Sammy, Marino, and I are. Normally I'd suggest since you know her and were with her last night, it's not a good idea for you to be present. But you're here. You might have helpful observations. It's up to you if you'd be more comfortable leaving."

"My biggest concern is another victim," I reply. "Especially if we're dealing with poisonings, and I think you know that's what I'm worried about."

"You and me both."

"You might be the only one who can say if anything looks out of place," Chang says to me. "So it would be helpful if you look around with me." His camera flashes and the shutter clicks as he photographs the handset under the bed.

The help he wants from me is something else entirely, and I know what he's doing. I recognize his approach and that it is the correct one. Sammy Chang has earned my respect as the day has worn on, and I don't underestimate him or what he is considering, and I don't blame him. In fact, I expect it. He's a shrewd investigator, bright and observant and highly trained, and his job is to be objective and relentless, and no matter what he's come to think of me, he would be foolish not to get every scrap of information he possibly can. He would be negligent if he didn't observe me carefully, and he has no choice but to eye me with suspicion even if there is no hint of it in his professional interactions with me.

"So far I'm not noticing any indication that someone other than Jaime has been in here since Marino and I were with her," I start with that.

"Anything going on between the two of them?" Chang asks.

"Beyond work? Not that I know of, and it would be hard for me to imagine. He took two weeks off from the CFC to come down here and help her with the Jordan case. As I understand it, he's been working with her in this apartment."

"What about at an earlier time? They ever have more than a professional relationship?"

"I can't imagine it," I repeat, as Colin sets a digital thermometer on the bedside table.

He manipulates the body's stiff right arm until he can bend it and tucks a second thermometer into the armpit.

"Why would it be hard for you to imagine it?" Chang asks, and the questioning has begun.

I could put a stop to it. I could say I'm not going to have this conversation without my lawyer, Leonard Brazzo, present. But I won't.

"There's never been any indication that Jaime and Marino have ever had anything but a professional relationship," I tell Chang. "And I certainly can't imagine him having any motivation whatsoever to harm her."

"Yes, but you know him. It's hard to be objective when we know people. It would be hard for you to think anything bad about him." Chang is on my side. The game of good cop/bad cop, as old as time.

"If there were a reason to think something bad about him, I would be honest about it," I answer.

"But you don't know what went on between the two of them in private." He is looking at the handset he collected from under the bed, holding it in two gloved fingertips, touching as little of its surfaces as possible. "This probably is going to be a waste of time," he considers. "Since she's probably the only one who touched it. But to be on the safe side, maybe I should take it in. Do you agree? What would you do?" He looks at me.

"If it were me, I'd want it checked for prints and DNA. I'd retain additional swabs for chemical analysis if that becomes a question."

"Someone might have poisoned her telephone?" he says, with a straight face.

"You asked what I would do. An exposure to chemical

and biological poisons can be transdermal, through the mucous membrane, through the skin. Although I doubt that's what we're dealing with or I would expect there to be more victims. Including us."

"No chance you used the phone back here at any point." His gloved finger presses the menu button.

"I wasn't in this area of the apartment at any point last night."

"A nine-one-seven number at one-thirty-two this morning." Chang checks the last number Jaime dialed on the handset.

"New York," I reply, and I'm aware of the burnt-fruit odor of the Scotch again, and it triggers a jolt of emotion.

"Looks like that's the last call she made, on this phone anyway," and he recites the rest of the number out loud as he jots it on a notepad.

The number is familiar, and it takes a moment for me to realize why.

"Lucy. My niece. That used to be her cell phone number when she lived in New York," I explain, not showing what I'm feeling. "When she moved to Boston she changed it eventually. Early this year, maybe in January. I'm not sure, but that number isn't hers anymore."

Jaime must not have known Lucy had a new number. When she told Lucy she didn't want any contact with her ever again, apparently she meant it. Until very early this morning.

"Any idea why she might have tried to call Lucy at one-thirty-two in the morning?"

"Jaime and I were talking about her," I reply. "We were talking about their relationship and why it ended. Perhaps she got sentimental. I don't know."

"What kind of relationship?"

"They were together for several years."

"What kind of together?"

"Partners. A couple."

Chang places the handset inside an evidence bag. "You left her at what time last night?"

"I left her this morning at about one."

"So maybe a half hour later she calls Lucy's old number and then fumbles with the phone when she's hanging it up. It ends up under the bed."

"I don't know."

"Indicating something might have been really wrong by that point. Or she was really drunk."

"I don't know," I repeat.

"You told me the last time you'd been in here prior to last night was when?"

"I told you I've never been in this apartment prior to last night," I remind him.

"And you'd never been here before. You'd never been inside this room, the bedroom, prior to now. You didn't come in here last night or really early in the morning before you left, maybe to use the bathroom, the phone."

"No."

"What about Marino?" Chang is squatting near the bed, looking up at me as if to give me a false sense of dominance.

"I'm not aware of him coming back here at any point

last night," I answer. "But I wasn't with him the entire time. He was already here when I arrived."

"Interesting he has keys." Chang stands up and begins to label the evidence bag.

"Possibly because both of them were using this place as an office. But you'd have to ask him about the keys." I expect that at any minute he is going to escort me out and read me my rights.

"It strikes me as a little unusual. Would you give him keys if you had a place?" he asks.

"If there was a need, I'd trust him with keys. I understand my opinions don't matter, so I'll stick with the facts," I then say, responding to his suggestion that I can't be objective about Marino. "The facts are that except for the sushi, Jaime brought in the food. She served food and drinks to us in the living room. Afterward, and I'm estimating this would have been close to ten-thirty, maybe quarter of eleven, Marino left us alone for a while. He returned to pick me up in front of the building at approximately one a.m., at which time Jaime seemed fine except intoxicated. She'd had wine and Scotch and was slurring her words. In retrospect, she might have begun having symptoms related to something besides alcohol. Dilated pupils. Increased difficulty in speaking. Her eyelids were drooping slightly. This was about two and a half, maybe three hours, after eating the sushi."

"Dilated pupils wouldn't be opioids but could be a lot of other drugs." Colin presses his gloved fingers into an arm, a leg, making a note of blanching. "Amphetamines, cocaine, sedatives. And alcohol, of course. Did you happen to notice if she might have taken anything while you were with her?"

"I didn't see her take anything or have a reason to think she might have. She was drinking while I was here. Several glasses of wine and several Scotches."

"What happened after you left? What did you do? Where did you go?" Chang asks.

I don't have to answer. I should tell him I'll be happy to cooperate under certain conditions, such as with my lawyer present, but that's not who I am. I have nothing to hide. I know Marino did nothing wrong. All of us are on the same side. I explain that we spent some time driving in the area where the Jordans lived, discussing that case, and returned to the hotel around two a.m.

"You see him go into his room?"

"He'd forgotten something in his van and went back out to get it. I went on up to my room alone."

"Well, that's a little bit curious. That he walked you in and then returned to his van."

"There was a valet on duty who should be able to say whether Marino did what he said he was going to do and got groceries out of the backseat, or whether he drove off again," I reply pointedly. "And the van was having serious mechanical problems that made Marino take it to a body shop this morning."

"He could have gone on foot. The hotel's maybe a twenty-minute walk from here."

"You'll have to ask him."

"Ambient temp's seventy-one degrees. Body temp is seventy-three degrees," Colin says, as he moves Jaime Berger's body off the side of the bed.

Her arms and head are unwilling, and he has to apply pressure to coax them, and it is difficult to watch. I've broken rigor thousands of times, countless times, really, and don't give it a thought when I'm forcing the dead to give up their stubborn and unreasonable positions. But I can scarcely bear to look. I think of the take-out bag I offered to carry upstairs and feel guilt. I feel to blame. *Why didn't I question the person who materialized out of the shadows on the dark street last night? Why wasn't I concerned when Jaime indicated she hadn't ordered sushi?*

"Anything else in here you think I should be aware of?" Chang continues to ask me questions that have little to do with what he really wants to know.

"The turned-over glass. And I would swab what appears to be spilled Scotch on the table. But you might want to wait until we're dealing with the leftover food and what's in the trash. All of it needs to be handled the same way. Anything she might have eaten or drunk."

I keep my hands in my pockets as we begin to walk around. I tell Sammy Chang the same thing I told him earlier at the prison. I will look and explore as long as he approves, and I will touch nothing without his permission. We start with the master bath.

27

The mirrored medicine cabinets are open wide, their contents strewn over shelves and the granite countertop, in the sink, and all over the floor, as if a storm blew in or an intruder ransacked the master bathroom.

Scattered about are cuticle scissors, tweezers, nail files, eyedrops, toothpaste, dental floss, teeth-whitening strips, sunscreens, over-the-counter pain relievers, body scrubs, and facial cleansers. There are prescription medications, including zolpidem tartrate or Ambien, and anxiolytic lorazepam, better known as Ativan. Jaime wasn't sleeping well. She was anxious and vain and not at peace with aging, and nothing she had on hand to relieve her routine discomforts and discontentedness was going to defeat the enemy that confronted her the final hours and minutes of her life, a violent attacker that was sadistic and overpowering and impossible to see.

As I interpret her death through the symbols of her postmortem artifacts and her chaotic clutter, it is clear to me that at some point early this morning she suffered an onset of symptoms that caused her to search desperately for something, for anything, that might mitigate panic and physical distress so acute that it looks as if an intruder pillaged her apartment and murdered her somehow.

There was no intruder, only Jaime, and I imagine her dumping out the contents of her pocketbook, perhaps looking for a medication that might relieve her suffering. I imagine her rushing inside the master bath for a drug that might offer remedy, and sweeping and knocking items off the shelves, frantic and crazed by the torture of what had seized her. Only it wasn't another person killing her, not directly. I believe it was a poison, one so potent it transformed Jaime's body into her own worst enemy, and I wasn't here.

I hadn't stayed. I'd left earlier, so relieved to get away that I'd waited outside in the dark under a tree for Marino to pick me up, and I can't stop thinking that had I not been hurt and angry, I might have noticed the warnings. It might have occurred to me that something was wrong, that she wasn't merely drunk. I was defensive of Lucy, and she's always been my weakness, and now someone she loves, maybe the love of her life, is dead.

"If you don't mind." I indicate to Chang that I want to look and touch as he takes photographs.

Had I been here during Jaime's crisis, I could have saved her. There were signs and symptoms, and I ignored them, and I don't know how I will explain that to my niece.

"Sure, go ahead," he says. "Any reason for you to suspect she might have had something inside this apartment that someone else wanted to get hold of? I notice several computers and what looks like case records and other confidential documents in the living room. What about sensitive information on her computers?"

"I have no idea what's on her computers. Or even if they're her computers."

I could have gotten a squad here. I could have given her CPR, I could have breathed for her until paramedics took over with an Ambu bag as they rushed her to the ER. She should be in a hospital now, on a ventilator. She should be all right. What she shouldn't be is cold and stiff on her bed, and I will have to tell Lucy I failed Jaime and I failed her. I'm not sure Lucy will forgive me. I wouldn't blame her if she didn't. All these years she has made the same comments to me again and again, repeating the same objections because I make the same mistakes. *Don't fight my battles. Don't feel my feelings. Don't try to fix everything, because you only make it worse.*

I made it worse. I couldn't have made it any worse, and I'm saying to Chang, "I think you're aware of what Jaime's been doing in Savannah, and therefore the nature of the documents you're referring to. But to answer your question, I wouldn't know if she had something inside her apartment that someone might have wanted. I have no idea what's on the computers in the living room."

"When you were with her, did she say anything to give you the impression she was worried about someone wanting to harm her?"

"Only that she'd gotten increasingly security-conscious," I reply. "But she didn't mention anything specific about being afraid of anything or anyone."

"Don't know what jewelry and other valuables she might have brought down here from New York, but her watch is still sitting there." He indicates a gold Cartier watch on a black leather strap on the counter near a glass that has a small amount of water in it. "Seems like that would have been worth stealing. I'm wondering if she started rummaging for medication or something when she was drunk."

I pick up a box of Benadryl out of the sink, noting that the top has been ripped off as if the person was in a frantic hurry. On the floor is a silver packet with two of the pink tablets missing.

"I'm no longer sure she was drunk. At least not as drunk as she seemed." I look at the price sticker on the Benadryl box. "Monck's Pharmacy. Unless there's more than one, it's in that shopping area near the GPFW where the gun store is."

"She bought this since she's been down here, since she's been interviewing people at the prison. Maybe she had allergies," he says. "You have an idea when she first came to Savannah and rented this place?"

"She indicated to me that it was several months ago."

"Maybe April or May. The pollen was really bad this spring. It was like everything had been spray-painted yellowish-green. For a while I couldn't run or bike outside. I'd breathe in all this pollen and my eyes would swell, my throat would close up." He is making conversation, being amicable, the good cop chatting with me.

Sammy Chang is being collegial, and I know the game. Loosen up, open up, I'm your friend, and I intend to treat him as my friend because I'm not the enemy. I have nothing to hide. I'll take a polygraph. I'll swear to the facts under oath. I don't care that he hasn't read me my rights, and I don't care what he asks. I will admit freely that I feel guilty, because I do. But I'm not guilty of causing Jaime Berger's death. I'm guilty of not preventing it.

"I'm going to guess she took Benadryl last night based on the torn-open box and the packet on the floor," I say to him. "If she took two tablets, she must have been suffering significant symptoms, possibly was having trouble breathing. But we won't know until her tox is back whether she has diphenhydramine on board."

"Maybe she had a severe allergic reaction to something she ate. Maybe the sushi. Was she allergic to shellfish?"

"Or she thought she was having a severe allergic reaction because she was having difficulty breathing or swallowing or keeping her eyes open," I tell him, as I pick up other toiletries to see where she bought them.

"It's been reported, as you know from being at the prison a few hours ago, that Kathleen Lawler was having difficulty breathing after she came in from the exercise cage. Supposedly she had trouble speaking and keeping her eyes open. Symptoms one might associate with flaccid paralysis."

"Which is what, exactly?"

"Nerves are no longer stimulating muscles, usually starting with the head. Drooping eyelids, blurred or double vision, difficulty speaking and swallowing. As paralysis progresses downward, breathing becomes labored, and this is followed by respiratory failure and death."

"Caused by what? What might she have been exposed to that could do what you describe?"

"Some type of neurotoxin is what comes to mind."

I bring up Dawn Kincaid. I tell him that Kathleen Lawler's biological daughter, who is charged with multiple violent crimes in Massachusetts, including the attempted murder of me, experienced difficulty breathing inside her cell at Butler this morning and went into respiratory arrest. She appears to be brain-dead, and I explain that officials there are concerned she was poisoned.

"I'm not aware of Jaime being allergic to shellfish, unless she developed a sensitivity recently," I continue. "Although an anaphylactic reaction to shellfish could cause flaccid paralysis and death. As could other types of poisoning. It appears Jaime did a lot of her shopping at the same pharmacy, Monck's. It would be good to pay close attention to anything she might have purchased there, anything from there that's in the apartment. Any product or over-the-counter meds or prescriptions, including anything she might have gotten in the past that we're not seeing now. Just to rule out she didn't do this to herself or that something she bought there wasn't tampered with."

"You mean if someone tampered with something on the shelves inside the store."

"We need to consider every possibility we can think of, and we need a careful inventory of everything in this apartment," I reiterate. "The last thing we want to do is overlook a potential poison that gets left behind and hurts or kills someone else."

"You're thinking suicide's a possibility."

"I'm not thinking that."

"Or that maybe she accidentally got hold of something."

"I have a feeling you know what I'm thinking," I answer him. "Someone poisoned her, and it's deliberate and premeditated. My overriding question is poisoned her with what?"

"Well, if something was put in her food," he then says. "Any ideas what could cause the symptoms you described? What might you put in someone's food that within hours would kill them from flaccid paralysis?"

"There's nothing I would put in any person's food."

"I didn't mean you personally." He continues to photograph every item in the bathroom, every toiletry and bath product, every beauty aid, even the bars of soap, and he is jotting notes in his notebook, and I know what he's doing.

Buying time and gathering information, methodically, painstakingly, patiently. Because the more time we spend, the more I talk. I'm not naïve, and he knows I'm not, and the game plays on because I choose not to stop it.

"And a neurotoxin would be what? Give me some examples." He probes for information that might tell him I murdered Jaime Berger or the others or know who did.

"Any toxin that destroys nerve tissue," I answer. "The list is long. Benzene, acetone, ethylene glycol, codeine phosphate, arsenic."

But I'm not worried about any such thing. I don't believe Jaime was exposed to benzene or antifreeze, or that some household product like nail polish remover or a pesticide was laced in her sushi or mixed with her Scotch or that she got into the cough syrup. Those types of poisonings are usually accidental or irrational acts. They aren't the stuff of my nightmares. There are far worse things I fear. Chemical and biological agents of terror. Weapons of mass destruction made of water, powder, and gas, killing us with what we drink, touch, and breathe. Or poisoning our food. I mention saxitoxin, ricin, fugu, ciguatera. I suggest to Sammy Chang we should be thinking about botulinum toxin, the most potent poison on earth.

"People can get botulism from sushi, right?" He opens the door of the shower stall.

"Clostridium botulinum, the anaerobic organism that produces the poison or nerve toxin, is ubiquitous.

The bacterium is in the soil and the sediment of lakes and ponds. Virtually any food or liquid could be at risk for contamination. If that's what she was exposed to, the onset was unusually fast. Usually it takes at least six hours for symptoms, and more commonly twelve or thirty-six."

"Like when you have a can of vegetables that's bulging because of gas and you're always told not to eat something that looks that way," he says. "That's botulism."

"Food-borne botulism is commonly associated with improper canning and poor hygienic procedures or oils infused with garlic or herbs and then not refrigerated. Poorly washed raw vegetables, potatoes baked in aluminum foil and allowed to cool before they're served. You can get it from a lot of things."

"Shit, well, that just ruined a lot of foods for me. So if you're the bad guy . . ."

"I'm not a bad guy."

"Saying you were, you'd cultivate this bacteria somehow and then put it in someone's food so they die of botulism?" Chang asks.

"I don't know how it was done. Assuming we're talking about botulinum toxin."

"And you're worried we are."

"It's something we need to consider very seriously. Extremely seriously."

"Is it common to use in homicidal poisonings?"

"It wouldn't be common at all," I answer. "I'm not

aware of any cases. But botulinum toxin would be very difficult to detect if you didn't have a history and a reason to suspect it."

"Okay, if she couldn't breathe, was having all these awful symptoms you've described? Why wouldn't she call nine-one-one?" He photographs bath salts and candles on the side of the tub. Lavender and vanilla. Eucalyptus and balsam.

"You'd be surprised how many people don't," I reply, as I indicate I'd like to examine the prescription drugs, and, of course, he doesn't mind. He doesn't care what I do as he continues to lead me down the path he wants me on. "People think they'll be okay or can help themselves with home remedies, and then it's too late," I add.

I open the bottle of Ambien, and information on the label indicates the prescription was filled ten days ago at the same pharmacy near the prison where I stopped by yesterday after using the pay phone. Thirty ten-milligram pills, and I count them.

"Twenty-one left." I return the pills to the bottle, and next look at the Ativan. "Filled at the same time and by the same pharmacy as the other, where she purchased most things in here, it seems. Monck's. A pharmacist named Herb Monck."

Possibly the owner, and I remember the man in the lab coat I bought the Advil from yesterday. A pharmacy that does home deliveries, it occurs to me. *Same day, right to your doorstep,* the promise on signs posted inside, and I wonder if Jaime had more than food delivered.

"Eighteen one-milligram pills left," I inform Chang. "Carl Diego is the prescribing doctor for both."

"Most people who want to kill themselves take the whole bottle." Chang takes off his gloves and reaches into a pocket of his cargo pants. "Let's see who Dr. Diego is." He has his BlackBerry out.

"Nothing to indicate a suicidal overdose," I emphasize.

I open drawers and cabinets, finding perfume and cosmetic samples Jaime must have gotten free at a department store or more likely from shopping online. Things delivered. Life brought to her door, and then death handed over in a take-out bag. Handed to me.

"We don't want to get hung up on thinking she caused her own death when there's someone out there who might do it again," I say to Chang. "Multiple deaths already. We don't want more."

I'm suggesting rather bluntly that he doesn't want to make the mistake of getting hung up on Marino or me. If Chang looks too hard at us he won't look anywhere else.

"A doc in New York on East Eighty-first. Maybe her GP up there, who called in her prescriptions down here." Chang is checking the Internet, and what he's really doing is giving me plenty of room to get trapped. "If something was put in her food deliberately, it would have to be odorless and tasteless, wouldn't you assume? Especially in sushi?"

"Yes," I agree. "As much as we know about what's tasteless."

"What do you mean?"

"Who tastes a poison and lives to report on it?"

"Examples of really strong poisons that would be odorless and tasteless?" As if I have a malignant truth he can coax out of hiding. "Tell me what you would use if you were a killer." He pushes harder.

"There is nothing I would use, because I wouldn't poison anyone, even if I might know how." I look him in the eye. "I wouldn't help another person poison someone, even if I thought we could get away with it."

"I didn't mean literally. I'm just asking what you think would have done the job. Something you can't smell or taste, and you put it in her sushi. Besides the bacteria that causes botulism. What else, for example?" He returns his BlackBerry to his pocket and pulls on fresh gloves, tucking his used ones in an evidence bag and sealing it so they can be disposed of safely.

"Hard to know where to begin, and these days it's also hard to know what might be out there," I say to him. "Really scary chemical and biological agents made in labs and weaponized by our own military."

28

We step back inside the bedroom, where Colin is pacing as he talks on his cell phone, giving instructions to the removal service. He has covered Jaime's body with a disposable sheet, an act of kindness and gesture of respect that wasn't necessary, and I'm struck by the irony. He has shown Jaime far more consideration than she ever showed him.

"You're going to want to double-bag her at least," he is saying over the phone, as he paces past the windows, the drapes still drawn. It is hard to know what time of day it is, and I realize it's raining just as hard. I can hear rain drumming on the roof and spattering the glass. "That's right, just use the same precautions as if it's infectious and we don't know that it isn't, and we always treat every body as infectious anyway, right?"

"Fentanyl and the so-called date rape drug Rohypnol, nerve agents such as tabun and sarin, oksilidin, anthrax," I go down the list with Chang. "But some of these are very fast-acting. If someone put Rohypnol or fentanyl in her food, for example, she wouldn't have made it through dinner. I think the priority is to screen for clostridium botulinum."

"Botulism. Wow, that's scary. Why are you thinking of that as opposed to something else?" He places his bagged contaminated gloves on the foot of the bed.

"The symptoms as they've been described."

"It's just strange to think of poisoning someone with a bacteria."

"Not the bacteria but the toxin produced by the bacteria," I explain. "That would be the way to do it, and it's what the military has in mind. You don't weaponize the bacteria. You weaponize the toxin, which is odorless, tasteless, as best anybody knows, relatively easy to get hold of, and therefore difficult to trace." I add to his suspicions about me. "We don't have time for a mouse assay. Not a nice thing to do to a mouse, by the way. Injecting it with serum and waiting days to see if it dies."

Colin covers the phone with his hand and says to me, "What about botulism?"

I tell him we should screen for it.

"You got a place in mind?"

I tell him I have an idea about it.

He nods and gets back to the removal service. "Exactly. The regular way with a removal cot, bags that don't leak. I know all of them do, let's be honest, but double or triple up and autoclave or incinerate them after the fact, along with soiled protective clothing, gloves, whatever's contaminated. The same drill if you were worried about hepatitis, HIV, meningitis, septicemia. For God's sake, don't reuse the bags, is what I'm getting at, and wash everything down, disinfect really good. Bleach . . . Yes. I would."

"Your idea?" Chang asks me.

"An aggressive one. A blitz attack," I reply. "Screen for anything that is a reasonable possibility, and botulinum should be first on the list, all serotypes. And do it as quickly as possible. I mean immediately. Two people have died in twenty-four hours, and a third is on life support. We don't have the luxury of waiting days for an old-fashioned assay when there are newer and faster methods. Monoclonal antibodies or using electrochemi-luminescence, ECL, which I know is being done at US-AMRIID, the U.S. Army Medical Research Institute of Infectious Diseases at Fort Detrick. I'm happy to contact them and see if I can help facilitate testing if needed. But I think it would be more practical and expeditious to deal with the CDC. That's my vote. A lot less red tape, and I'm sure they would have an analyzer that can test for biological agents such as botulinum neurotoxins, staphylococcal enterotoxin, ricin, anthrax."

"USAMRIID?" Colin says, as he gets off the phone.

"Why are we thinking about the military, and what the hell is this about clostridium botulinum, and did I just hear 'anthrax'?"

"I'm simply suggesting possibilities based on not just this situation but others," I reply. "Three cases, and the reporting of the symptoms is similar if not the same."

"You thinking this is a national security issue or terrorism? Because USAMRIID's not going to help unless it is. Of course, I realize you probably know people."

"The accurate answer at the moment is we don't know what this is," I reply. "But what's going through my mind is the other cases you've told me about. Barrie Lou Rivers and other inmates who died suddenly and suspiciously at the GPFW. An onset of something and people quit breathing. Nothing is found on autopsy or on a routine drug screen. In those cases, you didn't have specimens tested for botulinum toxin, I assume."

"Wouldn't have been a reason for that to occur to me or anyone," Colin replies.

"I'm just going to say it. Right now I'd be worried about a serial poisoner. Nobody hopes I'm wrong more than I do," I tell them, and I go into more detail about the delivery person who rode up on a bicycle last night as I was about to enter this building.

I describe the impression I got that Jaime might not have placed the order for the sushi and that the person who delivered it mentioned the restaurant had Jaime's credit card on file. She said that Jaime had food delivered regularly.

"As I look back on it," I add, "the person offered a lot

of information. Too much information. I'm vaguely aware of having an unsettled feeling at the time. Something seemed strange."

"Maybe trying to convince you she was a delivery person because maybe she wasn't," Colin considers. "Someone who placed an order, picked it up, poisoned whatever it was, and pretended to be a delivery person for the restaurant."

"If someone who works at the restaurant is responsible, that won't be hard to track," Chang remarks. "That would be really risky. Stupid, in fact."

"I'm more worried it wasn't a restaurant employee," Colin says. "And that it's going to be hard as hell to track. If this is someone who's been doing it for a while, the person is anything but stupid."

"Certainly would have to know her patterns." Chang looks at the sheet-draped body on the bed. "Have to know where she orders food and what she likes and where she lives and all the rest. Has Marino mentioned her having any other associates or friends in the area?"

I reply that he hasn't and insist that sushi didn't appear to be on the menu last night. By all appearances, Jaime had no intention of eating sushi or serving it to us, and in fact would have known that neither Marino nor I eat it. I describe arriving at the apartment and being told that Jaime had walked to a nearby restaurant for takeout, and when she returned it was with more than enough food for the three of us. Even so, when she was presented with the option of having sushi, she joked that she was addicted to it and said she had it sent in at least three times a week, and she ate the take-out delivery and was the only one who did.

"Kathleen Lawler also ate something that wasn't on the menu," I remind them. "Her gastric contents indicate she ate chicken and pasta, and possibly cheese, while the other inmates were served their usual meals of powdered eggs and grits."

"She didn't buy chicken and pasta in the commissary," Chang says. "And her trash was missing, plus there was something weird in her sink. If it was poison in her sink, though, it wasn't colorless and odorless."

"Unless she was escorted somewhere for a special meal, obviously somebody delivered chicken and pasta, and possibly a cheese spread, to her cell," I tell them. "You probably noticed Jaime had security cameras installed, out front and outside her apartment door. Question is whether they record, and Marino will know the details. I think he helped her with the installation or advised her about it. Or I suppose you might find the digital video recorder somewhere, if there is one."

"They're her cameras? The one out front in particular is hers and not the building's?" Colin asks.

"They're hers."

"Perfect," Chang says. "Do you remember what the person looked like?"

"It was dark, and it happened fast," I tell him. "She had lights on her helmet and a bicycle and some type of bag or backpack that the take-out food was in. White female. Fairly young. Black pants, light-colored shirt. She gave me the take-out bag, recited what the order was, and I handed her a ten-dollar tip. Then I went inside and took the elevator up here to Jaime's apartment."

"Anything unusual about the take-out bag?" Colin asks.

"Just a white bag with the name of the restaurant on it. Stapled shut with the receipt attached, and Marino opened it, placed the sushi in the refrigerator, and Jaime served herself and ate most of it. Various rolls and seaweed salad. There should be one seaweed salad left that I placed inside the refrigerator when I helped her clean up last night, or more exactly, after midnight, around twelve-thirty, quarter of one. We need to get the containers out of the trash, gather up all of the leftovers."

"Including the bag and the receipt," Chang says. "I definitely want those going to the labs for fingerprints, DNA."

"I'm estimating she's been dead at least twelve hours." Colin finishes packing up his crime scene case. "So early morning. How early, I can't be precise. Between four and five is a safe estimate. I'm not seeing anything that tells the story of what happened to her except the obvious, and if the other two are poisonings as well?" He means Kathleen Lawler and Dawn Kincaid. "Then how is that possible? How do you do that to inmates who are incarcerated a thousand miles apart and then to this person?" He means to Jaime. "The good news, if there's any good news to be found in all this, is the path for the drug or toxin, the route of administration, likely is something that was ingested and not intradermal or inhaled. So hopefully the rest of us are okay."

"Nice to know," Chang says. "Since we've been poking around in one victim's prison cell and now are about to dig in another victim's trash."

I return to the living room, and the clutter on the coffee table is similar to what was in the bathroom, items scattered, as if Jaime upended her pocketbook and dumped everything out. A bottle of an over-the-counter pain reliever. Lipsticks. A compact. A brush. A small bottle of perfume. Breath mints. Facial tissues. Several blister packs that are empty, ranitidine and Sudafed. Chang looks inside a crocodile wallet and finds credit cards and cash. He reports there's no obvious sign of anything stolen, and I let him know he might want to check for a concealed weapon. The handgun he pulls out of a side compartment of the big brown leather bag is a Smith & Wesson snub-nosed .38, and he points it up toward the ceiling and pushes in the ejector rod, unloading six rounds into the palm of his hand.

"Speer Plus P Gold Dots," he says. "She didn't mess around. Only I don't think what got her was anything she could shoot."

"I'd like to get started with the trash." I walk into the kitchen. "What I can do is place each take-out container in a plastic garbage bag. I noticed a box of them last night when I was helping clean up. The heavier-duty the better. Thirty-gallon garbage bags should work just fine temporarily."

I go into the cabinet under the sink and begin to shake open black trash bags, deciding to package each take-out container from the sushi restaurant separately. While I deal with the kitchen garbage can, Chang goes into the refrigerator and looks at what's inside without touching anything.

"I'm assuming you've got some waterproof tape with you," I say to him, as the rancid stench of rotting seafood wafts up from the metal can.

"Damn, that stinks," he complains.

"She didn't take out the trash last night, and I didn't volunteer to do it for her, and now I'm glad. Thank God for that. We need to make everything as watertight as possible," I explain. "What we don't want is anything leaking, especially if you plan to transport evidence in your car."

"Maybe there's a better way." He returns to his scene case and places rolls of evidence tape on the counter. He puts on a face mask and hands me one. "Maybe we should get HazMat in here."

"If that was necessary, I wouldn't still be around to help you."

I cover the counter with plastic bags and don't bother with the face mask. My nose is my friend, even if I don't like what I'm smelling.

"I touched all of this when I was helping clean up and didn't have the benefit of wearing gloves or knowing there was any reason for concern," I continue. "I'm sure Colin has contacts at the CDC, and if not, I do. I suggest making a call and letting them decide exactly how they want to handle transport, for example, which will be subject to regulatory control, since what we're talking about is the potential of pathogens or toxins present in body fluids and tissues collected at autopsy, and in foods and food containers, et cetera. But the first step for us is to package all this as rigorously as possible, triple-bag it, document everything. I don't know if you or Colin have biohazard labels or infectious-substance labels or any other type of leakproof packaging. And we need to get all of this back to the lab and immediately refrigerate it."

"We usually don't deal with stuff like this, I'm happy to report. I don't have any special biohazard boxes or containers."

"We'll do the best we can. Like this." From the refrigerator, I retrieve the container of seaweed salad left over from last night and make sure it's sealed tightly shut. "It goes in one bag, which I'll wrap around and tape into a tight little package, then that goes into a second bag, and I'll do exactly the same thing, and finally a third bag, again the same thing," I describe. "Probably would pass the four-foot-drop test, but I believe we won't press our luck. I can take care of this or you can help or you can stand here and watch. Or, if you prefer, Colin can do it."

"Who's volunteering me for what?" Colin says, as he walks down the hallway.

"You got any ideas about how to get this stuff to the labs?" Chang asks him. "She says it should be refrigerated."

"And what you're saying is you don't want potentially

poisonous garbage inside your candy-ass air-conditioned SUV."

"I prefer not."

"I'll throw it in the back of mine," Colin says. "Open air and I just hose her off, decon her good, and Lord knows I've done it before. Just can't use bleach on my fine upholstery."

Chang carries his scene case to the desk near the stacks of expansion files with their different-colored gussets, and he begins to process the two laptops. He swabs keyboards and mouse pads, making sure he won't wish he had done so long after the fact if there is reason to believe someone might have tried to get into Jaime's computers.

"I'm going to take these in," he says, "but I want to look first. Whatever isn't password-protected." He moves a gloved finger on the mouse pad. "Bingo," he says. "If your delivery lady is real, we're about to meet her. This baby's got a DVR card. Looks like it goes with that camera out front and the one outside the apartment door."

I shake open more black plastic trash bags, and Colin and I individually package the containers that I placed in the trash early this morning.

"And it's got audio," Chang lets us know. "A pretty fancy camera she's got outside, we'll start with that and see who shows up. Long-range, pans and tilts three hundred and sixty degrees. And thermal infrared, so it works in complete dark, fog, smoke, haze. What time did you say you got here last night?"

"Around nine." I dig chopsticks out of the trash.

"We probably should package her whisky glass," Colin decides. "And swab the bedside table, like you said. Let's make sure we don't forget."

"The Scotch is in there"—I indicate which cabinet—"but I doubt that's it, because the bottle was unopened when she first got into it. And here's the wine bottle." I lift it out of the garbage and set it on top of a plastic bag, and the memory of drinking pinot noir and talking on the couch tightens my stomach. It almost takes my breath away.

"Nothing like day-old seafood." Colin makes a face.

"Shrimp bisque. Scallops."

"Rather smell a floater. Lord, that's bad." He bags an empty container.

"Well, this is really strange," Chang says from the desk where he's seated. "What the hell happened to her head? Now, this I've never seen before. Well, shit. That really sucks."

We take off our soiled gloves and walk over to see what he's complaining about.

"Let me back up to when she's first picked up by the camera." Chang's finger moves on the mouse pad.

The images are high-resolution and remarkably clear in shades of white and gray. The entrance of the brick building, the iron railing of the front step, the walkway and the trees. The sound of a car going by and a flash of headlights, then she's there, a distant figure on the street. Chang pauses the recording.

"Okay. She's off to the left, right out here in front." He indicates the street below us in front of the building.

"You can barely make her out with the bicycle." He points at the upper-left area of the computer screen.

"There you are, pressing the intercom button, and here she comes in the distance. But she's not on the bike. She's walking it across the street," Colin observes. "That's a little unusual."

"And no safety lights on," I comment, as I look at what's on the screen. "As if she doesn't want anyone to see her."

"I'm going to guess that's the point," Colin agrees.

"It gets better." Chang touches the mouse pad, and the recording resumes. "Or worse, actually."

The figure moves again in the distance on the dark street, and I can see the vague shape of her, but I can't make out her face. A shadow in shades of gray moving the shape of a bicycle closer, and I catch a movement of her right hand lifting up and suddenly a hot spot. A shocking white glare. What looks like a ball of white fire has obliterated her head.

"Her helmet," I suggest. "She switched on the safety lights on her helmet."

"Why would you turn on helmet safety lights if you're not riding?" Colin says. "Why would you wait until you've reached your destination?"

"You wouldn't," Chang answers. "She was doing something else."

29

It is almost nine p.m. when Marino and I arrive at the hotel, the back of his van packed with bags of groceries and other necessities of life, including cases of water, a set of pots and pans and cooking utensils, a toaster oven, and a portable butane stove.

After he picked me up in front of Jaime's building as Chang and Colin were clearing the scene, I had him take me on a series of errands. First we visited a Walmart for whatever items I deemed essential to set up camp, as I put it. Then it was a Fresh Market for basic food supplies, and after that a liquor store. Finally we stopped at the specialty market on Drayton Street that Jaime recommended last night for its selection of nonalcoholic beer, and I was reminded of what some might view as the coincidence of proximity on the one hand and the sense-lessness of it on the other.

While I understand the concept of fundamental randomness, the favored theory of physicists that the universe exists because of a Big Bang roll of the dice, and therefore we can expect a mindless messiness to rule our everyday lives, I don't accept it. I honestly don't believe it. Nature has its symmetries and laws, even if they are beyond the limits of our understanding, and there are no accidents, not really, only labels and definitions that we resort to for lack of any other way to make sense of certain events, especially god-awful ones.

Chippewa Market is only a few blocks from Jaime's apartment and the Jordans' former home, and around the corner from the former halfway house on Liberty Street where Lola Daggette was a resident when she was arrested for murder. But Savannah Sushi Fusion is some fifteen miles northwest of where Jaime lived, and in fact is closer to the Georgia Prison for Women than to Savannah's three-and-a-half-square-mile historic district.

"The locations are telling us something. There's a reason for them, and a message there," I'm saying to Marino, as we climb out of the van into the steamy night air, and water pours from gutters and drips from trees, and puddles in the city's sea-level streets are the size of small ponds. "Jaime put herself right in the middle of some sort of matrix, in the backyard of evil, and the sushi place is the odd man out, way off to the northwest, as if you're heading to the airport or the prison, which might be how she discovered it. But why didn't she use a place closer to where she lived if she was going to have takeout delivered several times a week?"

"It's advertised as having the best sushi in Savannah," Marino says. "That's what she told me one time when I was with her and she had it brought in. I said how do you eat that shit, and she said it was supposed to be the best in town, but it wasn't as good as what she got in New York. Not that any of it's good. Fish bait is fish bait, and tapeworms are tapeworms."

"How does one make a delivery on a bicycle from there? Some of it would be highway. Not to mention the distance in this weather."

"Hey, I need a couple of carts," Marino yells for a bellman. "No way I'm letting anybody haul this shit upstairs," he lets me know. "If you're going to all this trouble to make sure everything's safe, then we don't let anything out of sight. Zero possibility of our stuff being tampered with. I'm not going to say you're kooky as hell. But I'm sure it looks kooky to anybody watching. Like the Brady Bunch is on summer vacation and can't afford to go out for a burger or order a pizza."

I trust nothing. Not a cup of coffee, not a bottle of water, unless I buy it. Until we have a better understanding of what is going on, we're staying right here in Savannah, and no food or drink will be delivered to us by restaurants or room service, and we're not touching prepackaged food or eating out. I've also given fair warning that there will be no housekeeping. Nobody outside our circle is to come into our rooms, period, unless it is a police officer or an agent we trust, and someone needs to be in residence at all times to make sure no one enters and touches anything, because we just don't know who or what we're up against. We will make our own beds, empty our own trash, and clean up after ourselves as best we can and eat what I prepare as if we are in quarantine.

Marino rolls two luggage carts to the back of the van, and we start unloading cookware, appliances, and water and nonalcoholic beer and bottles of wine, and coffee, and fresh vegetables and fruit, and meats and cheese and pasta, and spices and canned goods and condiments. As if we are the Boxcar Children settling in.

"I don't see how it's coincidental." I continue to talk about the geography. "I want us to get an aerial view, maybe Lucy can get a satellite map up on the television screen and we can take a really close look, because it means something." We roll our overloaded carts through the lobby, past the front desk and the crowded bar, and people stare at the couple in investigative uniforms who appear to be moving in or setting up an outpost, and I suppose we are.

"But Jaime wasn't around when it happened," Marino says, as we push onward to the glass elevator. "She wasn't staying in that apartment in the middle of the matrix or the evil backyard or whatever. She wasn't here in 2002 when the Jordans were murdered." He taps the elevator button several times. "So whatever the locations might have meant back then, they wouldn't mean the same thing now. It's apples and oranges. It's you being spooky. I don't know about the sushi place and the bicycle, though."

"It's not apples and oranges."

"Except if you were going to poison her food, it wouldn't be all that hard if she was a regular customer of some place and had stuff delivered all the time," he says. "That's the only connection I'm seeing. A place she used all the time. Didn't matter where it was."

"And how would you know Jaime used that place all the time and had her charge card on file unless she was in sight? Within range? Unless both of you were common to the same environment somehow?"

"How the hell do you think so much? I don't have any thoughts left in my damn head, and I'm dying to smoke, I admit it. See? No evasiveness. I didn't buy any cigarettes during our shop-a-thon. But I'm letting you know I need one really bad, and I might go through two six-packs of Buckler, whatever it takes."

"I can't tell you how sorry I am," I again say to him, as the elevator doors slide open and we roll our provisions inside, plastic bags swaying from the frames of the carts.

"Plus, I'm hungry as hell. Like one of those times when nothing I'm going to do will make me feel good," he says, and he is getting grouchier by the minute, about to come out of his skin.

"I'm going to whip up a very simple spaghetti and salad of mixed greens."

"Maybe I want a damn cheeseburger with bacon and

fries from room service." He irritably taps the button for our floor, then taps it again, then taps the button for the doors to shut.

"It won't take me long. You drink all the Buckler you want and take a hot shower. You'll feel better."

"A damn cigarette is what I want," he says, as the glass elevator takes off like a lazy helicopter, rising slowly above floors with their vine-draped balconies. "You need to quit telling me I'm going to feel better. This is why people go to meetings. Because they feel like fucking shit and want to kill everyone who says they're going to feel better."

"If you need to find an AA meeting, I'm sure we can."

"No way in fucking hell."

"It's not going to help if you go back to things that hurt you," I say to him.

"Don't lecture me. I can't take it right now."

"I don't mean to lecture you. Please don't smoke."

"If I have to go to the bar to bum one, I'm going to. You don't want me to be evasive, right? So I'm telling you. I want a damn cigarette."

"Then I'll go with you. Or Benton will."

"Hell, no. I've had enough of him for one day."

"You have every right to be devastated and disappointed," I reply quietly.

"It's not got a damn thing to do with disappointment," he retorts.

"Of course it does."

"Bullshit. Don't tell me what it has to do with."

We can barely see each other around all the bags and

boxes as we argue about what he doesn't feel, and I know that at the root of his anger is his pain, and he's crushed. He had feelings for Jaime that I'm aware of at some level, but I'll likely never know the extent of them and whether he might have been attracted to her or was in love with her, and I know for a fact he had attached his future to hers. He was going to help her out, and he hoped to do so in this part of the world, where he likes the lifestyle and the weather. Now all of that is changed forever.

"Look," Marino says, as the elevator stops on the top floor. "Sometimes nothing makes anybody feel better. I can't stand what was done to her, okay? It makes me crazy that we were right there eating with her in her own damn living room and had no idea. Jesus. She's eating poison right before our eyes and is going to die and we got no clue, and I leave and then you do. Goddamn it. And she was all by herself going through hell like that. Why the hell didn't she call nine-one-one?" He asks the same question Sammy Chang did, the question most people would ask.

We are rolling our carts along the balcony that wraps around the hotel's atrium, heading to a series of rooms that make up our camp, a suite for Benton and me, with a connecting room on either side: one for Lucy, one for Marino.

"She was drinking," I reply. "And that certainly didn't help her judgment. But the more relevant factor is human nature, and it's typical for people to put off doing something as drastic as calling for an ambulance. Strange thing is, people will call the police quicker than they will ask for a rescue squad or the fire department, because we tend to feel ashamed and embarrassed when we hurt ourselves or accidentally set our house on fire. We're much more comfortable siccing the police on someone."

"Yeah, like the time I had the chimney fire, you remember that? My old house on Southside? I refused to call. Climbed up on the roof with the hose, which was stupid as hell."

"People delay, they put it off," I say, as we roll our carts along, and hanging vines growing from the balconies on every floor remind me of Tara Grimm and all the devil's ivy in her office that she lets grow out of control to teach people a life lesson.

Be careful what you let take root, because one day that's all there is. Something took root in her, and all that's left is evil.

"They keep hoping they'll feel better or can fix the problem themselves and then reach the point of no return," I tell Marino. "Like the lady with the bucket. Remember her? She dies of CO poisoning while acting like a bucket brigade, house burns up and firefighters find her charred body next to her bucket. It's worse for those who work in the professions we do. You, Jaime, Benton, Lucy, me, all of us would be reluctant to call police or paramedics. We know too much. We make terrible patients and usually don't follow our own rules."

"I don't know. If I couldn't breathe, I think I'd call," Marino says.

"Or you might take Benadryl or Sudafed or root around for an inhaler or an EpiPen, and when nothing worked, you probably wouldn't be in a condition to call anyone."

Benton must have heard us making our way along the open-air balcony, and the door to our suite opens before we get there. He steps outside, holding the door open wide, and his hair is damp and he's changed his clothes, showered and fresh, but his eyes are clouded by what has happened and what worries him, and I imagine Lucy worries him most of all. I haven't talked to her since I saw her last when I was on the elevator in Jaime's building, on my way to discover an answer I would give anything to change.

"How are things?" It's my way of asking him about my niece.

"We're okay. You look exhausted."

"Like a train wreck. That probably would be a more apt description," I reply, as he helps us get the carts inside, and I pause to take my boots off. "I'll clean up in a minute, but let me get things set up and dinner started. I promise I'm safe. In non-air-conditioned vehicles all day, rained on, and I look like hell and don't smell good, but nothing to worry about."

As if they've never been exposed to me after I've been at crime scenes or in the morgue.

"Sorry I didn't have access to a locker room when I left the apartment." I continue to talk and apologize because there's no sign of Lucy, and that can't be good.

I'm sure she knows we're here, but she's not come out to see us, and I interpret that as a danger sign.

"But it's almost a certainty it's something Jaime ate," I'm explaining. "I'm very suspicious of botulinum toxin in her food, possibly in Kathleen Lawler's food. MGH should be testing Dawn Kincaid for it, but they've likely thought of that, and I'm sure they have access to fluorescent tests, which are highly sensitive and quick. You might want to mention it to someone up there. One of the agents working her case," I reiterate to Benton.

"Apparently she hadn't eaten anything when she started having symptoms," he says. "I don't think it's believed she was poisoned with food, but I've passed along your suspicions about the possibility of botulism."

"Maybe something she drank," I reply.

"Maybe."

"Possible you can get a detailed inventory of what was in her cell, of what she might have had access to?"

"It's not likely you're going to be allowed to have that information," Benton says. "I'm probably not going to be allowed to have it, either, for obvious reasons. Considering what Dawn Kincaid has accused you of."

"Your mistake was not hitting her harder with the fucking flashlight," Marino says.

"Well, I certainly can't be blamed for what's happened to her now," I reply. "What about the sushi restaurant? Do we know anything more about that?"

"Kay, who would be telling me?" Benton says patiently.

"Yes, everybody's going to be secretive when all I want to do is stop the person from killing someone else."

"All of us want the same thing," he says. "But your connection to Dawn Kincaid, to Kathleen Lawler and Jaime, creates more than a minor problem when it comes to sharing information. You can't work those cases, Kay. You just can't."

"The fact is I'm not going to transfer a neurotoxin like botulinum from my clothes or boots, of course, but I'm going to get out of them anyway," I decide. "Unfortunately, no rooms come with a washer and dryer, so there was no way around that. If you could find the trash bags I just bought," I say to Benton. "My shirt and pants are going in one, and I'll send them out to be laundered or, better yet, pitch them. I might just pitch my boots, too. Maybe everything, I don't know. Maybe you could get me a robe."

"Believe I'll go clean up." Marino grabs two nonalcoholic beers, doesn't matter that they aren't chilled, and walks through the living room to his connecting door.

I find sanitizing wipes in my shoulder bag and clean my face, my neck, my hands, as I've done multiple times this day, and Benton finds a robe for me and opens a trash bag. I take off the uniform I've lived in since the sun came up, the black cargo pants and black shirt that Marino packed in a go-bag weeks ago when a plan was being hatched and it wasn't what he thought. Jaime tricked all of us. I don't know the extent of her deception or her motivation or ultimately what she had in mind. It wasn't right or fair, and much of it was unkind, but she didn't deserve to die and to die so cruelly.

The kitchenette has cupboards with dishes and silver-ware, and a refrigerator and a microwave, and I set up the butane stove and the toaster oven, and we begin to put away food and supplies. There is no sign of Lucy. Her room is off the dining area to the right of the living room, and the door is shut.

"What I didn't get a chance to do was go to a pharmacy." I unwrap cookware and pull tags off utensils I bought. "One with home healthcare, some things we should have on hand, but nothing was open after six, not the sort of pharmacy I have in mind that has home medical equipment and supplies. I'll give Marino a list, and maybe he can pick up what I need in the morning."

"Seems to me you've got everything covered," Benton says, with a calmness that makes me only more unnerved, as if it portends a bad storm.

"An Ambu bag, I should at least have one of those. So simple, but the difference between life and death. I used to keep one in my car. I don't know why I don't do it anymore. Complacency is a terrible thing."

"Lucy's been in her room working on her computers," Benton says, because I haven't asked about her directly and he knows why. "She went out for a run and both of us went to the gym. I think she's in the shower, or she was a few minutes ago."

I wash a new cutting board and two new pots.

"Kay, you're going to have to handle it better than this," Benton says, as he places bottles of water in the refrigerator.

"Handle her or handle what's happened to Jaime? What is it I'm supposed to handle in this situation where nobody wants me to handle anything at all?"

"Please don't get defensive." He finds a corkscrew in a drawer.

"I'm not." I peel the skin off a sweet onion and rinse green peppers while Benton decides on a bottle of Chianti. "I'm not trying to be defensive. I'm not trying to be anything except responsible, to do what's right and safe." I begin to dice. "To do anything I can. I admit I feel I've gotten all of you into this, and I don't know how one apologizes for such a thing."

"You didn't get us into anything."

"You're here, aren't you? Latchkey in a hotel room in Savannah, Georgia, with someone who finds it necessary to throw her clothes away. A thousand miles from home and afraid to drink the water."

Benton opens the wine, and we seem headed for a repeat of our last night together in Cambridge before I came to Savannah against his wishes. In the kitchen, cooking and cutting vegetables, and boiling water, and drinking wine and having heated discussions and forgetting to eat.

"I haven't talked to Lucy all day because of where I've been and what I was doing," I then say, and he silently watches me, waiting for what I'm really feeling to come out. "And I thought it best to talk to her in person," I say next. "Not over the phone while I'm riding around in Marino's loud van."

Benton hands me a glass of wine, and I'm not in a mood to sip. I'm in a mood to drink, to throw back the entire glass. One swallow and I feel the effect instantly.

"I don't know how to handle her." I'm suddenly tearful and so tired I can barely stand. "I don't know what she must think of me, Benton. How much does she know about what's happened? Has she been told that Jaime was slurring her words and her eyelids were drooping when I was with her last night and I left her anyway? That I was furious and disgusted with her and just walked out?"

I begin pouring bottled water into a pot, and Benton stops me. He takes the bottle from me. He sets it down and carries the pot to the sink.

"Enough," he says. "I seriously doubt the tap water has been poisoned, and if it has, then nothing we might do is going to save us or anyone anyway, okay?" He fills the pot and sets it on the stovetop and turns on the burner. "Do you understand your vigilance and that, while much of it is appropriate, some of it isn't? Do you have any insight into what's going on with you right now? Because I think it's pretty obvious."

"I could have done better. I could have done more."

"Your default is to feel that way about everything, and you know why. I don't want to get into the past, your childhood and what certain events did to you. It would sound simplistic right now, and I know you get tired of hearing me say it."

I sprinkle salt into the water on the stovetop and open cans of crushed plum tomatoes.

"You took care of a parent who was dying and couldn't save him after years of trying, and that was most of your childhood," Benton says what he has said before. "Kids take things to heart in a way adults don't. They get imprinted. When something bad happens and you didn't stop it, you blame yourself."

I stir fresh basil and oregano into the sauce, and my hands aren't steady. Grief moves through me in waves, and most of all I'm disappointed in myself because I absolutely could have done better. Despite what Benton is saying, I was negligent. The hell with my childhood. I can't blame my negligence on that. There's no excuse.

"I should have called Lucy," I say to Benton. "There's no good reason for my not doing it except avoidance. I avoided it. I've avoided it since I saw both of you last at the apartment building."

"It's understandable."

"That doesn't make it right. I'll go in and deal with her unless she won't talk to me. I wouldn't blame her."

"And she doesn't blame you," he says. "She's not happy with me, but she doesn't blame you. I've had a few talks with her, and now it's your turn."

"I blame myself."

"You're going to have to stop."

"I was incensed last night, Benton. I stormed out."

"You've really got to stop this, Kay."

"I almost hated her for what she did to Lucy."

"You'd be more justified in hating Jaime for what she did to you," he says. "It's bad enough what she did to Lucy, but you don't know the rest of it."

"The rest of it is what we found in her apartment today. She's dead."

"The rest of it begins in Chinatown. Not two months ago, as Jaime's led you to believe, as she led Marino to believe when he took the train to see her in New York. It began in March. In other words, it began not long after Dawn Kincaid tried to kill you."

"Chinatown?" I have no idea what he's talking about.

"She manipulated to get you down here to Savannah, to get your help, and she manipulated the FBI, and she sure as hell manipulated Marino," Benton says. "Forlini's. I know you remember that place, since you've been there with Jaime on a number of occasions."

A popular watering hole for lawyers, judges, NYPD cops, and the FBI, Forlini's is an Italian restaurant that names its booths after police and fire commissioners, the very sort of political officials that Jaime claimed ran her off the job.

"Obviously I don't know all the details she might have told you last night," Benton continues, "but what you relayed to me later over the phone was enough for me to ask some questions, to look into a few things, not the least of which was the names of the two agents who supposedly came to her apartment and interrogated her about you. Both of them are from the New York field office, and neither of them ever went to her apartment. She talked to them at Forlini's one night in early March and chummed the water, as Jaime certainly knew how to do."

"Chummed the water with information about me? Is

that what this is leading to?" I decide on a pasta. "So she could put me in a weakened position and show me how much I needed her help?"

"I think you're getting the picture." Benton's face is hard, but he's also sad. I see his disappointment in the slant of his shoulders and the shadows of his face. He liked Jaime very much, in the old days he did, and I know what he would think of her now, alive or dead.

"That's a pretty despicable thing to do," I reply. "Gossip to the FBI that maybe there's some basis for Dawn Kincaid's defense. That I'm unstable and potentially violent or was motivated by jealousy. God only knows what she said. Why would she do that? How could she do that?"

"Increasingly desperate and unhappy. Certain that everybody was out to get her, was jealous and competitive and less deserving, when in fact she was the one," Benton says. "We could analyze her for the rest of our days and never really know. But what she did was wrong. It was unforgivable, setting you up, placing you in harm's way so you'd do what she wanted, and you weren't the only person she'd been undermining of late. When I talked to a couple of agents who were around her a fair amount, I heard the stories."

"Do you have any ideas about what's happening? About who might have killed her? About who might be doing this? Does the FBI?"

"I'll be very forthright, Kay. We don't have a fucking clue."

I crush fresh garlic and dribble olive oil into the sauce

and look for the container of grated fresh Parmigiano-Reggiano. It's in the refrigerator in a drawer, where Marino put it, and everywhere I look for food or spices or whatever I need, it's in the wrong place and I feel I'm walking in circles and can't think straight.

"Maybe you can help me set the table," I suggest to Benton, as the door opens to the right of the dining area, and I stop what I'm doing. I stand perfectly still.

Lucy's hair is wet and combed straight back. Barefoot, she's in pajama bottoms and a gray FBI T-shirt she's had since she went through its academy.

I want to say something to her, but I can't.

"There's something you need to see. Something you need to hear, too," she says to me, as if nothing has happened, but I recognize the puffiness around her eyes and the set of her mouth.

I know when she's been crying.

"I logged in to the security camera," she says, and I look at Benton, and his face is unreadable but I know what he would think of what she's done.

He wants nothing to do with it and begins to stir the tomato sauce, his back to us. "I'll finish up here," he says. "I think I remember how to boil pasta. I'll let you know when it's ready. The two of you talk."

"Did Marino give you the password?" I ask Lucy, as I follow her into her room.

"He doesn't need to know about this," she says.

30

Two red tugboats with black tire bumpers push a cargo ship west along the river, multicolored containers stacked high like bricks, reminding me of what I must guide and carry. It feels like more than I can manage. I'm not sure I can, and I pray for strength.

Dear God, I used to address the Almighty when I was a child, but I haven't of late, not in many years, if I'm honest, not knowing who or what God is, in fact, since He or She is differently defined by everyone I might ask. A Higher Power or a majestic being on a golden throne. A simple man carrying a staff traveling a dusty path or walking on the water and showing kindness to the woman at the well while inviting those without sin to cast the first stone. Or a female spirit found in nature or the collective consciousness of the universe. I don't know.

I don't have a clear definition of what I believe, except there is something and it's beyond me, and I think to myself, *Help me, please.* I don't feel strong. I don't feel justified or sure of myself. It might just destroy me if Lucy holds me up to the light like a crystal or a gemstone and points out the flaw that she never knew I had. I will see it in her eyes, like shades pulled down in a window or the hesitation in someone who wants to fire you or replace you or doesn't respect or love you anymore. I stare Jaime Berger's death in the face, and it is a mirror I would give anything to escape. I'm not who Lucy thought I was.

Lights flicker along the shore, the stars out and the moon bright, as I move the only extra chair in Lucy's room, an armchair upholstered in blue. I drag it from the window overlooking the river, across the carpet, to the desk where she has set up a workstation or cockpit, as I call it, that includes her own secure wireless network. She might hack into whatever she wants, but others aren't going to do unto her what she does unto them.

"Don't be upset," she says, as I sit down.

"Funny you would be the one saying that to me," I remark. "We need to talk about last night. I need to talk about it."

"I didn't ask Marino for the password because I wouldn't put him in that position, not that I needed anything from him," she says, as if she didn't catch my reference to Jaime and the fact that I abandoned her because I was angry and now she's dead. "And Benton's going to have to be blind and deaf and have amnesia. He needs to get over himself."

"We have to do things . . ." I start to say that we have to do things the right way, but I can't get the words out. I didn't do things the right way last night, so who am I to tell Lucy what to do. Or anybody. "Benton doesn't want you getting into trouble," I add, and it sounds ridiculous.

"There's no way I wasn't going to view the security footage. He needs to quit being so fucking FBI."

"Then you've already seen it."

"Sitting around waiting, playing by the rules, while that piece of shit is trying to frame you," Lucy says, staring at a computer screen. "Out there free as a bird, and here we are, holed up in this hotel, afraid to eat the food or drink the water. She'll kill someone else, maybe a lot of people, if she hasn't already. I don't have to be a profiler, a criminal intelligence analyst, to tell you that. I don't have to be Benton."

She's angry with him, and I know why. "What piece of shit? Who?" I ask.

"I don't know. But I will," she promises.

"Benton has an idea about who it is? He told me he didn't. That the FBI has no idea."

"I'm going to find out, and I'm going to get her." Lucy clicks the mouse pad of a MacBook and types in a password I can't see.

"You can't take matters into your own hands." But

there's no point in saying it. She already has, and I don't have a right to say it.

I took matters into my own hands when I came to Savannah, and then last night and also today. I did what I thought was best or simply what I wanted to do, and Jaime is dead and it could be said that I've compromised the case, certainly the crime scene. All because I was determined to rid myself of guilt and hurt, to somehow fix what can't be fixed. Jack Fielding is still gone, and what he did is still terrible, and now I feel guilty about everyone, and others have died.

"Benton did what he thought was best for you," I say to Lucy. "I know you're upset with him for keeping you out of the apartment."

"It's not accidental you happened to be at the building when she showed up with the take-out bag," she says, as a printer starts, and she's not going to discuss Jaime or Benton.

She's not going to allow me to confess that I was negligent, that I broke the oath I've sworn to. I did harm by doing nothing.

"She wanted to hand it to you," she goes on. "She wanted you to carry it inside. So maybe your prints are on it, your DNA. You're on camera clear as day, walking into the building with that bag of sushi you ordered."

"I ordered?" I think of the forged letter sent to Kathleen Lawler, allegedly by me.

"I called Savannah Sushi Fusion before anybody else did."

"That probably wasn't the best idea."

"Marino told me about the delivery, and I called and asked. Dr. Scarpetta placed the order a few minutes after seven last night. Sixty-three dollars and forty-seven cents. You said you'd pick it up."

"I never did."

"And it was picked up about seven-forty-five."

"Not by me."

"Of course not by you. Payment wasn't a credit card. It was cash. Even though her credit card was on file." She means Jaime's was.

"And the person who delivered the bag knew the credit card was on file. She mentioned it to me."

"I'm aware," Lucy says. "It's recorded on the security DVR. Cash is cleaner. No follow-up phone calls. No questions asked. No discussion about why someone named Scarpetta would have a right to charge something to another person's credit card. Small family-run restaurant, doesn't have a lot of seating and most of their business is takeout. The person I talked to doesn't have a good recollection of what this individual looked like, the one who showed up for the order."

"On a bicycle?"

"Doesn't remember, and I'll get to the bicycle in a minute. Youngish woman. White. Medium-size. Spoke English."

"That fits the description of the person I encountered outside Jaime's building, for what it's worth."

"You would think Dawn Kincaid was doing all this, but she has the minor problem of being brain-dead in Boston."

"How could this person know I was meeting Jaime and at the precise time I was opening the front door of the apartment building when even I didn't know I was meeting with her until the last minute?" It doesn't seem possible.

"Watching you. Waiting. The old mansion and the square across the street that take up the entire block. The Owens-Thomas House is a museum now and not open at night, and there isn't much activity in the square. A lot of huge trees and bushes, a lot of dark shadows to lurk around in if you're waiting for someone," she says, as I remember standing outside in front of Jaime's apartment late last night, waiting for Marino to pick me up. I thought I saw something move in the shadows across the street.

Lucy collects pages from the printer and straightens their edges, making a neat stack, the top sheet of paper a photograph from the security camera. A zoomed-in image in shades of gray, a person walking a bicycle across the street, the mansion in the background, hulking hugely against the night.

"Or I was followed from the hotel," I suggest.

"I don't think so. Too risky. Better to pick up the food and hang out across the street and wait."

"I don't see how she could have known that I was going to be there."

"The missing link," Lucy says. "Who's the common denominator?"

"I don't have an answer that makes sense."

"I'm about to show you. I'm living up to my reputation," she adds.

"It must seem I've not lived up to mine," I reply, but it's as if she doesn't hear it.

"The rogue agent. The hacker," Lucy repeats what I told her Jaime said to me last night.

"And when I had to listen to that, I got upset," I continue to confess, and she continues to ignore it. "I got very angry, and I shouldn't have."

She is clicking through a menu on the MacBook. Two other computer notebooks on the desk display programs that are running searches, it seems, but nothing I'm seeing is intelligible, and there is a BlackBerry plugged into a charger, which I don't understand. Lucy doesn't use a BlackBerry anymore. She hasn't for a while.

"What are we looking for?" I watch data speeding by on the two notebooks, words, names, numbers, symbols flowing too fast to read.

"My usual data mining."

"Might I ask for what?"

"Do you have any idea what's available out there if you have a way to find it?" Lucy is content to talk about computers and security cameras and data mining, about anything that doesn't include my evening with Jaime and my need to be absolved for her death in the eyes of a niece I love like a daughter.

"I'm sure I can't begin to imagine," I reply. "But based on WikiLeaks and everything else, there don't seem to be many secrets anymore, and almost nothing is safe."

"Statistics," she says. "Data that are gathered so we

can look for patterns and predict. Crime patterns, for example, so the government remembers it had better give you funding to keep all those bad people off the street. Or stats that will help you market a product or maybe a service, such as a security company. Create a database of a hundred thousand or a hundred million customer records and produce histograms you can show to the next person or business you want as a client. Name, age, income, property value, location, prediction. Burglaries, break-ins, vandalism, stalking, assaults, murder, more predictions. You're moving into an expensive house in Malibu and starting your own movie studio and I'm going to show you that it is statistically improbable anyone is going to break in to your residence or buildings or mug your staff in the parking lot or rape someone in a stairwell if you have a contract with my company and I install state-of-the-art security systems and you remember to use them."

"The Jordans." She must be looking for their alarm company information.

"Customer data is gold, and it's sold constantly and at the speed of light," Lucy says. "That's what everybody wants. Advertisers, researchers, Homeland Security, the Special Forces that took out Bin Laden. Every detail about what you surf for on the Web, where you travel, who you call or e-mail, what prescription drugs you buy, what vaccinations you or your children get, your credit card and Social Security numbers, even your fingerprints and your iris scans because you gave your personal information to a privatized security screening service that has checkpoints at some airports and for a monthly fee you bypass the long lines everybody else stands in. If you're going to sell your business, whoever acquires it wants your customer data, and in many cases that's all they want. Who are you, and how do you spend your money? Come spend it with us. And from there the data gets sold again and again and again."

"But there are firewalls, I assume." I don't want to know if she's hacked her way through.

"No guarantees that secure information doesn't end up in the public domain." She's not going to tell me if what she's doing is legal. "Especially when a company's assets are sold and their data end up in someone else's hands."

"As I understand it, Southern Cross Security wasn't sold. It went bankrupt," I point out.

"That's incorrect. It ceased operations, went out of business, three years ago," Lucy replies. "But its former owner, Darryl Simons, didn't go bankrupt. He sold Southern Cross Security's customer database to an international firm that supplies private protection and security advice, a soup-to-nuts outfit that will offer bodyguards or oversee the installation of a security system or do threat analysis if you're being stalked, whatever you want. In turn, this international firm probably sold their customer database, and on it goes. So I'm doing things backward, like deconstructing an elaborate wedding cake. First I find the wedding cake in the bakery of cyberspace, and then I have to search for the original itemsets, datasets that were mined when patterns of interest were extracted from data repositories."

"This would include billing information. Or details about false alarms."

"Whatever was on Southern Cross Security's server, and that certainly includes false alarms, trouble on the line, police response, whatever got reported, and this information got cooked up into statistical analyses. So the Jordan information is out there or in there somewhere. A teaspoon of flour I've got to uncook. Ultimately what I'm really looking for is the intranet link that Southern Cross Security had to its archived files. In other words, a dead site that would have the detailed billing information of individual customers. I hate that the process is slow."

"When did you start the searches?"

"I just did. But I had to write the algorithms before I could run them. Now I'm autotrolling. That's what you're seeing on these two screens."

"It might be a good idea to include Gloria Jordan," I suggest. "We don't know what name the account was in. Could have been an LLC, for that matter."

"I don't need to single her out, and I'm not worried about an LLC. Her data will be connected to his and to their children's and to companies and tax returns—to anything in the media, to blogs, to criminal records, everything linked. Think of a decision tree. Did she say anything to you last night about worrying someone was following her, watching her, maybe showing up at her building?"

"Jaime," I assume she means.

"Any reference at all, maybe somebody who gave her a weird feeling? Maybe someone who was too friendly?"

"I didn't ask."

"Why would you think to ask?" Lucy's gaze is fixed on data streaming by.

"The security system and camera," I reply. "And she'd started carrying a gun. A Smith and Wesson thirty-eight loaded with high-power hollowpoints."

She is silent, watching data roll by.

"Your influence?" I say to her.

Lucy answers, "I don't know anything about a gun. I would never recommend that for her. I never did, never got her one, never gave her lessons. A bad candidate."

"I'm not so sure it was simply a case of the jitters because she felt out of her element in the Deep South, and I should have asked if she was feeling frightened or threatened or unstable or irrational or just plain miserable, and if so, why. But I didn't." It's a relief to get it out, but I feel ashamed as I wait for her to turn on me, to blame me. "Just as I didn't bother to make sure she was okay when I left last night. Remember what I used to tell you when you were growing up?"

Lucy doesn't answer.

"Remember what I always said? Don't go away mad."

She doesn't respond.

"Don't let the sun go down on your wrath," I add the rest of it.

"What I used to call your *dead talk*. Everything predicated on the possibility of someone dying or something that could cause death," she responds, without looking at me. "Childproofing whatever it is, no matter the age and decrepitude of the person. Venetian blind cords or stairs or balconies with low railings or hard candies you can choke on. Don't walk with scissors or a pencil or anything pointed. Don't talk on the phone while you're driving. Don't go for a jog if it's about to storm. Always look both ways, even if it's a one-way street." Lucy watches data streaming by, and she won't look at me. "Don't go away after arguing. What if the person gets killed in a car wreck or struck by lightning or blows an aneurysm."

"What an annoying person I must be."

"You're annoying when you think you're somehow exempt from feeling what the rest of us do. Yes, you, quote, 'went away mad' last night. I know how angry you were. You went on and on about it over the phone until three o'clock in the morning, remember? And you should have been angry. It was okay to be angry. I would have been, too, if the shoe had been on the other foot and she was saying things like that about you. Or had done that to you."

"I should have stayed and sorted it out with her," I reply. "And if I had, maybe I would have been more aware of what was going on with her physically. Maybe I would have realized she was having symptoms unrelated to alcohol."

"I wonder if there's such a thing as Hackers Anonymous," Lucy muses, as if I didn't just say what I did. "HA, that's about right. A joke to think people like me won't get into something if we can. You can't cure a chipped plate. All you can do is live with it or throw it out."

"You're not a chipped plate."

"Actually, what she used to call me was a cracked teacup."

"You're not that, either, and that's unkind. It's a cruel thing to say."

"It's true. Living proof." She indicates the computers on the desk. "You know how easy it was for me to get into her DVR? In the first place, she was careless about passwords. Used the same ones repeatedly so she didn't forget and lock herself out. The IP address was child's play. All I did was send myself an e-mail with my iPhone while I was standing under the security camera, and that gave me the static IP address of that connection."

"You thought to do that while I was inside her apartment?"

"Benton and I were standing out there in the rain, under the overhang."

I don't know whether I should be amazed or horrified.

"Holding on to my arm, but I was polite about it, civilized about it. He's lucky I was. I almost wasn't. He's damn lucky as hell."

"He was trying—"

"I had to do something," Lucy cuts me off. "I saw there was an outdoor bullet camera that looked new—in other words, recently installed—an okay system with a varifocal lens, the sort of thing Marino would pick out, but I wasn't going to ask him, and I haven't," she makes that point again. "And I figured there was a DVR some-where, and there's no way I wasn't going to do some-thing. Who the hell wants to sit around in life waiting for fucking permission? The assholes don't. The pieces of shit who cause all the trouble don't. She's right. I can't be fixed. Maybe I don't want to be fixed. I don't. Hell, no."

"You were never broken." I feel the anger again. "*Primum non nocere*. First, do no harm. I've made prom-ises, too. We do the best we can. I'm sorry I've let you down." The words sound lame as they come out of my mouth.

"You didn't do any harm. She did it to herself."

"That's not true. I don't know what you've been told. . . ."

"She did it to herself a long time ago." Lucy clicks the mouse pad and the paused image of Jaime's building and the street in front materializes on the MacBook screen. "She filed that flight plan when she decided to lie, and she ended up in a crash even if someone else was at the controls when it happened. I'm aware that literally she was murdered and my philosophical point of view is ir-relevant at the moment."

"That's the suspicion, but it's not been proven," I re-mind her. "We won't know until the CDC finishes its analysis. Or maybe we'll find out about Dawn Kincaid first, assuming we're dealing with serial poisonings by the same neurotoxin."

"We do know," Lucy says flatly. "Someone who thinks she's smarter than the rest of us. The link, the common denominator, is the prison. Has to be. All of you have that place in common. Even Dawn Kincaid, because her mother is there. Was there. And they were writing to each other, true? Everyone is linked because of the GPFW."

Party stationery and fifteen-cent stamps come to mind. Something sent from the outside to Kathleen. Maybe she sent something to Dawn. I envision indented writing, the ghostly fragments written in Kathleen's distinctive hand. A reference to a PNG and a bribe.

"I'm going to get you," Lucy says to the image of Jaime's building on the computer screen. "You have no idea who you're fucking with. It wouldn't have mattered if you'd stayed with her longer," she then says to me, but she won't give me her eyes.

She hasn't looked at me once since I sat down, and it hurts and unnerves me even though I'm well aware that if Lucy's been crying she won't look at anyone.

"She sounded drunk," Lucy says, as if she knows. "Just shitface drunk, the way she's sounded before when she's called."

"Called when you were together. Or do you mean since then?" My attention returns to the BlackBerry on the desk as it begins to occur to me what has happened.

"You told me she was drunk, or more exactly, you said you thought she was drunk," Lucy says, as she types. "You never hinted you thought she might be sick or that anything was wrong with her. So you can't blame yourself. And I know you are. You should have let me go inside her apartment."

"You know why I couldn't do that."

"Why do you shelter me as if I'm ten years old?"

"It wasn't about sheltering you," I say, as I feel my honesty flitting away on the sweet breeze of my good intentions. A lie disguised as something lovely and kind. "Well, it was about that more than anything else," I tell the truth. "I didn't want you to see what I saw. I wanted your last memory of her—"

"To be what?" Lucy interrupts. "My partner being the prosecutor and telling me why I must never have contact with her again? It wasn't enough to break up with me, she had to make it sound like a restraining order. You are dirty. You are scary and destructive. You are crazy. Be gone."

"Legally, you couldn't be in the apartment, Lucy."

"You shouldn't have been in there, either, Aunt Kay."

"I already was, but you're right. It poses problems. You don't want your prints or DNA in there, anything that might cause the police to be interested in you," I tell her what she already knows. "It was wrong of her to talk to you that way. It was dishonest of her to make you the problem instead of dealing with what was so intolerable to her about her own self. But I should have made sure she was all right before I left. I could have been more careful."

"What you're really saying is you could have been more caring."

"I was very angry, and I didn't care enough. I'm sorry. . . ."

"Why should you have cared? Why was it up to you to give a shit?"

I search for the true answer, because the right one is false. I should have cared because one should always care about another human being. That's the right thing to do. But I didn't. I honestly didn't give a damn about Jaime last night.

"The irony is, she was done anyway," Lucy says.

"We don't get to decide that about anyone. She might not have been done. I'd like to believe she might have had insight at some point along the way. People can change. It's wrong that someone has robbed her of that chance." I'm deliberate and careful, as if feeling my way along a stony path that might trip me up and break my bones. "I'm sorry that my last encounter with her had to be so unpleasant, because there were many others that weren't like that at all. There was a time when she was . . ."

"I won't forgive her."

"It's easier to be angry than sad," I say.

"I won't forgive or forget. She set me up, and she lied. She set you up, and she lied. She began lying so much there was no reference point of truth left, and so she believed her bullshit."

Lucy moves the cursor to *play* and clicks the mouse pad, and the digital recording begins. Bricks and steps and iron railings in shades of gray, and the sound of cars driving along the street in front of Jaime's building, their headlights flashing past. Lucy opens another window and clicks on another file as a figure appears in the distance on the dark street, someone slender and on foot, the same young woman, I assume, but there is no bicycle, and she isn't dressed the way she was last night. She begins to cross the street, and then the shocking hot spot of white glare as if she is an alien or a deity. She walks up to the entrance of the building, comfortable and at ease, her head flaring like a nimbus.

"That's not the way she was dressed," I tell Lucy.

"Stalking," she says. "Dry runs. So far I've found five of them for the last two weeks."

"Last night she had on a light-colored shirt. So what I just saw on the recording was from when . . . ?" I start to ask, but I'm stopped by the sound of Jaime Berger's voice.

". . . I realize that once again I'm breaking the no-contact rule that I myself made." The familiar voice drifts out of a speaker, and Lucy clicks on the volume and turns it up as the figure in the video recording disappears down the dark street in front of Jaime's building. "I guess you know by now Kay is here and will be helping with a case of mine. We just had dinner, and I'm afraid she got perturbed with me. Always the lioness when it comes to you, and that didn't help. Jesus God, it never helped. An unfortunate triangulation is putting it kindly. Somehow I always felt she was in the room no matter what room. Lights out, hello, Auntie Kay, are you there? Oh, well. We've been through all this ad nauseam . . ."

"Stop," I tell Lucy, and she pauses both files. "Did she call you on your new number? When did she do that?" But I have a feeling I know.

Jaime's voice is halting, and she is slurring her words. She sounds very much like she did last night when I left her, but slightly more impaired and nastier. I look at the BlackBerry plugged into the charger on the desk.

"Your old phone," I say to Lucy. "You didn't change your number, you simply got a new one when you switched to an iPhone."

"She didn't have my new number. I never gave it to her, and she never asked," Lucy says. "I don't use it anymore." She indicates the BlackBerry.

"You kept it because she's continued to call it."

"That's not really the only reason. But she's called it. Not often. Mostly late at night when she's had too much to drink. I save all of the messages, download them into audio files."

"And you listen to them on your computer."

"I can listen to them anywhere. That's not the point. The point is to save them, to make sure they're never lost. They're all pretty much the same. Like this one. She doesn't ask me anything. Doesn't say she wants me to call her back. She just talks for a couple of minutes and abruptly ends it without saying good-bye. Sort of the way she ended it with us. Pronouncements and her talking at me and not listening, and then disconnecting."

"You save them because you miss her. Because you still love her."

"I've saved them to remind myself why I shouldn't miss her. Or love her." Lucy's voice quavers, and I hear her grief and frustration and rage. "What I'm trying to tell you is she didn't sound sick or in physical distress." She clears her throat. "She just sounds like she was drinking, and that was a half hour after you were gone. So she probably didn't sound even as bad as that when you were still with her."

"She didn't mention she felt bad or strange. She didn't mention anything."

Lucy shakes her head. "I can play all of it if you want, but she doesn't say anything like that."

I imagine Jaime in her maroon bathrobe, walking from room to room in her apartment, sipping expensive Scotch and looking out the window at Marino's van driving off. I don't know the precise time we left, but it was no more than thirty minutes later that she called Lucy's old phone number and left the message. Clearly, her symptoms didn't become severe until later, and I envision the nightstand with its spilled drink and empty base unit, the phone under the bed, and also what I saw in the master bath, medications and toiletries scattered everywhere. I suspect Jaime might have drifted off to sleep and possibly around two or three a.m. woke up short of breath and barely able to swallow or speak. It was probably at this point she frantically searched for something to take that might relieve her terrifying symptoms.

Symptoms, it occurs to me, that were eerily similar to what Jaime described when we were talking about Barrie Lou Rivers and what may be in store for Lola Daggette if she is executed on Halloween. Cruel and unusual, an awful way to die, and, according to Jaime, deliberately cruel. I thought she was trumping up a dramatic story to make her case, but maybe she wasn't. Maybe there is more truth to what she was alleging than she knew. Not scared to death but scared of it.

"Your mind is awake, but you can't talk. You can't move or make the slightest gesture, and your eyes are shut. You look unconscious. But the muscles of your diaphragm are paralyzed, and you're aware as you suffer the pain and paific of suffocation. You feel yourself die, and your system is in overdrive. Pain and panic. Not just about death but about sadistic punishment," I describe what Jaime was saying about death by lethal injection and what happens if the anesthesia wears off.

I think about how a killer might expose someone to a poison that stops breathing and renders the person unable to talk or call for help. Especially if the intended victim is incarcerated.

"Why would anyone send an inmate twentysome-thing-year-old postage stamps?" I get out of my chair.

"Why not sell them?" I ask. "Wouldn't they be worth something to a collector? Or maybe that's where they came from. Maybe they were recently purchased from a collector, a stamp company. No lint, dust, dirt, nothing stuck on the back, not wrinkled or grungy like they might be if they'd been in a drawer for decades. And allegedly sent by me in a counterfeit CFC envelope that included a forged letter on my counterfeit letterhead? Possibly, maybe? She seemed to think I'd been generous with her when I hadn't been. A big envelope allegedly from me, and extra postage. Something else in it. Maybe stamps." Lucy finally gives me her eyes, and I can see what's in them. A deeper green, and they are immeasurably sad and glinting with anger.

"I'm sorry," I say to her, because of how dreadful it is to imagine Jaime's death the way I just described it.

"What kind of stamps?" she asks. "Tell me exactly what they looked like."

I tell her what I found in Kathleen Lawler's prison cell, tucked inside a locker at the base of her steel bed, a single pane of ten fifteen-cent postage stamps issued in an earlier era when glue on the back of them, and on labels and envelope flaps, had to be licked or moistened with a sponge. I describe the letter to Kathleen that I didn't write and the strange party stationery that she couldn't have gotten from the commissary. Someone sent her stamps and stationery, and it very well may have been me or, more precisely, someone impersonating me.

Then the stamp is on the computer screen. A wide white beach with sprigs of grass, and an umbrella with red and yellow panels is propped against a dune beneath a seagull flying through the cloudless sky over bright blue water.

31

It is midnight, and we are picking at a dinner that Benton has managed to overcook and wilt, but no one is particular at the moment or preoccupied with food, at least not in a good way. Right now I can easily imagine not wanting to eat ever again, as everything I look at turns into a potential source of disease and death.

Bolognese sauce, lettuce, salad dressing, even the wine, and I'm reminded that a peaceful, healthy coexistence on this planet is shockingly fragile. It takes so little to cause disaster. Shifting tectonic plates in the earth that create a tsunami, clashing temperatures and humidity unleashing hurricanes and tornadoes, and worst of all is what humans can do.

Colin Dengate e-mailed me about an hour ago with information he probably shouldn't be releasing to me, but that's who he is, a redneck, as he describes himself. Armed and dangerous, he likes to say, roaring around in that ancient Land Rover of his in the blistering heat and afraid of nothing, including bureaucrats, or bureausaurs, as he calls people who let policies, politics, and phobias get in the way of doing what is right. He's not going to shut me out of any investigation, certainly not when efforts to frame me are blatant enough to bury any reasonable doubt that I'm the one running around poisoning people.

Colin let me know that Jaime died in good health, just as Kathleen Lawler did. There was nothing on gross examination to show what caused Jaime's death, but her gastric contents were undigested, including pinkish, reddish, and white tablets or pills that he and I suspect are ranitidine, Sudafed, and Benadryl. He explained that Sammy Chang passed along lab results that probably don't mean anything unless it's possible Kathleen died of heavy-metal poisoning, and Colin certainly doesn't think so, and he's right, she didn't. Specifically, he wanted to know if trace elements of magnesium, iron, and sodium might hold any special meaning for me.

"I understand that." Benton paces back and forth past windows overlooking the Savannah River, lights scattered along the opposite shore, where shipyard cranes are etched faintly against the distant dark sky. "But what you need to understand is the following. They could be deadly poisonous," he is saying to Special Agent Douglas Burke from the FBI's Boston field office.

I can tell from what I'm overhearing that Douglas

Burke, a member of the task force that has been working the Mensa Murders, is resistant to answering Benton's questions beyond confirming the statement that Massachusetts General Hospital has released to the media. Dawn Kincaid has botulism. She remains on life support, and her brain is no longer viable. Benton has asked point-blank if fifteen-cent postage stamps featuring a beach umbrella might have turned up inside her cell at Butler.

"She got hold of the toxin somehow," he pushes. "Poisoned, in other words, unless she got it from Butler's food, which I seriously doubt. Anybody else at Butler with botulism? . . . Exactly. The glue on the stamps could be the source of the exposure."

"That was pretty good, but no offense to Benton, he should stay out of the kitchen." Marino pushes away his bowl of unfinished Bolognese sauce without pasta, which turned out gummy. "The Botox Diet. All you got to do is think about botulism. That will make you lose weight. Doris used to do her own canning," he adds, talking about his ex-wife. "Creeps me out to think about it now. You can get it from honey, you know."

"Mostly that's a risk for infants," I reply distractedly, as I listen to Benton's conversation. "They don't have the robust immune systems adults do. I think you're fine to eat honey."

"Nope. I stay away from sugar, fake sugar, and I sure as hell don't want honey or home canning or maybe salad bars, either."

"You can get the stuff for like twenty bucks a vial from China." Lucy has her MacBook on the dining-room table, typing with one hand as she eats a piece of bread with the other. "Fake name, fake e-mail account, and you don't have to be a doctor or work in a lab. Order what you want from the privacy of your own home. I could do it as I sit here. I'm surprised something like this hasn't happened before now."

"Thank God it hasn't." I begin to clear the dishes while I continue to debate whether I should call General Briggs.

"The most potent poison on the planet, and it shouldn't be this easy to get," Lucy says.

"It didn't used to be," I reply. "But botulinum toxin type A has become ubiquitous since its introduction into the treatment of numerous medical conditions. Not just cosmetic procedures but migraine headaches, facial tics and other types of spasms, hypersalivation—drooling, in other words—crossed eyes, involuntary muscle contractions, sweaty palms."

"How much of it would you have to use, saying you could order vials of it off the Internet?" Glass clanks as Marino drops empty bottles in the recycle bag inside the kitchenette, where he's followed me.

"It comes in a crystalline form, a white powder, vacuum-dried clostridium botulinum type A, that you reconstitute." I turn on the water in the sink and wait for it to get hot.

"Then you just inject it in a package of food, for example," Marino says. "Or a take-out container."

"Very simple. Frighteningly so."

"So if you got hold of enough of it, you could wipe

out thousands of people." Marino finds a dish towel and begins to dry as I wash.

"If you tampered with some product, like a prepackaged food or beverages that aren't heated sufficiently to destroy the toxin, yes," I reply, and that is what scares me.

"Well, I think you should call Briggs." He takes a plate from me.

"I know you do," I reply. "But it's not that simple."

"Sure it is. You just friggin' call him and give him a heads-up."

"It sets things in motion before we have lab results." I hand him a wineglass to dry.

"Dawn Kincaid's got botulism. That's one lab result." He opens cabinets and starts putting away dishes. "You ask me, that's the only confirmation you need when you think of everything else we're finding out and start putting the pieces together. Like the shit in Kathleen Lawler's sink that fits with the burns on her foot."

"It might fit with that. I'm speculating."

"The person you should be speculating with is him."

He means General Briggs, the chief of the Armed Forces Medical Examiners, my commander and an old friend from my earliest days when I began my career at Walter Reed Army Medical Center. Marino wants me to tell Briggs that Kathleen Lawler's gastric contents appear to be undigested chicken and pasta and cheese that possibly were poisoned with botulinum toxin, and that scanning electron microscopy and energy-dispersive X-ray analysis of the odd-smelling residue recovered from her sink revealed magnesium, iron, and sodium. The answer to Colin Dengate's question about whether the finding of these elements in the chalky residue means something to me is yes. Unfortunately, it does.

When water is added to food-grade iron, magnesium, and sodium or salt, the result is an exothermic reaction that rapidly produces heat. Temperatures can reach up to one hundred degrees centigrade, and it is this technology that is the basis for the flameless ration heaters used to cook or warm up food eaten by soldiers in the field. MREs, meals ready to eat, offer dozens of different menus, including chicken with pasta, and many of the tough tan plastic bags they're packaged in offer additional rations, such as cheese spread. Each of these self-contained meals includes a water-activated flameless ration heater packaged in a sturdy polybag, an ingenious device that requires a soldier in the field to do nothing more than cut off the top, add water, and then place the bag under the MRE, propping both against "a rock or something," according to the operating instructions.

I realize it's possible there might be other explanations for why swabs of the residue in Kathleen's sink show trace elements of iron, magnesium, and sodium, but it is the combination of evidence that offers a possible nightmarish answer that can't easily be explained away. The unpleasant odor that reminded me of a shorted-out blow-dryer or overheated insulation strikes me as consistent with a chemical reaction producing heat, and Kathleen had burns on her left foot that prison officials claimed she could not have sustained while incarcerated in Bravo Pod. I believe she accidentally dripped a hot liquid on her bare skin, and it may very well have been the boiling water from a flameless ration heater.

The first-degree burns were recent, and I can't dismiss from my thoughts her obsession with food and certain comments she made to me, and I wonder if a missing diary or more than one might have contained what Kathleen was doing and thinking and possibly eating since she'd been moved to Bravo Pod. Tara Grimm was taking care of her, was good to her, and Kathleen was more than happy to be a *test kitchen*. She had sweet buns and packages of noodles in her cell and knew how to turn Pop-Tarts into strawberry cake, fancying herself the *Julia Child of the slammer*. Maybe Tara Grimm was seeing to it that Kathleen got an occasional treat in exchange for cooperation or other favors, and early this morning the treat was a ready-to-eat feast that had been injected with poison.

"Plus, there's the shit about the camera," Marino continues to lecture me about what I should do. "Defeating infrared with infrared, a strip of tiny IR LEDs on her bike helmet, assuming Lucy's right about that. Whatever this person did, the camera got defeated with something, and that's a fact, completely whiting out her head the instant she got close enough for her face to be recognizable on the camera, and Lucy says the recording can't be fixed or restored. Like the damn Chinese blinding our spy satellites with lasers. You should call him."

"It will be sounding an alarm that could end up in the Oval Office," I say what I've said before. "General Briggs will have to pass the information up the chain, straight to the Pentagon, the White House, if there's even the slightest possibility that the bigger target is our troops— that what we're dealing with is the preliminary if not plenary stages of a terrorist plot," I'm explaining, as Benton appears.

"She isn't going to say it outright." He tells me about his conversation with Special Agent Douglas Burke, who is a woman. "But reading between the lines, the answer is yes. Fifteen-cent stamps matching the description we have were found in Dawn Kincaid's cell. A pane of ten with three removed that are on a letter she didn't get around to mailing. A letter to one of her lawyers."

"The question is, where might she have gotten the stamps?" I ask.

"Dawn received mail yesterday afternoon from Kathleen Lawler," Benton says. "Douglas wouldn't confirm that the stamps were included, but the fact that she is letting me know about the letter suggests it."

"Written on party stationery?" I ask.

"She didn't say."

"Mentioning something about a PNG and a bribe? In other words, derisive comments, probably about me?"

"Douglas didn't go into that level of detail."

"Fragments of indented writing I could make out while in Kathleen's cell. What struck me as sarcastic, and understandably so, if she were under the impression that I sent her the stamps and stationery, what would appear to be cheap leftovers, something I didn't want," I say, as I recall Kathleen's snide comment about people sending inmates their detritus, things left over and expired that they no longer want. "That I might try to butter her up or bribe her with such a stingy gift," I continue. "Only it wasn't from me. The forged letter likely accompanying these items was mailed in Savannah on June twenty-sixth, meaning there was ample time for Kathleen to mail a pane of these same stamps to Dawn."

"It seems she did, but Douglas wouldn't go into detail, and she didn't refer to you," Benton replies. "Although I certainly was clear about obvious forged documents and a campaign on the part of an individual or individuals to set you up and that none of it is plausible."

"An accident," I decide. "Her incarcerated mother sends her incarcerated daughter stamps so they can be prison pen pals, having no idea the glue on the back has been tampered with. But Kathleen was too selfish to send the good ones."

"What good ones?" Marino frowns.

"She had current stamps, forty-four-cent ones, in her cell, but she didn't share those. Just the ones that were, quote, 'shit' other people didn't want anymore. Ones she thought were from a PNG. From me."

"That's what stinginess will get you. She gives away her daughter and thirty-two years later gives her botulism," Marino says as Benton empties the serving bowl of pasta into the trash and it lands in a solid mass.

"Sorry about that," says my husband, who is rather worthless in the kitchen. "And washing the lettuce in hot water wasn't the best idea, either."

"You'd have to boil lettuce a good ten minutes to destroy botulinum toxin, which is very heat-resistant," I inform him.

"So you ruined it for nothing," Marino is happy to let Benton know.

"If Dawn wasn't an intended victim, that tells us something," Benton says.

"The stamps didn't poison Kathleen. It doesn't appear she ever touched the stamps, and that tells us something, too," Marino says, as we return to the dining-room table, where Lucy is working on her computer and has committed the only act that she considers a crime.

Paper. She doesn't believe in printouts, but there is too much information to sort through, so much to look at and connect. Images, security-company billing information and logs, decision trees, datasets, and her searches continue. Out of consideration for the rest of us, she is doing her best to make it easy, sending files to the printer in the other room.

"It's looking like she got killed by what she ate, right? Maybe chicken and pasta and cheese spread, and not the stamps." Marino pulls out a chair and sits. "That's really something. Maybe she's lucky she didn't live to learn that her daughter licked three of those stamps to put on the letter to her lawyer. How much botulism could you get on three stamps?"

"About three hundred and fifty grams of botulinum toxin is enough to kill everyone on the planet," I reply. "Or about twelve ounces."

"No fucking shit."

"So it wouldn't take much on the back of stamps to

create a potent poison that would have caused a rapid onset of symptoms," I add. "My guess is that within several hours Dawn Kincaid was feeling really bad. If Kathleen had used the stamps when she first received them, I wouldn't have been able to interview her because she would have been dead."

"Maybe that was the intention," Benton says.

"I don't know," I reply. "But you have to wonder."

"But that's not what killed her, and that's what's weird." Lucy hands out stacks of whatever she's printed so far. "Someone sends her stamps spiked with botulinum toxin but doesn't wait for her to use them. Why? Seems to me she would have used the stamps eventually, and when she did, she was going to die."

"It might suggest that whoever sent them doesn't work at the prison," Benton remarks. "If you didn't have access to Kathleen or what was in her cell or witness mail going out, you might assume the stamps were ineffective, not realizing she simply hadn't gotten around to using them. So the person doing the tampering decided to try again."

"The stamps sure as hell aren't ineffective," Marino comments.

"And how would the poisoner know what's effective?" Benton points out. "Who do you test your poisons on to make sure they work? Certainly not yourself."

But you might test your poisons on inmates—a possibility I've considered throughout the evening—and that a warden might be inclined to allow it in certain cases, if she is driven by a need to control and punish, the way Tara Grimm seems to be. I remember the hard look in her eyes that wasn't disguised by her southern charm when I sat in her office yesterday, and her obvious displeasure with the idea that a wrongfully convicted woman soon to be executed might go free or that a deal was in the works that could release Kathleen Lawler early. There could be no doubt that Tara resented Jaime Berger's meddling in the lives of inmates and overriding the wishes of their respectable, highly praised warden, the daughter of another prominent warden, who designed the very facility that she considers rightfully hers.

It no longer seems possible Tara Grimm wasn't aware of the kite Kathleen slipped to me. The warden probably knew all about it and not only didn't care but considered my meeting with Jaime a gift, the ideal opportunity to have me intercepted by someone with a take-out bag that I suspect contained a potent dose of botulinum toxin serotype A injected into sushi or seaweed salad. Tara had known for almost two weeks that it was in the works for me to come to her facility, and somehow the woman with the take-out bag knew I was headed to Jaime's apartment, and perhaps, as Lucy has suggested, this person was waiting in the nearby dark for me, possibly waiting all night and well into the morning, watching the silhouette of her victim walking past windows, waiting for lights to go off and back on, waiting for death.

People stalked and followed and spied on, and manipulated like puppets, by someone who is cunning and meticulous, a poisoner who is patient and precise and as cold as dry ice, and I can't think of a more vulnerable population, a captive one like rats in a lab, especially if anyone working at the correctional facility is in collusion with whoever might be masterminding such sinister research. Figuring out what works and what doesn't as you design a much bigger attack, biding your time, fine-tuning for months, for years.

Barrie Lou Rivers died suddenly while she was awaiting her execution. Rea Abernathy was found dead inside her cell, slumped over the toilet, and Shania Plames appeared to be a suicidal asphyxiation, supposedly hog-tying herself with her prison uniform pants. Then Kathleen Lawler, and Dawn Kincaid, and now Jaime Berger, all of the deaths disturbingly the same. Nothing is found on autopsy, the diagnosis one of exclusion. There was no reason, at least not in the earlier cases, to suspect homicidal poisonings that would elude routine toxicology screens.

It is almost two o'clock in the morning, and I don't remember the last time I called General John Briggs at this hour. Whenever I've been as inconvenient as I'm about to be, I've had an ironclad reason. I've had proof. Lucy adds to my pile of printouts, and I take them with me. I go back to the bedroom and close the door as I imagine Briggs snapping up his cell phone wherever he's sleeping or working. It could be the Air Force base in Dover, Delaware, the headquarters of the AFME and its port mortuary where our military casualties are flown in and given dignified transfers and sophisticated forensic examinations, including three-dimensional CT and explosive-ordnance scans. He could be in Pakistan or Afghanistan or Africa, maybe not the MIR space station, but we speculate about it, not really joking, because AFMEs could end up any place where deaths are the jurisdiction of the federal government. What Briggs doesn't need is one more thing to worry him needlessly. He doesn't need me and my intuition.

"John Briggs," his deep voice answers in my wireless earpiece.

"It's Kay," and I tell him why I'm calling.

"Based on what?" he says what I knew he would.

"Do you want the short answer or a more involved one?" I prop pillows behind me on the bed and continue scanning the information Lucy has been printing out.

"I'm about to get on a plane in Kabul, but I have a few minutes. Then you're not going to get me for about twenty-five hours. Short answers are my favorite, but go ahead."

I give him the case histories, starting with suspicious deaths at the GPFW that Colin has told me about, and from there I move on to what has happened in the past twenty-four hours. I point out the obvious concern that the one confirmed poisoning by botulinum toxin serotype A, Dawn Kincaid, suggests an enhanced delivery system, something we've not seen before.

"While it's theoretically possible that death or severe illness due to botulinum toxin can occur in as few as two to six hours," I explain, "usually it's more like twelve or twenty-four. It can take longer than a week."

"Because the cases we're accustomed to seeing are food-borne," Briggs says, as I go through the printouts Lucy generated, studying an enhanced surveillance image of the woman who delivered the take-out bag of sushi last night.

A sadist, a poisoner, I believe.

"We don't see cases of exposure to the pure toxin," Briggs says. "I can't think of a single one."

The woman's head and neck are completely whited out, but Lucy has produced sharply defined and enlarged images of the rest of her, including the silvery bicycle she walked across the street and leaned against the lamppost. She is in dark pants, running shoes and socks, no belt, and a light-colored short-sleeved blouse tucked in. The only flesh exposed is her forearms and her hands, and a close-up of her left ring finger shows a baguette-cut square band that might be white gold or yellow or platinum, I can't tell. All of the images are infrared and in shades of white and gray.

"Food contaminated by the clostridium botulinum spores that produce the toxin," Briggs is saying, "and it's got to work its way through the digestive tract, usually becoming absorbed in the small intestine before it gets into the bloodstream and begins attacking neuromuscular proteins, basically attacking the brain and preventing the release of neurotransmitters."

The woman in the surveillance footage also has on a watch: what Lucy shows through other image files is a dark-faced Marathon wristwatch with a high-impact fibershell and waterproof and dustproof case, made by contract with the U.S. and Canadian governments for issuance to military personnel.

"What if a pure, extremely potent toxin was exposed to mucous membrane?" I propose, as I continue to worry that the killer has some sort of military connection.

Someone with access to military personnel, perhaps her real target.

"Think about people who apply drugs to the mouth, vagina, rectum," I add. "Cocaine, for example. We know what happens. Imagine a poison like botulinum toxin."

"A really big problem," Briggs says. "No cases I've ever heard of, no precedents, nothing to compare it to, in other words. But could only be bad."

"The pure toxin in the mucous membrane of the mouth."

"Much faster absorption, as opposed to ingestion of the actual microbe, the bacterium clostridium botulinum and its spores, what is actually in contaminated food," Briggs contemplates. "The bacteria have to grow and produce the toxin, all of this taking hours, possibly days, before paralysis starts in the face and spreads down."

"Nothing worked its way through the digestive tract, John. It would seem these people had an exposure that actually induced gastroparesis," I reply, and I can see what Lucy wants me to realize about the bicycle.

It appears lightweight, with very small wheels, and she has included an article she pulled off the Internet. A folding bike. Someone possibly with a military connection and a folding bike.

"Could also be induced by severe stress," Briggs says.

"Fight-or-flight syndrome, and your digestion quits. But that would be true only if the onset of symptoms was rapid. Again, no cases to compare it to. A direct hit to the bloodstream, and everything vital starts shutting down, my guess. Eyes, mouth, digestion, lungs."

A seven-speed bike with an aluminum frame that has quick-release hinges, the entire bike folding into a 12x25x29-inch package, and in a series of zoomed-in and enhanced photographs from the security camera, Lucy shows the woman taking off a backpack, opening it, and pulling out the take-out bag from Savannah Sushi Fusion. The next page is an ad from a sports and out-doors online site where one can order what appears to be the same type of backpack for $29.99. Not an insulated bag for delivering food but a folding bike backpack for carrying or transporting the bike when one isn't rid-ing it.

"But the truth is, we don't know what extremely po-tent doses of botulinum toxin manufactured in a lab might do," Briggs continues, as I listen intently and go through paperwork on the bed, my thoughts moving rapidly in multiple directions that somehow point at the same thing.

But who or what and why?

"I'm just not aware of any deaths from that, any homicides, as I've said," he adds. "Not one."

A folding bike that's nothing more than a ruse, a prop, an explanation for the helmet that interferes with security cameras, Lucy is implying. It would look suspicious to be wearing a bike helmet with safety lights on it if you didn't have a bike, and it would look equally odd if you were wearing a lighted hat or headband. That's why the woman was walking the bike across the street when she appeared at Jaime's building at almost the same moment I did, it occurs to me. The woman with the baguette ring and military watch wasn't riding the bike at all, and probably had a car parked somewhere.

"It's about dosage," Briggs continues. "Almost anything can be a poison if you get too much of it, including water. You can be poisoned by your wallpaper if there's enough copper arsenide in it. That's what happened to Clare Boothe Luce, paint chips falling from her bedroom ceiling when she was the ambassador to Italy."

"I'm just wondering if there's been anything new in efforts to weaponize botulinum toxin," I say to him. "Any technologies that a violent sociopathic person might have gotten hold of. A rogue military person, for example. Like the Army scientist who was working on an improved anthrax vaccine and carried out anthrax attacks that left at least five people dead."

"You always have to pick on the Army," says Briggs, who couldn't be more Army. "Nice of him to do us the courtesy of killing himself before the FBI could arrest him."

"Any other scientists who have been banned from labs where such research is going on?" I ask. "Especially anyone with military ties."

"If it becomes necessary to look for that, we could," Briggs says.

"In my opinion, it's necessary."

"Obviously that's your opinion, which is why you're up all night and calling me in Afghanistan."

"No new technologies that the military might know about?" I again ask. "Anything classified, you don't have to tell me what. Just that we should be considering such a possibility."

"No, thank God. Nothing I'm aware of. A gram of pure crystalline toxin could kill a million people if it was inhaled, and to weaponize it, you'd need a way to produce a large aerosol. Fortunately, there's still no effective method."

"What about a small aerosol distributed to a lot of people?" I ask. "In other words, an approach that is different, more painstaking. Or a distribution of small packages of poison that are mass-produced like MREs."

"I'm curious about why you're mentioning MREs specifically."

I tell him about Kathleen Lawler, about the burns on her foot and the trace evidence in her sink, and that her gastric contents were similar to an MRE menu of chicken and pasta with a ration of cheese spread.

"How the hell would an inmate get hold of an MRE?" he asks.

"Exactly," I reply. "Almost any food could have been poisoned, so why an MRE? Unless someone is experimenting with them to use on a bigger target."

"That would be pretty damn awful, and it would have to be a systematic approach, a highly organized one.

Someone working in the factory where rations are being produced and packaged, otherwise you're talking about a lot of vials of the toxin and hypodermic needles and hijacked delivery trucks."

"You wouldn't need a systematic approach if the point is terror," I reply.

"Well, I guess that's true," he reconsiders. "Have a hundred or three hundred or a thousand casualties at once in theater or on military bases or in operational areas, and the impact would be destabilizing. It would be disastrous to morale, would empower the enemy, and further cripple the U.S. economy."

"So not anything we're doing or working on," I make sure. "Not research our government might be involved in to damage morale and cripple the economy of the enemy. To terrorize."

"It's just not practical," he replies. "Russia's given up trying to weaponize botulinum toxin, as has the U.S., for which I'm grateful. A terrible idea, and I hope no one ever cracks the technology, but that's just me. A point source aerosol release, and ten percent of the people downwind of it up to a third of a mile away are going to be incapacitated or dead. God forbid it drifts to a school or a shopping mall. One thing we need to figure out is why some people are dead while others aren't or weren't intentional targets."

"We don't think Dawn Kincaid was intentional."

"But you think her mother was, and also the prosecutor."

"Yes."

"And based on what you're telling me, you think that whoever is responsible really wanted the prosecutor . . ."

"Jaime Berger and Kathleen Lawler. Yes, I believe whoever is responsible really wanted them dead."

"Then they're not necessarily what you're considering research, like the deaths of inmates, if what you suspect is true. A science project. I don't mean to trivialize the death of anyone who might have been killed with botulinum toxin. A hell of a way to die, for fuck's sake."

"I feel as if something changed," I reply. "I feel as if whoever is doing this is meticulous and has a plan, and then something came up she wasn't expecting. Possibly because of Jaime. Somebody doesn't like what she was doing."

"You believe this person is female."

"A woman delivered the sushi last night."

"Well, if that's confirmed."

"I suspect it's going to be, and then what?" I say to him.

"Three cases of homicidal poisoning by botulinum toxin that include a tampered-with MRE? All hell's going to break loose, Kay," he says. "And you need to stay out of the way. A million miles from it."

32

The sun is high in another washed-out sky, the heat wave tenaciously holding its grip on the Lowcountry, and what Colin Dengate claims simply isn't true. Not everyone gets used to riding around with no air-conditioning in weather like this, although Benton was thoughtful enough to bring me clothes, summer khakis, so I'm not baking in all black.

It's July 2, Saturday, almost ten a.m., and Colin's staff isn't working except for whoever's on call, and he had to swap a few favors to set up what I need, he said. Then he had to pick me up at the hotel, because I don't have a way to get around on my own. Marino is off with a shopping list for medical supplies that I want to have on hand, and he just dropped off Lucy at the local Harley-Davidson dealership. She intends for her transportation to be a motorcycle while she's here, and I wasn't going to leave Benton without the rental car, although his plan at the moment is to stay at the hotel. When I left him he was making phone calls, and FBI agents are on their way to Savannah from the Atlanta field office so he can brief them thoroughly as we wait for the news from the CDC to have its impact.

Botulinum toxin serotype A has been confirmed in Kathleen Lawler's and Jaime Berger's gastric contents. The toxin has been confirmed in the empty container of seaweed salad and also the leftovers in the refrigerator from the bag of take-out sushi that a serial poisoner delivered to Jaime's apartment building Thursday night. I haven't given the latest information to Briggs, who is in transit on a military airlifter out of the Middle East, but I don't need him to repeat what's expected of me, which is to do nothing. I don't want to hear him tell me that again, and I'm grateful I can't, because I don't intend to comply, at least not quite.

The investigation is locked down and off-limits in anticipation of what we expect to be a rapid and decisive diverting of jurisdiction to Homeland Security, the FBI, whatever the federal government decides, and I know when I'm supposed to stay out of the way, to use what I call the ten-foot-pole rule. Don't go anywhere near these poisoning cases, and were Briggs or anyone else to ask me, I would say that technically I'm not. The nine-year-old murders of a Savannah family and the mentally impaired woman who was convicted of them are of no interest to the FBI, the Department of Defense, the Pentagon, the White House, or scarcely anyone else at this moment.

Those cases are still closed, and Lola Daggette is still scheduled to die because Jaime never filed the petition to vacate her capital-murder convictions. The new DNA results are languishing in a private lab, awaiting some other criminal defense attorney to step in and finish what Jaime started. Until then, the Jordan murder cases are cold and old and irrelevant, when attention is on a serial poisoner, who might be a terrorist planning mass murder. As I've sorted through all that has happened, I continue to ask why. But the *why* of a terrorist plan to cause incapacitation and casualties among innocent civilians or military personnel isn't my question. Unfortunately, there's a long line of disturbed people in the world who would covet the chance to cause such destruction. What has my attention is something else.

If earlier deaths at the GPFW were vengeful murders that also served as research for a poisoner planning a widespread attack, then how do Kathleen Lawler and Jaime Berger fit with the modus operandi and ultimate goal? Jaime's reopening the Jordan case shouldn't matter to a poisoner planning terror, unless Jaime was tampering with something that alarmed this person enough to take the risk of getting Jaime out of the way. By murdering her and Kathleen, and inadvertently poisoning Dawn Kincaid, the killer has only drawn attention to herself when before there was none. A cluster of homicidal poisonings with botulinum toxin that might include tampering with military rations, and the entire

U.S. government is going to come down on the killer's head. Ultimately, she won't get away with it, and to take that chance after quiet years of painstaking premeditation can't be attributed to a loss of self-control or an escalated urge to torture and murder. Something unexpected happened.

Pathologists—and certainly this is my natural inclination—focus more on cause than effect. I'm less interested in the gore of blood and tissue spattered everywhere than I am in the angle of an entrance wound that might suggest it wasn't the victim who pulled the trigger, and I don't care about the drama of symptoms beyond the suffering they cause. My method is to track down the disease, to reflect away distractions, and to dissect to the bone, if need be, or, in the Jordan case, return to the crime scene as best I can. I intend to look at the photographs and all the evidence as if they've never been examined, and I might visit the Jordans' former home if I determine there's anything left to see that matters.

"The same records you were looking at yesterday," Colin is saying, as we walk along the deserted corridor, mobiles of bats and bones slowly twirling from the ceiling inside his empty lab building. "The knife recovered from the kitchen. Clothes, some other items that I collected at the scene and sent in with the bodies then. All of it submitted as evidence at trial, unless the prosecutor considered it irrelevant. My path tech Mandy will be in the room with you. Nice of her to come in, since we can't afford overtime. Anyway, same drill as before. And I'll be in my office, because I know damn well you'd rather take a look and not listen to opinions, meaning mine. You get to interpret the evidence the same way I did, and I won't be breathing down your neck."

Mandy O'Toole, in scrubs and examination gloves, is arranging a pair of children's pajamas on white butcher paper that covers the conference room table, the case records I started looking at yesterday out of the way, stacked on a chair.

"It's the kids' stuff that's really, really hard for me," she says, and I recognize most of what I'm seeing from photographs I began to review yesterday.

Neatly spread out on the white paper are two sets of children's pajamas, one SpongeBob, the other a football design with helmets of the Georgia Bulldogs. A pair of men's boxer shorts and a T-shirt must have been what Clarence Jordan was sleeping in when he was stabbed to death in bed, and a blue floral and lace nightgown obviously was his wife's. All of the garments are stained dark brown with old blood, and riddled with small slits and punctures from at least one sharp instrument, and there are multiple small holes where fabric was removed for DNA analysis.

I pull gloves out of a box on the table and put them on, then pick up evidence labeled and marked by the court: a knife, and I leave it inside its bag, examining it through the plastic. The blade is approximately six inches in length, the wooden handle smudged with old blood. White, filmy partial fingerprints and an intact one are permanently fixed in superglue on the nonporous smooth surfaces of the steel and lacquered wood, and while the knife may have been used by the killer to make a sand-wich in the kitchen, I don't believe it killed anyone.

The kitchen knife is a clip point, or "granny," used for such tasks as removing the eyes from potatoes or peeling vegetables and fruits, and as suggested by the name, the blade has been clipped off from the middle of the spine all the way to the point, leaving a dull edge for resting your thumb. Any knife with a false curved edge will be less effective in piercing, and therefore not a good choice in stabbings. Furthermore, the blade at its widest point is almost two inches, which is inconsistent with what I saw on body diagrams in the autopsy reports. I walk to the other end of the table and look through the thick files on the chair, sifting through documents until I find what I remember looking at yesterday morning, a de-scription of the wounds.

The cause of death in all four cases is multiple sharp force injuries, and I'm particularly interested in the stab wounds to the chest and neck, because areas of the body that offer a thickness of tissue and hollow spaces can be a good indication of the length of the blade. On Clarence Jordan's right lateral chest, the wound measures one inch long and extends to a depth of three inches, penetrating the pericardial sac and the heart. On his right lateral neck, the wound track travels front to back and down-ward, and to a depth of three inches, severing his carotid artery.

Other measurements of the other victims' wounds suggest the blade was at most three inches in length and an inch wide, with some sort of guard at the top of the handle that left four parallel but irregular abraded contusions spaced one-eighth of an inch apart. Such a pattern injury couldn't have been inflicted by the granny knife or any kitchen knife I can think of, and it was Colin's conclusion at the time that the weapon was unknown and inconsistent with anything recovered from the scene. It would seem that the killer carried in what must have been an unusual cutting instrument, and afterward left with it.

Clarence Jordan has no incised wounds or defensive injuries of the arms or hands, arguing against him struggling or even being awake when he was attacked. Toxicology findings of a blood alcohol concentration of .04 and what would be considered a therapeutic level of clonazepam paint a picture of him having a drink or two and taking a modest dose, perhaps a milligram of the benzodiazepine, to calm anxieties or to help him sleep. That thought leads me around to the other side of the table, where a plastic evidence bag that isn't marked for court contains half a dozen prescription bottles, only one of them with Clarence Jordan's name on it, the beta blocker propranolol. Other bottles belonged to his wife, including antibiotics, an antidepressant, and clonazepam, and while it isn't uncommon for someone to take another person's medication, it surprises me that Clarence Jordan would.

He was a physician with easy access to samples, to any medication he wanted, and it is illegal to share prescription drugs. That doesn't mean he didn't get into his wife's clonazepam the night of January 5 when he returned home from his volunteer work at an area men's emergency shelter around dinnertime. It also doesn't preclude the possibility that he didn't take the sedative willingly. It would be easy to crush pills to mix in someone's drink, and I continue to think about the security system event logs I reviewed.

According to the actual data from the alarm company's internal archives, the Jordans armed and disarmed the alarm repeatedly through November of 2001, but something changed in December, when it appears the false alarms, allegedly caused by the Jordan children, began to be a problem. The last month the Jordans were alive, there were five faults that set off the alarm, all involving the same zone, the kitchen door. The police did not respond, and the alarms were cleared because the subscriber, when called by the service, said the alarms were false. The arming of the security system became increasingly erratic through the holidays, based on my review of the logs, but it continued to be set most nights, which is why I find the data for Saturday, January 5, rather odd. The alarm wasn't set at all that day until almost eight o'clock at night. Then it was disarmed at not quite eleven and never reset, and this seems to be contrary to what has been supposed by journalists and the police over the years.

In fact, it would appear that Dr. Jordan returned home from his volunteer work and set the alarm, then three hours later someone disarmed it, and that detail in addition to his having a sedative on board not prescribed to him disturbs me. I spread out scene photographs of the bloody massacre in the Jordans' master bedroom, looking at images of the couple's bodies in the bed, the covers pulled up to their necks, and that bothers me, too. People aren't manikins when they're being murdered, and bedcovers aren't neatly arranged over their dead bodies unless the killer or someone does so for psychological reasons, to restore order or cover up what they've done. Colin has commented that the bodies may have been displayed to mock the victims, and I sort through more photos that were taken after he removed the top covers so he could examine Dr. and Mrs. Jordan's bodies in situ.

He is on his back, his head on a pillow, staring straight up with an open mouth, his arms straight down by his sides, his genitals protruding through the slit in his boxer shorts, and I doubt this was his position at death. Someone rearranged him, and the more I see, the more I understand the hatred that the police, the prosecutor, and others must feel toward Lola Daggette as they imagined her inside this room, enjoying herself after she's slaughtered everyone, demonstrating blatant degradation and contempt.

The T-shirt and the waistband of Dr. Jordan's white boxer shorts are completely saturated with blood that has soaked the sheet under him, spreading in a stain that extends to the edge of the mattress and under the body of his wife, the entire fitted sheet bloody. He was stabbed a total of nine times in his chest and neck, and there is no indication he struggled or attempted to ward off the vicious attacks of a knife with an unusual guard that left parallel contusions on his skin. His wife is on her right side, her hands tucked under her chin, facing away from her husband, toward the window that overlooks the street in front and the old cemetery on the other side of it, and I certainly don't believe she was in this position when she died. Her body was rearranged, staged to look almost pious, as if she is praying, yet her gown is hiked up to her waist and her breasts are exposed.

I pick up her flannel gown, long-sleeved, with buttons up to the neck and a lacy collar that seems to fit with the demure serious-looking woman in the Christmas portrait taken not even a month before she was to be photographed again, this time vulgarly positioned on her blood-soaked bed. Flakes of old dark blood drift to the white paper covering the table as I look at every perforation and cut left by a blade that stabbed her a total of twenty-seven times, her face, her head, her chest, her back, her neck, her throat slashed for good measure. The gown is stained front and back, so saturated with blood that only areas of the sleeves and the bottom of the hem indicate the flannel is a pattern of floral blue.

I'm aware of Mandy O'Toole sitting in a chair she's moved near a window to stay out of my way. She's watching me intently, curiously, as I arrange the gown on top of the paper, putting it back the way I found it, dried blood making some areas of the fabric as stiff as petticoat netting. Mandy doesn't say a word or interfere, and I don't offer my thoughts, which are getting darker and uglier by the minute. I check Gloria Jordan's case file again. I study body diagrams and review laboratory reports of blood samples taken from her gown, confirming the presence of her DNA, as one would expect, but also her husband's and their five-year-old daughter's. Why Brenda's blood?

I notice from Colin's measurements and descriptions that the wound to Gloria's neck begins behind her left ear and travels down in one clean incision, under the chin, below the right earlobe, consistent with her having her throat cut from behind. If she didn't see it coming and her carotid was severed, that would explain the lack of defensive injuries Colin mentioned, but it raises more questions than it answers. Next I notice another photograph of her on the bed, a close-up taken from the foot of it. Blood spatters are on the tops of her feet, and the soles of them are bloody, which doesn't seem possible if she was lying down when she was cut and stabbed. But it's hard to say. There was so much blood everywhere, and I try to imagine an assailant cutting Mrs. Jordan's throat from behind if she was lying down, sound asleep, drugged out on clonazepam.

I follow blood that is streaked, smeared, pooled, stepped in, and splashed on the stairs, and then the arterial pattern that may have been from the slashing of the knife, perhaps to the neck, perhaps Gloria Jordan's neck, the spatter arching in rhythm to the beating of a heart that was about to quit. But whose heart, and which direction was the person heading, up or down, in or out? Crime scene investigators, even good ones like Sammy

Chang, can't swab every blood drop or streak or mop up every pool and puddle at a scene, and the labs couldn't possibly analyze all of it.

Down the stairs to the landing at the bottom, and I pause in the area near the entryway and front door where Brenda collapsed as I try to come up with an explanation for why her blood would have been transferred to the nightgown of her mother, who supposedly died in bed. I look for any evidence that efforts were made to clean up blood in the foyer, on the stairs, in the hallway, or anywhere in the house, but I see nothing that hints of it, and there is nothing to suggest it in any of the reports I've seen. I continue going back to the area of the entryway, to Brenda's body, a sight that must have horrified police when they arrived at the house after the next-door neighbor discovered the broken glass in the kitchen door and called 911.

No normal person likes to look at dead children, and it's a temptation not to look closely enough. The flooring in the area of the entryway is a chaotic pattern of drips and spatters cast off by a weapon, and smears and puddles, and bloody prints left by footwear and also marks that appear to have been made by bare feet. Toe prints and a heel that are too large for a child's, and I pick up the SpongeBob pajamas again. They have footies. The marks left by bare feet could not have been left by Brenda when she was fleeing downstairs toward the front of the house and the door, and I find myself back to the same conundrum, the cut, which is significant, on her mother's left hand.

Colin speculates Mrs. Jordan sliced open her thumb while pruning in her garden, and I follow the thread of this theory through photographs, returning to the sunporch and the garden in back. I revisit the round drops of dried blood, approximately eighteen inches apart on terra-cotta tile and flagstone and foliage, Mrs. Jordan's blood, believed to be unrelated to the case and excluded from evidence at the trial. If what Colin suggests is correct, and I don't think it is, she must have injured herself almost immediately after she began pruning. But there's no tool anywhere in any of the pictures I review, not a cut branch or side shoot or sucker in sight, the garden bleak and in need of a winter cleanup it never got.

When Marino questioned Lenny Casper, the former next-door neighbor who happened to notice Mrs. Jordan in her garden the Saturday afternoon of January 5, Casper made no mention of her appearing to have hurt herself. Maybe he didn't notice, but most people taking their dog out or looking through a window might be aware of someone hurrying back into the house, dripping blood. A casual observation by a neighbor and drops of Gloria Jordan's blood that didn't make sense in the context of such gory homicides led to the conclusion that she cut her thumb earlier in the day. She returned to the house, forgot to clean up the sunporch and the hallway near the guest bath, and didn't bandage her injury or let her physician husband tend to it when he arrived home from the men's shelter. I just don't believe it.

According to her toxicology report, when Mrs. Jordan died she had alcohol and clonazepam on board, higher blood levels than her husband's, and she was taking the antidepressant sertraline. After the murders, these prescription drugs were collected from the master bathroom, from what appears to be her side of the sink, and I look at them again in their evidence bag, noticing a detail that eluded me earlier.

"You want to help me with something?" I ask Mandy, who is observing everything I do with her cobalt blue stare.

"You bet." She's already out of her chair.

"The Barrie Lou Rivers case file? I believe it's electronic, not printed, because her death occurred after the office became paperless."

"Want me to print it?" she asks.

"Not necessary. But I'm interested in a document, if you can find it in her file."

"Can you wait one minute so I can get my laptop?"

"I'll stand in the hallway." I step outside the conference room.

33

Mandy O'Toole returns from the histology lab with a laptop and begins a search of Barrie Lou Rivers's records while I search Lola Daggette's clothing for anything that might have been missed.

I examine the Windbreaker, the blue turtleneck and tan corduroys that she was washing in her shower, an incriminating act that was the sole basis for her being charged with multiple counts of first-degree murder and sentenced to death. Much of the blood was washed away, only traces of a pattern left, areas of dark discoloration on the thighs of the pants, and drips and smears on the cuffs and on the front of the Windbreaker and its sleeves. Lola would have had blood on her shoes, and my thoughts keep going back to that.

"Got her file. Tox and other lab reports, autopsy records," Mandy says, sitting in the chair by the window, the computer in her lap. "What are you looking for, exactly?"

"Something you might not have but Jaime Berger did. A one-page document included with the autopsy protocol and tox reports," I reply. "A chain-of-custody form from the GPFW relating to the execution drugs. The prescription was filled but never used because Barrie Lou Rivers died before they could execute her. Just a strange piece of paper that doesn't belong with the autopsy record but somehow ended up in there."

"My favorite thing," she says. "Details that aren't supposed to be included. But they are."

As I continue looking at Lola Daggette's clothing, I think about what the victims had on when they died and how much blood there was. The crazed trail of footwear prints on the black-and-white checkered kitchen tile and the fir wood floor indicate that the killer was tracking blood throughout the house or someone was or more than one person was. Not all of the tread patterns look the same. Contamination by people disrupting the crime scene after the police got there, or did Dawn Kincaid have a partner in her hideous crimes?

It wasn't Lola. Had she been walking around the Jordans' house that early morning, her shoes would have been bloody. Yet she wasn't washing shoes in the shower when the volunteer healthcare worker walked in. She wasn't washing her underwear or socks. She was never examined for injuries, such as scratches, and it wasn't her DNA or fingerprints recovered from the victims' bodies or the scene, and it's tragic no one paid attention to these facts. Dawn Kincaid's DNA but her fingerprints aren't a match, and I remember what Kathleen Lawler said about giving her *children* away. As if she had more than one.

"Paydirt," Mandy says, and I think of *Payback*.

A monster most assume Lola made up.

"Yes, exactly what I'm looking for," I reply, as I read the form on the screen, a lethal prescription filled by a pharmacist named Roberta Price, the drugs delivered to the GPFW and signed for by Tara Grimm at noon on the day of Barrie Lou Rivers's execution, two years ago, March first.

Boxes checked on the form and blanks filled in indicate the sodium thiopental and pancuronium bromide were stored in the warden's office, then moved into the execution room at five p.m. but never used.

"Mean something? You're looking like you're thinking something," Mandy can't resist asking, as I hand the computer notebook back to her.

"As far as you know, these are the only items of clothing belonging to Lola Daggette?" I answer her question with one of my own, as I pick up the evidence bag of prescription drugs, checking labels on the orange plastic bottles. "In other words, no shoes."

"If this is what Colin's got, what the GBI still has stored, then that's all there was, I feel sure," she says.

"As bloody as the killer would have been, impossible

to think the shoes weren't bloody, too," I comment. "Why wash your clothes in the shower but not your bloody shoes?"

"One time Colin scraped gum off the bottom of a high-heeled shoe that came in with the body and recovered a hair, then the DNA of the killer. We had T-shirts made. Colin Dengate the Gum Shoe."

"Would you mind finding him? Tell him I'll meet him outside. I'd like to take a ride. Do a retrospective visit, if possible."

Lola Daggette didn't wash her shoes in the shower, because a pair of shoes wasn't included with the bloody clothes planted in her room. She didn't murder anyone, and she wasn't inside the Jordans' antebellum mansion the early morning of the murders or on any occasion. I suspect the troubled teenager would have had no reason to meet the distinguished and wealthy Clarence and Gloria Jordan or their beautiful blond twins and probably didn't have a clue who they were until she was interrogated about their murders and charged with them.

I strongly suspect Lola also didn't have a clue who to blame, a person or persons motivated by more than drugs or petty cash or the thrill of killing, a monster or a pair of them with a grand plan that a mentally impaired teenager in a halfway house wouldn't have had any reason to know about. Or if she did, she'd probably be dead, too, just as Kathleen Lawler and Jaime are. I suspect there was an orchestrated scheme that included framing Lola, just as someone is trying to frame me now, and I don't believe these manipulations are the sole handi-work of Dawn Kincaid.

I dig my phone out of my shoulder bag and enter Benton's number as I emerge from the lab building, finding a spot near bottlebrush bushes with brilliant red blossoms where I'm eye to eye with a hummingbird, and the blazing sun is a relief. I'm chilled, even my bones are cold from being inside the air-conditioned conference room surrounded by evidence so obvious it seems to shout its grotesque secrets, and I'm not sure who's going to respond.

I can count on Colin, and, of course, Marino and Lucy will pay attention, and I've sent both of them text messages asking if the name Roberta Price means anything, and asking what else can we find out about Gloria Jordan? There's very little about Mrs. Jordan in news stories I've read, few personal details and nothing to suggest there were problems, but I'm sure there were, and the timing couldn't be worse.

If Benton weren't my husband, I have no doubt he wouldn't listen to what will sound like a tale of horror, a sensational yarn, something made up. What I strongly suspect happened nine years ago isn't going to be of interest to the FBI or Homeland Security right now, and I understand why, but someone needs to hear me out and do something about it anyway.

"Sounds like your friends from Atlanta arrived," I say to Benton, when he answers his cell phone, and voices in the background are loud, a lot of people with him.

I'm about to try his patience. I can feel it coming.

"Just getting started. What's up?" Distracted and tense, he is moving around a noisy room as he talks.

"Maybe you and your colleagues could look into something."

"What's that?"

"Adoption records, and I need you to pay attention," I reply. "I know the Jordan case isn't a priority at the moment, but I think it should be."

"I always pay attention, Kay." He doesn't sound annoyed, but I know he is.

"Whatever pertains to Kathleen Lawler, to Dawn Kincaid, although that wasn't her name when she was born and I have no idea the name of the first family who adopted her. Dawn was passed around to a number of different foster homes or families, and eventually ended up in California with a couple that died. Supposedly. Anything you can find that the FBI hasn't already found, specifically relating to Dawn's contacting someone. She had to have contacted someone, possibly an agency down here in 2001 or 2002, when she decided to learn the identities of her biological parents. She had to have gone through the same process anybody else would."

"You don't know that what Kathleen Lawler told you is true, and it would be best to discuss this later."

"We know Dawn paid a visit to Savannah in early 2002, and we need to discuss it now," I reply, as I envision Kathleen Lawler in the contact interview room, talking about being locked up in the *big house* when she went into labor, and I keep thinking of her comments.

Something about being locked up like an animal and having to *give your children away* and what was she supposed to do, give *them* to a twelve-year-old boy, to Jack Fielding?

"That really hasn't been proven, either," Benton says, and when he's in a hurry and doesn't want to have a discussion, he gets contrary.

"Retested DNA places her in the Jordans' house in 2002," I say to him. "But you're going to have to request different testing, and I'll get to that. Did she come all the way from California to meet her biological mother, or was there another purpose?"

"I know this is important to you," Benton says, and what he means is Dawn Kincaid's alleged visit to Savannah in 2002 isn't important to him. The Bureau and the United States government, perhaps even the president, are preoccupied with potential terrorism.

"What I'm suggesting is the possibility of someone else she wanted to meet in addition to her mother." I go on anyway. "Maybe there are records no one has thought to check into. This is important. I promise."

He's moving around, and a voice in the background says something about coffee, and Benton says thanks and then to me, "What are you contemplating?"

"How it's possible to leave bloody fingerprints on a knife handle and a bottle of lavender soap at a crime scene if you had nothing to do with the crimes."

"What about the DNA of those bloody prints?"

"The victims' DNA and also an unknown donor, a profile that we now know is Dawn Kincaid. But the prints aren't hers," I answer. "The Jordans' DNA and Dawn's, supposedly. But some other person's prints."

"Supposedly?"

"Bloody transfers by whoever had bloody hands and touched the kitchen knife, the soap bottle, but the fingerprints aren't Dawn Kincaid's. They've never been identified, supposedly from contamination, from a lot of people being on the scene, including journalists, maybe walking through blood and picking up evidence, touching it, or even cops, crime scene techs. Apparently the scene wasn't well contained. That's the explanation I've been given."

"It's possible. If people didn't have their prints on file for exclusionary purposes and they handled things. I'm going to have to go, Kay."

"Yes, it's possible, especially when everyone involved is eager to accept such an explanation because they've got Lola Daggette and aren't looking for anyone else. That seems to be the problem across the board, overlooking, not questioning, not digging deep enough because the case is solved, the murders committed by someone who was caught washing bloody clothes and told all sorts of lies that bordered on nonsense."

"Tell her I'll call back in a few minutes," Benton says to someone else.

I watch Colin walk out of the building. When he sees I'm on the phone, he gestures that he'll wait for me in the Land Rover.

"See what you and your agent colleagues can find out about Roberta Price," I say to Benton, who isn't saying anything. "The pharmacist who filled Gloria Jordan's prescriptions nine years ago. Who is she, and is she connected to Dawn Kincaid?"

"I remind you that if someone is a head pharmacist, their name is on every prescription bottle, even if they didn't fill it."

"Probably not if it's a script called in by a prison doc or one who's an executioner," I reply. "If you're the head pharmacist and didn't fill the prescription for sodium thiopental and pancuronium bromide, you might not want your name on it. You might not want your name even remotely associated with anything having to do with an execution."

"I have no idea what you're getting at."

"Two years ago a pharmacist named Roberta Price, presumably the same person who filled Mrs. Jordan's prescriptions, also filled the prescription for the sodium thiopental and pancuronium bromide that would have been used in Barrie Lou Rivers's lethal injection, had she not mysteriously died first. The drugs were delivered to the GPFW, and Tara Grimm signed for them. It's hard to imagine she and Roberta Price aren't acquainted."

"A pharmacist at Monck's Pharmacy. A small pharmacy owned by Herbert Monck." Benton must have searched Roberta Price's name as he was listening to me.

"Where Jaime shopped, but Roberta Price's name isn't on Jaime's prescription bottles. And I wonder why," I reply.

"Why? I'm sorry, I'm confused." Benton sounds completely distracted.

"Just a hunch that maybe when Jaime went into Monck's Pharmacy, Roberta Price kept her distance," I add, and I recall the man in the lab coat who sold the Advil to me mentioning the name Robbi, someone who must have been inside the store a moment earlier and then suddenly wasn't. "I don't guess you can tell me what kind of car Roberta Price drives, and if it might be a black Mercedes wagon," I say to Benton.

A long pause, and he says, "No car registered to her, at least not by the name Roberta Price. Could be in some other name. Did Gloria Jordan get her meds from this same pharmacy?"

"One close to her home. A Rexall back then that's been replaced by a CVS."

"So at some point after the murders, maybe Roberta Price changed jobs, ending up in a smaller pharmacy very close to the GPFW," Benton says to me, as he tells someone else he'll be right there. "There's no probable cause to go after a pharmacist just because she filled prescriptions for Gloria Jordan, for the GPFW—and probably tens of thousands of other people in this area, Kay. I'm not saying we won't look into it, because we will."

"A pharmacy that must not have a problem aiding in executions at the GPFW, possibly the men's prison, too. It's unusual," I point out. "Many pharmacists see themselves as drug-therapy managers responsible for promoting a patient's best interests. Killing your patient usually isn't included."

"It tells us Roberta Price doesn't have ethical issues about it or just feels she's doing her job."

"Or takes pleasure in it, especially if the anesthesia wears off or something else goes wrong. They had a case like that here in Georgia not so long ago. Took at least twice the usual time to kill the condemned inmate, and he suffered. I wonder who prescribed those lethal drugs."

"We'll find out," Benton says, but he's not going to do it this minute.

"And someone needs to contact the DNA lab Jaime was using," I tell him, whether he thinks it's a priority or not, as I walk in the direction of Colin's grumbling Land Rover. "I suspect they're not going to be up to speed with the new technologies being used by the military."

I'm referring to the Armed Forces DNA Identification Lab, AFDIL, at Dover Air Force Base, where DNA technology has reached a new level of sophistication and sensitivity because of the challenges posed by our war dead. What happens when identical twins end up in theater and one of them is killed or, God forbid, both? Standard DNA testing can't tell them apart, and while it's true that their fingerprints wouldn't be the same, there may be nothing left of their fingers to compare.

"IEDs and the devastating injuries, in some cases almost complete annihilation," I add. "The challenges of identification when all that's left is a mist of contaminated blood on a shred of fabric or a fragment of burned bone. I know AFDIL has the technology to analyze epigenetic phenomena, using methylation and histone acetylation for making DNA comparisons not possible with other types of analyses."

"Why would we need to do something like that in these cases?"

"Because identical twins may start out in life with identical DNA, but older twins are going to have significant differences in their gene expression if you have the technology to look for these differences, and the more time twins spend apart, the greater these differences become. DNA determines who you are, and eventually who you are determines your DNA," I explain, as I open the passenger's door, hot air blasting out of the blower.

34

The man who answers the door is sweating, the veins standing out like ropes in his big tan biceps, as if he was in the middle of a workout when we showed up unannounced.

He is visibly displeased to find two strangers on his porch, one of them in range pants and a GBI polo shirt, the other in a khaki uniform, an old Land Rover parked in the shade of a live oak tree next to trellises of jasmine separating this property from the one next door.

"I'm sorry to disturb you." Colin opens his wallet, displaying his medical examiner's shield. "We'd really appreciate a few minutes of your time."

"What's this about?"

"Are you Gabe Mullery?"

"Is something wrong?"

"We're not here on official business, and nothing's wrong. This is a casual visit, and we'll leave if you ask us to. But if you'd give me a minute to explain, we'd be most grateful," Colin says. "You're Gabe Mullery, the owner of the house?"

"That's me." He doesn't offer to shake our hands. "It's my house. My wife's all right? Everything's okay?"

"As far as I know. Sorry if we scared you."

"Nothing scares me. What do you need?"

Quite handsome, with dark hair, gray eyes, and a powerful jaw, Gabe Mullery is in cutoff sweatpants and a white T-shirt emblazoned with *U.S. NAVY NUKE: If you see me running, it's already too late.* He blocks the doorway with his muscular body, clearly not the sort to appreciate strangers dropping by without calling first, no matter the reason. But we didn't want to give the man who lives in the former Jordan house the chance to say no. I need to see the garden and figure out what Gloria Jordan was doing in it the afternoon of January 5.

I don't think it was pruning, and I want to know why she returned to her garden very early the next morning, possibly to the old root cellar, possibly because she was forced back there in the pitch dark about the time she and her family were murdered. I have an imagined scenario that is based on my interpretation of the evidence, and information Lucy e-mailed to me during the drive here only strengthens my conclusion that Mrs. Jordan wasn't an innocent victim, and that's putting it kindly.

I suspect that on the night of January 5 she may have spiked her husband's drink with clonazepam, ensuring he would settle into a hard sleep. At around eleven, she went downstairs and disarmed the alarm, leaving the mansion and her family vulnerable to a break-in that she couldn't have anticipated would end the way it did. What she probably had in mind was wrong, and most of all it was foolish, not so different from a lot of schemes devised by unhappy people who want out of their marriages and are seduced into believing they're entitled to take what they think they deserve.

Mrs. Jordan probably never meant for her children to be harmed, and certainly not herself, and possibly not even her husband, whom I suspect she'd come to resent deeply, if not hate. She may have been determined to get away from him, but probably what she wanted was a secret source of cash, something of her own, and not necessarily for him to be dead. A simple plot, a simple burglary on a January night after a day of intermittent thunderstorms and chilly blustery winds, Lucy let me know the weather back then. One doesn't decide to clean up the garden in such conditions, not that there's any evidence Mrs. Jordan actually pruned so much as a branch stub or a watersprout the afternoon before her death.

What was she doing by the crumbled walls and depressed earth, what looked to me in photographs like the ruins of a root cellar from an earlier century? Maybe attempting to outsmart her accomplice or accomplices, and the grim irony is she wouldn't have survived even if she'd been honorable. She didn't recognize the devil she'd befriended and come to trust, and must have assumed all would be forgiven if a fortune in gold I suspect she'd promised to share was nowhere to be found because she'd decided to keep all of it for herself and had hidden it.

"Look, I wouldn't blame you for not wanting to be bothered about this," Colin is saying on the hot front porch, with its stately white columns and view of a cemetery that dates from the American Revolution. Puffs of hot wind carry the scent of cut grass.

"Not that damn case," Gabe Mullery says. "You and reporters, and the worst are the tourists. People ringing the bell and wanting a tour."

"We're not tourists, and we don't want that kind of tour." Colin introduces me, adding that I'm returning to Boston in the next day or two and want to take a look at the garden in back.

"I don't mean to be rude, but what the hell for?" Mullery says, and past him, through the open doorway, is the fir wood staircase, and the landing near the foyer where Brenda Jordan's body was found.

"You have every right to be rude about it," I reply, "and you're not obligated to let me look."

"It's my wife's thing, and she completely redid it. Her office is out there. So whatever you think you're going to see probably doesn't exist anymore. I don't understand the point."

"If it's all right, I'd like a quick look anyway," I reply. "I've been reviewing some information. . . ."

"About that case." He exhales loudly in exasperation.

"I knew it was a mistake to get this place, and now with her execution coming up of all times on fucking Halloween. Like we can be in town for that. Close up the fucking place and call in the National Guard, would if I could, and wait it out in Hawaii, you got that straight. All right."

He steps aside to let us in.

"Ridiculous having this conversation at all," he continues irritably, "but not outside in this heat for all the world to see. Buying this damn place. Jesus Christ. I shouldn't have listened to my wife. I told her we'd be on the tour route and it wasn't a good idea, but she's the one here most of the time. I travel pretty much constantly. She should live where she wants, it's only fair. You know, I'm sorry people died in here, but dead is dead, and what I hate is people violating our privacy."

"I can understand that," Colin says.

We walk into the grand foyer of a house that looks so familiar it's as if I've been in it before, and I imagine Gloria Jordan on the stairs, barefoot and in her blue floral-printed flannel gown, padding toward the kitchen, where she waited for company and a conspiracy to unfold. Or perhaps she was in some other area of the house when the door's glass shattered and a hand reached in to unlock the deadbolt with the key that shouldn't have been there. I don't know where she was when her husband was murdered but not in bed. That's not where she was when she was stabbed twenty-seven times and her throat was slashed, overkill, what I associate with lust

and rage. Most likely that attack took place in the area of
the foyer where she stepped barefoot in her own blood
and in the blood of her slain daughter.

"You probably can tell I'm not from here," Mullery is
saying, and at first I thought he might be English, but his
accent sounds more Australian. "Sydney, London, then
to North Carolina to specialize in hyperbaric medicine at
Duke. I ended up here in Savannah long after the murders, so stories about this place didn't mean much to me
or I sure as hell never would have gone to see it when it
went on the market a few years ago. We looked, and it
was love at first sight for Robbi."

*Not the marriage made in heaven it was painted to
be,* Lucy e-mailed me, and attached information from
records she searched that paint a portrait of a miserable
woman with a self-destructive past who married Clarence
Jordan in 1997 and immediately had twins, a boy and a
girl named Josh and Brenda. A Cinderella story, it must
have seemed to those around her when at the age of
twenty she was hired by Dr. Jordan's practice as a re-
ceptionist, and apparently this is how they met. Maybe
he thought he could save her, and for a while she must
have stabilized, her earlier years ones of chaos and trouble, pursued by collection agencies as she cashed bad
checks and got drunk in public, moving from one low-
rent apartment to the next every six or twelve months.

"Kings Bay?" Colin assumes Gabe Mullery is affiliated with the Atlantic Fleet's home port for Trident II
submarines armed with nuclear weapons, less than a
hundred miles from here.

"A diving medical officer in the reserves," he says. "But my day job is here at Regional Hospital. Emergency medicine."

Another doctor in the house, I think, and I hope he's happier than Clarence Jordan must have been, trying to control his wife and do so discreetly, possibly relying on his publicized friendship with the chairman of the news service that owned a number of newspapers and television and radio stations back then, someone Dr. Jordan served with on committees and charitable foundations and who had the ability to manipulate what might end up in the press.

The media didn't report a word about Mrs. Jordan's recurrence of bad behavior, the series of sad and humiliating events beginning in January of 2001 when she was arrested for shoplifting after hiding an expensive dress under her clothes and neglecting to remove the security tag. A cry for attention, for help, but possibly more treacherous than that, it went through my mind, as I was going through Lucy's e-mail.

Mrs. Jordan was striking out in a way that might actually punish a husband who neglected her and had rigid expectations about his wife's role and behavior, and she retaliated by targeting his pride, his image, his impossibly high standards. Not even two months after her shoplifting incident at Oglethorpe Mall, she ran her car into a tree and was charged with DUI, and four months after that in July, she called the police, intoxicated and belligerent, claiming the house had been burglarized. Detectives responded, and in her statement she claimed the housekeeper had stolen gold coins worth at least two hundred thousand dollars that were kept hidden under insulation in the attic. The housekeeper was never charged, the accusation dismissed after Dr. Jordan informed police he'd recently relocated the gold, an investment he'd had for years. It was safely inside the house, and nothing was missing.

But what became of the gold between July and January 6? Dr. Jordan could have sold it, I suppose, although the price was at an all-time low throughout 2001, averaging less than three hundred dollars an ounce, Lucy pointed out, and it seems odd to think he wouldn't have waited for the value to go up, especially if he'd had the gold for a while. There's no evidence he needed money. His 2001 tax return showed earnings and dividends on investments totaling more than a million dollars. Whatever became of the gold, it seems a fact it was gone after the murders. There's no reference to stolen property, and investigative reports indicate that jewelry and the family silver didn't appear to have been touched.

Certainly Gloria Jordan didn't end up with a small fortune in gold, since it likely was she who relocated it the last time, likely the afternoon before her murder, and although I don't think anyone will ever know exactly what happened, I do have a theory based on the facts as I now know them. I think she staged a burglary to explain the disappearance of what she herself intended to steal, and then decided she wouldn't have to share the loot with a coconspirator, or more than one, if she pretended she couldn't find it. Her husband must have hidden the gold yet again, and she was dreadfully sorry but it wasn't her fault.

I can only imagine what she might have said when her accomplice, or most likely two of them, showed up, but I believe Mrs. Jordan was up against a force of evil far more brilliant and cruel than she could conjure up in her worst dreams. I suspect that on the early Sunday morning of January 6, she was forced to reveal the gold's hiding place and perhaps while she was in the garden near the old root cellar she received her first cut. Possibly as a warning. Or maybe the beginning of the attack, and she fled back into the house, where she was killed, her body carried upstairs to be lewdly displayed in bed next to her slain husband.

"So we're looking around and it's a great place, and I'm impressed, I admit," Gabe Mullery is saying to us. "And an amazingly good price, and then the Realtor went into detail about what had happened here in 2002, and no wonder it was a deal. I wasn't thrilled about the association or the karma or whatever you might want to call it, but I'm not a superstitious person. I don't believe in ghosts. What I have come to believe in is tourists, in idiots that have the sense and manners of pigeons, and I don't want a carnival atmosphere now that her execution's back on."

There will be no execution. I will make sure of it.

"Damn shame it didn't go down as planned, that the judge delayed it. We want it over with so it will settle to the bottom, out of sight, and be forgotten. Hopefully someday people will stop asking for the nickel tour."

I'll do whatever it takes to make sure Lola Daggette never sees the death chamber, and maybe the day will come when she'll have nothing to fear. Not Tara Grimm, not corrections officers at the GPFW, not *Payback*, as in paying the ultimate price, and maybe that ultimate price is one with the first name of Roberta. Anything can be a poison if you have too much of it, even water, General Briggs said, and who would know more about medications and microbes and their fatal possibilities than a pharmacist, an evil alchemist who turns a drug meant to heal into a potion of suffering and death.

"Tell me what you want to look at," Gabe Mullery says to me. "I don't know if I can help you or not. Another owner lived here before we bought the place, and I really don't know the details of what it was like when those people were killed."

The kitchen is unrecognizable, completely renovated, with new cabinets and modern stainless-steel appliances and a black granite tile floor. The door leading outside is solid with no panes of glass, just as Jaime said, and I wonder how she knew, but I have a guess. She wouldn't have hesitated to walk here and insert herself, possibly feigning she was a tourist wandering around, or she might have boldly said who she was and why she was interested. I notice the laptop computer on an area of the counter where there is no place to sit and work. There is a wireless keypad on top of a table and contacts in every window I see, an upgraded security system that might include cameras.

"Well, you're smart to have a good security system,"

I remark to Gabe Mullery. "Considering the curiosity people have about this place."

"Yeah, it's called a Browning nine-mil. That's my security system." He grins. "My wife's into all the gadgets, glass breaks, motion sensors, video cameras, the nerdy one. Always worrying people will think we got drugs in here."

"Two urban myths," Colin says. "Doctors keep drugs in the house and make a lot of money."

"Well, I am gone all the time, and she does sell drugs for a living." He opens the kitchen door. "Another urban myth that pharmacists keep a stash at home," he says, as we go down stone steps to a hyphen of flagstones and grass, and I hear music on the sunporch, which is set up as a gym and probably where Gabe Mullery was when we showed up. Before that, he probably was cutting the grass.

I recognize the red terra-cotta tile floor behind glass where there's a bench and racks of free weights, and leaning against the back of the house are two bicycles with small wheels and hinged aluminum frames, one red, with the seat and handlebar raised high, the other one silver and for someone shorter. Next to them are a lawnmower, a rake, and bags of clippings.

"I guess the best thing is to let you wander around," Mullery says, and I can tell by his demeanor he's not the least bit wary of us and has no idea that maybe he should be. "Gardening's not my thing. This is Robbi's domain," he says, as if he's not particularly interested in it, and nothing that once was there is left.

The tea olives and original shrubbery, the statuary, the rockery, the crumbling walls, have been replaced by a limestone terrace built directly over what I suspect was once a root cellar, and behind the terrace is a small outbuilding painted pale yellow with a shingled mansard roof and a vent rising from it that looks industrial, and under the eaves are bullet cameras. So far I've counted three, and tucked behind boxwoods are an HVAC and a small backup generator, and storm shutters cover the windows as if Gabe Mullery's wife is expecting a hurricane and a power outage and is worried about trespassing and spying. The building is blocked on three sides by privacy screens, white-painted lattices climbing with crimson glory vine and firethorn.

"What sort of work does Robbi do in her office back here?" I ask her husband what would be a normal question under normal circumstances.

"Getting her Ph.D. in pharmaceutical chemistry. Online studies, writing her dissertation." He would never volunteer any of this if he weren't an innocent, a big, strong warrior who doesn't know he lives with the enemy.

"Honey? Who's here?" A woman's voice, and she appears around the side of the house, walking calmly but with purpose, not toward her husband but toward me.

In bone-colored linen slacks and a fuchsia blouse with her hair pulled back, she's not Dawn Kincaid, but she could be if Dawn wasn't brain-dead in Boston and was more filled out, was very fit. I notice the baguette ring and the big black watch and most of all, her face. I see

Jack Fielding in her eyes and nose, and the shape of her mouth.

"Hello?" the woman says to her husband as she stares at me. "You didn't tell me we had company."

"They're medical examiners and wanted to look around because of the murders," says her handsome husband, who's a busy doctor in the Naval Reserves and is gone a lot, leaving her alone to do what she wants. "Why home so early?"

"Some big ole bad-boy cop came in," she says to him while she looks at me. "Asking a lot of strange questions."

"Asking you?"

"Asking about me. I was in back but could hear the whole thing, and I thought it was annoying." She looks at me with Jack Fielding's eyes. "He was buying an Ambu bag and wanted to know if we had a defibrillator, was chatting up a storm with Herb, then the two of them were outside smoking. I decided to leave."

"Herb's a moron."

"A lot of loose grass clippings," she complains to him, but she doesn't look around. She looks at me. "You know how much I don't like that. Please make sure you rake the rest of them up. I don't care if they're good fertilizer."

"Hadn't finished. Wasn't expecting you home so soon. I think it's time to hire a yard man."

"Why don't you get us some water and some of those cookies I baked. And I'll give our visitors a tour."

"Colin? While I look at the garden, what's left of

it, maybe you can give Benton a message for me," I say to him, but I don't take my eyes off her, and I know Colin senses something is wrong.

I give him Benton's cell phone number.

"Maybe you could let him know he and his colleagues really need to see what Robbi has done to her garden, converting the old root cellar into a remarkably functional office, unlike anything I've ever seen. Robbi for Roberta, let me guess," I say to Colin, as I look at her, and I can hear him on his phone.

"Yes, in the backyard," Colin says quietly, but he doesn't recite the address or where we are, and I suspect that Benton might already be on the way.

"It's exactly what I'd like to do at home, build an office in back that's as secure as Fort Knox, an area where maybe gold once was kept before it was stolen," I say to Roberta Price's face. "With backup power and special ventilation, plenty of privacy and security cameras I could monitor from my desk. Or better yet, remotely. Keeping an eye on who comes and goes. If you don't mind my husband and his colleagues dropping by," I say to Roberta, as the kitchen door shuts, and I wonder if Colin is armed.

"Price or Mullery?" I ask her. "You probably took your husband's name, Mullery. Dr. and Mrs. Mullery in a lovely historic house that must hold special memories for you," I tell her stonily, as I'm vaguely aware of a loud engine in the distance.

She steps closer to me and stops. I see her anger seething because she's finished and she knows it, and I again wonder if Colin is armed and I wonder if she is, and while I'm wondering about all of this I'm worried most about the husband boiling out of the house with his nine-millimeter. If Colin points a gun at Roberta or tackles her to the ground, he very well might end up beaten to death or shot, and I don't want Colin shooting Gabe Mullery, either.

"When your husband comes out of the house," I say to her, as Colin moves closer to us, "you need to tell him the police are coming. The FBI is on the way even as we speak. You don't want him getting hurt, and he'll get hurt if you do anything rash. Don't run. Don't do anything, or he'll get in the middle. He won't understand."

"You won't win." She slips her hand inside her shoulder bag, and her eyes are glassy. She is breathing hard, as if she is extremely agitated or about to attack, and the sound of the loud engine is close, a motorcycle, as her husband emerges from around the side of the house, carrying bottles of water and a plate.

"Take your hand out of your bag. Slowly," I tell her, as the engine roars close and suddenly stops. "Don't do anything that makes us do something."

"Looks like we got more company." Her husband strides across a yard strewn with fresh grass cuttings, and he drops the bottles and the plate as Roberta Price withdraws her hand from her purse and she's holding a canister that is boot-shaped and white, and a gunshot explodes near the house.

She takes one step and drops to the ground, blood streaming out of her head, an asthma inhaler nearby on the grass, and Lucy is running across the yard, a pistol gripped in both hands as she shouts at Gabe Mullery not to move.

"Sit down nice and slow." Lucy keeps the pistol aimed at him as he stands in his backyard, shocked.

"I've got to help her," he cries out. "For God's sake, let me help her!"

"Sit down!" Lucy yells, as I hear car doors shut. "Keep your hands where I can see them!"

TWO DAYS LATER

The bell in City Hall's gold-domed tower rings in slow, heavy clangs on a hazy Independence Day that won't include fireworks for some of us. It's Monday, and while the plan was to get out early for the long flight home, it's already noon.

By the time we land at Hanscom Air Force Base west of Boston it will be eight or nine p.m., our delay not due to the weather but to the winds of Marino's moods, which are gusting in fits and starts and constantly changing direction. He insisted on returning his cargo van to Charleston, where he wants us to land en route, in case he decides to return home with us, because he's not sure, he said. He might stay down here in the Lowcountry and do some fishing or thinking, and he might look for a preowned johnboat or decide to take a sabbatical, as he put it. He might end up back in Massachusetts, it was hard to say, and as he deliberated over what he should do with himself he discovered other ways to stall.

He needed more coffee. He might make one last run for steak-and-egg biscuits he can't get up north. He should go to the gym. He should return the rented motorcycle to the dealership so Lucy doesn't have to do it. She's been through enough with all the police and FBI interviews, all the red tape, as he put it, that goes with a shooting, and it's a bad feeling to kill someone and realize the person wasn't reaching for a weapon but a wallet or driver's license or an inhaler. Even when the dirtbag deserved it, you'd rather it didn't go down like that, because someone's always going to question your judgment, he went on and on, and that's what stresses you out more than having the person dead, if you're honest about it. He didn't want Lucy on a motorcycle right now, and began worrying about her flying because of what he imagines is her state of mind.

Lucy is fine. It's Marino who's not. He ran errand after errand, and when at last he was ready to set out for the two-hour drive to Charleston, he decided he wanted all the provisions I'd bought, which can't fit in the helicopter anyway, he pointed out. Not that I'd planned on hauling extra pots and pans and canned foods and a butane two-burner stovetop all the way back to New England, but he insisted he have them. He hasn't had a chance to set up his new place in Charleston, he explained, as he piled everything he could find into boxes he got from a liquor store, including open bags of chips and trail mix and used containers and bottles of cleansers and hand-washing detergent, even a travel hair dryer he doesn't need for his bald head and a travel iron and ironing board he'll never use on his synthetic blends.

He grabbed spices, and several almost-empty jars of olives, pickles, relishes, and fruit preserves, and a banana, condiments and crackers, paper napkins, plastic silverware and plates, foil wrap, a stack of folded shopping bags. Then he went from room to room and gathered up the hotel toiletries as if he's turned into a hoarder.

"Like those pickers or whatever they're called on TV," I decide. "Digging through other people's castoffs and junk and never throwing anything out. This is a new compulsion."

"Fear," Benton says, a computer notebook in his lap, his phone on the table next to his chair. "Afraid he might get rid of something or lose sight of it and then he needs it."

"Well, I'm texting him again. No excuses, he's coming home with us. I don't want him down here by himself when he's not thinking clearly and in the throes of some new compulsion. We're landing in Charleston, no matter what he says, and if need be, I'll go to his condo and haul him out of there."

"Not many compulsions left for him to choose from," Benton says, as he skims through electronic files. "No booze, no cigarettes. He doesn't want to get fat, so he's not going to turn to food, and he starts hoarding. Sex

is a better compulsion. Relatively inexpensive and requires no storage space." He opens another e-mail that
I can tell from where I sit is from the FBI, possibly an
agent named Phil whom Benton was on the phone with
a short while ago.

It has been a busy morning inside the living room of
our hotel suite, our camp with its dramatic view of the
river and the port. Since the sun came up, Benton and I
have been preparing to return north while processing
information that continues to be gathered at what seems
the speed of light. I'm not accustomed to an investigation being worked like a war, with multiple attacks on
multiple fronts made by different branches of the military and law enforcement, all of it executed with a force
and pace that is dazzling. But most cases I work aren't a
threat to national security and of interest to the president, and labs and investigative teams have pulled full
pitch, as Lucy put it.

So far information has been well contained and kept
out of the news as the FBI and Homeland Security continue their relentless quest to make sure that nothing
Roberta Price was tampering with might have found its
way into a military base exchange, on a destroyer or airlifter loaded with troops, in a submarine armed with
nuclear missiles, in the hands of soldiers in combat or
anywhere. DNA and fingerprint analyses and comparisons have been confirmed, and it is a fact that Roberta
Price and Dawn Kincaid are different sides of the same
evil, identical twins, or clones, as some investigators have

been referring to siblings who grew up without each other and then reunited to form a catalyst that created hideous technologies and caused untold numbers of deaths.

"The fear of it," I say. "That's what has Marino running in circles and out of town. He sees death every day, but when it's cases you work, you are deluded into feeling you can control it or that if you understand it well enough, it won't happen to you."

"Smoking that cigarette at Monck's Pharmacy got too close for comfort," Benton says, as his cell phone rings.

"After what he saw in the root cellar? I guess so," I agree. "He certainly knows what could have happened."

"I can give you a suggested approach," Benton says to whoever's just called. "Based on the fact that this is someone who feels completely justified. She's done the world a favor by getting rid of bad people."

I recognize he's talking about Tara Grimm, who's been arrested but not yet charged with any crime. The FBI is making deals, willing to negotiate with her in exchange for information about others at the GPFW, such as Officer Macon, who might have assisted her in meting out the punishment she decided certain inmates deserved, and doing so hand in glove with a diabolically clever poisoner who needed to practice.

"You have to appeal to her truth," Benton says over the phone. "And her truth is she did nothing wrong. Giving Barrie Lou Rivers a last smoke with a cigarette that had a filter impregnated with . . . Yes, I would say it that directly, but couching it in your understanding of why she wouldn't think it was wrong. . . . Yes, a good way to put it. About to be executed, was going to die anyway, a merciful ending compared to what she did to all those people she chronically poisoned with arsenic. Well, right. It wasn't merciful, smoking something with botulinum toxin, a horrible way to die, but leave out that part."

Benton finishes his coffee, listening, staring out at the river, and says, "Stick with what she wants to believe about herself. Right, you hate bad people, too, and can understand the temptation to take justice into your own hands. . . . That's the theory. Maybe Tara Grimm, whom you should refer to as Warden Grimm, to acknowledge her power . . . It's always about power, you got it. Maybe she will offer it up, that it was a cigarette or the last meal, whatever, but all she did was ensure that Barrie Lou Rivers and the others got what they deserved, had done unto them what they'd done to their victims, an eye for an eye with a little something extra. A twist of the knife for good measure."

"I don't know what's going to give him insight about it," I say when Benton gets off the phone, because as bad as Marino feels about what happened to Jaime, it's his nature for him to feel worse about what might have happened to him.

"He's not exactly strong in the insight department," Benton replies. "He took a stupid chance. It's like drinking and getting into a car and then driving on a highway that's had a lot of accidents. I hope Phil does what I said," he then says, and Phil is one of many agents I've met these past two days. "Someone like that and you have to appeal to their belief in what they've done. Feed right into their narcissism. They were doing the world a favor."

"Yes, people who believe that. Hitler, for example."

"Except Tara Grimm wasn't obvious," Benton says. "Came across as the great humanitarian who ran such an exemplary prison she was held up as a model. Job offers, officials showing up for tours."

"Yes, I saw all the awards on her walls."

"The day you were there," he adds, "a group from a men's prison in California had gotten the royal tour and were thinking of hiring her as their first female warden."

"Would be an irony if she ended up in Bravo Pod. Maybe in Lola Daggette's former cell," I reply.

"I'll pass it along," Benton says drily. "That and Lucy's suggestion about Gabe Mullery being the next of kin who decides to pull Dawn Kincaid's plug."

"I don't know what's going to happen," I answer, although Gabe Mullery won't be the one deciding to disconnect Dawn Kincaid's life support.

Apparently he'd never heard of her beyond a vague recollection of the name or a similar one that was in the news, relating to murders in Massachusetts. He knew his wife, Roberta Price, had been raised by a family in Atlanta that they sometimes saw on the holidays, but he knew nothing about a sister.

"My guess is she'll be transferred to a different facility," I suppose. "A ward of the state, kept alive on a ventilator until the day comes she's clinically dead."

"More consideration than any of the victims got," Benton says.

"That's usually the case. I just feel bad I didn't listen to Marino when he pointed out the elevated adrenaline and CO levels, and that smoking has been banned from prisons, so why might Barrie Lou Rivers have had that, and I didn't pay attention because I wasn't interested at the time. I was focused on something else. Maybe if I tell him that, he won't be so hard on himself for not paying attention when he stopped by Monck's Pharmacy and bummed a cigarette."

"Maybe you won't be so hard on me for the same reason." Benton looks up and meets my eyes, because we've had a few cross words about it. "You told me something important, and I had my mind on something else. Understandably."

"I can make us another coffee," I decide.

"May as well. It's not putting a dent. I'm sorry I wasn't nice."

"So you've said." I get up from my chair as a container ship glides by our windows, stacked high and pushed by tugs. "You don't have to be nice when it's work. Just take me seriously. That's all I ask."

"I always take you seriously. I was just taking other things more seriously at the time."

"Jaime, and then he bums a cigarette that could have killed him, and yes, he's traumatized," I say, because I

until soon after 9/11, when Dawn set out to learn the identity of her biological parents, which led to the discovery that she had an identical twin.

In December 2001, they met for the first time in Savannah, both of them cursed with what Benton terms severe personality disorders. Sociopathic, sadistic, violent, and incredibly bright, the two of them had made eerily similar choices in life. Dawn Kincaid talked to an Air Force recruiter about enlisting after college, interested in cybersecurity or medical engineering, and thousands of miles east a twin sister was investigating scientific training programs in the Navy.

Separately and independently on opposite coasts, Roberta and Dawn were rejected because of their asthma, and they enrolled in graduate programs. Dawn studied materials science at Berkeley, while Roberta attended the College of Pharmacy in Athens, Georgia, and in 2001 she began working at the Rexall drugstore near the Jordans' house. On weekends and holidays she dispensed methadone at Liberty Halfway House, where she would have encountered Lola Daggette, a recovering heroin addict.

Recent statements Lola has made to investigators are consistent with what she said to Jaime. Lola had no personal knowledge of what happened on the early morning of January 6, a Sunday, when Roberta was scheduled to dispense methadone from the medical clinic, which happened to be on the same floor as Lola's room, and none of the residents' rooms had locks.

A drug addict with significant intellectual limitations and problems with anger management was an easy target for framing, and although it isn't possible to reconstruct exactly what happened, it is theorized that Roberta entered Lola's room at some point and took a pair of corduroys, a turtleneck sweater, and a Windbreaker from her closet, which she or Dawn wore during the commission of the murders. Afterward, Roberta entered Lola's room while she was sleeping, left the bloody clothing on the bathroom floor, and by eight a.m. was dispensing methadone in the medical clinic.

"Death is an intensely personal and lonely enterprise, and no one is really prepared for it, no matter what we convince ourselves of otherwise," I'm saying to Benton, as I sit back down with my coffee. "Easier for Marino to focus on everything he thinks is wrong with Lucy right now. Or to be obsessed with making sure his cupboards are overflowing."

"He's in the bargaining stage."

"I guess so. If he stocks his kitchen, has plenty of food and accoutrements, he's not going to die," I reply. "If I do A and B, then C won't happen. He had skin cancer, and suddenly he decides to become a private contractor and basically quit his job with me. Maybe that was bargaining, too. If he makes a big life change, it means he still has a future."

"I think Jaime was the bigger factor." Benton checks e-mails as he talks. "Not his skin cancer. She always had a way of making Marino see the pie in the sky. The best thing hasn't happened to him yet. Something magical is yet to come. Being with her validated his self-deluded belief that he doesn't need you, Kay. That he's not spent half his life following you from pillar to post."

"That's a shame if I don't make him see pie in the sky," I muse, as the doorbell rings. "It's worse if he feels he's wasted half his life because of me."

"I didn't say he's wasted it. I know I haven't wasted anything." Benton kisses me.

We kiss again and hold each other, then go to the door. Colin is there with a baggage cart that we don't need, because Lucy's already taken our luggage to load on the helicopter.

"I don't know about this," Colin says, as he pushes the empty cart toward the elevator. "I've gotten mighty used to having you around."

"Hopefully next time we'll bring something better to town," I reply.

"You northerners never do. Turn our church bells into cannonballs, burn up our farms, blow up our trains. We're taking a slight detour, going to SCH instead of the airport. Realize it's not much closer, but Lucy doesn't want to deal with the tower and all the people running around in pickle suits, which I imagine she doesn't mean literally."

"Military," Benton says.

"Okay, flight suits, green ones, I guess. I wondered what she meant when she was talking a mile a minute about it, and I was imagining people dressed like pickles," Colin continues, and I'm not sure if he's being funny. "Anyway, I guess things are pretty buttoned down, there and at Hunter. Apparently they're doing ramp checks, and she's already been ramp-checked once and wants out of there but has instructed me to let her know when we're close. She doesn't want to wait at the hospital and have to move if a medflight comes in. Which isn't likely at SCH, but better safe than sorry."

We board the elevator, and our glass car begins to glide down, passing below balconies draped with vines, and I envision women inmates working in the prison yard and walking the greyhounds, all of them ghosts of their former selves, abusers and the abused, and then ware-housed in a place engaged in a secret enterprise of death. I imagine Kathleen Lawler and Jack Fielding first laying eyes on each other at that ranch for troubled youths, a connection that set in motion a series of events that has changed and lost lives forever, including their own.

"You get tickets for the Bruins or, better yet, the Red Sox, and I just might visit sometime," Colin says.

"Well, if you ever think of leaving the GBI." We pass through the lobby, on our way to heavy heat and a hot, windy ride.

"I wasn't hinting about a job," he says, as we climb into the Land Rover.

"You always have an invitation at the CFC," I reply. "We've got good barbershop quartets up there, and this thing certainly has heat," I add, as he turns on the blower. "It probably would do just fine in snowdrifts, blizzards, ice storms."

I get Marino on the phone, and I can tell from the noise that he's still in his van, riding toward Charleston or maybe away from it, I have no idea what he's up to.

"Where are you?" I ask.

"About thirty minutes south," he says, and he sounds subdued, maybe sad.

"We should land in Charleston by two, and I need you to be there," I reply.

"I don't know. . . ."

"Well, I do, Marino. We'll have a late dinner, celebrate the Fourth up north with something good to eat and get the dogs back from the nanny, all of us together," I tell him, as the old hospital comes into view.

Founded not long after the Civil War, Savannah Community Hospital, where Kathleen Lawler delivered twins thirty-two years ago, is redbrick with white trim and provides full-service but not acute care. It's not often helicopters land here anymore, Colin says. The helipad is a small grassy area with a rather ragged orange wind sock in back, surrounded by trees that thrash and churn as the black 407 thunders in and sets down lightly on the heels of its skids.

We shout good-bye to Colin over the thudding of the blades, and I climb into the left-front seat and Benton gets in the back, and we buckle up and put on headsets.

"Pretty tight spot in here," I say to Lucy, dressed in black, scanning her instruments, doing what she likes best—defying gravity and clearing obstacles.

"Old place like this, and they never bother trimming the trees back," I hear her voice in my headset as

I feel us get light, then lift, and the hospital is under our feet.

Colin gets smaller on the ground, waving, as we ascend vertically, straight up, high over trees. We level off and nose around toward the buildings and rooftops of the old city, and beyond is the river, and we follow it to the sea, heading northeast to Charleston and then home.

NOW THAT YOU'VE FINISHED READING

Red Mist

YOU MIGHT BE INTERESTED IN READING

Port Mortuary

AND

The Scarpetta Factor

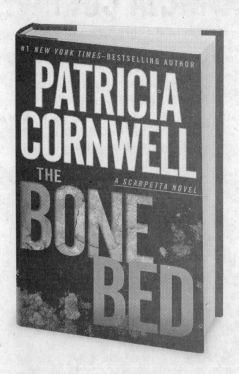

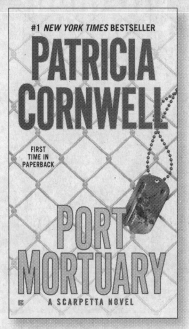

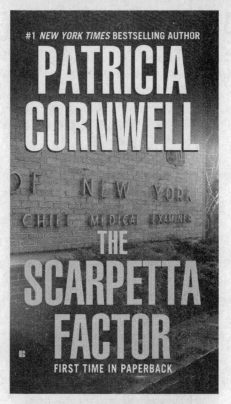